Unexpected Interruptions

A Novel

By Trice Hickman

Platinum Books

Published by Platinum Books

Copyright © 2007 by Trice Hickman.

Cover photography and design by Kea Taylor for Imagine Photography

Printed in the United States of America
ISBN-13: 978-1-60751-341-4

This book is dedicated to the loving memory of Allene Trice

October 27, 1927 – February 4, 1986

A great lady who left this world much too soon

Acknowledgements

My dream of writing a novel has finally been realized, and I am deeply grateful to God for the gifts he has allowed this journey to bring into my life. He has blessed me, in spite of myself, and I am humbled by his grace.

Thank you to my parents, Reverend and Mrs. Irvin and Henalmol Hickman, for always loving me, guiding me, and showing me the way. Thank you to my sister Melody, you were the physical inspiration for the main character (you made the cover hot, girl!), and your love and support mean the world to me. Thank you to my brother Marcus, for your caring spirit. Thank you to all my relatives, too numerous to name individually, but you all know who you are!

Thank you to Sekou Murphy and David Jannarone. You men are HOT Cover Boys!

Thank you to Brian K. Little, your friendship has always been true blue. Thank you to Barbara Marie Downey, you have been my girl through the years.

Thank you to my dear friend Melanie Trottman, from the book's infancy you encouraged, inspired, and supported with your words and actions. Thank you to Cerece Rennie Murphy and Carmen Lathan for reading the manuscript and giving me valuable feedback, friendship, and support.

Thank you to my amazing sister friends; Tammi Johnson, Vickie Lindsay, Sherraine McLean, Terri Chandler, Tiffany Dove, Carolyn Mitchell, Rita Ingram, Sondra Stephenson, Sheila Reynolds, Theresa Dillon, Vielka Sims, Denise Holmes, Bernadette Gatlin, and Kim Riley. You ladies are simply the best!

Thank you to Linda Duggins, for your listening ear and expert advice. Thank you to Janell Walden Agyeman, your literary suggestions helped to make the story better. Thank you to Tynisha Thompson, a lady who knows her stuff! Thank you to authors, Marissa Monteilh, Cydney Rax, Jean Holloway, and Diane Dorce. You ladies are wonderful sistahs, and I appreciate your support of this book.

Thank you to all my friends in the Hands Together Neighborhood Club in Washington, DC, for your support and encouragement.

Thank you to the following talented artists; Trina Cox, your layout design on the pages made my words come to life; Kea Taylor, God has blessed you with a gift that is beyond words; and Will Armstrong, you are a talented designer.

Thank you to the many readers who have supported me. You could have done many things with your hard earned dollars, I'm appreciative that you used them to purchase this book.

To those who have helped me, but are not mentioned, I'll "holla" in the next book!

I've saved the best for last. Thank you to my husband, James. I could not have done this without your stead-fast support, unwavering love, and immense understanding.

Peace and Blessings
Trice Hickman
Visit me at www.tricehickman.com

Unexpected Interruptions

Chapter One

Not Necessarily In That Order......

"Why is my life so damn complicated?" Victoria asked herself as she steered her car past her circular driveway, toward the car pad in the back. She turned off the engine and sat for a few minutes, reflecting on the last twelve hours of her day. Work and men, not necessarily in that order, had thoroughly wrecked her nerves.

She grabbed her handbag, leather attaché and umbrella from the passenger seat, took a deep breath, and readied herself for the cold Atlanta rain that had been falling all day. Looking overhead at the evening sky, Victoria could see that it was just as unsettled as her mood. She stuck out one leg, planting her size-nine, black Ferragamo onto the cold wet pavement. *"Damnit, it's days like this that I wish I'd never turned the garage into a home gym,"* she cursed, quickly pushing her umbrella open as she made a mad dash for the door. She fumbled with her key until it slid into the lock.

"Home sweet home," she said out loud. Each time Victoria walked through her door she felt an immediate sense of comfort. After patiently saving money, buying high-end furniture, scouring antique stores, and then garnering her treasured finds in a storage unit she'd rented, Victoria had finally found her dream home. This month made one year since Sherry Smith, realtor extraordinaire, had led her to 1701 Summerset Lane.

"Sherry, this house is beautiful!" Victoria had marveled, pulling her long black hair behind her ear as she and Sherry approached the large Tudor style house.

"I came by first thing this morning to check it out for myself," Sherry smiled, flashing her perfect, cosmetically whitened teeth. "This home is a lovely split level with three large bedrooms including a master suite. There's even an extra bonus room that'll be great for a home office. Victoria, I know you'll just adore the large living and dining room; they're perfect for entertaining. And wait 'til you see the hardwood floors, high ceilings and crown moldings throughout. Believe me, this house is *you* dear," Sherry gushed, already calculating her sizeable commission.

Things had been very different twelve months ago when Victoria walked into her dream home—out of a recent nightmare. And as she replayed today's events in her mind, she had a funny feeling that her life was about to take an unpredictable turn. Her day began with an interesting twist when Ted Thornton knocked on her office door.

Warm Cinnamon Sugar......

"Hi Ted, how are you?" Victoria smiled, startled to see him as she looked up from the stack of papers on her desk.

"I'm well, thank you," he smiled back, allowing his eyes to quickly dart over both Victoria and her office.

Ted Thornton had been hired at ViaTech seven months ago. Lamar Williams, the Founder and CEO of the company, had successfully wooed him from Asco Systems, one of their toughest competitors. Lamar was retiring next spring, and had handpicked Ted as his successor to run the company he'd built from a small storefront into a telecommunications powerhouse. Ted was well known and highly regarded throughout the telecom industry, which made Lamar confident in his choice of the man he both admired professionally and respected personally. It was even rumored that Ted had negotiated a deal with Lamar to become part owner of the privately held company once he assumed the permanent CEO position next spring.

For a man of forty-five, Ted looked younger than his years. He was very handsome…one could even say outrageously so. His ocean blue eyes, tall, lean body and confident allure attracted all the women at ViaTech, many of who boldly flaunted themselves at him. He could have his pick of women, but he was careful, never giving them so much as a second glance. His non-chalance served to make him even more intriguing to his many admirers, par-ticularly since it was no secret that his marriage of over twenty years was about as sunny as London in the fall.

"Victoria, do you have a minute?" Ted asked.

"Sure, have a seat," she said, motioning to the chair in front of her desk. Victoria had only seen Ted twice in the seven months he'd been with ViaTech. Their first encounter had been during her department's senior management meeting. He'd only been with the company for less than a week, and no one had expected him to attend department meetings so soon, or without warning. He had come in, stayed for a few minutes, then left as suddenly as he'd entered.

The second time was two months later when he'd requested individual meetings with senior staff in the Atlanta headquarters office. Their meet-ing had gone well. They'd started out discussing business strategies and ViaTech's future, then shifted to a more casual conversation; his adjust-ment from L.A. to Atlanta and her preference of Atlanta over her home-town of Raleigh, North Carolina. They even touched on their personal lives. Nothing too deep. Just nice get-to-know-you questions—Where did you grow up? What are your hobbies and interests? Their meeting ran well over the scheduled thirty-minutes, and even Jen, Ted's personal assistant, had said that was a good sign because Ted Thornton wasn't a man prone to wasting time on idle chatter. But up to this moment, Victoria hadn't heard from him since that day many months ago.

Now, he was standing in her office and her mind raced to figure out why the hell he was there. She knew it wasn't every day that the acting CEO just happened to pop in for a visit. Victoria watched as he pulled out one of the leather chairs in front of her desk, unbuttoned the jacket of his gray, cus-tom-made suit and took a seat. Even though most telecom companies prac-ticed a relaxed dress code, ViaTech employees, save for the engineers, dressed like Wall Street investment bankers. *He's very handsome,* Victoria thought to herself, watching him settle comfortably into the chair.

"You have an incredible office," Ted observed, surveying the room. "The way you've decorated with art on the walls and plants all around…it feels more like a room in your home than an office at work. And it smells good too."

Victoria smiled. "It's my job to make our employees feel comfortable when they come to me with problems or concerns, and I believe a welcoming environment helps to foster that." Although she appreciated his discerning eye and obvious good taste, she thought it was an unusual observation to make, given that most of the men at ViaTech could care less about her office's décor and had never commented on the fragrant smell that filled the room. But she noticed that Ted had taken in every detail.

"I like your style, Victoria," Ted smiled.

"Warm cinnamon sugar," she spoke up.

"I beg your pardon?"

"That's what you smell, it's warm cinnamon sugar scented potpourri."

"Ahh...very nice," Ted paused, giving himself a moment before proceeding with the speech he'd been rehearsing for days. "Victoria, as you know, ViaTech is the number two telecom company in the region. But our goal, and my plan, is to make us number one. The only way to hit that target is through the strength of our human capital. Only the best and the brightest can lead this company forward."

Victoria nodded in agreement, but wondered where he was going with the conversation.

"Five years ago the executive management team developed a highly selective year-long mentoring program to identify individuals who show great leadership potential. You're familiar with the program, are you not?" he asked.

"Yes, I'm very familiar with the Executive Mentoring Program. Our department handles the announcements." *Who doesn't know about EMP?* Victoria thought, letting out a frustrated sigh—but only in her head.

The EMP nominations for the upcoming year were due to be announced next week. Victoria was sure that Patricia Clark, the senior director of compliance, would be nominated from their department for the prestigious honor. But she couldn't figure out why Ted had come down to her office to share that information.

"Then all that's left to say is congratulations, Victoria. I'd like to personally nominate you for the program," Ted smiled.

Victoria sat in stunned silence. At thirty-three, she was one of the youngest senior directors in the company. She'd started in the marketing department when she came to ViaTech six years ago after leaving Queens Bank. But after working for a short time in the all-white, male dominated department, the only upward mobility she saw available required a willing libido; which for her was out of the question. So when the HR department posted an internal search to replace the director of employee relations, Victoria seized the position. A few years later she was promoted to senior director. She excelled in her job, which was a piece of cake compared to the rigors of having worked for Queens Bank. In return for her hard work, ViaTech rewarded her with a handsome salary, bonuses, and perks.

But despite her corporate success, Victoria longed for something else entirely. Her plan was to leave ViaTech next summer and do what her heart had been calling her to do for as long as she could remember—open her own event planning and catering business. She'd started Divine Occasions a year ago, shortly after she bought her house. Slowly, she'd begun to build a client roster and was putting plans into motion to run her business full-time. Being nominated for EMP was the last thing she'd expected, or wanted for that matter.

"Ted, I'm…um…honored. I really don't know what to say," Victoria stammered. She came from behind her desk as Ted rose to his feet on her approach. She sat down in the chair beside him, crossed her long legs, and quickly tried to organize her thoughts.

Ted carefully inspected her from the top of her head to the tip of her pointed toe shoes, all done so smoothly she didn't even notice. Her silk blouse, slim fitted skirt, and double strand pearls and matching earrings gave her a decidedly feminine look he loved. "Just say you'll accept my nomination," he encouraged.

"Well, it's just that I'm really shocked by this…I wasn't expecting it at all." Victoria's mind raced. All she could think about were her plans to leave ViaTech.

She knew that start-up costs for her business would be high, so she'd decided to work until next June so she could stash extra money under her belt before fleeing the corporate dungeon. Victoria knew that her father would gladly give her as much financial backing as she needed, even without presenting the business plan she'd been working on for months. His guilt, if for nothing else would dictate that. But this was something she wanted to do on her own. So instead of accepting his money, she planned to apply for a low-interest loan just like any other bank customer. Besides, she knew that her cousin Jeremy who was now helping to run Queens Bank, which her father owned, would probably demand a perusal of her business plan. In Victoria's opinion, Jeremy was a first-class asshole.

She knew she had to ease out of the EMP nomination without giving away her plans. Her father had taught her the golden rule of corporate America—never let them know all your business!

Ted sensed her trepidation. "Victoria, you seem a little hesitant?" He was trying to figure out why a go-getter like her wasn't jumping at the golden opportunity he'd just laid before her.

"Actually, I am. The truth is, I have a lot on my plate right now." She could see the surprise on Ted's face, but she continued. "It's just bad timing. I believe in giving one-hundred percent, and if I don't see that it's possible for me to do my best, I don't commit. That's why as much as I'm flattered by the nomination…"

"Victoria," Ted interrupted, "I understand your concerns. And yes, committing yourself to this program will require extra hours and projects, in addition to your normal workload. But I'll see to it that you have the support and resources you'll need."

Ted hadn't planned on Victoria turning him down, and now he was scrambling to convince her to accept his nomination. He'd been looking for a way to spend time with her since the first day they met. But without a legitimate work related project, the acting CEO couldn't spend leisure office time with one of his many employees unless there was a damn good reason.

Initially, Ted questioned his decision for choosing Victoria. Was it because he was attracted to her, or because she deserved to be in the program? In the end he realized it was both. Her outstanding reviews, high praise from the executive team, and her record of achievement made her a prime candidate. And an added bonus was that he would finally be able to spend time with the woman he'd been thinking about and desiring from afar.

"Ted…again, I appreciate the consideration and vote of confidence. But as I said, it's bad timing."

"I must say, I'm disappointed." Ted leaned back in his chair, quickly plotting his next move. "The nominations won't be finalized until next Friday. I'd like you to take a week and think it over," he asked, masking his desperation. He stood and buttoned his suit jacket, signaling that he was about to leave.

Victoria rose on cue. "All right, I'll think about it," she said, even though she knew her answer wouldn't change.

As she watched him walk out of her office, she could feel there was something arrestingly different about him. He wasn't like most executive types she knew. He seemed familiar, almost like she knew him, even though this was only their third encounter.

Just as she returned to her desk to finish her paperwork, Denise, her administrative assistant, walked through the door. She stood there, arms crossed and staring. "Girlfriend, what kind of excuse are you gonna come up with for not accepting that man's EMP nomination? Telling him you can't dedicate one-hundred percent is some bullshit that ain't gonna fly."

"Have you been out there listening?"

"Absolutely. You know I gotta get the 411," she grinned.

Victoria pictured Denise standing outside her door with a glass cupped to her ear like a detective in a 1960's spy movie. Denise called Victoria by her given name in the presence of their colleagues, but when they were alone she affectionately referred to her as "Girlfriend."

Denise was impeccably dressed, well-organized, and knew her job inside-out. She was an unabashed woman who could read you like last weeks news, yet be gentle as a lamb when the occasion warranted. There were three things about Denise that were constant; she always smelled of Chanel No. 5, her pretty, apple-shaped face always boasted a smile, and she always shot straight from the hip, never sugar coating anything. She had an Associates degree in Administrative Office Technology and a PhD. in common sense. She was sharper than a J.A. Henckles carving knife, and Victoria relied heavily upon her insight.

"Denise, why didn't you tell me that Ted Thornton was coming to my office? I was completely caught off-guard."

"Sorry. He must've come by my desk while I was in the copy room," Denise said, handing Victoria a thick stack of papers. "When I came back your door was half-closed. I was going to come in and see what was going on, but then I heard you two talking, and well...I listened because Mr. Thornton never comes down to anyone's office," she said, placing her hands on her ample hips.

"I'm shocked. I just knew that Patricia had the nomination in the bag, at least that's what she's been telling everyone. Can you imagine how embarrassing it's going to be for her when she finds out that she's not one of the ten nominees?"

"That's *her* problem. This is one time she can't throw her legs open to get what she wants. That woman is so shady, I wouldn't trust her with the keys to the shit house."

"Damn!" Victoria laughed. "You're right about that. But seriously, Ted Thornton can give me a week or even a month, I'm not going to change my mind."

"And you shouldn't. You've put your dream on hold long enough. You have to make yourself happy, Girlfriend."

"Tell me about it. I'm tired of running my business on the side and try-ing to maintain this job at the same time. It's really taken a toll over the last year. I just wish I'd had the courage to make this decision sooner," Victoria lamented.

"Things don't always work out the way we want them to. Things happen over time, not overnight."

"Yeah, that's true. And it's time for me to stop letting other people's expectations and my own fear impede my happiness," Victoria said with confidence, thinking about the sacrifices she'd made to please others; like when she wanted to attend culinary school after high school graduation.

She could still hear her father's words ringing in her ear. "No child of mine with a near-perfect SAT score is going to school to learn how to cook and throw parties for a living. What kind of profession is that anyway? Your mother and I want so much more for you. Who knows, maybe one day you'll take over the bank," he'd hinted.

"But Daddy," Victoria challenged, "event planning and catering can be a lucrative profession, just like any other service…like the bank. Besides, I'm good at it. Look how well the homecoming party turned out that I planned. Everyone said it was the best party Alexander Prep has ever seen!"

"Planning a homecoming party in a gymnasium, and mapping out your future are two entirely different things," her father cautioned. "Victoria, you're my little Queen, and it's my responsibility to make sure that I prepare you for the real world."

After months of arguments and listening to her mother's pleas of intervention, Victoria appeased her father. She enrolled at Spelman College, majored in finance, and minored in coordinating birthday parties, graduation celebrations, and any other kind of festive event she could plan. After graduation, she went on to earn her MBA from Wharton, her father's alma mater—again, obeying his wishes. She'd surprised herself when she discovered that she actually enjoyed the curriculum, knowing that her training would come in handy one day when she started her own business. But in the meantime, she put her dreams on hold and went to work at her father's bank, which he'd named in honor of her and her mother—his two Nubian Queens.

Victoria focused on marketing and community relations at the bank. She planned and executed promotional campaigns, community outreach events, and employee programs. She frustrated her father by doing what he called "fluff work" instead of digging into the "meat" of the bank—dealing with operations and finance. After they butt heads one too many times, Victoria decided to leave. She dusted off her resume and started looking for a new job. Within a month she landed a position with ViaTech. She packed her bags and moved to Atlanta, putting her back in the city where she'd gone to college and had grown to love.

"Girlfriend, you know I got your back and your front, whether I'm helping you with memos here or planning a party with Divine Occasions," Denise said.

"Thanks, you're such a good friend."

"No need to thank me, you're my girl. Now, you better get ready for your lunch date with Mr. Might-be-Right."

"I just hope he's Mr. I-Am-Sane! I'm really not up for any drama."

"This is your first date in over a year. Just be positive. You know that saying...we get back what we bring forth."

"Preach, Oprah," Victoria teased as they broke into laughter.

You Like Adventure Don't You?......

I hope he's gonna be worth me getting out in this cold rain, Victoria thought as she glanced at her Baum & Mercier dangling from her wrist, and realized she was running late for her lunch date.

"Victoria, I know you'll love him," her friend Debbie had said with enthusiasm. "Vincent is tall, handsome, and *really* nice. Now, he's a little on the shy side and doesn't talk a whole lot, but he's very sweet. And oh yeah, he's a consultant. I know you two will hit it off!"

Debbie and her husband Rob had met Vincent a few weeks ago at the gym, and she thought he'd be perfect for Victoria. Debbie Long was a professor in the art department at Emory University, and one of Victoria's closest and dearest friends. They'd been roommates in graduate school, helping each other labor through insanely demanding course work. But after a semester of Probability and Statistics, Debbie decided that business school wasn't for her. She changed her major, breezed through the History of Art curriculum, then accepted a faculty position at Emory. When Victoria had moved back to the area, Debbie was thrilled that they were in the same city once again.

Victoria was both nervous and excited as she turned her silver Audi into the restaurant's parking lot. This was truly out of character for her. She'd never been on a blind date, let alone agreed to go out with someone she'd never even spoken to over the phone. Debbie had set up everything because she was afraid that if left to Victoria, the date would never happen. She knew her college buddy would just find another excuse for not getting back into the dating scene, and Debbie thought it was high time her friend jumped back in with both feet.

Boy, this is a nasty day. But at least it's Friday, and who knows...this lunch date might be the beginning of a good weekend. Just think positive, Victoria encouraged herself, walking into the restaurant with a spring in her step. She shook out her umbrella, ran her fingers through her long, silky mane, and looked around for Vincent. Debbie told her that he'd meet her at the hostess stand, so Victoria knew that the first tall, handsome, black man she saw standing up front would be him. She saw a man coming toward her.

"Whassup baby, you must be Victoria. Damn, a sistah's fine!"

Oh my God. How does this man know my name? Victoria wondered.

"I'm Vincent Frank," the man said, extending his hand. "I been waitin' about ten minutes, but now I see it was well worth it," he grinned, looking Victoria up and down like she was an item on the menu. "C'mon baby, let's get our eat on." He motioned for Victoria to walk in front of him as they followed the hostess back to their table.

Victoria was in shock and had to remind herself to breathe. The hostess seated them and gave Victoria a look that said *"you poor thing"* before walking away.

"Well, well, well, I hit the jackpot witchu' baby. Debbie said you was beautiful and all, but you know how some white folks be thinkin' that just 'cause you a sistah, that you all exotic and shit. So they think you look good, know what I'm sayin'? But baby she was right about you...you a stone cold killa!"

Victoria bristled at his words, feeling as though the air had been sucked out of the room. *Breathe, breathe,* she told herself. Vincent was talking, his lips were moving, but she couldn't hear a word he was saying. She was too busy trying to process the visual before her eyes. He was wearing two-tone alligator shoes and a green suede pantsuit. A playboy bunny medallion dangled from a thick gold rope chain around his neck, so big she could have snatched it off and started a game of Double Dutch. His gold tooth was centered in the front of his mouth, and each time he smiled it gleamed against the flickering light of the votive candle on the table. When he lifted his hand to stroke his goatee, Victoria nearly choked at the sight of his large, diamond encrusted gold watch, accented by a gold nugget ring on his pinky finger. The crowning touch were his two-carat diamond studs, blinging loud in each ear. Victoria stared at him, feeling faint.

She thought about Debbie's description of Vincent, and so far she was only half right. She'd said he was tall, handsome, shy and educated. *He's tall and cute, in a slick bad-boy, hustler-on-the-street kinda way. But he's definitely not shy, and he doesn't sound educated. Come to think of it, Debbie never mentioned where he went to college?*

Victoria had just assumed that because he was a consultant, he must have an MBA and work for one of the major firms. Her mind was swirling with confusion.

Snap, snap! Vincent popped his fingers, breaking Victoria's trance. The server was standing at the table, ready to take their order.

"Hey, baby, I know you captivated and all," Vincent smiled, using his hands to showcase himself like a game show prize, "but let's get some drinks goin' on."

"What will the lady have to drink?" the server asked.

"I'll have a glass of Pellegrino, please."

"I like a woman who ain't afraid to get her drink on durin' her lunch hour. You like adventure don't you?" Vincent winked.

"It's not alcohol, its sparkling water," Victoria blinked with disbelief.

"Oh, you a sophisticated sistah," he grinned. "I'll have a Bud."

Oh My God! I'm gonna kill Debbie! Victoria repeated in her head. *But wait…slow down. Maybe I'm being too judgmental. He's not the kind of guy I usually go for, but maybe I should give Vincent a chance.*

"Yeah, I think we gonna hit it off real nice, know what I'm sayin'? You tall, dark and luscious and I'm the real deal. You lookin' at a total package right here baby," Vincent said, making a fist and pounding his chest.

Can this get any worse? Victoria was beginning to think that her first impression had been right on target.

"I usually date redbones, but you look so good I'm willin' to make you the exception 'cause that body is tight. And I love a sistah wit' good hair all down her back," Vincent grinned. "Yeah, I can tell it's real. It ain't no weave, that's all you baby…you the shit, you know that?" Vincent smiled, licking his full lips. He leaned against the side of the booth, pleased with himself, like he'd just given Victoria a real compliment.

Did his simple ass just say what I think he said? This fool is clearly hauling around a heavy load of plantation luggage! Victoria was pissed. "I didn't know you had a hair and skin-color requirement, or was that a back-handed compliment you just slapped across my face?" she said in her best *go to hell* tone. Vincent's complexion was the color of light caramel, sufficiently qualifying him to pass the dreaded brown paper bag test.

Vincent threw his hands up in surrender. "Whoa, whoa, baby girl. You fine as hell, no matter what the color. I'm just tryin' to be real about my shit. I usually date light skinded babes, know what I'm sayin'? But wit' all that junk in yo' trunk, a brothah's got to get wit' that!"

Okay, this jackass has lost his damn mind! Victoria tried to restrain herself by taking another deep breath. She cleared her throat before she spoke. "Debbie gave me the impression that you were...well...not as *extraverted* as you appear to be," she said, struggling to hold back her displeasure.

"I like the way you use them big words," he smiled as Victoria's eyes bucked wide at his statement. "Well, you know how you gotta play the role wit' white folks, talkin' all proper...like you sound. You know, make'em feel comfortable and what-not. But witchu'...you family, I can be myself, know what I'm sayin'?"

What the hell? Okay, that's it! Victoria looked at Vincent with near disgust. She was ready to leave, but being a human resources professional she had to know what reputable firm was foolish enough to hire the asshole sitting in front of her.

"Tell me, Vincent...what firm are you with?"

"Oh, I work for my family's company."

"And that would be?"

"Franks' Pest Control," he said with pride.

Victoria looked puzzled. "But Debbie said you told her that you're a consultant?"

"Yeah, I am. You see, I go to a client's house and evaluate what kinda pest or rodent problem they have and then I consult wit'em on how to treat it. Know what I'm sayin'...I'm a consul'ant, baby."

Oh, Hell No! Victoria couldn't take it any longer. Vincent's racial snides, profanity, misrepresentation and flashy jewelry had all pushed her well beyond her limit.

"Mr. Frank, my name isn't baby, it's Victoria...Ms. Small to you." And with that, Victoria grabbed her belongings and started to slide out of the booth.

"Where you goin'?" Vincent asked with surprise.

"Anywhere you're not!"

"I can't believe you snooty, educated bitches! Y'all sistahs always cryin' the blues 'bout how you want a good black man, but when you get one you can't handle us. Don't know how to 'preciate a good brothah. I got a good job, ain't got no kids, ain't never been arrested, and I got a top of the line Sentra parked out front...fully loaded. I got females sweatin' me left and right tryin' to get wit' this," Vincent said loudly, pounding his chest again.

People sitting at the surrounding tables and booths began to look in their direction. Just then, the server came back with their drinks as Victoria pushed past him and stood. "Your stupid ass is crazy," she hissed, just loud enough for Vincent to hear.

"Go 'head then, step off. I'm tired of dealin' wit' sistahs that be trippin' anyway. That's why I'ma get me a white woman. They know how to 'preciate a good man," Vincent sneered, taking his glass of beer from the server's tray.

Mortified, Victoria let out a small gasp. She looked over her shoulder and saw a gray-haired older white woman put her hand to her mouth in shock. She wanted to grab her glass of sparkling water and throw it in Vincent's face, but instead she simply held her head high, walked away and never looked back. The server just stood there—speechless.

*I*sn't It Incredibly Cool?...

"What were you thinking, setting me up with that jackass?" Victoria asked Debbie, speaking into her hands-free headset as she drove back to work.

"What're you talking about? Vincent is a really sweet guy."

"Yeah, about as sweet as strychnine! He was putting on an act for you. He's not shy at all. He was just quiet around you so you wouldn't find out how crazy he really is."

"I don't get it…what did he do to make you so upset?"

"Well, for one thing he was wearing a green suede pant suit, and tons of jewelry. He looked like a reject from a low-budget rap video."

Debbie shook her head on the other end of the line. "God, Victoria. You've always been picky as hell when it comes to clothes and men. Loosen up why don't you?"

"You've got to be kidding!" Victoria nearly screamed. But what did she expect from a woman whose wardrobe consisted of tie-dye shirts and broomstick skirts. Debbie was a free spirit and liked guys with an edge. She'd stunned her family and friends when she settled down and married a guy as straight-laced and normal as Rob. The truth was, the only reason Victoria had agreed to the date was because Rob had given Vincent his stamp of approval. Victoria loved her friend, but she knew that she and Debbie had very different tastes.

They were complete opposites. Victoria was tall, African-American, and refined. Debbie was short, Caucasian, and a wild, artsy-fartsy kinda gal. Victoria wore heels, while Debbie wore Birkenstocks. Victoria ate Sushi, while Debbie preferred Ramen Noodles. Victoria sipped mocha lattes, while Debbie drank hot water and Valerian Root. But over the years they'd become as close as any blood sisters could be.

"When I met him he was wearing the cutest t-shirt and shorts," Debbie countered, trying to defend Vincent.

"That doesn't count. It's hard to foul up workout gear!"

"Okay, so what if he's not the best dresser? You can't just throw out the baby with the bath water!"

"Debbie, he had a *gold* tooth."

"I know, isn't it incredibly cool?"

"I don't believe you just said that," Victoria strained. She had one hand on the wheel and the other on her head. Things like this brought up their differences. To Debbie, a gold tooth was *incredibly cool*. To Victoria, it was the equivalent of the grim reaper's kiss of death.

"Victoria, I think you're overreacting. You need to be more open-minded."

Victoria ignored her statement. "Debbie, he was loud, obnoxious and completely uncouth. But I've saved the best for last. Let me tell you the absolute *worst* part of this bullshit date, and the real reason why I'm so upset! That idiot told me he was making an exception by going out with me because he normally only dates light skinned women, but because I have a nice ass and *good* hair, I get a pass. Then he told me that he puts on his "good guy" act for white folks…like you…to make *y'all* feel comfortable with his stupid ass," Victoria huffed. "I should've walked away when I first saw him, but *nooooo*, I was trying to be *open-minded!*" she shouted, ending her tirade.

"Oh shit," Debbie whispered in a low voice. "Victoria, I'm so sorry. I had no idea Vincent was like that. I guess I made a terrible, terrible mistake."

"I can't believe Rob thought that asshole was cool. He usually has better judgment about people."

"Well, actually…um…he and Rob only played basketball one time. Vincent's in my aerobics class, and honestly, he seemed so nice. When I found out he was single, I immediately thought about you. You know, because it's been so long since you've gone out with anyone. Not since…"

"Don't say his name," Victoria snapped.

"I wasn't going to…Victoria, you're my friend and I care about you. It's been a year…"

There was a silent pause.

Debbie was one of the most sincere and caring people Victoria knew, and was sensitive to a fault. She knew that her friend meant well, and she felt bad for yelling at her. "I guess I should've talked to that fool myself before agreeing to go out with him. And you're right, I do need to start dating again, this just wasn't the guy to do it with," she said, softening her tone.

"I'm really, really sorry," Debbie apologized again. "So…do you forgive me? Are we cool?"

"Yes, I forgive you. And we're always cool, you know that."

"Good," Debbie breathed with relief. "Hey, are you still meeting us at Sambuca tomorrow night? You better say yes, I'll even buy all your drinks… it's the least I can do."

Damn, I forgot about tomorrow night, Victoria sighed to herself. She'd promised her friends she would join them, and she knew that if she bailed out once again she'd never hear the end of it. "It's time for you to start going out again," she could hear them saying. So in spite of her reluctance, she told Debbie she would be there.

After ending their call, Victoria pulled into the ViaTech parking garage and headed into the building. She tried to brush off her frustration as she rode the elevator up to her office, but all she could think about was the name that Debbie had almost called out, and the pain that still lingered from the man tied to it.

The Nerve……

Victoria sat at her desk and checked her email as she filled Denise in on the details of her horrifying lunch date.

"Girlfriend, tell me you're lyin'!" Denise said, shaking her head.

"I lie to you not."

"Humph, that's a damn shame for anyone to act that way. His attitude was loud and wrong. My grandmother always said to stay clear of people with two first names…can't be trusted."

Victoria nodded, but then frowned as she read her most recent message. "I just got an email from Patricia. This woman is so obnoxious."

"What does it say?"

"Brace yourself for this," Victoria said as she read the email aloud.

Date: Fri. October 1 2:01 p.m.
From: patricia.clark@ViaTech.net
To: victoria.small@ViaTech.net

Subject: SME Report: URGENT!

I want to make sure you have the SME report on my desk before the
Wed. Oct. 6, deadline. I need to get started on this project ASAP, as
my workload will increase once the EMP nominations are announced.
Naturally, my nomination will dictate that I spend the majority of my
time on program related issues. Make sure you get this to me on time.
PC

Patricia Clark had always considered herself a perfect ten. She loved her
creamy porcelain complexion, super thin body, and Angelina Jolie-like lips. She
thought her only shortcomings were her small eyes, outlined with crow's feet,
and her slightly wrinkled neck, announcing her membership in the forty and
over club. That notwithstanding, her crowning glory was her platinum blonde
hair, compliments of L'Oréal, and her big boobs, compliments of Dr. Jerry
Steiner & Associates Surgical Center. *What more could you ask for?* was her attitude. She didn't have a college degree, but she'd managed to work her way up
the corporate ladder with what she called "friendly ingenuity," or sleeping her
way to the top, as everyone else accurately pinned her tools for success.

Patricia had it in for Victoria from the first day they met. When Victoria
turned in her reports, her work was error-free, which made Patricia suspicious.
She believed that Victoria was getting other people to do the work for her.
How else could she do such a good job? she often thought, discounting the fact that
Victoria held an MBA from one of the top business schools in the country.
And she didn't understand how Victoria could work twelve-hour days and still
find time to bake homemade treats to bring to the office. Everyone loved
Victoria, and Patricia couldn't stand it.

"The nerve," Denise fumed. "Like she's even being considered for EMP. I
wish you would accept Mr. Thornton's offer just so I could see her shit a brick.
She's more fake than those flotation devices she masquerades as breasts. She's
one sneaky bitch. I'm telling you right now, you gotta watch her."

Victoria knew Denise was right. That's why she decided she would come in
this weekend and work on the SME report to make sure it was ready in time
for the Wednesday deadline.

And that was how her day had gone...so far.

Chapter Two

D̲ead On The Money......

Victoria stepped into the mudroom, stuck her wet umbrella in the porcelain umbrella stand and hung her raincoat on the brass wall hook. She walked into the kitchen, dropping her handbag and attaché on the long granite island. Her kitchen was her favorite room in the house. When she'd hired a contractor to update the room a month after moving in, she'd remodeled it to serve a combination of both style and function. From the travertine tile on the floors, to the custom cherry wood cabinets, to the Viking and Sub-Zero appliances, Victoria had designed the space with epicurean care.

She opened the refrigerator, looking for something to scrounge up for dinner. "No leftover anything," she said aloud. After her long day she didn't feel up to preparing a meal, but she was starving because her disastrous blind date had robbed her of lunch. She reached for a truffle from the nearly empty box of Godiva Chocolates sitting on the counter, as she scanned through her stash of delivery and take-out menus. Nothing appealed to her. Finally, she decided to take herself out. "I deserve it. Especially after the lunch I had, huh…more like didn't have," she mumbled between bites of the decadent chocolate treat. "How in the hell do I always find myself in the middle of drama? Is that what I'm bringing forth?"

Satisfied with her plans to go out, Victoria headed upstairs. She flipped on the light and stood in the middle of her spacious master bedroom, which resembled a hotel-quality suite. This was her second favorite room in the house. Her four-poster teak wood bed was covered with a luxurious Dupioni silk comforter and a mix of silk and chenille pillows, making it so inviting she wanted to crawl into it. But the hunger pangs in her stomach called her to action. She undressed piece-by-piece as she walked past the sitting room and into her large walk-in closet, depositing her clothes into the hamper. She quickly changed into a cowl neck sweater and a pair of black wool trousers. She walked back out to the sitting room and admired her reflection in the full-length mirror.

At five-foot ten, Victoria Small was a strikingly beautiful woman. She carried her slender, shapely frame with the grace of a dancer. Her smooth, deep-brown skin was flawless, exposing her regal features. She owed the debt of her good looks to her mother. People in her hometown always said, "Girl, with the exception of your coloring and your height, you look just like Elizabeth." And like her mother, she believed in attending to the details of her appearance.

Victoria reached for her compact sitting atop the vanity and lightly dabbed a small amount of Whipped Cocoa pressed powder over her T-zone for a perfect matte finish. She reapplied her berry colored lipstick and gave herself a spritz of her favorite Diptyque perfume behind each ear. *I forgot to call Mom back,* she remembered, reaching for the phone.

"Hey Mom."

"Hi sweetheart, how're you doing?" her mother asked in her usual happy voice.

"I'm okay. I had a long day and I just got in a few minutes ago. I meant to call you earlier, but I've been swamped."

"That's all right, I know how busy you are. I just wanted to see how you were doing. You know I worry about you."

"Don't worry about me. I'm fine."

"*Mmm-hmm.*" Elizabeth Small knew her daughter just like she knew every crease and line in the palm of her own hand, and since Victoria's break-up a year ago, she'd been very concerned about her only child. "Sweetheart, you sound stressed."

"Yeah, I am…a little."

"Is it work?"

Victoria quickly told her mother about the EMP nomination and her dilemma over finding a graceful way to turn down the incoming CEO without revealing her plans.

"This sounds like a delicate situation. You should talk to your father," Elizabeth said. "John," she yelled into the background, "Pick up the phone dear, Victoria needs to talk to you about some business matters."

Now Victoria's father was on the line. "How's my Queen?" John Small asked in his deep baritone.

"I'm fine, Daddy." Victoria felt conflicted whenever she talked business with her father. It wasn't that he didn't offer sound advice, because she considered him to be one of the smartest men she knew. He was the same man who had opened the first black owned, black operated, and black financed bank in Raleigh. And today, Queens Bank boasted three branches in town and had plans for a fourth location in the neighboring city of Durham. But she harbored resentment of him for manipulating her career and trying to turn her into the corporate banker he'd always wanted her to be. Victoria wished they could go back to the close relationship they once shared when she was growing up, when she was truly his little Queen.

Being a teacher by profession, Elizabeth had seen to it that Victoria excelled in academics. And being a successful businessman, John was determined that his only child would carry on his legacy. He always knew that Victoria was destined for great things. She was special. When her friends bought Barbie dolls and bubble gum with their allowance, Victoria bought magazines like *Gourmet* and *Better Homes and Garden*. She would invite girls from the neighborhood over for tea parties. She'd take out her pink and white tea set and don a pair of little white gloves her mother had bought her to wear with frilly church dresses for Sunday service. She'd serve her young guests Hawaiian Punch in dainty teacups, and coconut cookies from a matching plastic serving tray. She was a gracious hostess at the tender age of seven.

But as the years went on, it frustrated John that what he saw as a cute hobby for his little Queen had turned into a career aspiration. His own father had made his fortune in the tobacco fields of South Carolina, where he'd managed to acquire two large farms, several parcels of land, and rental property; a monumental achievement for a black man during those days. He'd worked his fingers to the bone so that John could make his fortune wearing a suit and tie like the white folks in town.

So for John, the thought of his beautiful, intelligent daughter wasting her talent slaving over a hot stove and entertaining people for a living, made his blood pressure rise. In the early eighties, people like B. Smith, Preston Bailey and Colin Cowie weren't household names. John was from the old school, and to him, his daughter's dream sounded frighteningly similar to a glorified cook. Or worse yet…a domestic. He vowed he'd die before he allowed that to happen.

"What kind of business advice do you need, Queen?" John asked.

Victoria explained the situation to her father, going into greater detail with him than she had with her mother. He listened carefully before he spoke, "My advice to you is to either leave now or accept the nomination."

"Explain each position," Victoria asked in business-like fashion.

"If you stay with the company after turning down a lucrative opportunity that's been offered from top brass, they'll know you're not a serious player. They'll try to find ways to get rid of you, or they'll make your life so miserable you'll wish you were gone. Either way you lose. But if you leave now, no bridges will be burned and you'll be that much closer to establishing your business full-time. Isn't that what you've always wanted?"

His last remark stung. "Daddy, you above anyone else should know that's exactly what I've always wanted. But I planned to work through next June so that I'll have a little cash cushion to carry me through the lean times, at least until Divine Occasions starts to turn a profit. Besides, I still haven't finished my business plan for the loan I'll need."

"Don't let money or finishing the business plan be an issue. I've been offering you seed money for over a year. And knowing you the way I do, I know you've got a nice little nest egg tucked away that'll carry you through."

Despite her discomfort, Victoria laughed to herself because her father was always dead on the money. "Daddy, I don't want your *guilt*, I mean seed money," she said with an intentional slip, which her father recognized for the flippant remark it was. "I'll meet with Jeremy at the beginning of the year and present my business plan, then I'll negotiate a low interest loan and use my own savings to supplement my income."

Victoria could hear her mother sighing on the other end.

John cleared his throat. "Listen, I know you're still a little resentful because I pushed you in a different direction from the one you wanted to take, but it's time to put that aside. This is business," he said.

"Strictly," Victoria bounced back with an edge in her voice. She could hear her mother's sighing getting louder in the background.

"Queen, I'm trying to make amends. I'm trying to help you."

Victoria knew he was trying…trying hard, and that she was being a real bitch about it. Since she'd left Queens Bank their relationship had improved, but it still wasn't like old times. "I know your trying to help, Daddy. But this is something I need to do on my own, she said"

"Well, the offer still stands in case you change your mind…you know, it's been a year and people are still talking about the black-tie ball you planned for the bank. You're a natural," John praised. "I'm so proud of you. And whether you take my advice or not, watch your back at work. And remember…"

"Never let them know all your business," they both repeated.

"Love you Queen." And with that, John was off the phone.

"Victoria, your father's right. We're both so proud of you," her mother said.

"Thanks Mom, but I wish he'd said that fifteen years ago."

"Sweetheart, you've got to start somewhere. He's extending an olive branch."

"I know, but he didn't value my talent until I pulled together that ball and everyone raved about it."

"Why do you hold on to things? You need to let that go. He's supporting you now. Can't that be enough? All he wants you to do is meet him halfway."

Victoria knew that her mother was right. "Okay, I'll try," she finally said.

"Good. Now listen, it's nearly eight o'clock and you just got home. I think you're working yourself into the ground."

"Mom, I'm fine, really."

"I was just telling your Aunt Phyllis the other day that I don't know when I'm going to get any grandchildren out of you because you won't even take the time to get a man. Patsy and her husband have two children already, and even that peculiar acting Jeremy has a wife and a child on the way. Sweetheart, when was the last time you went on a date?"

Here we go again, Victoria thought. "Mom, why does everyone think that being single is like having a debilitating disease? I have a lot going for me. So what if I'm not seeing anyone?"

"Victoria, I'm your mother and you need to listen to me. There's going to come a time when you'll need someone by your side to help take care of you. Someone you can come home to at night. Someone you can count on."

"Mom, I can take care of myself, and I've been doing a pretty good job of it for quite some time. Besides, I enjoy the peace and quiet of coming home alone…no *unexpected interruptions*," Victoria said, trying to convince herself.

"Mmm-hmm." Elizabeth could see through her daughter's words like they

were floating in a glass. "The right man just hasn't come into your life yet. I know it's been difficult since you broke up with…"

"Mom, please…don't mention his name," Victoria said in a quiet voice.

"Sweetheart, if you had an old pair of shoes that had been worn down to the soles, you wouldn't keep them in your closet would you? You'd throw them away and get a new pair, wouldn't you?"

"Yeah, so what's your point?" Victoria asked squarely.

"Don't get fresh with me young lady. You know I'm only saying this because I love you. You've moved forward with so many things in your life. You bought your house, you started your business, now it's time for you to move on with a new relationship. Sweetheart, I just don't want you to end up alone."

"Mom, I didn't mean to snap at you. I had a long, frustrating day," Victoria sighed, "I guess I do need a little down time, but listen, I've gotta run because I'm getting ready to go out to dinner."

"Oh, you have a date. Why didn't you tell me?" Elizabeth perked up.

"No, Mom. I don't have a date. I'm taking myself out and I'm going to enjoy the pleasure of my own company."

"Mmm-hmm."

"Mom, I've gotta go. I Love you," Victoria said before ending the call.

As she headed out the door, Victoria thought about her mother's words; *someone to come home to at night, someone to count on.* Deep down, she wanted those things and more.

Chapter Three

Okay, That's My Cue......

Victoria was hoping that tonight's dinner would make up for her lunch from hell. The Cheesecake Factory in Buckhead was a casual dinning spot, popular with the yuppie crowd. She'd been craving cheesecake all week and was thankful for the short wait. *One of the few times that being a party of one has its advantages,* she thought to herself.

As the hostess led her to her table, Victoria noticed two attractive men sitting in the booth directly across from where she was being seated. She slid off her coat, aware that they were watching her, and draped it across the extra chair that no one would be occupying. She took her time as she sat down and scanned the menu. When she looked up in the direction of the two men she had to steady herself...the man staring at her was gorgeous!

He hadn't taken his eyes off her since she'd entered his view. Victoria fumbled with her napkin before getting up the nerve to look at him again. When she did, he smiled and revealed the most perfect set of pearly white teeth she'd ever seen, and dimples so sweet it made her want to smile back at him. His bald head and clean-shaven face added to what she thought was a delicious sex appeal. Her weak attempt to smile back made him grin even harder.

Thank goodness, Victoria thought when the server came by to take her order. Any distraction was welcome. She stumbled through her order, feeling naked under the gorgeous man's gaze. She had to gather herself before she made her next attempt at innocent flirtation because she couldn't believe she was letting a man's stare have this kind of effect on her. She was used to walking into a room and turning heads. That was the way it had been since she'd turned thirteen and started developing curves. She was about to throw a sexy smile his way when she noticed there were half empty glasses sitting in the vacant spaces beside each of the men.

Damn! It figures. He's here with someone, but where is she? Probably in the ladies room, Victoria thought as she heard the rhythmic chime of her cell phone. She was surprised when she looked at the caller ID. "Tyler, to what occasion do I owe the privilege of a Friday evening phone call?" she asked her best friend. Tyler's wife usually saw to it that Victoria's phone access to him was limited after work hours ended.

Tyler Jacobs had been her *boy* since her freshman year of college. He'd been a sophomore at neighboring Morehouse when they met one weekend at his fraternity's house party. They talked all night, sealing an inseparable friendship. "What's this I hear about your lunch date with Snoop Dog?" Tyler laughed.

"Umph…you talked to Debbie?"

"Yeah. She called me. She feels bad about the whole thing. It sounds fucked up."

"It was."

"I could've told you not to let Debbie set you up on a date. I love her like a play sistah, but damn, you know her taste is, uh, out there."

Victoria laughed, noticing that Mr. Gorgeous was still eyeing her. "Tyler, you should've seen him. The brother had a gold tooth in the front of his mouth, and enough on his body to melt down and make a statue."

"Get outta here, you kiddin'?"

"I wish. He told me that black women didn't know how to appreciate a good man like him, so he's gonna get himself a white woman. Well, a white woman can have his sorry ass," Victoria said, lowering her voice.

"See, that's the kinda shit that gives brothah's a bad name."

"Tell me about it. I've never been so mad and embarrassed in my entire life. But I'll have to tell you all the gory details at another time, I've gotta go."

"Why? Whatcha doin'?"

"I'm having dinner at The Cheesecake Factory, and I don't want to air my business in this crowded restaurant."

"Oh, who ya with?"

"I'm with the best company I could have…me, myself and I," Victoria said, trying to sound convincing for the second time tonight.

"Tell that to somebody who doesn't know you like I do. As fine as you are, why the hell are you sittin' up in The Cheesecake Factory by yourself, on a Friday night? How long has it been since you've been on a date…I mean a real date?"

Just then, Victoria saw two women approach the table where the men were sitting. Both women were attractive and petite in stature, but that's where their similarities ended. One looked like a typical BAP (Black American Princess) poster girl. Her bobbed, shoulder length hair was relaxed ridiculously straight to within an inch of its' folliclely manipulated life. Her tailored herringbone skirt, silk blouse, expensive pumps and understated jewelry said, *I've got style and I know how to wear it.* The other woman was her counterpart's exact opposite. Her long, bouncin'-n-behavin' blondish brown extensions, cropped cargo pants, trendy tight-fitting shirt, and three-inch stilettos said, *I just stepped off the set of Jay-Z's latest video.*

Mr. Gorgeous stood up to let the video chick slide into the space next to him. Victoria thought they made an odd pair. *He looks so sophisticated and she looks so…not!* she thought to herself. The video chick leaned in close to him, but he looked uncomfortable.

"Are you listening to me?" Tyler asked, pulling Victoria's attention back to their conversation.

"Look, I really don't need another lecture about my love life."

"What love life?"

"Tyler, please. You know what I've been through."

"Yeah, but you know I gotta keep it real. You've shut yourself off for over a year now. It's time to get back in the game. You need to get beyond that shit that went down between you and…."

"Tyler, don't you dare say his name," Victoria hissed in a low voice.

"Hey, you know me better than that. I was just gonna say that you need to get beyond what happened between you and ole' boy. Let it go. Victoria, don't allow what happened to keep holdin' you back."

"I hear what you're saying, and honestly, I agree with you. It's just hard, you know?" Mr. Gorgeous was still looking in her direction, so she tried not to show the sadness on her face that she felt in her heart.

"You know you're my girl, and I'm here for you. True blue baby," Tyler paused, then became silent as his wife's voice roared in the background. "Hey, I gotta jet. Allison's calling me and we're running late for dinner with her parents."

"Oh, you're dining with the king and queen tonight?" Victoria smirked through the phone.

Tyler paused again. "Somethin' like that." He was ready to change the subject. "Hey, you still comin' to Sambuca tomorrow night?"

"Yeah, I'll be there."

"Okay, catch you later. And don't forget, you owe me blow by blow details of your lunch date...Peace."

Even after his companion had returned to join him, Mr. Gorgeous was still starring in Victoria's direction. She breathed with relief when the server approached her table again. Ironically, her food came out the same time as the couples' across from her. Mr. Gorgeous and his friend had ordered hearty steak entrées, while the two women had both ordered salads. Victoria's chicken dish took up nearly half her plate and was accompanied by a huge serving of mashed potatoes and vegetables. Together with her basket of bread, it looked like she'd ordered for two. Mr. Gorgeous looked at her plate piled high with food and smiled.

I must look like a freakin' pig! Why didn't I order a salad like most weight conscious women? Like those women! Victoria silently admonished herself. Then, a little voice inside her said...because you're hungry, you love food, and you love to eat! She put Mr. Gorgeous out of her mind and grabbed her knife and fork.

She cleaned all the food off her plate and had conquered an entire slice of chocolate mousse cheesecake by the time she finished. Mr. Gorgeous and his friend were eating dessert while their dates took small sips of their after dinner coffee. He'd been stealing glimpses of Victoria throughout the evening and she'd caught each one of them. She also saw the video chick following the direction of her man's eyes, and the woman looked pissed in a major way. If it was one thing Victoria knew, it was that attractive women always noticed other attractive women, especially if their man was within eyesight.

After leaving a generous tip, Victoria reached for her coat and handbag, ready to return home—alone. She added extra sway to her hips and gave Mr. Gorgeous one last glance as she glided by his table like an elegant gazelle. Out of nowhere, a server came hurrying by and bumped into her with a tray full of food. Victoria lost her balance and her graceful exit suddenly turned into a giant fiasco.

The collision with the server sent her flying into Mr. Gorgeous' table, hurling her and his half eaten strawberry shortcake to the floor with a hard crash. She fell to her knees, looking about as graceful as a bull on rollerblades. She put her hand to her head, dizzy with embarrassment. The server began apologizing a mile a minute as Mr. Gorgeous jumped out of his seat and knelt down by her side. "Are you okay?" he asked. His voice was like a freshly brewed cup of coffee—strong, rich, and full of flavor.

"Um, yes, um, I'm okay…thank you," Victoria answered, trying to regain her composure. She felt like a klutz. *Damn, I'm having shitty luck in restaurants!*

Mr. Gorgeous gently held her arm, helping her up from the floor. When he stood, his muscular body towered over her—a good sign in her book. His hands were strong, and warm to the touch. He held her with the delicate care one would use if handling a rare antique. "You sure you're okay? he asked again.

Just then, Victoria heard another voice rushing up from behind. A wiry, nervous looking man approached. "I'm the general manager and I saw what happened. Are you all right?" Is there anything we can do?"

At this point Victoria wished she could snap her fingers and disappear into thin air. But since that wasn't possible, she had to pull herself together and walk out with what little dignity she had left. She turned to the manager and the server, assured them that she was fine and that all she wanted to do was get out of there and go home. The manager looked relieved as he and the server walked away amidst the busy restaurant noise.

The next task was to face Mr. Gorgeous. "Really, I'm fine. I'm sorry for ruining your dessert," Victoria apologized. Her eyes were on the floor, examining the reddish-pink mess she'd made of his strawberry shortcake. Slowly, she looked up at him, feeling a sensual heat rise between their bodies.

"Please don't apologize. You didn't ruin anything…quite the opposite," Mr. Gorgeous smiled. "Are you sure you're okay?" he asked, shifting his tone. His voice was now official and commanding, like he was used to asking questions and giving orders.

"She said she's fine," the video chick leaned over, interrupting.

Mr. Gorgeous turned in the woman's direction, giving her an uncomfortable stare.

"Have a good evening and try to make it home in one piece," the woman snapped, flipping her long synthetic locks.

Okay, that's my cue to either get going right now, or curse this heifer the hell out. "Sorry for the trouble," Victoria apologized again, this time returning the video chick's wicked stare."

She and Mr. Gorgeous stood frozen in place, looking at each other one last time. She knew he felt the same heat that was creating a tingling sensation below her waist. It was in his eyes. She watched as he picked up her coat and bag, handing them to her. "Thank you," she nodded, then turned away and resumed her glide out of the restaurant. She didn't know it, but he remained where he stood, watching the door even after she'd disappeared.

That night her dreams were filled with his face, his smile, and his touch. She wondered who the mysterious, gorgeous man was who'd managed to occupy her mind and her heart in just one night.

A Surprising Comfort......

The next morning Victoria rose early and went downstairs for a heart-pumping workout in her home gym. After a couple of miles on the treadmill she was ready to start her day. Later that afternoon, she sat in her office at work, rubbing her eyes from slight fatigue. *I'll finish this up when I come in on Monday morning,* she thought to herself as she put the large stack of documents away.

She'd been pouring over the senior management evaluations, or SME's as they were called. SME was Victoria's brainchild. It was a new type of annual review she'd developed to allow non-exempt employees to evaluate their managers and directors.

After putting away the papers, she rose from her desk and was taking a long stretch when she looked up to find Ted Thornton standing at her door.

"You're very dedicated. Only we die-hards come in on Saturday," he smiled.

This was the second time in two days that he'd startled her. Victoria knew he was in the building because she'd seen his black, vintage Jaguar parked in his reserved space in the parking garage when she came in. Ted was notorious for keeping late night and weekend hours. He was a very driven man, and Victoria admired that.

She noticed how different Ted looked outside of his standard corporate uniform, which consisted of expensive ties and custom-made suits. She examined his simple khakis, white button down, navy blazer, and brown loafers. The look was classically preppy, yet somehow it was very chic on him. His appearance made Victoria aware of her own.

Her black, lycra knit top, snug fitting low-rise jeans, and chunky heeled black boots was an ensemble more fitting for afternoon errands around town, which she planned to do once she left the office, than for work. She wasn't revealing any skin, but she was definitely showing her curves. She hadn't expected anyone else to show up in her department on a cold, rainy Saturday. *Why is he here in my office? Is he checking up on me?* she wondered. "Hi Ted, I'm just finishing up a little work on the SME report," she answered.

"How's it coming?"

"Very well," Victoria said, shifting her weight to one leg. "As a matter of fact, my report will be ready by Monday."

"Good, then you'll be a day ahead of schedule."

"A day?"

"Yes, Tuesday…that's the deadline Patricia stated in the email she sent to the executive team yesterday. Is that not correct?"

Damn, she's trying to set me up, Victoria quietly seethed. *That bitch specifically told me that the report was due on Wednesday.* "It was communicated to me that the deadline is Wednesday. Nevertheless, it's almost complete. I'm sure Patricia chose different deadline dates for her own reasons," Victoria responded, hoping Ted would catch her hint.

"Great," he said, seemingly oblivious to her intent.

Victoria wanted to shake her head, but instead she concentrated on the overstuffed manila envelope in Ted's hand. "So, what brings you down to my office?"

"I was on my way out and thought I'd drop this off on Denise's desk so you'd have it when you come in on Monday morning. But since you're here, I can give it to you now." He handed Victoria the envelope. "It's the EMP application packet. I also included some additional reading material I thought would be helpful to you."

Ted had been on his way out when he spotted Victoria's car in the parking garage. A few months earlier, he'd seen her leaving work late one afternoon and remembered that the silver Audi parked in the reserved spaces for senior management belonged to her. He came back into the building, retrieved the EMP packet off his assistant's desk, and added a few additional items before heading two floors down to Victoria's office.

"Thank you, Ted, but you didn't have to do this. As I said, I don't think I..."

"You never know, you might have a change of heart," he interjected.

She nodded, trying to play it cool. "Okay, I'll look over it this weekend."

"I hope you're not going to spend your entire weekend working? Otherwise, I'm sure your boyfriend will think I run a sweatshop operation,"

Ted hinted with a tease. He was venturing into bold territory, but his curiosity was eating away at him. He knew from her personnel file and from the bare ring finger on her left hand that she wasn't married. But that she didn't have a man in her life was still up for question.

Victoria bit her lower lip, speaking slowly. "There's no boyfriend to worry about how I spend my time."

"I didn't mean to be presumptuous. I just thought that you were…"

"It's okay…really. I was involved with someone, but it ended over a year ago. It's actually been a long time since I've even been on a date." *My god, why did I just tell him that?*

The truth was that she felt a surprising comfort with him. It was like he was just another guy. But she was very aware of who he was, so she knew that she had to be careful.

Ted looked at her with disbelief. He couldn't imagine why she wasn't seeing anyone. He'd been fully prepared for competition.

Victoria noticed the puzzled look clouding Ted's face. "I'm sorry," she began, "I don't know what came over me. I'm sure you don't want to hear about the details of my personal life."

"I'm the one who brought up the subject, you just answered honestly, and I'm glad you did. Victoria, I hope to work closely with you in the EMP program over the next year, and that means we'll get to know each other better. I admire you as a colleague, and it's my hope that we'll form a good friendship."

Ted Thornton wants to be friends with me? Victoria was a little shocked, especially when she heard herself say, "I'd like that."

They walked out to the parking garage and stood by her car, laughing and talking for another hour before they each drove off to live their lives in different worlds.

I Hope That's Not A Bad Thing……

Later that evening, Victoria stood in the middle of her closet trying to decide what to wear. It was cold outside and the forecast called for rain the entire weekend. She wanted nothing more than to curl up on her couch, sip herbal tea, and read through a few cooking magazines. But her friends were expecting her at Sambuca and she'd told them that she would be there.

"What am I going to wear?" Victoria pondered out loud, looking over her neatly organized garments draped on wooden hangers. "I have to make sure I look good. You never know who you might meet!"

She decided on her black, silk jumpsuit with wide leg bottoms. She slipped a pair of Swarovski crystal cuff links into the French cuffs of her sleeves, fastened the posts of her diamond earrings securely into place, and completed her look with an antique pavé diamond cocktail ring. Victoria loved accessories and believed they were the finishing touch to any outfit. She slid on her sling backs, spritzed a whiff of Cartier behind each ear, and did a once over in the mirror before throwing on her wrap and heading out the door.

Sambuca was a hip jazz supper club with a sophisticated clientele and a reputation for great live bands and killer martinis. When she arrived, her friends were already there. Debbie, Rob, Tyler, and Allison were sitting at a table in the middle of the room. Victoria was painfully aware that she'd become a hopeless fifth wheel, but she put on a smile and sashayed over to the table, snapping her fingers and moving to the beat of the music surging throughout the room. "Hey gang, what's up?" she said, sliding into the empty seat they'd saved for her.

A minute later, the server came over to take their order for appetizers. Debbie asked around the table to see what everyone wanted. "It doesn't matter to me," was the response from Rob and Tyler, two men who were easy to please. But before Victoria or Debbie could offer a suggestion, Allison turned to the waitress and ordered for everyone. The two friends looked at each other and counted to ten, knowing it would be a long night.

After thirty minutes of lively conversation over appetizers and a second round of drinks, Debbie and Rob hit the dance floor. The band had just announced the beginning of the love song set, which meant the next set of songs would be slow and romantic. Tyler and Allison didn't move. Victoria knew they probably wanted to dance, but out of courtesy, at least on Tyler's part, they remained seated. "Why don't you two get out there on the floor?" she coaxed.

"Nawh, we're cool," Tyler nodded, giving Victoria a sincere smile. But the look that Allison shot him clearly said, *speak for yourself.*

"I know you're just sitting here so I won't be alone, but I'm fine. Besides, maybe if I'm solo I'll get some action," Victoria teased, giving Tyler a wink.

"Great, come on, Tyler," Allison said, grabbing her husband by the elbow as she practically pushed him onto the dance floor.

Victoria looked at them and shook her head. She couldn't stand Allison. It was hard to believe that just a few weeks ago she and Tyler had celebrated their first wedding anniversary. Tyler and Allison had met at a fundraiser for the Atlanta Symphony Orchestra. Allison had been there with her parents, who were faithful patrons of the arts and long standing members of Atlanta's tightly woven black bourgeoisie community.

Victoria had asked Tyler to accompany her to the event against his protests. "It'll be stiff and boring as hell," Tyler had complained about the affair. As the executive director of the Youths First Initiative (YFI), a successful non-profit organization he'd founded for at risk youth, Tyler was more interested in grassroots organizing than blue blood social events, so he'd prepared himself for a dull evening.

But when he and Victoria found their numbered table, he brightened at the sight of Allison sitting there. Her pretty, oval shaped face was framed by a sophisticated pageboy that distracted from the coldness behind her eyes. Cordial greetings were exchanged before the inquisition from Allison began. Tyler said he thought it was refreshing to meet a woman who was interested in getting to know him. But Victoria saw through her shallowness. Then her parents jumped in, asking questions about Tyler's profession and his background. They deemed Victoria inconsequential to their conversation. It was clear to her that they were interviewing for a son-in-law, and she didn't understand why Tyler couldn't see through these people, who she thought were about as comforting as an ice water bath.

Less than a year later, Allison made the perfect bride. Some cried during the ceremony, but it hadn't been tears of joy that flowed. Everyone who knew Tyler wanted it to be his ex-girlfriend, Juliet. She was the one he should've been standing beside, reciting his vows. Juliet was sweet and caring, full of fun and laughter. She was the one who got away.

If Tyler's parents had been alive, they would have undoubtedly been opposed to him marrying a woman like Allison. But they'd been gone for over twenty years, so the show went on. Sitting in the second row pew beside her parents and her new fiancé, Victoria smoothed the wrinkles in her silk dress and glanced down at her sparkling engagement ring. Silently, she prayed for the best as she watched Tyler slide the platinum band onto Allison's finger, but deep down she knew it was the beginning of the end for her best friend.

Watching them now, she still wondered what Tyler saw in his wife. *That's how they should be,* Victoria thought as she watched Rob holding Debbie in his arms, whispering and smiling into her ear as they danced cheek to cheek. Tyler was holding Allison, but there was no intimacy in their rhythm. He seemed distant. *His dinner with the in-laws must not have gone well.*

Victoria noticed a few men looking her way, but none had come over. She was about to return the stare of a fine brother sitting three tables over when she felt a tap on her shoulder. She turned around and was shocked by who she saw. "Hey, what're you doing here?" she asked Ted, surprised and strangely happy to see him. "I've seen you more in the last two days than I have since you've been at ViaTech."

"I hope that's not a bad thing."

"Oh no, it's not a bad thing at all." She gave him a warm smile to prove it.

Ted pulled out the chair beside her and took a seat. "I come here at least once a month. The bands are great, and the martinis...well, they speak for themselves."

Victoria nodded in agreement. "I didn't know you liked jazz. I figured you for an Eric Clapton, Bruce Springsteen kinda guy."

"I like them too, but my real love is jazz. My roommate in college played the sax. One weekend he went to New York to scout a few clubs for jam sessions and asked me if I wanted to tag along. I've been hooked ever since."

"Do you play?"

"No, I wish I did. Jake, he was my roommate, he taught me a few tunes but I was never any good. I'm a lousy musician, but an excellent listener," he joked.

Victoria smiled. "I grew up on jazz. My father loves it, so our house was filled with the music. There's something freeing about it," she said, realizing the irony of her words. The man who'd introduced her to that freedom was the same person who made her feel completely loved, yet at times utterly suffocated.

Ted nodded. "Yes, I know what you mean."

"Are you here by yourself?" Victoria asked. If the rumors she'd heard about his marriage were true, she knew that chances were he was flying solo tonight.

"No, I'm here with a good friend of mine from Boston. He loves this place too, so we come whenever he's in town on business." Ted looked over his shoulder in the direction of an average looking middle-aged man sitting at a table tucked away in the back of the room. The man had his eyes fixed on them and smiled when he saw them look his way.

Why is his friend staring at us like that? Is that a smirk or a smile on his face? Victoria wondered. Then a thought came to her...*I wonder if Ted is gay?* As she gave it more thought, she realized it would explain a lot of things. Like his estranged marriage, and why he'd never so much as glimpsed in the direction of any of the women at work. And even today when they were in the office, he'd paid no attention to her attributes, and she knew that most men took a second look when she wore her booty huggin' jeans. It would also explain his friend who was sitting in the back of the room, staring at them like a jealous lover.

Now it all made sense to her. That's why she felt so comfortable with him; not threatened in any way. It explained why he'd noticed the décor of her office, and even the scent of potpourri. *Like they say, the good ones are either married or gay. Good Lord, he's both!* Victoria thought. "So, are you two having a good time?" she asked with a knowing smile.

"Yes, we are. The band is really hot tonight."

The band began playing a rhythmic melody that Victoria instantly recognized as her favorite. Ted's voice softened when he heard it too. "This is my favorite song," he said, tilting his head to let the music float into his ears. The band was playing *In a Sentimental Mood*.

He'd startled her yet again. "It's my favorite too," Victoria said with surprise.

They shared a brief stare before she looked away, listening to the seductively hypnotic beat of the music.

Ted wondered if she knew how much he wanted her, that he was basically putty in her hands. His friend Barry had to talk him into getting up the nerve to go over and say hello.

"Ted, what the hell's wrong with you? I've never seen you act like this," Barry had said. "But I have to say, you were right. She's stunning, but she's still just a woman, so get some fucking balls and go over there before someone else beats you to the punch. You're her boss for Christ sakes. You're the one with the power. You're the one in control."

Boy was he wrong, Ted thought.

"Penny for your thoughts? You look a million miles away," Victoria said.

"Oh...just thinking."

"I can see. It must really be something."

Ted looked into her eyes and smiled. "Yes, something wonderfully unexpected."

Victoria stared back at him, wondering what his life was really like. They'd talked for an hour after they walked out to their cars earlier that afternoon. They even ventured a little further into each other's personal lives and laughed about Victoria's horror story of a lunch date that she'd had the day before; although she gave him the abbreviated version, leaving out some of Vincent's more colorful moments.

"Give me some advice, Ted. As a married man, how do you know when you've found the right one?" Victoria had asked.

"I'll let you know when I find that out myself," he replied as they shared a nervous laugh.

Now, Victoria knew where his strange comment had come from. "Well, Ted, I guess that's what makes life interesting…the unexpected," she smiled.

"Yes, Victoria, it does."

After the love song set ended, the band broke for intermission and everyone returned to the table. Victoria quickly introduced Ted to the group. They exchanged friendly hellos before he excused himself and headed back to his table. After he left, all eyes were on Victoria.

"Who was that?" Debbie asked in an excited voice.

"Oh, Ted? He's the acting CEO of ViaTech," Victoria answered.

"Yeah, and he wants to get with you," Tyler grinned, taking a sip of his Ketel One.

Victoria laughed. "I can assure you he's not interested in me. But you or Rob on the other hand, are probably more his flavor," she whispered with raised brows.

"He's gay?" Debbie whispered back.

Tyler shook his head. "Gay men don't look at women the way he was lookin' at you."

"What do you mean? How was he looking at me?"

"Like someone just handed him a one-way ticket to heaven. Trust me, I'm a man, and I know that look."

"Well, you're wrong. As a matter of fact he's here with his boyfriend. They're sitting in the back, in the far left corner. But don't look now," Victoria cautioned.

But as soon as she finished her sentence, the entire table turned and looked at the same time. "He looks so masculine. He doesn't seem gay," Debbie commented.

"Not all gay men are effeminate," Victoria said, taking a sip of her cosmopolitan.

Tyler spoke up again. "He might be here with another dude, but that doesn't mean he's gay. I'm tellin' you, he was lookin' at you the way a man looks at a woman when he's interested."

Rob nodded his head in agreement. "I've got to agree with Tyler," he said, "he looked like he was into you."

"See, I told you. I know that look," Tyler said again. He knew it because it was the way he used to look at Juliet—the one who got away.

"Is that the way you look at me?" Allison asked abruptly. Tyler didn't answer. His avoidance was blatant, causing a heavy tension to fall over the table.

Debbie cleared her throat, breaking the chilly mood. "We have some good news," she announced with a cautious smile. "Rob just got a promotion. He's been promoted to director of accounting."

"Congratulations!" everyone said in unison.

"Thanks, I'm really excited about this opportunity," Rob smiled. Debbie tried to share his enthusiasm but her mood was growing tepid.

Victoria could sense her friend's change in disposition. "Debbie, what's wrong?" she asked.

"Oh, Victoria, she's fine," Allison smirked in her usual crass manner. "What wife wouldn't be when her husband is *finally* moving up? That's a look of relief if you ask me."

Rob and Debbie shot Allison a look that could've killed a rattlesnake, while Tyler shook his head in frustration, taking a big gulp from his glass.

The nerve of this heifer, Victoria slowly simmered, giving Allison a death stare. "Well, I wasn't asking you"...*bitch,* she wanted to say, but refrained. "I was asking Debbie." The tension returned, and the table fell silent as Joe Sample's piano serenaded in the background.

Debbie turned her glare away from Allison and began to speak. "Victoria, you know me so well." Rob took her hand and held it tight. "Rob's promotion is for a position in his company's Miami office. We'll be moving in a few weeks. It's all happening so fast. We have to find a new home, and we'll be leaving you guys," Debbie sighed.

"Debbie," Tyler said, "You've been saying you need a break from teaching, so maybe this'll be an opportunity for you to do that. You'll even have time to start painting again."

"Yeah, girl. Look at this as a new beginning," Victoria encouraged. "I'm going to miss you, but miles can never separate us. Besides, ViaTech has an office in Miami, so you know I'll be down there to see you, at least through next June," she teased, leaning over and hugging her friend.

"Let's order champagne to celebrate," Tyler roused. After everyone's glass was filled with bubbly, Tyler made a hilarious toast that put everyone back in a good mood.

"I have some news to share that's...quite interesting," Victoria announced.

"Oh, you finally found a man?" Allison asked, causing the table to fall silent again.

Victoria took a deep breath and ignored the comment. "I'm being nominated for a prestigious year-long executive mentoring program at work."

"But you're leaving next June, right?" Debbie asked.

"Yeah, that's my plan. But I have to admit, it's a flattering offer when I think about it. But of course I'm going to turn it down because my future isn't with ViaTech. I have to devote my time to building my business."

"Victoria, I'm a little concerned that you'll be stretching yourself too thin," Allison said as she reached for a stuffed mushroom.

"Why're you concerned about anything that I do?" Victoria asked, surprise and caution lacing her voice.

"You spend so many hours at work that you barely have time for a social life, let alone to meet anyone new. And now with your little party business…"

"It's called *Divine Occasions,*" Victoria corrected.

"Yes that. Anyway, given all the work you'll have on your plate, you definitely won't have time for a relationship."

Victoria's forehead was getting hot. "Thank you for your *concern*. But my life is made up of more than just sitting around waiting for Mr. Right to come along."

By this time Debbie and Rob were watching the exchange like dialogue from a movie, while Tyler stared blankly into his drink.

"True," Allison retorted, "but nothing beats having someone to come home to. I know it's been hard since things between you and Steven ended, but you have to move on with your life," she said, feigning a look of concern that hid a conniving smile.

"Be quiet, Allison!" Tyler hissed at his wife.

There…she'd said his name. Everyone who knew Victoria firmly understood that Steven's name was off limits. To Victoria, his name was like a spinning tornado, or a wild fire out of control, or an erupting volcano—it was a natural disaster. Her heart raced and her face turned hot. His name hung in the air like Gulf Coast humidity. Tyler looked at Victoria, his mouth didn't move, but his eyes said I'm sorry.

The good mood was broken once again, and this time no happy announcement or bubbly drink could bring it back. They remained at the club just long enough to pay the bill before their "friends-night-out" came to an abrupt end.

Chapter Four

Like Alka-Seltzer in a Glass of Water......

Victoria's fun evening out had turned into another disappointing disaster. "I need a bubble bath and a drink...bad!" she said to an empty room. She peeled out of her clothes and wrapped herself in her silk robe. She walked into the bathroom, lit her favorite Jo Malone Black Vetyver candle, then sprinkled her special home concocted blend of scented bath foams and sea salts under the running water. She went downstairs, grabbed the last two chocolates in the Godiva box, and poured herself a glass of wine before heading back to her private spa retreat.

The combination of wine and warm water felt good to every inch of her body as she slid down into her Jacuzzi tub, submerging herself in the thick, fragrant bubbles. But even as she tried to relax, her ears still stung from Allison's words. Victoria had to admit that it would be nice to have someone to come home to. To actually talk out loud to another person, instead of to herself. Even her mother had said those very words just the night before. And she knew her mother was right because she had the experience to qualify her words.

John and Elizabeth Small shared a love that was strong, unquestionable, and true. They'd survived racism in the segregated south, the devastating loss of their first child, a stillborn baby girl, and had weathered the painful storm of indifference from Elizabeth's "color-struck" family. Her relatives had only tolerated her marriage to John because he hailed from the wealthiest black family within a hundred mile radius of their small South Carolina town. But their narrow-minded prejudice against his dark skin was so strong, it caused a dramatic blowout that resulted in bitter words, hurt feelings, and eventual estrangement. Yet through it all, Elizabeth and John remained dedicated to each other. Their love was enviable and Victoria desperately wanted a relationship like the one her parents shared. She thought she'd found that with Steven.

Even though he lived in Washington, DC, and she lived in Atlanta, the distance only served to make their time spent together more precious. Steven was the man Victoria thought she was going to marry, have children with, and build a happy life with—it lasted two years...............

They met at a telecommunications seminar in DC. Steven had been a rising regional senior sales director with Verizon, well on his way to a VP position. When Victoria first saw him, the attraction was instant. His skin was like a Hershey's Kiss and his smile was like happiness wrapped around a pair of lips. He pursued her with veracity.

Steven was different from the men she'd been with in the past, most of whom shared a similar background to her own: educated family, affluent upbringing, summer camps, vacations abroad and membership in the right social organizations. Steven had grown up in the projects of Chicago, the youngest child of five in a single-parent home. Between his academic scholarship and the money his mother earned from working two jobs, he managed to attend a top private school in the suburbs. That meant making a two-hour commute each day by bus and train. When he graduated with honors from Stanford, he'd made his mother proud.

After the three-day seminar ended, Victoria decided to stay an extra day and take Steven up on his offer to be her personal tour guide of the nation's capital. They visited several museums and enjoyed an afternoon stroll along the National Mall. They ended their day with a romantic dinner, flirting throughout the evening while sparks ricocheted between their bodies. When Steven took her back to her hotel room, he tried to talk his way in for a little late night goody. But Victoria wasn't having it. Instead, she let him enter her door halfway, thanked him for a wonderful evening and said good night. But Steven wasn't giving up that easily. He pulled her in close and kissed her softly. "You're an amazing woman, Victoria," he whispered into her ear.

"Steven, I really like you, but I'm sorry, you're not gettin' any tonight," she said, pulling away from him.

All he could do was smile. He kissed her one last time before closing the door.

Two weeks later after dozens of hour-long phone calls, emails, and roses, Steven flew Victoria back to DC for a visit. He wouldn't hear of her staying at a hotel, and insisted that she spend the weekend in his spacious townhome. When she arrived, she put her bags in his guest bedroom without prompting. She wanted him to know that just because she was spending the weekend in his home, that didn't mean they would be sleeping together. But she remembered the kiss they'd shared and brought her red, silk babydoll and matching thong...just in case.

That night they held hands in their seats at the tightly packed Constitution Hall, swaying to the rhythm as Maxwell crooned with passion. After returning home, Steven put on one of Luther's love making CDs to cap off the romantic evening. They kissed and caressed each other on his leather couch. Victoria was attracted to Steven like bees to honey and she could feel herself getting wet; slowly losing control. She knew she had to pull back. "I think I'm going to call it a night," she said in between his sensual kisses.

"But, Victoria," Steven whispered, his tongue gently grazing her earlobe, "the night's still young." His erection was growing harder by the minute.

"I'm really tired from the early morning flight and all the running around we did before the concert. I had a great time though," she said before withdrawing from his arms and walking back to the guest bedroom.

After a few minutes, Steven gathered himself off the couch and headed back to his bedroom, disappointed at the thought of sleeping alone. He took off his shirt and was unzipping his pants when Victoria appeared. She stood in his doorway, draped in delicate red lingerie.

"I, um...wanted to give you a proper good night kiss...if that's all right with you?" she purred.

He undressed her, pulled off his pants and brought her to his bed. He kissed her hard, sucking her nipples as he gently massaged the wetness between her legs, making her moan while his fingers sank deep inside her. He reached into the nightstand, retrieved a condom, slipped it on and entered her with a force that let her know he was hungry for her. She felt his breath, warm on her neck, drowning her in his seduction. He was going deep inside her and she could feel herself begin to dissolve and fizz like Alka-Seltzer in a glass of water.

Steven leaned back until only the tip of his penis remained inside her. He pushed her knees to her shoulders, caressed her throbbing clit with his thumb, then slowly slid back inside with a pulsating rhythm. He moved his hips like a trained professional. Victoria knew this man was beyond good when she had her first orgasm within minutes. She'd been with her fair share of men, but none had ever made her feel the way Steven did. He rocked her until she was sore, yet wonderfully tender, and left her begging for more.

Steven was affectionate, funny, and he spoiled her to no end. They saw each other as often as their busy schedules would allow. They were opposites in almost every way, but they made it work. She introduced him to things he would have never considered doing; watching foreign films and going to Broadway musicals. And she experienced new things with him; taking in her first professional heavyweight fight and snorkeling off the Florida Keys. Neither of them cared much for the other's brand of entertainment, but it didn't matter as long they were together.

But by the end of the second year of their relationship, things had started to change. What began as an appreciation for each other's differences had become a major source of their constant battles. She liked jazz and neo-soul, he liked hip-hop and rap. She liked candle light dinners at home; he preferred trendy restaurants out on the town. But it wasn't so much their differences that frustrated Victoria, as much as it was Steven's sudden inability to meet her halfway.

"Victoria, he's a weak ass brothah," Tyler had told her after meeting Steven during one of his weekend visits. "He's up to no good. He thinks he's the shit with his designer clothes and expensive gifts, don't be fooled by his sweet talk," Tyler warned.

Tyler's opinion meant a lot to Victoria, and it bothered her that her best friend didn't like her man. She thought Tyler was being over protective as usual. He'd always found fault with the men she dated, no matter how suitable they seemed to be. She once teased that she could've dated Jesus Christ and Tyler would have said he needed a haircut, shave, and a new pair of sandals!

Victoria knew that Steven was city slick, but that was part of his appeal. He excited her; especially in the bedroom. He sexed her the way she wanted it and needed it—slow and steady, bold and uninhibited. The bedroom was the only area where Steven was completely unselfish, always attentive to her needs. Many nights he wouldn't let her rest until she came several times, sufficiently satisfied.

But Victoria started to grow suspicious of Steven, thinking more and more about Tyler's comments. Despite her doubts, she didn't want to give up on their relationship. She felt she'd invested too much time and emotion to walk away from someone she loved. And to make matters worse, Steven's mutual dislike of Tyler didn't serve to help the situation.

"Somethin' must be wrong with him if he's known you all these years and he's never tried to sleep with you," Steven once told her.

"Not all close relationships between a man and woman have to be sexual," she countered.

"Vic, let me break it down to you, baby. It's impossible for a man and woman to remain as close as you two are, and not have somethin' goin' on. It just doesn't happen."

"What're you getting at?"

Steven shrugged. "I'm just sayin'…it's a very unusual friendship."

"Tyler's like a brother to me. And besides, he has a girlfriend. Remember Allison? He loves her, even though she's wrong for him."

"That don't mean nothin' baby," Steven smirked in his city slick street vernacular that he allowed to slip out on occasion. "Every man gets a lil' taste on the side."

Victoria eyed him suspiciously but refused to follow up on his comment. The fact that she didn't confront him both shocked and scared her. Deep down, she knew that was a sign to end things, but instead, she tried to hold on……………

Victoria had been soaking in the tub so long her fingertips looked like raisins. She thought about what her therapist had said after the break up. Her family and friends had been supportive, but she needed someone else to talk to. She needed someone who'd be objective, who wouldn't say, "It's a good thing you didn't marry that asshole. Count your blessings," as Denise had told her. Or, "Screw him, it's his loss," as Debbie had offered, giving her a pat on the back. Tyler simply took her out to dinner, supposedly to console her, but Victoria believed it was really to celebrate—he even ordered champagne.

"Don't run away, confront your fears. Only then can you operate in truth," her therapist had said during one of their sessions. In her professional life, Victoria was direct and in control, not letting anything ruffle her feathers, never wavering from a position. But in her personal life, her desire to please others nearly crippled her. She'd compromised her dreams to please her father, and had subjugated herself in her relationships with men to appease them too. She knew that a change was in order.

"What's wrong with me?" she shouted out loud, pounding her fists against the porcelain tub, splashing water onto the floor. She hopped out of the tepid bath and wrapped herself in her robe. She took a deep breath, picked up the phone and began to dial by memory.

"Hello," said the male voice on the other end. Victoria knew from experience that Steven always checked his caller ID, just as she did. So she knew, that he knew, that it was her.

"Hello, Steven…its Victoria."

There was silence until Steven's voice broke through. "Vic, it's been a long time. I can't believe it's you," he said in a faint whisper.

Victoria could hear the surprise in his voice.

"I didn't think I'd ever hear from you again. You wouldn't accept any of my phone calls or respond to my emails, and you sent back all my letters…unopened," he said.

"I know, I should've put closure on things a long time ago, but I couldn't. It was too hard. Too painful."

"I know. I really messed up…I hurt you, and I'm so sorry for that. But Vic, I loved you. I've never stopped loving you," Steven said in a low voice.

Victoria couldn't see his face, but she could hear his longing. She hadn't expected to feel the weight of emotions that made her heart quicken as she listened to Steven's voice, seduced by its timber. She had loved this man.

"How are you Vic? Tell me what's been going on in your life, are you seeing anyone?"

"Things are going well. I bought a new house last year and I finally started my business. I'm doing it on the side because I'm still at ViaTech, but, um…things are good."

"That sounds great, I'm happy for you…but are you seeing anyone?"

There was another brief silence.

"No," Victoria answered. "Actually, I haven't dated since we broke up. That's why I'm calling. Steven, I…"

"Oh Vic, I knew there was still a chance for us. I've prayed for this day for so long. We were so good together, baby…remember?" Steven whispered softly. "I miss you, Vic. I miss touching you, and you touching me. I miss us," he breathed into the phone.

This wasn't turning out the way Victoria had expected. His sex was her weakness. When she looked back on it, and was really honest with herself, *sex* was part of the reason their relationship had lasted for as long as it had. The sex had been out of this world, and it clouded a multitude of issues that arose in their path. Victoria knew she had to focus. "Steven, that's not why I called. I just wanted to tell you that I forgive you. That's the only way

I can move on with my life."

"I don't understand," he said in a whisper.

"We just weren't meant to be, and I understand that now. I've been angry with you to keep from being angry with myself—for a lot of different reasons. Some of which have nothing to do with you. But I'm releasing it. It's too much to hold on to."

The tension drained from Victoria's shoulders. She hadn't realized that she'd been sitting slumped over with anxiety from the moment Steven answered the phone. But now she was sitting up straight, feeling ten pounds lighter.

"Baby, you don't mean that," Steven said in a hushed and pleading whisper. "I still love you, Vic…we can work things out. I know you were angry with me, especially after what you did…"

"Steven, I'm not proud of what I did that night. And every time I think about it I feel sick. But you deserved it. That's one thing that I won't apologize for."

"Baby, I didn't mean to bring up that whole ugly scene. It was all my fault. I know that. I just want you to give us another chance," he begged softly.

"*Steven?*" a female voice called out in the background. "Steven are you on the phone?"

"Give me a minute," he yelled back in an irritated tone.

Unbelievable! That explains all the whispering. That's not longing, that's bullshit! Victoria said to herself. "Listen, I see that you're busy, so I won't interrupt your evening any further. I just wanted to tell you that I'm not angry with you any more."

"Vic, it's not what you think. That was my friend's cousin. I'm letting her stay with me until she finds a place of her own…you know how outrageous real estate is in the District." He was whispering again. "Look baby, we can still work things out. I miss you."

His lie was almost laughable to her. "You really think you're slick, don't you?"

"Vic, I'm not tryin' to be slick. I love you. That's one thing I never lied about. I know that after what happened between us you have some trust issues, but..."

Victoria had been composed up to this point, but now she lost it. "*Trust issues!* Are you fucking kidding me? Of course I have trust issues after the shit you put me through. Do you really think I'm gonna fall for your unoriginal bullshit again?" Victoria took a deep breath, trying to calm herself.

"I'm not going down this road with you, Steven. I've said what I had to say."

"Steven, are you still on the phone?" the woman called out again.

Victoria let out a laugh. "This is my final goodbye, so please don't bother trying to contact me after tonight. Have a good life."

Click…

Victoria felt good, releasing her anger with Steven. She sat by the phone trying to decide whether she should call her father. She knew that if she could let go of the anger she'd harbored for Steven, a man who'd shown her disingenuous love at best, that she could forgive her father, the one man who'd loved her unconditionally all her life. Finally, she decided to go to bed. One soul cleansing per night was enough. The conversation with her father was something she needed to do at another time. But she felt good inside, knowing she had the strength to make things right.

That night, Victoria slept like a baby. For the first time in over a year she dreamt about a man—Mr. Gorgeous. They were on the beach, lying on a blanket near the shore, wrapped in each other's arms. Tonight, he was making love to her in her dreams.

Chapter Five

Everyone Makes Mistakes......

Victoria started her Sunday morning early. She was laying on a cushioned mat in her home gym, performing slow, steady poses with the instructor on her yoga DVD. She'd just finished her cool down stretch and was about to head upstairs to change for eight a.m. church service when her doorbell rang. *Who's at my door at seven o'clock on a Sunday morning?* she wondered.

It was Tyler, and he looked terrible. His eyes were red, as though he hadn't slept all night. "Tyler, what's goin' on?" Victoria asked, shivering as the cold morning air whipped around her bare arms.

"Can I come in?"

"Of course." Victoria moved to the side to let him through. He walked past her and back toward the den where she and her friends always hung out. The room was large, but the chocolate colored walls gave it a cozy, intimate feel. The soft lighting and big fluffy pillows on the over-sized furniture were tailor-made for relaxing. Tyler sank down into the soft chenille sofa and rubbed his temples, trying to give himself therapeutic relief. "I see you're doin' your workout thing this morning," he said, trying to smile.

"Tyler, what's wrong? You look like hell."

He let out a sigh. "Allison and I are over. We're done…finished."

"What brought this on?" Victoria asked casually, folding her arms across her chest. She didn't know whether to jump up and click her heels, or sit down and comfort him.

"Things haven't been good between us for a long time. All we do is argue. I stayed in it for as long as I could, tryin' to make it work, but in the end there was nothing left between us."

Victoria's heart went out for him. She and Tyler had known each other for fifteen years, and lately, he hadn't been himself.

Tyler had boyish good looks and a natural charm that came as easy to him as breathing air. He was medium height, with broad shoulders and a slim build. His thick black hair was closely cropped, and his café au lait complexion still showed evidence of minor scaring from adolescent acne. But it was his big hazel brown eyes and sincere smile that made you notice only the goodness in his face and the brightness of his spirit. Tyler was charming, drawing people to him like a magnet, and his sense of humor rivaled Richard Pryor's. He was educated and polished, yet possessed a bad boy quality that gave him *edge*, compliments of his Brooklyn born accent and homeboy swagger which balanced out his suburban upbringing. And women loved him! "Victoria, who's that cute brother who comes to visit you?" one of her graduate school classmates once asked. "Can you hook a sistah up? He's adorable."

Tyler was blessed with his mother's maiden name as his birthright. His father had been a prominent Pediatrician, and his mother, a professor at NYU. Like Victoria, he was an only child. His parents were what many in their social circle called "bohemian" and "eclectic." They were socially conscious, and were raising their son with the same values. They were Tyler's heroes.

He was thirteen years old when they were killed in a car accident, on their way to Morehouse College for his father's alumni reunion. They'd decided to drive instead of fly so they could enjoy the lush greenness of the south's landscape. On their way down the Interstate they were hit by a car of teenagers who'd skipped school in favor of drinking and joy riding. After the funeral, Tyler moved to Virginia to live with his mother's older sister, who had never married or had any children of her own. His Aunt Beatrice was an accomplished business woman, and she took Tyler in, raising him with the same humanitarian values she knew his parents would have approved of.

Tyler had surprised everyone when he asked Allison to marry him. She was the opposite of everything he stood for. She was elitist, status seeking, and pretentious. She didn't *fit* him. But his background, on the other hand, did fit into the fairy tale life that Allison wanted. And the fact that Tyler had a nice inheritance that had matured when he'd turned twenty-one sealed the deal. The trust his parents had the foresight to setup for him would sustain him comfortably for many years to come. Allison believed that over time, and with her influence, she could convince Tyler to give up his "down with the people" mentality, forgo his silly non-profit venture, and settle into a respectable corporate job.

Victoria returned from the kitchen with two cups of coffee. "Columbian Blend with lots of sugar and a dash of cream, just the way you like it," she smiled, handing the cup to Tyler. She sat on the opposite end of the couch, sipping the hot brew. "Tyler, you know I never cared for Allison, but honestly, I'm sorry that you're hurting right now."

"Actually, I feel relieved that we're getting a divorce."

Victoria looked startled. "You're really serious this time, aren't you?" She knew that Tyler had threatened to end his marriage once before. A month after his wedding, he'd confided to her that he was thinking about separating from his new wife.

"I think that Allison and I need to reevaluate things," he'd said. "We moved too fast, and made a big mistake. So many things change once you say 'I do'."

But after he talked with Allison, she managed to connive her way back into his good graces with sweet lies and sugar-coated promises to work on the problems of their marriage; mainly her overbearing attitude and meddling parents.

Tyler took a sip of his coffee. "I know I'm doin' the right thing. I told her I wanted a divorce six month's ago, but she talked me into giving it another try."

"I knew you two were having problems shortly after the wedding, but you didn't tell me that you tried to end things six months ago," Victoria said with surprise.

"Yeah, well, it's been crazy and I didn't want to bother you with it again. I felt bad when I dropped that news on you a few weeks after we got married. You'd just broken up with…well, you were goin' through some shit of your own. So I decided this time I'd deal with things myself."

"You're such a knucklehead. After all we've been through together, you know you can count on me to be there for you. No matter what."

"I know, I just thought it was something I could handle on my own. But after last night, I knew it was over. Her attitude was fucked up," he paused. "I should've made her apologize to you on the spot. I'm sorry for that."

Victoria leaned over and patted him on the knee. "Don't worry about it. Listen, I know I've asked you this question a dozen times, but why in the hell did you marry Allison in the first place?"

Tyler looked Victoria squarely in the eyes. "Because I knew that even if the marriage ended, I'd be okay. I knew she couldn't hurt or disappoint me. If I lost her, I wouldn't be devastated," Tyler admitted. "You see, when I first fell in love with Juliet I was cautious, 'cause I was afraid that one day I might lose her. But hell, after a while I couldn't help it. I loved that girl."

"But you broke her heart," Victoria softly reminded him.

"I was a different man back then, young and stupid. I didn't want to go through the kind of pain I felt when I lost my parents. After Juliet accepted the job offer in New York, I took it as a sign, so I broke it off. Crazy, right?"

"Everyone makes mistakes," Victoria tried to console.

"Yeah, and that was a big one. That's why I'm gonna undo what should've never been done. I'm going by my lawyer's office tomorrow morning so I can file the divorce papers. He told me a couple of months ago that I could get one of those quickie divorces, that way I won't have to go through the standard year-long separation period, as long as Allison doesn't contest it. And she won't. She's upset right now, but she'll get over it."

"What makes you so sure she won't contest it? She's held you off twice already," Victoria asked, finishing the last of her coffee.

"For one thing, her parents will probably have her married off to some Cliff Huxtable type before the ink dries on the divorce papers. Plus, as of this morning we're no longer living under the same roof."

"Where are you going to stay in the meantime?" Victoria asked, ready to offer up her guest room for as long as it would take for Tyler to find a new place.

"Whadda you mean where am I gonna stay? I'm stayin' in my house," Tyler balked, picking up his cup and gulping now that his coffee had cooled.

"So you put her ass out?"

"You damn skippy. She's back at her folks' place. That's why I haven't slept in almost twenty-four hours. We spent all night and well into this morning movin' her stuff. And it's a good thing it stopped raining shortly after midnight or we'd still be hauling clothes and shoeboxes right now."

"Wow! I'm stunned."

"We just finished the last trip an hour ago. I would've been here sooner if I hadn't had to wait for the locksmith."

"You changed the locks?"

"You better believe it."

"Tyler, you don't think she would do anything crazy, do you? I mean, I know she's a bitch…but damn, she's not stupid."

"You never know what a person is capable of under certain conditions," he answered slowly.

Victoria knew the true indictment behind Tyler's words. They were both ruminating over the same thought—the thing she'd done to Steven. "I know what you're thinking," she said, shaking her head. "Sometimes I still can't believe I did that. Looking back on that entire situation, I was so pathetic."

Tyler reached for Victoria's hand and held it firmly in his. "You were hurt. The shit he did was fucked up, and a heart that's been hurt knows no bounds."

"I let Steven bring me down to a level that I'll never allow myself to sink to again," Victoria said with resilience. She could see the shock on Tyler's face at the mention of Steven's name coming from her lips. "I called him last night," she continued, clearing her throat, "and I told him that I'm not angry with him anymore. I'm moving on and closing that door, and I can't tell you the last time I felt this alive. I feel like *me* again."

Tyler pulled Victoria into his arms for a long hug. "I'm happy for you, sweetie. That asshole wasn't worth it. I always thought you were too good for him anyway. I told you he was a weak ass brothah from the get go."

Victoria leaned back and looked at Tyler. "*Please*, just like I told you about Allison from the jump."

Tyler smiled and nodded his head. "Sometimes we see what we want to see."

Those Booty-Huggin' Jeans……

Victoria skipped church and spent the day with Tyler, who served as her sous chef, prepping the food she planned to prepare for dinner; roasted red pepper soup with cilantro, herb glazed lamb chops with mustard seed vinaigrette, rosemary new potatoes, and honey glazed carrots. That evening Debbie and Rob came over to join them. Victoria hailed the night's feast as a victory dinner to celebrate Tyler's new freedom. After they cleaned their plates, Victoria brought out a freshly baked apple cranberry pie, while Debbie carried the Ben & Jerry's in one hand, and a carafe of coffee in the other.

"To new adventures," Tyler toasted. They all lifted their mugs, then dug into their dessert. "And on that subject," he smiled, looking around the table, "I'm gonna get back with Juliet."

"*What?*" the group asked, speaking in one voice.

Tyler nodded. "Yeah, I'm gonna call her tomorrow. I got the 411 on her from her girl, Gigi," he paused, nodding toward Debbie and Rob, "she's Juliet's best friend from undergrad."

"And she's wild and crazy as hell," Victoria added.

"Yeah, Gigi's a piece of work. But we keep in touch. Anyway, we talked a few months ago and she told me that Juliet's seeing some guy, but it's not serious, so I'm steppin' in."

Victoria listened with caution, remembering Tyler and Juliet's last encounter.

They'd dated in college. After graduation, Tyler started YFI, while Juliet entered law school at Emory University. After she graduated, she was recruited by a large firm in Manhattan. It was a great opportunity, and would place her back home near her family. She and Tyler agreed that their love was strong enough to survive the distance, but after a few months he ended things.

Juliet had called Victoria in tears. "What's wrong with him, Victoria? Is it another woman? He hasn't returned any of my phone calls. You're his best friend and you know him better than anyone else. Please tell me why he's doing this?" Juliet had pleaded.

"I don't know why Tyler's acting this way, but I do know that he loves you. You need to go to him and talk to him for yourself." Victoria didn't know what else to say.

The following weekend Juliet came back to Atlanta to confront Tyler. After that, the relationship was officially over. Tyler never talked about the details of what happened, but Victoria knew he wasn't seeing another woman.

Victoria looked at Tyler with skepticism. "What if the guy that Juliet's seeing is more serious than Gigi thinks? You spoke to her a few months ago. A lot can happen in that time." She hated to ask the question, but she wanted Tyler to be prepared.

"I hear you, but I'm gonna do whatever it takes to win her back. Whoever that brothah is, he's just wastin' his time," Tyler posed with confidence.

"Wow," Debbie said. "This is too much for me to process. We're moving in a few weeks, Tyler's getting a divorce and then reuniting with Juliet.

And the biggest kicker of all...Victoria called Steven and told him to kiss her ass!"

"I didn't tell Steven to kiss my ass," Victoria laughed.

Debbie grinned, "I know, but you should have."

"Amen to that," Tyler agreed.

"Well, hold on because I have another announcement to make," Victoria said. "I've decided to turn in my resignation tomorrow morning."

"What happened to waiting until next June?" Debbie asked.

"Turning down the EMP nomination sends up a red flag. And like my father told me the other night, it's a no win situation. I know that Ted will be disappointed because not only am I turning down his personal nomination, I'm resigning at the same time. But I gotta do what I gotta do."

"He'll be disappointed all right," Tyler grinned. "I bet he was really looking forward to *mentoring* you."

"Tyler, I told you. I think he might be gay," Victoria sighed.

Tyler shook his head. "Rob, will you tell her that the man's not gay. He just wants a little brown sugar. Or in your case, a little milk chocolate," he winked.

Rob laughed, nodding in agreement "What makes you think he's gay?" he asked. "Have you heard rumors about him at work or something?"

"No, not about him being gay, but Ted is estranged from his wife. I heard they even take separate vacations. She's probably just a cover for him, his beard. And he's never been known to even look in the direction of a woman."

Tyler laughed. "That's circumstantial evidence. It doesn't prove anything."

"Oh yeah? Then why is he into home décor? He even asked me about the potpourri in my office. And what about his boyfriend last night...who's conveniently from out of town," Victoria posed.

Rob looked at Victoria with surprise. "Just because he's in a bad marriage but doesn't chase after other women, and he has good taste and hangs out with his friends when they come to town, that doesn't mean he's gay."

Victoria had to admit that under cross examination, her theory had more holes than Swiss cheese. "Well, there's something about him that doesn't add up."

Rob asked his next question with caution. "Victoria, have you ever dated a white guy?"

"What does that have to do with anything?" she asked.

"I can answer that," Tyler said in between bites of his pie. "If you're not a seven foot tall, money-havin', expensive cologne wearin', well-educated, well-dressed, well-hung Mandingo, Victoria ain't havin' it!" he laughed.

"Tyler, you know that's not true," Victoria quipped, "I don't put a dollar amount on how much a brother has to make. But Rob, to answer your question…no, I haven't dated white men." At this point Victoria was becoming slightly defensive.

"Maybe you're not taking Ted seriously because he's white," Rob said.

"Rob!" Debbie snapped. "You know Victoria's not like that."

Victoria remained silent.

"I'm not saying that she doesn't like white people for God's sake," Rob defended himself, "I just think that maybe because she hasn't dated white guys, it might affect how she looks at Ted." He turned his attention back to Victoria for her reaction.

"To be perfectly honest, I've never really considered white men as a romantic option," she said resolutely.

Debbie looked stunned. Now it was her turn to be silent. She and nearly everyone she knew had dated people of different races. She'd always known that Victoria was attracted to a certain type of man, and as Tyler had said, they all fit the same mold. But until tonight, in all the years they'd known each other, Debbie had never thought that her friend might disqualify a potential mate because of race.

"Regardless of who you've dated or what you think, that white man wants you," Tyler said.

"There's evidence to the contrary," Victoria countered in frustration. "Yesterday when I went into the office, Ted was there. I was wearing my *Juicy Couture* jeans and he didn't even look at my behind…didn't even try to sneak a peak."

Tyler put down his spoon. "You mean those booty-huggin' jeans you wore to my Labor Day party last month?"

"Yep, and he never looked below my neck."

"*Damn!*" Tyler said. "There's got to be an explanation. I guarantee you he looked. You just didn't see him. Hell, I'm your best friend, I have no romantic interest in you whatsoever, and even *I* looked at your ass in those jeans."

Although Rob wanted to comment, he didn't. It was one thing to look at your wife's best friend's ass, but it was another to admit to it out loud. So he exercised good judgment and kept his mouth shut.

"Umph, I never thought my friends would think I was so desperate that they'd try to push me off on a man who might be on the down low…and married!" Victoria balked.

"As far as the married thing goes, Victoria does have a point," Debbie agreed, recovering from her silence."

Victoria was ready to change the subject. "Anyway, I'm resigning tomorrow and I'm getting on with my business, and my life. And you guys are right, I need to start dating again. As a matter of fact, I can't stop thinking about this guy I met the other night. And before you ask…yes, he's black."

Debbie leaned into the table. "Where, when, and is he fine?"

"The Cheesecake Factory…Friday night…and yes girl, he's fine," Victoria giggled.

Tyler spoke as he polished off the last of his pie. "You told me that you were having dinner by yourself."

"I was. He was seated at a table across from me." Victoria talked with a dreamy look in her eyes as she told her friends about her encounter with Mr. Gorgeous.

"Get a grip, Cinderella," Tyler interrupted, "he should've been looking at his woman, not makin' goo goo eyes at you. If that brothah was there with someone else and he still tried to step to you, stay the hell away from him. He's no good."

Victoria shook her head. "I got a good vibe from him. It might sound crazy, but even though I don't know his name or anything about him, we made a connection."

"He sounds interesting," Debbie said. "Maybe you'll run into him again."

"If you do, just be careful," Rob warned.

Each person at the table had been rendered silent at one point during the evening. Now it was Tyler's turn. He didn't say a word.

Please Send Me A Good Man……

Later that night as she lay in bed, Victoria replayed her dinner conversation with her friends over and over in her mind. She had to admit that there was something intriguing about Ted Thornton.

On the surface, Ted possessed the very qualities she loved. He was intelligent and kind with a good sense of humor, and to top it all off he was very handsome. But she also thought he was the kind of man who seemed too good to be true, and in her experience, if they seemed too good, there was usually something bad hidden in the shadows.

Then her mind drifted to Mr. Gorgeous. Even though he was apparently taken, she still hoped she'd meet him again. She didn't know if it was just pure and simple physical attraction, or a rare and wonderful spiritual connection, but whatever it was it had made her tremble inside. When she looked into his eyes and heard the concern in his voice after her fall, she wanted to kiss him right there on the spot. When he knelt close beside her, he smelled like citrus and spice, exciting her senses. She remembered that he hadn't been wearing a ring, and that his hands were soft and smooth, like those of an artist or a pianist.

Meeting him had awakened carnal desires that Victoria had pushed away for over a year, and now, thinking about him was making her body ache for a man's touch. She needed relief. She hopped out of bed and took a long shower to calm her urges. But when she crawled back under her warm comforter all she could think about was Mr. Gorgeous and the intense throbbing between her legs. She lay in bed and said a prayer.

"God, please send me a good man who's kind and gentle, and who knows how to treat a woman like a lady and take responsibility for himself as a man. Please send me a man who's drug-free, baby-mama-drama-free, debt-free, educated, straight, has no criminal record, and is respectful of others. And God, please let him be an honest man because I can't tolerate any more deceitful liars. And please send me a man who'll love me even after he discovers that I'm quirky, stubborn, and slightly neurotic. Please let him be the kind of man who loves children, and laughter, and long walks in the park, and traveling to exotic places, and eating rich food, and drinking good wine, and telling silly jokes. God, let him be patient, and understanding. And please, please let him be the kind of man who knows how to fix things around the house. And Lord, send me someone who's good to look at. He doesn't have to be Denzel handsome, but if he could be somewhere in that ballpark I'd really appreciate it. And God, I know I'm asking a lot, but I have one last request…Please send him fast! Amen.

Chapter Six

*B*lack. No Sugar. No Cream......

Victoria arrived at the office two hours early on Monday morning. She finished the recommendations for the SME report, made copies, then stuffed them into a large envelope and slipped them under Patricia's office door. There were only five evaluations that didn't meet company standards, and Patricia's was one of them. Her team had ranked her low in every category. One evaluator even blasted her by using expletives so ugly, it almost made Victoria feel bad for her nemesis.

Victoria had come in early because she wanted to tell Ted about her resignation before she broke the news to Bob Hoffman, the VP of HR. She felt that he deserved to hear it directly from her lips instead of through a memo or office gossip. She'd been thinking about her decision all morning.

She knew her father had been right, she needed to leave. She was starting to build her clientele and she knew that Divine Occasions could really take off if she concentrated her efforts full-time. A few months ago, Sherry, her realtor, had asked her to organize an office party and golf outing for her small realty company. Victoria planned an event that was fun and creative, earning her glowing praises from Sherry and the other employees. The good word of mouth led more business her way. She knew that now was the time, so she took a deep breath and picked up the phone. "Good morning, Jen. It's Victoria Small, how're you?" she greeted Ted's assistant.

"Good morning, Victoria. I'm doing well. Ted left me a note that he already delivered the EMP packet to you. Did you find everything okay?"

"Yes, um, actually I'm calling because I'd like to schedule a meeting with Ted…as soon as possible." She said her last words in a direct tone, emphasizing the importance of her request. She could hear Jen pecking away at her computer keys, accessing Ted's electronic calendar.

"Looks like his schedule is pretty full, is it something I can help you with?"

"No…I really need to speak with Ted."

"He should be in the office within the next half hour. I'll check with him and call you back. Can I tell him what this is in reference too?" Jen asked with heightened curiosity.

Victoria didn't know why, but she felt a bit nervous. "Um, I'd rather not say. It's something I need to speak directly with Ted about. Just tell him that it's important…please."

"Okay, Victoria. I'll give him your message and I'll call you back as soon as I can fit you into his schedule."

"Thanks, Jen." Victoria hung up the phone and took another deep breath. *Why is this so hard? I don't owe Ted Thornton anything.*

When Victoria smelled fresh coffee brewing, she knew that Denise had arrived. She walked from behind her desk, pulled out a cake platter and small paper plates from a large Williams-Sonoma bag, and sat them on her credenza. Denise came in smiling from ear to ear, carrying two steaming cups of Breakfast Blend.

"Wait a minute. Stop the press. I know that's not your cappuccino pound cake!"

"I went on a little baking binge yesterday," Victoria smiled, handing Denise a slice of cake. "Tyler, Debbie and Rob came over for dinner. We ate a whole pie, but didn't touch this cake."

Denise sat down, preparing to dig in. *"Yuumm!"* she practically sang, taking a bite. "I shouldn't be eating this, but it's so good. I'll probably gain five pounds from one slice."

Victoria took a seat beside Denise in front of her desk. "Oh, go ahead, you only live once." She picked up her fork and attacked her slice of the densely moist, aromatic cake. "Now, tell me about your weekend, then I'll tell you my interesting news."

"Interesting news?" Denise asked with raised brow.

"Yeah, but you go first."

Denise told Victoria about the romantic weekend she and her husband shared after they sent their two teenagers to stay with her sister for the weekend. "Girlfriend, after sixteen years of marriage Vernon can still rock my world like it's comin' to an end," she grinned devilishly.

"I'm glad somebody's gettin' some," Victoria said as they both laughed. "I haven't had sex since I broke up with Steven. He was an insincere bastard, but he sure could screw!"

Denise put down her fork. She was speechless. "What brought this on?"

Victoria quickly told Denise about the events of her weekend, giving her the abbreviated versions of her encounter with Mr. Gorgeous, the incident at Sambuca, (although she left out the part about seeing Ted there with his boyfriend), her conversation with Steven, Tyler's breakup, and last but not least, her decision to resign as soon as she could schedule a meeting with Ted.

"That's a heavy load to handle in one weekend. But you know what, I'm glad that Tyler and The Wicked Witch are history, and I'm ecstatic that you're finally over that asshole! I never did like him."

"I guess all good things come in time."

"Yes they do, and I think you're making the right decision to leave now instead of waiting 'til next June. But Girlfriend, I'm gonna miss you like crazy. You'll just have to work hard so you can afford to hire me," Denise smiled.

"If my clientele continues to grow, it might be sooner than you think. Denise, I feel so good about the direction my life is taking. I'm even going to start dating again."

"Good, it's about time you resurrected your love life from the dead. The right man will come along, just have faith in God and pray on it. And oh yeah, while you're at it, ask him to send you a man who can take care of business in the bedroom...a whole year? Please!" Denise teased as they broke into laughter.

Just then Ted knocked on the door. "Good morning ladies, I hope I'm not interrupting?"

Victoria looked up and could've sworn the man standing in front of her had just stepped off the pages of a magazine. She took in his navy three-button suit, French blue shirt, and raspberry-colored silk tie. He was a sight that made both women pause.

"I was just leaving," Denise said. She walked toward the door, then turned toward Ted. "Mr. Thornton, would you like a cup of coffee?"

"Denise makes the best coffee," Victoria offered.

Ted smiled, "In that case, how can I refuse? And please, call me Ted. My father was Mr. Thornton."

"Okay, Ted, one cup of coffee coming up. How do you take yours?"

"Black. No sugar. No cream," he said, turning to look at Victoria. His yearning was seeping out, so he quickly looked away.

Denise smiled, then gave Victoria a curious glance before walking out the door.

Ted wondered if Victoria had noticed his slip. Her eyes didn't indicate recognition, so he cleared his throat and began. "Jen gave me your message. She said it sounded rather urgent. Is everything okay?"

He was hoping that Victoria couldn't see how anxious he was. He'd asked Jen to cancel his nine-thirty appointment, then took the elevator down to Victoria's office. He'd spent his entire weekend thinking about her, fantasizing about what it would be like to hold her close. *Does she know?* he wondered.

When he saw her in the office over the weekend, he could barely contain himself at the sight of her body, nicely melted into her clingy top and snug fitting jeans. He tried his best not to stare. And he thought he'd done a pretty good job, but when she turned to gather her things from her desk as they were leaving, he couldn't help savoring her smooth curves. He replayed his actions in his mind. He didn't think she'd caught him because he'd been very discreet. When he saw her later that evening at Sambuca, he'd successfully fought the urge to lean over and kiss her. He wasn't sure, but he could've sworn that the two men at her table had seen the intention in his eyes. And he knew he was the subject of conversation among the group because once he returned to his table, they all shifted their stares in his direction at the same time. Then shortly after that all the talking and laughing between them ceased. When he looked toward the group again, they were leaving, and none looked too happy. He wondered what had happened.

"Yes, everything is fine," Victoria answered, snapping Ted out of his thoughts. "Please have a seat," she said, motioning to the empty chair beside her where Denise had been sitting. "I was waiting for Jen to call me back. I hadn't expected you to come down."

He could see that Victoria was uneasy. Her body language seemed stiff, almost as if she was bracing herself for something. "So, tell me what's on your mind. Have you reconsidered the EMP nomination?" he asked.

They were interrupted when Denise walked back into the room. "Here you go. One coffee, straight." She handed Ted the cup, gave Victoria another curious look, then headed out again.

Victoria walked over to her credenza. "Have a slice of cake to go with your coffee," she said, trying to keep her nerves in check. She picked up the knife, cut a slice and handed it to him.

Ted didn't want cake, he wanted answers. But he knew he had to play it cool. "Thanks," he smiled politely. He took a bite as he watched Victoria take her seat, enjoying the rise of her skirt as she sat next to him and crossed her legs. "This is delicious. Where did you buy it?" he asked.

Victoria beamed with pride. "I didn't buy it, I baked it."

She's beautiful and she cooks, he thought as he devoured the cake. "You're a woman of many talents," he complimented, quickly swallowing his last bite before refocusing on the mission at hand; getting to the bottom of why Victoria had requested a meeting with him. "So, back to the reason you wanted to meet with me?"

Victoria put her plate to the side. "I've come to a decision and I wanted you to be the first to know..." She paused for a moment when she heard Denise and Patricia speaking in harsh tones just outside her door. Patricia had eased in past Denise and was now eyeing Ted like a piranha ready to tear into flesh.

"Good morning, Ted. It's so good to see you. How are you today?" Patricia asked, leaning over and extending her delicately French manicured hand.

He answered with cool reserve. "I'm fine. And yourself?"

"I'm marvelous, but I'm also a little anxious...I can't wait until Friday," she hinted. She wanted to start up a discussion about the EMP nominations which would be announced at the end of the week.

"You're ready for the week to end already? It's just begun," Ted responded. He wasn't taking her bait. He'd dealt with women like Patricia before, and he had no interest in entertaining her games. She reminded him of his wife.

Patricia didn't know what to make of Ted's brush-off, so she didn't push it.

"Good morning, Patricia," Victoria spoke up, slightly annoyed. Patricia had entered her office and hadn't bothered to address her because she was too busy kissing up to Ted. Victoria suspected that Patricia had come by to discuss the SME report, and to make a case to have her evaluation omitted from the final report. But now that Ted was within her reach, it was apparent that the platinum ticking time-bomb's only interest lay with him

"Good morning, Victoria." Patricia gave her a smile that was about as genuine as a three-dollar bill.

"Patricia, would you like a slice of cake?" Victoria offered.

Patricia looked at the empty plate in Ted's hand. "I see that Victoria's at it again, trying to fatten up the office," she said, finger tossing her hair. She put her hands on her slim waist. "I'm very health conscious and I don't eat *that type* of fattening food. Victoria, I know that you don't really watch what you eat, but I do, so I'll pass," she smirked.

Victoria was about to respond when Ted stepped in. He sat his crumb-covered plate on her desk and rose to his feet. "Patricia, you'll have to excuse us, Victoria and I were about to have a meeting when you came in…have a good day," he said as he ushered Patricia to the door, then closed it behind her. When he came back to his seat, his cool demeanor belied his annoyance.

"Thank you, Ted. I couldn't have done it better myself," Victoria smiled. She wanted to slap him a high-five, but decided it might be going a little overboard.

"Arrogance, I can handle, but rudeness …it's uncalled for," Ted huffed. "I guess we got a little side tracked. What was it that you wanted to discuss?"

Victoria took a deep breath. "First, I want you to know that your offer of support and interest in my career development meant a great deal to me. It's nice to know that someone in executive management recognized my talent and the contributions I've made to the company."

"My admiration for you…for your work, is well deserved," he said. Ted knew that something was very wrong because Victoria was speaking in the past tense. This sounded like a resignation speech to him.

"Thank you," she paused, "what I'm trying to say is that after much thought and deliberation …"

"Victoria," Ted interrupted, "I just remembered I'm running late for a meeting." He stood abruptly and walked toward the door.

"But Ted, I…"

He looked at his watch and cut her off again. "I'm sorry, but I have to go. I'll have Jen put you on my calendar so we can talk at greater length when I have time."

Victoria didn't have a chance to respond because before she knew it, Ted was out the door. She walked back to her desk and thought about what had just happened. She didn't know why, but she found herself standing there—smiling for no good reason.

Ted pondered over his conversation with Victoria on the elevator ride back up to his office. His instincts had told him that she wasn't going to change her mind about the EMP nomination. He'd known it last week when he left her office, even though he'd asked her to rethink her decision. And now, what he feared was coming had just nearly happened; her resignation. He knew it was imminent. Why else would she have turned down his offer? But he wasn't ready to see Victoria walk away when he'd finally figured out a way to get close to her. He knew he had to think of another plan, and quick.

The Way He Looked At You......

Victoria told Denise about her conversation with Ted. "I wish he hadn't left before I had a chance to tell him," she sighed, "I hope Jen can get me on his schedule tomorrow."

"Hmmmm?" Denise gave Victoria another curious look.

"Why're you looking at me like that? You did it earlier this morning, what gives?"

Denise closed Victoria's door, then came back and leaned over her desk. "Girlfriend, I can't believe what I just saw."

"Believe what? Victoria asked, eyes filled with curiosity.

"That Ted Thornton has a thing for you!"

Victoria's back stiffened. "What in the world makes you say that?"

"Jen said he doesn't go to anyone's office for meetings. The man is way too busy, people have to come to him. And this is the second time he's popped up in your office."

"Denise, please. Just because he's come to my office..."

"Girlfriend, he's interested in you. I can tell by the way he looked at you this morning. He tried to hide it. He's good, but I'm better because it didn't slip past me. That black coffee comment took the cake, pardon the pun."

Victoria thought about what Denise had just said. Her other friends had all voiced the same opinion too, and they'd said it was because of the way Ted had looked at her. "Denise, I don't think Ted's interested in me. Actually, I got the impression he's gay."

Denise nearly lost her balance. "Are you crazy?"

Victoria spelled out the same rationale she'd used on her friends, making Denise shake her head. "Girlfriend, Jen would've told me something like that. She's his right hand and she would know. That man is not gay."

"I know she's your girl, but do you think Jen would really tell you something that private about Ted?"

"Yeah. When she worked for Lamar Williams she told me some things about that man that I'll carry to my grave. Jen knows who to trust. She's clever. That's why Ted kept her on in that position instead of bringing in someone from Vanguard Systems. She knows where the bones are buried."

Victoria shook her head. "Well, he may not be gay, but there's something about him that I can't quite shake."

"Yeah," Denise said with a smile, "it's call attraction and denial."

*C*ross The Race Line......

Victoria thought about her conversation with Denise all afternoon. Along with her mother and Tyler, she highly valued Denise's opinion. Denise had the kind of smarts that years of formal education couldn't match. She had common sense, and as her mother always said, common sense wasn't that common.

Victoria trusted her own judgment, but she knew that she wasn't wise like her mother, or intuitive like Denise, or crafty like Tyler. But she was smart and she approached things from a logical position. That's why she found it hard to believe that after having several conversations with Ted, she hadn't picked up on what everyone else seemed to think.

She'd been around the block enough to know when a man wanted more than just casual friendship. And she knew the signs all too well; a lingering glance, an innocent brush against the body that was too close to really be innocent, suggestive banter, and straight up mackin' as Tyler would say. But Ted had done none of those things.

Gnawing at the forefront of Victoria's thoughts was the question that Rob had asked—was she dismissing Ted because he was white? She'd always thought herself to be open-minded, but in her romantic relationships she'd only dated black men. From the lightest hue of beige to the darkest shade of onyx, they'd all been black. It was her requirement...period!

She felt it was a betrayal to cross the race line, and didn't want to become another contributor to the decline of the black family unit. She knew that on some level her views stemmed from her own dysfunctional family background, and the painful memories that still lingered her from her past. And despite all her success, good looks, and friends and family who loved her, sometimes she still felt like that seven-year-old little girl who sat at the edge of the stairs one night long ago, and lost herself.

This Was A Sign......

Victoria sped down the street through Friday afternoon rush hour, barely zipping past the traffic light before it changed to red. She'd had a busy week and she was on her way back to the office from an off-site meeting, rushing to make it in time for her appointment with Ted. She'd hoped to meet with him earlier in the week, but to her disappointment Jen had called and told her that his schedule was full, and that his first available appointment wouldn't be until five o'clock Friday afternoon. She'd been stressed all week just thinking about how she'd break the news to him. *Why are you acting like this? You don't owe Ted Thornton anything,* she kept telling herself.

"Damn!" she hissed as she came up to another light. This time it turned red before she could squeak through. She sat there, impatiently waiting for it to change to green when she saw someone familiar at the other side of the intersection. It was him! Mr. Gorgeous!

His light changed and she watched as he rolled through the intersection and past her car. It was as if he was driving in slow motion as she took in the moving details; the serious focus etched on his face, his lips moving as he talked on his cell phone, his left hand on the wheel as he steered his truck through traffic, his eyes focused on the road ahead. She craned her neck to watch him as he eased down the road and eventually out of sight. She didn't flinch another muscle until she heard the horn of the driver behind her, signaling that the light had changed.

Victoria knew this was a sign. She didn't know who he was, where he was going or what he was doing, but she knew that seeing him meant there was something great ahead. This wasn't just a coincidence, this was God's way of telling her that he'd heard her prayer and he was on the job!

Incredibly Sexy......

Victoria made it back to work just in time for her meeting with Ted. She rushed up to his office, only to find herself waiting because he was running late. She'd come dressed in her favorite Adrienne Vittadini suit. The fitted jacket accentuated her slim waist, and the pencil skirt hit just at her knee, showing off her shapely calves. The outfit gave her bold confidence, exactly what she needed in order to give her resignation speech.

She looked down at her wrist and noted the time, it was five-thirty. She'd spent the last half hour sitting in the waiting area outside Ted's office, fantasizing about Mr. Gorgeous. But now she was starting to get antsy. Even though her only plans for the evening included a trip to the library to do research for her business plan, she didn't want to spend any more time at ViaTech than she had to.

She glimpsed over at Jen, finding it hard to believe that she and Denise had gone to school together and were the same age. While Denise's smooth skin, bright eyes, and exuberant smile defied her forty years, Jen looked fifty if she looked a day. Mother Nature had dealt the slim brunette a devastatingly low blow, and years of sun worship had given her skin the look of well-worn leather. But despite her declining beauty, she had a smile that was pleasant enough to put even the most disagreeable person in a good mood.

Victoria was about to ask how much longer she'd have to wait when Jen's phone rang. She spoke quickly, then hung up. "Victoria, you can go in, he's ready to see you now. Have a good weekend." And with that, Jen turned off her computer and began to gather her things.

Ted rose from behind his desk to greet Victoria as she walked through his door. The sight of her brought a smile to his face. "Please come in and have a seat," he said, ushering her to the chair in front of his desk. "Sorry to keep you waiting. It's been a killer week and I miscalculated my time"

"I understand. You're a very busy man," Victoria replied, shifting her weight in the hard leather chair. "Ted, I'd like to pick up where we left off on Monday. As I said, I appreciate your support…"

"Excuse me," he gently interrupted. "I didn't want you to continue waiting, but I have one final report from the New York office to review. It should only take a few minutes. While I'm finishing up, I'd like you to take a look at the proposal the marketing department sent over for the SuperNet convention next June. Do you mind?"

Victoria was a little hesitant at first, but SuperNet had always been one of her favorite events since her early days in the marketing department, and she was curious about what kind of show ViaTech had planned for the upcoming year, even though she wouldn't be there to see it. "Sure," she said, taking the documents.

They both concentrated in silence. Victoria examined page after page of the proposal, while Ted took the opportunity to inspect her without having to use discretion. He'd purposely set their meeting for as late as he could at the end of the week. He knew that ViaTech was like a sinking ship on Friday afternoons, with everyone scrambling to desert the deck. And that was good because he didn't want anyone around. He wanted to have private time with Victoria so they could talk free of any *unexpected interruptions*.

Victoria was engrossed in her reading, so Ted waited for her to finish. He inhaled her seductive perfume that filled the air. After his small slip with the coffee comment, he'd beaten himself up the rest of the week. He couldn't believe he'd let his desires flow like a running faucet. He knew it was time to seriously think about what he was doing with this woman.

He was certain it would be inappropriate at the least, and possibly detrimental to his career, to risk getting involved with a colleague. It was something he had never done in his entire life. He'd known many powerful men who had been brought down because of office romances that eventually turned into ugly public scenes, and in some cases, sexual harassment lawsuits. Over the years he'd perfected the art of zoning out potential hazards like lips, hips, and other essential female body parts…between the hours of nine to five. Looking at women outside the office was one thing, but at work it was nothing but business. His wife had taught him how dangerous it could be to get involved with the wrong woman. But despite his forewarned knowledge, Ted found himself exploring Victoria's entire body whenever he had the opportunity.

He loved her spirit and energy. She was ambitious, but not ruthless, kind, but not a pushover. He thought back to the week he'd come on board at ViaTech. He had reviewed the personnel files of several people in senior level positions in the headquarters office because he wanted to assess the company's leaders. When he looked into Victoria's file, his interest was piqued. She'd received outstanding evaluations and had earned several employee achievement awards for exemplary performance. Her academic transcripts showed that she'd graduated in the top of her class from both undergraduate and graduate school. She was smart, a quality that Ted found incredibly sexy.

At the end of the week he'd made it a point to show up unannounced at the HR department's senior management meeting. He wanted to see Victoria Monique Small in person because even on paper, she'd intrigued him. When he walked into the room, everyone sat on edge in their seat except her. He spotted her right away because she was the only black person in the room. In her personnel file, African-American was circled under race, so he knew this had to be her. But what he hadn't expected was the feeling that came over him when he saw the beauty of her face and felt a sudden pounding of excitement in his chest. He took a seat in the back of the room so he could observe her from a distance. It was at that moment that he knew he had to have her.

"Hmmm," Victoria said, interrupting Ted's thoughts.

He put down his document; he hadn't been reading it anyway. "So, tell me what you think about our plans for SuperNet?"

"I think they're terrible. It's boring, unimaginative and unoriginal…should I go on?"

Ted pushed his papers aside, giving Victoria his full attention. "Please do."

"Well, where should I begin?"

"From the beginning."

Victoria explained in detail, the flaws of ViaTech's plans for SuperNet, from the layout and placement of products in their booth, to the overall event theme and ineffective use of company personnel. "That's it in a nutshell," she concluded.

"That's quite an assessment. Tell me what you would suggest to make it better?"

Victoria jumped at any opportunity to plan an event. She described her concept of a sleek, hip, sales-oriented theme for the company's presentation, and explained how they could streamline the most cost effective use of promotional incentives for the event. "You need bait to reel in fish," she said, leaning over and sitting the proposal back on his desk.

Ted smiled. He moved the proposal to the side and picked up a blue folder in front of him. "Please, let's have a seat over there," he motioned toward the other side of the room, "it's much more comfortable."

They walked over to the buttery-soft leather coach. Victoria tried to be patient as she took her seat, but the clock was ticking and she still hadn't discussed her resignation. After they settled into comfortable positions, Ted handed her the folder. "What's this?" she asked.

"The EMP nominations. Since we didn't announce them today, I'd like your department to post them first thing Monday morning."

Victoria opened the folder and read its contents. Her name wasn't on the list. "You knew I wasn't going to change my mind?" she said, looking over the list of nominees.

"Yes, I did. And I wanted you to read the SuperNet proposal for a reason."

"Why's that?"

"I knew you'd be able to give a critical assessment. SuperNet is our industry's biggest event, so we have to step up our game and find fresh and creative ways to bring in new customers."

"I agree," Victoria nodded.

"We need big results, so I'm making big changes this year. Instead of the sales and marketing departments running the entire show, I'd like to make you an instrumental part of the planning team for SuperNet."

"What?" Victoria was momentarily at a loss, completely surprised by his proposition.

"This does fall under your purview of special projects, doesn't it?"

"Yes...I participate in SuperNet every year, but I've never been involved in the actual planning." Victoria felt a jolt of excitement.

"It's a project that will involve a lot of work, but I know you can handle it. SuperNet is eight months away, which will creep up on us before we know it. Victoria, I'd like your help. What do you say?"

Victoria's creative juices had begun to flow the minute she started reading the proposal. She loved the idea of planning a hip, creative presentation for the telecom industry's party of the year, and an added bonus was that her talents would be showcased on a national scale. This would be yet another project she could add to her growing portfolio of work. And the timing was perfect because SuperNet was set for the second week of June, which meant she could coordinate the show and still resign as she'd originally planned. This opportunity was almost too good to be true, which also made her curious. "I'm flattered, but why me?" she asked with suspicion.

"I know you'll deliver the results I'm looking for. One of the qualities of a good leader is knowing people, and knowing how to maximize their strengths. I see your strengths."

Victoria leaned in close to Ted and was a little surprised when he didn't move...not even an inch. "Like I said, I'm flattered. But tell me, why are you doing this for me? There are a lot of smart, talented people in this company. I've learned that from the SME report I just completed. I know I'm smart and I know I'm good, but why choose me?" No matter what his answer, Victoria had already decided that she wouldn't resign until next June. She'd take on the SuperNet project.

Ted knew he could make up a politically correct statement and talk under and around his feelings, but instead he chose to tell her the truth. He leaned in even closer—now they were only inches apart. "I chose you for all the reasons I've already stated, plus...I like you, Victoria."

She searched his face, and she could see that he was being honest.

"Victoria, I'll also be very involved on this project because the success of SuperNet is one of my top priorities."

"So we'd be working together?" she asked.

"Yes. So, what will your answer be?"

Victoria extended her hand. "You've got yourself a deal," she smiled as Ted eagerly took her hand in his.

He breathed a sigh of relief that she'd accepted his offer. He'd spent all week trying to figure out how to persuade her not to resign. Finally, after diligent background work and a few conversations with Jen, he'd discovered that Victoria's forte was event planning, and that over the years she'd organized nearly all of ViaTech's social functions. He knew that SuperNet would be right up her alley. "I'm glad I can count on your help. I'll be out of town next week, but I'll have Jen schedule a meeting for the following week so we can get the ball rolling," he said.

Victoria looked at her watch. "It's almost six-thirty, and I need to get going, besides, I don't want to cut into your evening plans." She stood to her feet, preparing to leave.

Ted shrugged, "I'll be here the rest of the night."

"All work and no play will make you a very dull boy," Victoria teased, waving her finger at him as they shared a slow and easy laugh. "I hope you have a fun weekend planned since you're spending your Friday night here at the office."

"No, nothing exciting, unless you're into running. I usually just hit the treadmill at home or at the gym, but I'm taking the time to get out this weekend for a nice nature run.

Victoria looked Ted up and down, sizing him up. "You're a runner? Wow, so am I."

His face lit up. "I've been running since my high school track days. I'm a distance man. Cross country's my thing. There's nothing like getting fresh air in your lungs," Ted paused, then went out on a limb. "I'm going for a run over in Sunnybrook Park tomorrow morning, why don't you join me?"

"I haven't been for a run over there in ages. It's a beautiful area."

"Well then, it's settled," he said with a smile. He couldn't believe how easy this had been. "I have a morning meeting at nine, so is seven okay for you?"

Despite her slight hesitation, Victoria accepted. "Seven sounds good." They quickly exchanged cell phone numbers. "Call me if you can't make it," she smiled on her way out.

"Don't worry, I'll be there."

Chapter Seven

The Same Perfect Page......

It was six forty-five when Victoria arrived at Sunnybrook Park, fifteen minutes early. The air was cool and crisp; the perfect fall weather for an early morning run. Sunnybrook Park was an eye catching landscape of lush greenery and rugged trees. As she pulled into the lot adjacent to the park, she saw that Ted's car was already there. She parked beside him and sat for a minute with the engine running.

She spotted him stretching near the benches at the edge of the trail. When he saw her car slide in beside his, he smiled, waving his arms to get her attention. Looking at him standing there, eagerly waiting for her, gave Victoria a tingly feeling. *Must be this cool weather,* she thought, brushing off the sensation as she headed his way.

The sight of her made small bumps creep up on Ted's skin, an effect the chilly morning breeze hadn't been able to achieve. She was dressed in a black sports bra and matching lycra running pants and jacket. He watched her long legs stride toward him, accentuating the curvy slimness of her hips.

Her thick black hair that usually hung down her back was pulled into a ponytail sitting high on her head, revealing her long, slender neck. He thought she looked like the African queens he'd seen in history books. Her face was fully exposed, flaunting the natural beauty it possessed; high check bones, regal nose, inviting lips, and expressive brown eyes.

"Good morning," Victoria greeted him.

"Good morning," he smiled.

They stood beside each other, both beginning warm-up stretches to loosen their muscles. "Aren't you cold?" she asked, extending her leg to flex her calf. Ted's only clothing was a white t-shirt and a thin pair of black running shorts.

"No, I love cold weather. Growing up in Boston you get used to it," he answered, inhaling a deep breath of air.

As they continued to stretch, Victoria took a moment to study Ted, gazing at his pleasing complexion; not pale, and not exactly olive, but a nice blend in between. He had the kind of skin that could hold a nice tan in the summer. When he leaned forward, she appraised his svelte waist and narrow hips, and when he bent to stretch his legs she checked out his behind; high and tight. *Not bad for a white boy!* she said to herself. His chest was broad and his muscular arms looked strong and strangely inviting. All that, plus his six-foot three-inch frame made him look alarmingly good. *I need to stop looking at this man*, she thought to herself.

They both finished stretching at the same time. "The three mile trail is a little bumpy in a few places," Ted motioned toward the clearing ahead, "but it's an otherwise smooth run. I know you have much younger legs, but I'm a very advanced runner so don't be upset if you get dusted by an old man this morning," he joked. He felt playful, enjoying the tease.

"Talkin' trash already are we?" Victoria laughed, "Okay, old man, let's see whatcha got." She gave him a small shove on the shoulder, then sprinted ahead toward the trail. Ted ran after her, and they were off.

They started at a moderate pace, not knowing each other's gate or rhythm. But after only a few lengths, they quickly fell into sync and picked up their speed. Ted glanced over at Victoria, noticing her long stride. He knew she was fast because he was running at his usual rigorous pace and she was gliding smoothly beside him. When they came up to the point that signaled their last mile, Ted wanted her to see that he was still in great shape for a man twelve years her senior, so he quickened the pace. They challenged each other, running faster and harder, their competitive juices flowing.

When they reached the quarter mile point, as if on the same perfect page, they slowed their pace and started their cool down run. They were getting closer to the end and could see their cars parked in the distance. "Not bad for an old man, huh?" Ted panted in between quick breaths. Being very pleased that he'd shown her his vitality, and in a gesture to mimic her earlier playfulness, he gave Victoria a small shove on the shoulder. Then everything went wrong.

Victoria lost her balance and went tumbling to the ground. She fell hard, rolling off the side of the paved trail and onto the rocks and thorns near the bushes. When her fall ended, she was crouched on the ground several feet away, grabbing her ankle and screaming out in pain. It was as if it had happened in slow motion. Ted saw her falling and reached out to catch her, but even at their slower pace they were going too fast for him to stop what he saw happening.

"Oh my god, are you all right!" Ted was down on his knees, huddled beside her. "Victoria, are you all right? Are you okay?" he asked again.

She'd stopped screaming, but she was holding her ankle, wincing. When she looked up at him, he could see the pain on her face. Her right leg was bent in an awkward position and the material of her pants was ripped, blood trickling through. "My ankle," she said slowly, "I think it's bad."

Ted leaned in close. "Let me see." It was more a statement than a question.

When Victoria removed her hand from her ankle, all he saw was blood. She looked at the deep cut and moaned. She tried to remove some of the blood from her hand by wiping it on the freshly fallen leaves covering the ground.

Ted pulled off his t-shirt, making a tourniquet around her ankle. They were half a football field's length away from their cars, and judging from the looks of things, he knew that Victoria couldn't make it that far. "Hold on tight," he said. Without hesitation, Ted scooped her up into his arms and carried her to his car. After safely securing her in the front seat, he opened the trunk, reached into his gym bag, and threw on the extra t-shirt inside. Within seconds, they were on the road.

❧

You're What's Most Important......

Ted switched lanes in and out of traffic in his rush to get Victoria to the hospital. He'd already run two red lights, and was now handling his Jaguar like a veteran NASCAR driver. "We'll be there in just a few minutes," he said, trying to comfort her.

Victoria was slumped against the passenger door with her head against the window. Her ponytail grazed her shoulder, swishing from side to side with each bump in the road. Ted was driving with one hand on the wheel and the other gently, but securely, wrapped around hers. He'd been holding her hand since they left the Park.

Victoria knew she was in bad shape. When she'd fallen, she landed hard on several jagged rocks. She'd twisted her ankle to the side, then rolled over another sharp object. She didn't know whether it was broken glass or a piece of metal, but she knew it was damaging when she felt her skin rip open as soon as it made contact.

"This is all my fault," Ted mumbled, continuing to weave in between cars.

Victoria spoke slowly through the pain. "Ted, it was an accident, and accidents happen. Let's just make sure we get to the hospital safely." He'd just dodged in front of another car.

The Emergency Room was crowded but calm, not like the chaotic scenes on TV shows like *ER.* The large waiting area was full of people in varying states of illness and injury. Ted knew that emergency room visits could take a very long time, and unless you had a missing limb or gunshot wound, the wait could be hours. He walked up to the attendant and handed her Victoria's paperwork. "Chip Langston is a good friend of mine," he smiled. I'll be sure to tell him that his ER staff does a fine job the next time we're on the driving range." He dropped that bit of information to let everyone behind the desk know that he was friendly with the head of the ER. Five minutes later a nurse with heavily frosted hair came into the lobby and called Victoria's name.

After nurse frosty hair took Victoria back, Ted sat in the waiting area, praying he hadn't caused her any permanent damage. Two hours later, nurse frosty hair motioned for him to come back toward the double doors. He bolted to his feet, anxious to see Victoria.

They walked down a long hallway. "She's going to be just fine," nurse frosty hair said. "Ms. Small requested that we come and get you. When the doctor comes back he'll talk with you both. She's right in here," the nurse smiled, escorting Ted into the room.

Victoria sat slightly slumped over on a small examining table. A flimsy hospital gown and blue scrub pants had replaced her blood-stained running clothes. Ted looked down at her feet. Her running shoe dangled loosely on one foot, while neatly bandaged gauze covered the other. He walked over to her, reached for her hand and held it in his. "How're you feeling?" he asked softly. "Are you still in pain?"

"Yeah, they gave me something for it though," she said, rubbing her head. "Ted?"

"Yes?"

Victoria was tired and her voice was faint. "I knew you'd still be waiting, so I wanted to let you know that I'm okay. I know you have a meeting this morning that you're already late for. I can take a cab home. I'll be ok…"

"Shh," Ted quieted her. "Right now you're what's most important. I'm not leaving."

They looked down and studied their intertwined hands, firmly secured around one another. Even though Victoria was woozy from the pain and the medication she'd been given, she was aware of Ted's tenderness. When the pleasant-faced doctor entered the room, she turned her attention to him.

"Hello, I am Dr. Obikwelu," the tall, dark, reed-thin doctor said to Ted as he extended his hand.

Ted was still holding Victoria's hand, so he used his free one to greet the doctor. "Ted Thornton," he said, giving the man a firm shake.

Dr. Obikwelu looked down, glimpsing the hand lock that Ted and Victoria shared. A frown slowly spread across his face. Victoria was too preoccupied with her pain to notice, but Ted recognized the man's expression. "What's the verdict, doctor?" he asked with an edge.

Putting his bias aside, Dr. Obikwelu explained that Victoria hadn't broken any bones, but she'd badly sprained her ankle. She needed several stitches to close the wound above her anklebone, along with the deep gash on her upper thigh.

He wrote two prescriptions and handed them to Victoria. She was in no condition to comprehend, so Ted gently took them from her. Seeing that Ted would not be ignored, the doctor gave him a list of instructions on how Victoria should care for her wounds. Ted took in every word the doctor said, nodding in obedient agreement with the stack of orders—all for Victoria's sake.

"You are ready to go now, Ms. Small. Do you have any questions?" Dr. Obikwelu asked, begrudgingly looking in Ted's direction.

Victoria was tired and slightly dazed, an effect of the painkillers. The doctor's crisp Nigerian accent sounded like Mandarin to her ears. Slowly, she registered his question. "Can you give me something else for the pain?" she asked.

Dr. Obikwelu was startled by her request. An hour earlier when she'd complained that she could still feel the sting of the needle he was using, he gave her a double dose of Lidocaine to numb her as he sutured her wounds. And he'd just given her two painkillers before a final review of her chart. The doctor couldn't believe Victoria's high tolerance to the medication.

"Ms. Small, I just gave you Percocet not too long ago. I understand that you are in pain, but I do not want to over medicate you. Believe me, the narcotic will help to ease your discomfort. Just give it time to work," Dr. Obikwelu advised. "I gave you a strong dosage. You will be in…how do you say it?…la la land before you know it."

After the doctor left the room, Victoria was relieved that she would be able to finally go home. She fiddled with the string of the extra gown that nurse frosty hair had given her to cover up, then tied her jacket around her waist while Ted stuffed her ruined clothes into a plastic bag.

"She's lucky to have such a good friend to help take care of her," the nurse winked at Ted.

"I'm the lucky one," Ted winked back.

La La Land……

Ted was driving calmly now, still holding Victoria's hand. She'd been lucid enough to give him directions to the pharmacy in her neighborhood. After getting her prescriptions filled, Ted returned to the car and they headed to her house.

As they drove in silence, save for the soft jazz playing on the radio, Victoria ripped into the bag of medicine and swallowed a pill.

"Victoria, what are you doing?" Ted asked with concern, trying to keep his eye on the road.

"I'm taking something for the pain."

"But the doctor already gave you painkillers. Is it that bad?" Ted flicked on his turn signal and pulled off to the shoulder of the road. He reached over and took the bottle of pills from Victoria's hand, reading the directions as he dialed on his cell phone.

"What're you doing?" Victoria asked in a whiny voice.

He knew she wasn't herself. "I'm taking care of you," he told her. Once the pharmacist came on the line, Ted explained what Victoria had done, then listened for instructions. After a few minutes, he was relieved to learn that she wasn't in danger. "You've overmedicated," he said, rubbing her hand with care, "but the pharmacist said you're going to be fine." With yet another small scare abated, they were off again.

When they finally arrived at 1701 Summerset Lane, Victoria was too groggy to use the crutches they'd given her at the hospital, so Ted wrapped his arm around her waist and helped her to the door. As she reached into the pocket of her jacket, fumbling for her keys, she looked over Ted's shoulder and saw her next-door neighbor, Ms. Swanson, peering out the window. She gave the old lady a quick wave before she and Ted disappeared inside.

Victoria was glad to be home, and Ted was glad to be there too. He allowed the comfort to swallow him, knowing he was in her intimate space. The décor was layered with richly textured fabrics, a mix of contemporary and African art, and large-scale furniture. He managed to get Victoria to the sofa in her living room. "Where's your kitchen?" he asked.

Minutes later, he emerged from the kitchen with a box of crackers he'd found by searching her cabinets. "The pharmacist said you should eat this since you've taken so much medicine on an empty stomach."

"Thanks," Victoria managed to say. She was lying outstretched across the sofa.

Ted took a seat beside her. He'd been dreaming of being this close to her, but under much different circumstances.

"My car, it's still at the park," Victoria said in a sleepy voice, raking her fingers through her badly disheveled hair.

"I'll call my car service and have it towed here," Ted offered.

"No, you've done too much already."

"It's the least I can do. Remember, this was all my fault," he said, picking up his cell phone to make the arrangements.

"Stop saying that. You saved my life," Victoria smiled, doing her best not to slur her words. "You're the best friend in the whole wide *woooorld*," she said with a woozy grin.

Ted controlled his urge to laugh. *The doctor was right. She's in la la land.*

Just then Victoria's phone rang. She reached for it in a clumsy attempt, picking up on the third ring. "Hello?" she answered in a weak voice.

"Victoria, you sound weird. What's wrong?" Debbie asked.

"Oh, hey Debbie. I had an accident this morning, but I'm okay now." She was tired, barely releasing the words from her lips.

"What? What kind of accident?"

Ted had finished his call and could see that Victoria was fading fast. "Here," he motioned, reaching for the phone with one hand as he held hers with his other. "Let me speak to her. You need to rest."

His voice sounded so soothing and his touch felt so warm, that Victoria didn't put up an argument.

Ted proceeded to tell Debbie the entire story from start to finish, including how Victoria had come to be in her present drug-induced state. Debbie could hear the concern in his voice. "Rob and I are headed out of town to Miami in a few hours, but we're going to swing by on our way to the airport to check on her," she said. "And Ted, thanks for taking care of my friend."

"No need to thank me. I'll stay with her until you get here." Ted hung up the phone and looked at Victoria. He was still holding her hand.

She looked up at him and smiled. "Can you help me upstairs to my bedroom?"

A Special Brand Of Torture......

Victoria was in no condition to negotiate the stairs so Ted picked her up as he'd done in the park, carefully holding her in his arms. Her body heat and salty-sweet smell were an arousing combination to his senses. After what seemed like a climb up Mount Everest, they finally reached the top of the stairs.

"You smell woodsy... I like it," Victoria purred, nestling her nose against the side of his neck.

Ted was determined not to succumb to what he wanted. "Uh, Victoria, which way to your bedroom?"

"To the right," she breathed into his ear.

He carried her over the threshold. When he looked around, he saw a room that was as sensuous and beautifully adorned as the woman he held in his arms.

"Can you help me over to my bathroom, I need to *shooowwer*," Victoria said, slurring her words again.

"I don't think that's a good idea. You're too out of it from all the medication and you can barely speak straight. The pharmacist said you'll be this way for a while.

"But I wanna get clean," she whined.

"You might slip and hurt yourself even worse. Take a nap and sleep it off, you need the rest," he said, in a firm but gentle tone. He knew it was the drugs that had her behaving like his elementary school-aged niece.

"Okay," Victoria huffed, too weary to argue. "Can you help me over to my closet so I can change out of these hospital clothes?"

Ted helped her through the small sitting room, and over to her closet. It was the most neatly organized space he'd ever seen, with pristine rows of clothes, custom built-ins, and floor to ceiling shelves on one side that held more shoes than he thought possible for one person to own.

"Can you hand me my robe? It's on the hook of my bathroom door," Victoria said.

Ted walked over to the bathroom, retrieved the pink, silk robe, and handed it to her. He quickly turned away when she began to undress without warning, peeling down to her underwear. He resisted the urge to turn back around for a peek, deciding that this was a special brand of torture engineered to test his strength.

All Victoria could think about was how good it would feel to lay under her seven hundred thread-count Yves Delorme sheets. "I think you were right. I'm so tired," she said in a whisper, tossing her clothes to the side and pulling on her robe.

Ted brought her to her bed, laying her safely atop the comforter. Her robe shifted open, and for the first time he was able to take a good look at her bare, exposed leg. He winced when he saw the large gash on her thigh that had required stitches, and the small scrapes and bruises up and down her leg. And even though her ankle was bandaged, he could see that it was badly swollen. He closed her robe and touched her face with the back of his hand. She was sound asleep.

He went downstairs, and returned with her crutches and medicine. He reached into the bag, pulled out the prescription-medicated cream, and attended to her wounds as the doctor had instructed. He knew she was in deep slumber because she didn't flinch when he touched her painful looking flesh.

The Perfect Combination......

Downstairs, Ted explored Victoria's house, secretly delighting in the unsupervised private tour. This time when he entered her kitchen he wasn't fumbling through her cabinets looking for food or dishes. He had more time to take it all in. *So this is where she cooks,* he said to himself. He saw at least two dozen cookbooks on the shelf under her large island, and two boxes of Godiva

Chocolates sitting on the counter near the refrigerator. *Ahh, she likes chocolate.*

He walked around the corner, peeked into the den and then into her home gym. He headed back down the hallway that led to the dining room and stood there, admiring the antique dinning table, upholstered chairs, and bronze chandelier hanging above. *Nice,* he thought. He walked around the corner and found himself back in the living room. He hadn't noticed the photographs on the side table before, but now that he was more relaxed he went over to take a look.

There were various pictures of Victoria with family and friends. A large black and white photograph of an interracial couple caught Ted's eye. He picked it up for a closer inspection. The handsome pair was leaning against a dark-colored Buick as the tall black man towered above the small white women. He wore a light-colored shirt, plaid bell-bottoms, and sported a small afro, perfectly suited to his distinguished face. His skin was dark and his eyes shown so brightly through the picture that Ted felt as though the man was staring directly at him. He held his arm around the waist of a petite white woman wearing a mini-skirt, and platform heels. Her long black hair hung down her back. She was beautiful, with a happy smile. But what struck Ted was that the white woman bore a startling resemblance to Victoria.

After studying the picture for several minutes, his eyes were pulled to a more recent color photo of the couple, with Victoria standing in between them. The man was dressed in a Brooks Brother's looking suit. His once neatly manicured Afro was now a closely cropped tinge of receding hair. The photo revealed the true color of his deep black skin, and his eyes were still as piercing as they had been in his youth. The woman was wearing a yellow dress and pearls. Her hair was much shorter now, bobbed at her chin, and she still possessed the same beauty and happy smile. Looking at the photo, Ted noticed that the woman wasn't white as he'd originally thought. As he peered closer, he could see the light fawn hue of her complexion. He looked back and forth at the two pictures and smiled. *She's the perfect combination of them both.*

ⅆⅆ

Say What's On Your Mind......

The doorbell woke Ted from his sleep. He'd been flipping through a travel magazine he'd found in a basket beside the sofa when he drifted off after his private tour. He sprang to his feet and answered the door, greeting Debbie and Rob with an ease that made them all feel more familiar than they really were.

"How's the patient?" Debbie asked with concern.

"Better. She's been asleep since we spoke earlier. She was in a lot of pain, but she's resting comfortably now." Ted wanted to stay with Victoria for the rest of the evening, but he knew that he should leave. "Before I forget," he said, heading toward the door, "she won't need to take another dose of painkillers for at least two more hours."

Rob smiled, "Thanks again. We can see that Victoria was well taken care of." He shook Ted's hand again, this time more firmly, acknowledging his obvious affection for their friend.

Victoria heard voices downstairs. She was still groggy, but much more coherent than she'd been before falling asleep hours ago. She looked down at her leg and cringed at the sight. There was a greasy film covering her wounds... *Ted?* She heard his voice trail off, and the door close behind him. Victoria sat up in her bed. She wanted to see him, to thank him again, but he was gone.

"Hey, how ya feelin'?" Debbie asked, entering the room with Rob behind her.

"A little tired, but much better."

Debbie walked over to the bed and looked down at Victoria's leg, "Oh, Victoria..."

Rob took a quick glance, then turned his head. "I'll give you ladies a little privacy," he said, and with that he headed back downstairs.

"Did Ted just leave?" Victoria asked.

"Yeah, poor guy, he feels so guilty. I tried to tell him that your accident wasn't his fault. That you're just clumsy as hell and old as dirt," Debbie smiled. They both laughed until Debbie became quiet, changing to a serious tone. "Listen, I've been thinking about something you said last weekend."

"What's that?"

Debbie spoke slowly. "What you said...about dating white men..."

The two friends stared at each other in silence.

Finally, Victoria cleared her throat. "Debbie, just get it all out, say what's on your mind."

"Okay. You're dismissing Ted's attraction to you because he's white, and that bothers me. I never knew you felt this way about interracial dating."

Victoria sighed. "It's a complicated issue, but it's not that I dislike white men. I just love brothers. I've always felt a natural connection with men who share my same skin, culture, and ethnic background. Does that make me wrong?"

"No, but it damn sure limits your options."

"You may be right, but your argument is lost on Ted. The fact that he's white, and my boss, doesn't bother me nearly as much as the fact that he's married," Victoria sighed. "So for now, can you please give it a rest? I'm recovering and I need peace, not diversity training."

Debbie could see that Victoria was struggling, and it wasn't just from her injuries. "Okay, but this conversation isn't over. And for what it's worth, I like Ted. He's so *fiii-eeene!*"

"Well, I have to agree with you on that," Victoria blushed, "and you should see him in a pair of running shorts. Talk about hot!" She fanned herself as Debbie joined in for a good girlfriend-laugh.

❦

Just The Right Things To Say......

Ted thought about her touch, her smile, and the warmth of her breath against his skin. He didn't remember getting on the highway, turning down the winding streets, or inserting his key card into the main gate that served to guard the exclusive neighborhood where he lived. Only when he turned off the engine, sitting in his four-car garage, did he realize he was home.

He walked into the kitchen, headed straight to the refrigerator, and grabbed a cold beer and a sandwich that Rosa, his housekeeper, had left for him. He sat at the table in the breakfast nook and ate the quick meal in only a few bites.

What am I doing? I must be crazy! Ted thought to himself. He was surprised by what he'd done and the way he'd been acting. Yesterday, he'd given Jen instructions to leave once Victoria arrived for their meeting. His assistant always stayed until his meetings ended in case he needed her, but he wanted privacy for this occasion, so he'd told her to go home early and enjoy her weekend. And this morning he'd actually gone jogging with Victoria, then over to her house this afternoon ... *Damn! Why can't I get her out of my mind?* he wondered, allowing a smile to form at the thought of her.

"I'll be gone for the next two weeks," the raspy voice roared. Ted's wife jarred him from his daydream. "What are you smiling about?" she asked.

Trudy stood before him in the middle of the kitchen. She was dressed in a designer pantsuit, her golden locks cascading at her shoulders. Her tightly pulled face showed no trace of compassion, just pricey cosmetic procedures.

"Why do you care?" was Ted's unfeeling response.

"Whatever," Trudy said, brushing off his remark. "I'll be at the spa in Phoenix."

"Try not to spend too much of my money while you're at it," Ted growled, clearly pissed.

Trudy looked him dead in the eyes. "Don't mess with me, and I won't mess with you," she spat out. "And in case you've forgotten, it's *our* money that I'll be spending," she snapped, then turned on her heels and headed out the door.

Ted sat in his chair, gripped by regret and his own weakness...............

When they married, Ted had been twenty-four years old, and Trudy, one year younger. They'd met at a party that Ted and a few of his classmates had thrown to celebrate their graduation from Harvard Business School. A co-worker of Trudy's was dating one of the graduates, and had invited her to tag along.

Ted was instantly attracted to her youthful beauty and natural charm. She was smart, funny, and always seemed to know just the right things to say. She wasn't college educated, but he admired her curiosity for learning. She worked at one of the local museums, and had a passion for fine art. They enjoyed a whirlwind courtship full of romantic candlelight dinners and nights of wild, passionate sex.

But his best friend Barry had cautioned him about his new love. He and Barry had been like brothers since their prep school days. "Ted, she's hot and everything, but slow it down. Just give it a little time, don't rush into anything," Barry had warned.

Jake Johnson, Ted's friend and roommate from his undergraduate days at Princeton had warned him as well. "Man, be cool and use your head with this woman. You've only known each other a few months. Take your time. What's the rush?"

"Theodore, you really don't know a lot about this girl, or her family for that matter," his mother had said. "You never know someone until you look closely into their background. Trust me on this. I know what I'm talking about," Carolyn Thornton had warned with an eerie foreboding. "Your father and I are very concerned that you may be getting yourself into something you're not ready for."

Ted ignored them all. In less than two months, he and Trudy hopped a weekend flight to Vegas and stood before a Justice of the Peace. It wasn't the kind of ceremony that Ted's mother had dreamed of for her youngest son, but it was the way Trudy had wanted it. She'd said that she wanted to start her life with Ted as soon as possible.

But very quickly after they married, things began to change. Trudy quit her job at the museum, and Ted couldn't understand why. When they were dating, she couldn't stop talking about the museum and its interesting exhibits, paintings, and sculptures. She'd said she loved her job. But when Ted asked her why she'd quit, she simply shrugged her shoulders and said, "I think I need a change."

Meanwhile, Ted was busy building his career. Thanks to his well-heeled father, the Thornton name was synonymous with success, and through his influential contacts, he'd helped Ted to land a promising position with a large software company in the heart of downtown Boston. Ted knew that if he learned all he could, he would rise to the top. He was ambitious and smart. He worked long days and nights, determined to step out of his father's shadow and make his own mark. The top executives in the company were impressed by his tenacity and were grooming him to rise quickly through the ranks. On weekends, he tried to spend as much time with Trudy as he could, but she was growing more and more distant.

One evening, sitting at his desk in the new home he'd purchased for him and his bride, Ted went through his monthly ritual of budgeting their bills and reconciling their joint bank account. He stopped when he came across something unusual on their bank statement—a two-hundred fifty dollar check to Boston Women's Clinic. Trudy's doctor practiced at Mass General, so he couldn't understand why she would've gone to the clinic. He began to wonder if she was sick, if that was why she'd been so moody, withdrawn, and distant.

She's sick and she's trying to keep it from me so I won't worry! he thought. That night, he looked at his wife as she lay sleeping in bed. He wanted to wake her and ask her what was wrong? What was she hiding? He wanted to assure her that whatever it was, they could get through it together. But she was resting peacefully so he didn't disturb her.

The next morning, Trudy was still asleep when Ted headed out the door before the sun rose. He decided to leave work early that evening, bring dinner home, and talk about whatever health crisis his wife was facing.

But during dinner, Trudy barely touched the Moo Shoo Pork that Ted had lovingly laid out on their fine china, a wedding gift from his parents, despite his mother's strong reservations. They sat at the table in silence until Ted spoke up. "Trudy, I know there's something going on with you."

"I'm fine," she answered with irritation.

"No you're not. You quit the job you loved for no apparent reason. You've been moody and distant, and I can't remember the last time we made love."

Silence...

"I know about your visit to Boston Women's Clinic," he said.

That got Trudy's attention. She looked at him with an intense stare. "Oh, so now you know?" she responded in a chilly tone.

Ted wasn't sure what kind of game his wife was playing, but he didn't like it. He banged his fork against the intricate gold trim outlining his plate. "Trudy, whatever it is we can get through it together. I love you. If you're sick, we can get you treatment. Boston has some of the finest doctors in the country."

For the first time in weeks Trudy laughed; uncontrollably!

"What's so funny?" Ted demanded. "Tell me what the hell's going on!"

Trudy halted her laughter and peered into Ted's eyes. "I'm not sick. I had an abortion."

He sat in shock. Did his beautiful new wife just tell him that she was pregnant with their first child, and that she'd aborted it? He thought surely he must have heard her wrong. His head began to ring like a siren.

"You heard me. I killed it." Trudy's voice was harsh and maniacal. "I need to clear up a few things for you, Ted. I didn't marry you because I love you, but I do love what we can have together. You're ambitious and smart, and I'm beautiful, witty and fun. Together, we make the perfect couple. It looks good for a corporate man on the rise to have an attractive young wife on his arm. I'm good for your image, and I know how important image is to you and your elitist family, it's your birthright. I'll help you as much as you'll help me," Trudy said, rising from the table.

"In public, I'll play the dutiful wife and you'll be the adoring husband. We'll keep up appearances, and your career and squeaky clean reputation you hold so dear will stay intact. Take a close look into my background. You won't want the truth to come out," she threatened. "You should be more careful about the girls you sweep off their feet." Trudy walked past him and headed toward the bedroom before stopping midway, "And Ted, never forget...if you don't mess with me, I won't mess with you."

Ted sat at the table, his heart and mind pounding like a late summer storm. Over the next few weeks he received shocking information from Bo Powers, the private investigator he'd hired to dig into Trudy's past. He discovered that she was really seven years older than she'd claimed to be, and that she had a criminal record of arrests for theft and prostitution. She'd gotten the job at the museum as part of an outreach program for ex-offenders.

Trudy threatened to expose her seedy past to Ted's family, friends, and business colleagues if he tried to leave her. She vowed to put a stain on his otherwise pristine reputation. She knew that Ted's weakness was his pride, and his desire to become a powerful man like his father. Her torrid past would surely cause rumblings, but above all, his pride and that of his family's couldn't take the ridicule.

"How can a company trust the judgment of a man who would marry a thief and a whore he'd only known for two months?" Trudy laughed during one of their heated arguments. "And won't your high society Beacon Hill family and friends be surprised to learn that your beautiful new wife used to turn tricks on the pier in Atlantic City?"

Ted felt numb. He wondered how he could've been so blind. He lamented over his poor judgment night after night, too ashamed and angry to confide in anyone. He resolved that he would not let Trudy be the ruin of his reputation or his career. He'd made a terrible mistake, and now he would have to live with it. He would have to recover.

That evening changed Ted's life forever. From that point forward he watched everyone and everything around him, holding his feelings close, and his heart even closer. As the years passed he'd thought about leaving Trudy several times, but decided to concentrate on his career instead. Over time he matured enough to put his pride aside, realizing that the damaging truth about his wife's tawdry past would be overlooked. But now, it was about the finances of his situation. It would cost him more to divorce Trudy because she would surely try to take half of everything he'd worked so hard for. He couldn't let that happen, so they lived separate lives.

Chapter Eight

*B**agels or Croissants......*

The next morning Victoria sat up in bed and looked down at her leg. Even though her skin was bruised and cut, the medicated cream that Ted had applied the day before had helped. She knew it wasn't a flattering sight, but she was grateful that it wasn't worse.

When her phone rang, she looked at the caller ID and smiled. "What's shakin' in the big apple?" she said.

Tyler was in New York, visiting Juliet. He'd talked to her every day last week, desperately trying to persuade her to agree to his visit. At first she was reluctant, telling him that she needed time to think it over. But he told her that now was as good a time as any because he wasn't giving up. By the end of their third conversation she said yes.

"Things are good," Tyler said. "But I need to ask what's up with you. Are you okay? You know, you really need to get more coordinated."

"News travels fast."

"Yeah, Debbie hit me on my cell late last night after she and Rob landed in Miami. But I didn't call you because I thought you might be resting.

Besides, I didn't know if Prince Charming decided to drop back by and give you a little more TLC."

"Debbie has such a big mouth. Please don't start," Victoria sighed.

"Just admit it, the man wants to get with you. He stayed at the hospital with you, put up with your overdosing drama, and nursed you by your bedside. When a man goes the extra mile like that, he's either in the panties or tryin' to get there."

"Ted took care of me because he's a gentleman and a decent human being. Look, I've already told you, he's not interested in me…"

Tyler cut her off in mid-sentence. "I hope you're not talkin' that gay nonsense. Trust me, Prince Charming likes pussy, and the way I see it he's after yours," he laughed.

His joke hit a nerve. "Let's change the subject," Victoria said, a little uneasy. "Give me all the dirty details about how things are going with you and Juliet?"

"My girl is still fly as hell, just like I remember." Tyler said. Excitement sprinkled his words as he told Victoria about their reunion. He was happy to report that Juliet's relationship with the man she'd been seeing had ended almost as quickly as it had begun. And even though many years had passed, they were beginning to pick up the broken pieces, slowly making them fit together again. "As a matter of fact, I'm about to head back over to her place now."

"You mean you're not staying with her? Where are you…at a hotel?" Victoria asked.

"Yeah, I'm takin' it slow. The main objective of this visit is to let her know that I still love her and that I've never stopped. I'm doing things the right way this time."

"Tyler, that's so special," Victoria smiled, "I'll let you go so you can do your thing. Give Juliet a hug and a kiss for me," she said before hanging up the phone.

Although Tyler's comments about Ted had placed a frog in her throat, Victoria was still happy inside. She was glad that her friend was on the road to happiness again. And for the first time in over a year she felt hopeful about the possibility of the same. Getting over Steven was the beginning, and meeting Mr. Gorgeous had reignited her flame. He represented new hope, and had awakened desires she'd suppressed since that fateful night in the parking lot of Steven's condo……………

In the last year of her relationship with Steven, Victoria had started to suspect that he was cheating on her. During one of her weekend visits she found a pair of silk panties in his bedroom. When she confronted him with the evidence he denied any wrongdoing.

"Vic, those are yours," he said casually. "You must've left them from your last trip."

"Bullshit! I know my own underwear when I see them. You must think I'm some kind of fool!" Victoria yelled.

"Vic, baby, calm down. Don't you remember? I bought them for you," Steven spoke in a low and seductive tone as he walked toward her, wrapping his arms around her waist. "Remember when we went to LA a few months ago and I took you to that store, and bought you all that sexy lingerie?"

Victoria did remember that Steven had spent an obscene amount of money buying her lingerie at the Le Perla store during their weekend in LA. He loved it when she dressed in sexy undergarments and performed her own private striptease for him. But no matter how much he tried to convince her, Victoria knew those underwear belonged to someone else. When she was in undergrad, her friend Gigi, who was a serious man-eater, told her how she would strategically place a sexy piece of clothing under her man's bed, serving as a calling card to any other women who might come prowling around.

After her discovery, Victoria knew she had to reevaluate their relationship. A few weeks later she decided to break up with Steven. As much as it pained her to let him go, she knew she would end up being hurt even more if she stayed in the relationship.

She planned to do it when Steven came to town for Tyler and Allison's wedding. She knew that it wasn't the most appropriate occasion at which to execute a break-up, but Steven had already purchased his tickets months ago. She didn't want to do it over the phone or in a letter, so she decided to tell him face to face, as soon as he got off the plane. His bags would still be packed so he could turn around and catch the next thing smoking back to DC.

Victoria knew it was cold, ruthless even, but she had to do it this way. She was weak for him. She knew herself well enough to know that if they spent any amount of time together, he would persuade her to change her mind and she'd be back in his arms with her legs in the air before she even knew she was under the sheets!

She waited nervously for him at the baggage claim area. Steven walked toward her carrying a small suede duffel and a garment bag, no doubt containing a dashing designer suit. Victoria thought his gray wool trousers and black silk shirt made him look good enough to eat. *Be strong. Just tell him quickly and walk away. Don't linger, and don't let him talk softly into your ear,* she told herself.

Steven reached into his duffel and pulled out a neatly wrapped box of Godiva Chocolates. "Hey, Vic. I brought your favorites," he smiled. He reached for her, but she backed away. "What's wrong?"

"Steven, we need to break up."

"What?"

"We need to end this relationship. It's over. Now please, make this easy on both of us. The next flight back to DC leaves in another hour and a half and..."

"You're jokin' right?"

"No, we need to end things now."

Steven stood directly in front of her, letting the chocolates drop to the ground. "Vic, I've come here to be with you for your best friend's wedding, and to enjoy a weekend with the woman I love. And you meet me here to break up with me? Out the blue! At the fuckin' airport!"

"Steven, it's not out of the blue. You and I both know that things haven't been right between us for a while. We've been going in different directions for months." Victoria stopped, then looked into his eyes. "And I don't trust you. You say there isn't another woman, but too many things don't add up; mysterious phone calls in the middle of the night, days that go by when I don't hear from you, strange panties under your bed. I can't continue like this."

"Baby, I've never loved another woman the way I love you." Steven reached for her hand and held it in his.

Victoria wanted to believe him, but she knew she had to stand her ground. She tried to pull her hand away, but he held on. "*Steven, Do Not* create a scene in this airport because I promise you, I will show my ass if I have to," she said in a firm voice, this time successfully freeing herself from his grip.

"Vic, I know the last few months have been rough, but you're the only woman for me. You're the only woman I want to share my heart, my bed, and my life with." Steven knelt down on one knee and pulled a small, black velvet box from his duffel bag.

Victoria's eyes grew large. She started to tremble when he opened the box to reveal a large, flawless, brilliant cut diamond ring. The fire and ice reflected off the overhead fluorescent lighting, creating a small rainbow of colors.

"I was gonna wait for a more appropriate time to do this. But I think if ever there was a time, it's now. Victoria Monique Small, I love you. And if you do me the honor of becoming my wife, I promise I'll spend every day from this moment forward, loving you, and only you. Will you marry me?"

Victoria was overcome with emotion. The silence around them was cut when a woman from the small crowd that had gathered yelled out, "Say yes!"

Victoria teared up, looking into Steven's eyes, "Yes, I'll marry you." They embraced as the crowd cheered. It was a priceless moment.

How could I have been so wrong? He wants to spend the rest of his life with me, Victoria thought a week later as she boarded her flight to DC. She'd decided to surprise Steven with a weekend visit. He'd promised to be more understanding and attentive to her needs, vowing to work hard to regain her trust.

Three hours and a rental car ride later, she arrived at Steven's condo and rang the bell. When the door opened, a cute woman wearing one of Steven's t-shirts and nothing else answered. "You're not the Papa John's guy?" the half dressed woman said.

"Who the hell are you? Victoria asked in astonishment.

"I'm Steven's girlfriend. Who the hell are you?" the woman glared, hands on her hips.

"I'm his fiancé!" Victoria shot back. She looked past the partially clothed woman and saw Steven standing in the background, a towel wrapped around his waist.

"Vic, this isn't what it looks like," Steven said, walking toward the door, pushing the woman to the side.

"You lying bastard! You just proposed to me last week. Now seven days later some half naked bitch is answering your door!"

Steven had to hold the woman back as she lunged toward Victoria. "Yeah, well this bitch must be doin' something right because I'm the one sleeping in his bed," the woman shouted.

"How could you?" Victoria screamed at Steven, tears springing from her eyes. She turned and ran away, leaving him standing in the doorway.

Victoria drove around the city in a daze for an hour before she ended up in Arlington, a small Virginia suburb a few miles outside the District line. Before she had time to talk herself out of what she was about to do, she pulled her rental car into the parking lot of *Home Depot*. Inside, she purchased a carpet-cutting knife and a can of spray paint, then headed back to the District and into the parking lot of Steven's building. She lowered herself to the ground next to his tan Lexus and started slashing tires one by one. She picked up the can of spray paint and wrote "Cheating Bastard" across the doors and hood. After she finished, she stood up to inspect her handiwork. One of Steven's neighbors who she'd shared friendly chats with during her many visits, walked by and saw her. But the woman didn't say a word. She simply gave Victoria a look of pity before heading up to her unit.

Victoria stood in the middle of the parking lot with tears streaming down her face, the carpet knife in one hand, the can of spray paint in the other. She turned and looked at her reflection in the window of the car beside her, but hardly recognized the sad looking woman staring back. She was out of work for the next two weeks while her friends shared turns nursing her back from a broken heart…………..

Victoria switched her thoughts back to the present, swinging her body around the side of her bed. She was about to limp over to the bathroom to take a shower when the phone rang again. She picked it up when she saw that it was Ted. "Good morning, Ted," she smiled into the phone.

"Ahh, caller ID, don't you love it?"

"I don't know how we lived without it? Kind of like air conditioning."

"Yeah, but it kills the surprise."

"Hearing from you is a good surprise."

Her words made him smile. "I'm glad you think so. How're you feeling this morning?"

"Better…thanks to you. What are you doing up so bright and early? Don't you ever sleep in on the weekends?"

"Actually, no." Ted hadn't slept in on a weekend since his freshman year of college.

"I'm about to step into La Madeleine. Do you prefer bagels or croissants?"

"What?"

"I'm guessing that you haven't eaten this morning, right?"

"No, I haven't."

"So, do you prefer bagels or croissants? I'm bringing you breakfast. You've got to eat, don't you?"

"If I tell you not to go through the trouble, you're not going to listen to me, are you?"

"You're a smart woman. And believe me, it's no trouble."

"Okay, I should be presentable by the time you get here."

Ted pictured what she must look like first thing in the morning. He wanted to rush over that very moment. "I'm about to order, so which do you prefer, bagels or croissants?"

"I'll let you decide."

Cementing Herself......

Victoria greeted Ted wearing an over-sized Spelman sweatshirt and black shorts that exposed her bruised leg. She quickly ushered him in, shielding herself from the cold air outside.

When he walked in he immediately noticed the change. It was her hair. It was different, not the way she usually wore it. Today, it was a thick mass of glistening waves, in a style he found slightly wild and very sexy. He loved it.

Victoria hobbled along behind him as he walked straight back to the kitchen, like it was something he did everyday. "You look like an old pro on those crutches," Ted joked, unpacking the bags of food.

"Yeah, I hope I can ditch them next week, once the swelling goes down."

They stood for a moment, staring at each other. Victoria could feel his eyes penetrating her.

"Your hair. It's different?" he smiled, looking at her head as if trying to figure out the answer to a riddle.

Victoria wanted to laugh because she knew that black hair was a mystery to most white people, and *how* exactly black women could change their hair-style and lengths from day to day was an enigma in itself. She'd washed her hair the night before and let it dry naturally, not blow drying it straight as she normally did. "Black women go through all sorts of machinations with our hair," she said.

Ted wanted to ask her what kind of machinations, but he decided against it. "I think it looks very nice. I like it," he ended up saying.

Victoria watched Ted as he moved about her kitchen with ease. He was wearing dark denims and a sky blue cable knit sweater. She thought the color made his blue eyes come alive. And she noticed his scent again. It was the same woodsy fragrance she'd smelled yesterday. It suited him; not too over-powering, not too subtle.

They decided to eat in the den. Ted arranged the assortment of break-fast goodies on a large oval serving platter and sat it in the middle of the coffee table. "It all looks so good," Victoria said. "You made a great choice, I love croissants."

"I'm glad you approve." When he sat down beside her, Victoria reached for his plate and began to pile on the food. "You don't have to do that," he said.

"I'm an old fashioned southern girl, and this is called southern hospitality." Victoria handed Ted his plate and then prepared her own. "Excuse me," she whispered, bowing her head to say her grace. When she looked up, Ted was starring at her. "Does that offend you?" She knew that religion in any form made some people very uncomfortable. She hoped he wasn't one of them.

"No, it's just that I haven't seen anyone pray before eating in a long time."

"Do you believe in God?" she asked, popping a piece of fresh pineapple into her mouth. Victoria knew she was being blunt and probably a little intrusive, but she wanted to know.

"Yes, I do. Church on Sunday was a rule in my house when I was growing up. But to be honest, I can't remember the last time I went to church or practiced any form of organized religion."

"Do you pray?"

Ted smiled and reached for a croissant. "Sometimes." He thought about the small prayer he'd said yesterday when he was waiting for her in the emergency room.

Victoria looked at him for a long moment. "God hears your prayers even when you don't say them out loud, when you think them in your heart...if you believe." Victoria didn't know why she was talking to him in this deeply personal way, but somehow it felt as natural as breathing air.

She was cementing herself in his heart without even knowing it. She was asking him questions and telling him things that no other woman had ever cared to share or say. "That's comforting to know," was all he could manage in return.

"Am I being too?..."

"Nosy?" he teased as they both laughed. "No, I enjoy your company, and I enjoyed yesterday. Not your accident, of course. But it made me feel good being able to help you after what happened. Especially since it was my fault. I'm so sorry."

"Ted, please stop apologizing. Besides, after the way I acted," she paused from slight embarrassment, "with the pills and everything, I should be the one apologizing to you."

"Nonsense," Ted shrugged, shaking his head. "I'm just glad you're okay. Are you comfortable, now?" He reached over and propped a throw pillow under her ankle. "The doctor said you should keep your foot elevated." His eyes focused on her leg. He put his plate to the side and knelt before her, inspecting her injuries just as the doctor had done. "May I," he asked, moving his hand toward her leg.

Victoria didn't know what he intended to do but she said, "Yes."

He gently stroked her bandaged ankle, then her bruise covered thigh, smoothing in the remains of the thick, medicated cream she had unsuccessfully tried to apply. "The doctor said it should be smoothed directly onto the wounds. I'm not hurting you am I?" he asked in a low and soothing voice.

"No," Victoria answered back in the same tone. She liked the way his touch made her feel. *What in the hell is wrong with me? I'm enjoying this!*

Once Ted finished, he returned to the couch, sitting closer to her this time.

Victoria couldn't believe she was sharing breakfast with him on her sofa. This definitely wasn't her idea of what her relationship with Ted Thornton would be like. But when she looked at him she didn't see a colleague or a CEO. All she saw was an interesting, attractive man. "How old are you?" she asked.

"How old do you think I am?"

"I know you've been in the telecom industry for over twenty years, and you were recruited into corporate right out of B School from Harvard…"

"You've done your homework. What else do you know?"

Victoria gave him a sly wink, "I'm gonna say forty-four…forty-five."

"Very good, I'm forty-five."

"Wow."

For some reason, her *"Wow"* made him feel old. "What does *wow* mean?" he asked, munching on his croissant.

"It's just that you look much younger."

"Good save."

"No, I'm serious. I guessed your age because I knew your background, but if I didn't, I'd think mid to late thirties… easy."

Ted tried to hide his delight. "Really?"

"Yes, really. Do you have children?"

"No, I don't."

"Why not? I only ask because I see how you are…I mean, how kind you are. Despite your corporate suit of armor, you're a very patient, gentle person. You'd make a great father."

He took a sip of his orange juice. "Thank you," he said, almost as an afterthought. He let the question and her compliment breeze by, hoping to avoid the subject.

"So, either tell me to mind my own business or satisfy my curiosity," Victoria pushed. She wasn't going to stop until she got an answer, or he backed her down.

"It's a long story."

"I love long stories over good food."

To his surprise, Ted found himself telling Victoria about his marriage to Trudy. About how she'd deceived him, and how their life together was a big sham. He even admitted to having indiscretions of his own; a result of their separate lives. Victoria looked for a sign of anger, bitterness, sadness or anything that reflected the gut wrenching hurt of a shattered love. But she saw nothing. He was virtually emotionless in the telling of his story, as if he had extrapolated the ability to feel from the last two decades of his life.

"My God, Ted. How could you stay in a loveless marriage for all these years?"

"At first I was worried about my reputation and my career. Now I'm worried about my money. I should've divorced her a long time ago, but now I have entirely too much to loose. Especially given that I'm five months away from having control and part ownership of the company."

Ted had managed to keep Trudy in the dark about the true extent of the wealth he'd accumulated over the years. He had no intention of splitting any of his material possessions, from the rental properties in LA and fifty percent ownership in his friend Barry's consulting firm, to the significant stock and real estate holdings in Boston that he'd inherited when his father passed away several years ago. "I won't let her take anything else from me," he said.

"Ted, she's taken your freedom and your joy. I'm speaking from experience, from what I went through in my last relationship. You've got to let it go and free yourself. That's the only way you'll be able to really enjoy life again."

Ted shook his head. *Where have you been all my life?* he wanted to ask. "You've given me a lot to think about, Victoria."

They ate, listened to music, and talked well into the late afternoon. They discovered that they shared many things in common. They talked about how they'd grown up, their families and friends, and their likes and dislikes on everything from sports to politics. Victoria told him the details of her relationship with Steven, and the emotional pain she'd suffered from it. But she kept silent about her plans with Divine Occasions. Finally, after spending over half of his day with Victoria, Ted reluctantly left for home. "Remember to follow the doctor's orders, I'll be checking on your progress," he smiled before heading out the door.

Later that evening, Victoria thought about Ted. She remembered how he made her feel when he rubbed her leg. He knew how to touch a woman just so. There was something hidden and seductive in his fingertips. It was slightly erotic and had made the seat of her panties wet.

But she reminded herself that he wasn't a viable option. He was a sign that screamed STOP: CAUTION AHEAD! So she concentrated on putting him out of her mind, allowing her thoughts to turn to Mr. Gorgeous. He was out there, somewhere. She remembered that the night she'd seen him in the restaurant, he hadn't been wearing a wedding band. Ted was married, but he didn't wear a ring, so that wasn't a solid indicator of commitment. The woman he'd been with that evening could have been his girlfriend, fiancée, or just a casual lover. Victoria didn't know and didn't care because she could still dream, and there was no harm in that. Thinking about him, she drifted off into a peaceful sleep.

Chapter Nine

A Bowl of Milk......

"Girlfriend, you've been falling on your ass a lot lately," Denise said into the phone. "Are you sure there's nothing wrong, physically? You might have vertigo."

Victoria laughed. "No, I don't have Vertigo. The doctor thoroughly examined me at the hospital, and aside from my predilection for good desserts and bad men, I'm healthy as a horse."

"So you're gonna be out for the rest of the week?"

"That's the doctor's orders."

Initially, Victoria wasn't going tell Denise about the more personal details of what happened between her and Ted over the weekend. But she found herself divulging everything, starting with his offer to let her coordinate SuperNet. She tried to control the smile that kept creeping into her voice each time she mentioned his name. Their new friendship was turning into something she hadn't expected.

When Victoria first heard about the new CEO that Lamar Williams had hand picked to take over the company, she found herself oddly intrigued by the industry insider. Ted's reputation preceded him. He was known for his fearless leadership style and shrewd business negotiations.

She remembered the first time she met him. He'd shown up unannounced during an HR Department meeting on the day she was to present a proposal for the SME evaluation she'd developed. She had worked on her presentation for weeks.

When Ted walked into the room, everyone sat at attention. Victoria recognized him from the photos she'd seen in *Technology Today*, and realized that the pictures hadn't done him full justice. The other directors made a big fuss over him; offering up their seats, shaking his hand, and making congratulatory remarks. Victoria thought the whole scene was a bit much.

Instead of sitting at the conference table in one of the seats that her fellow ass-kissing colleagues had willingly offered up to him, Ted chose to sit in the back of the room. He said he wanted them to go on with their meeting as if he weren't there. *Yeah, right! How can we pretend he's not in the room?* Victoria thought to herself.

Bob Huffman, the Vice President of HR, asked everyone to go around the room and introduce themselves. When it was Victoria's turn, she had to stand slightly so she could make sure that Ted saw her from where he sat, even though she knew that not seeing her would be like not seeing a fly floating in a bowl of milk. When she spoke, she noticed that he didn't look in her direction; he was too busy writing in a leather portfolio perched atop his loosely crossed legs. *Probably taking notes on everyone? Shit!*

When the moment arrived for her to give her presentation, Victoria stood and gave a quick and virtually flawless performance, detailing the benefits that could be gained from having employees evaluate their supervisors.

"This type of evaluation won't work." Patricia threw out. "You can't seriously expect to get honest results using this method," she said, looking over at Ted, giving him a wicked smile. "Our non-exempt employees don't have the skills to evaluate us."

The truth was that Patricia was terrified at the thought of her staff evaluating her work performance and management skills. She began citing unfounded reasons as to why the new evaluation wouldn't work. But for each negative objection she hurled, Victoria countered with a positive resolution.

"I think it's an excellent idea," Ted's voice cascaded from across the room. Victoria was shocked, as were the rest of her colleagues. "It looks like this department is on the right track with new ideas. Have a good afternoon," he nodded, then quickly left the room. He'd made a lasting first impression.

After Victoria finished telling Denise about the details of her weekend with Ted, she waited for her friend's reaction. "So, what're you thinking?"

"Why ask a question you already know the answer to?"

"Denise, Ted and I are becoming friends, that's it."

"Girlfriend, you know he likes you, and it sounds like you're beginning to like him too."

"Yeah, as a friend."

"Mmm-hmm."

"Denise, he's married. And frankly, I'm shocked that as a married woman you're advocating infidelity."

"I'm advocating you gettin' some…A whole year!"

Incoming Mail……

After Victoria talked to Denise, she applied her medicated cream like a good patient and rebandaged her ankle. She was amazed at how quickly her leg was healing. Even though the bruising had mildly discolored her skin, the swelling to her ankle was already starting to subside. Pleased with her progress, she retrieved her company-issued laptop from her computer bag, grabbed one crutch, and hobbled downstairs. She logged onto the ViaTech system and checked her email while she ate a bowl of cereal. She was about to log off when she received a pop-up alerting her of incoming mail. It was from Ted.

Date: Mon. October 11, 8:45 a.m.
To: victoria.small@ViaTech.com
From: theodore.thornton@ViaTech.com

Subject: Progress Report

Ms. Small,

Just checking on your progress. I'll have Jen set up a meeting to discuss SuperNet when I return to the office next week. Also, please remember to follow the directions we discussed.

Best,
Thornton

Victoria smiled, quickly typed a reply, and hit send.

The Defining Moment......

Later that night, Ted smiled as he re-read the email that Victoria had sent from earlier that morning. His day had been stressful, ending with a meeting in which the newly appointed VP of Operations informed him of the disappointing production numbers for the New York office. The pressure of the telecom industry's forecasted decline, and how to save ViaTech in its midst, required all his waking energy. He was tired, but Victoria's message had put a bright spot on the tail end of his long day.

Date: Mon. October 11, 8:50 a.m.
To: theodore.thornton@ViaTech.com
From: iamSMALL@mailnet.com

Subject: It's Me......V

Mr. Thornton,

Thought I'd send you this address for future correspondence concerning my progress and other subjects. I'm pleased to say that things are coming along nicely, thanks to your assistance. Looking forward to seeing you soon.

V.

She'd sent him a message from her personal account. I am SMALL...he smiled to himself. It was an ironic title for someone who he thought was larger than life. Ted was thrilled that she wanted to share private conversations with him, and that she was looking forward to seeing him when he returned. This was another small step. He'd already started putting a new plan into action before he boarded his flight earlier that morning.

He'd be forty-six in five months, and he couldn't afford to play it safe any longer, especially not with a woman like Victoria. Each day that he waited brought the possibility that she might find comfort in another man's arms. In their long conversation the day after her accident, she'd told him that she was ready to start dating again. He couldn't stand the thought of her with someone else, so he knew he had to move fast and make changes.

That morning, before he left town, he'd done just that.

He'd called his attorney to set the wheels into motion. He was finally going to divorce Trudy. He knew that Victoria would never consider getting involved with a married man, but if he was legally separated and awaiting divorce, that might help his case. Next, he called his realtor and asked her to start scouting properties because he planned to move as soon as he could.

He knew he had strong feelings for Victoria, but he began to wonder about her feelings for him? He was reasonably sure there was at least a small attraction on her part. He remembered the way her leg trembled when he touched her. He didn't think his age would be an issue. It never had been with any of the women in his past, and he'd been with women younger than Victoria. But that was just for fun, for the pleasure of it. He didn't think their working relationship would pose a problem either. He knew that her time with ViaTech was short, especially once SuperNet ended next June. Her future plans were a mystery to him, but his instincts told him that ViaTech wasn't a part of them.

And then another thought crossed his mind. *Maybe she doesn't date white men?* But he quickly dismissed the notion. *She has white friends, and they seem very close, more than just casual acquaintances,* he reasoned.

Ted had been with a black woman in the past. It was during his senior year at Princeton, and the young woman was in one of his classes, a blow-off elective he took to even out his grueling schedule.

She was a pretty girl, with a pretty face and a bright smile. She wore her hair in a neat ponytail, and smelled of freshly picked flowers. Jake, Ted's roommate and one of his closest friends, who'd introduced him to jazz, took him to clubs, and who also happened to be black, had called her an *"Oreo"* because he'd never seen her hang around other black students on campus. Ted thought that Jake's statement was out of line. She was clearly a black woman, at least to him.

When Ted approached her after class, they hit it off right away. She was smart, with a lively personality, and seemed very interested in going out with him. After nearly a month, and several dates, Ted took her back to the off-campus apartment he shared with Jake. They slept together, and the most vivid memory he held of the evening was that it was nothing out of the ordinary. No spectacular acrobatics or forbidden sexual acts that he'd expected. The next week she cornered him after class and asked where their relationship was going. She said she wanted a commitment if they were to continue seeing each other. That was the defining moment; he thought—all women are the same.

Other Subjects......

Monday's were Victoria's longest days, and her prescription ordered bed-rest had made it seem to drag along even slower. But her evening livened up when she received a call from Debbie, sounding happy as a kid on the last day of school. After only two days of searching, she and Rob had found the perfect house, but the most exciting news was that she thought she might be pregnant.

She wasn't sure, but this was the second month she'd been late. She planned to take a pregnancy test after they returned to town. She asked Victoria to cross her fingers. She'd suffered three miscarriages over the last two years, so she was cautious. "Have faith," Victoria told her, "everything's gonna be all right."

This had been the perfect news to cap off her evening. Victoria was happy that her friends were moving ahead, living their lives to the fullest. It was something that she intended to start doing.

As her day came to an end, she decided to check her email one last time before going to bed. She lit up when she saw the message from Ted.

Date: Mon. October 11, 10:14 p.m.
To: iamSMALL@mailnet.com
From: ted1.runner@email.net

Subject: Other Subjects

Hello V,

I'm glad you sent your message from your personal account. I've returned the favor so we can discuss other subjects without peering eyes. I'm happy to hear that you're doing better.

V, I need to talk to you when I return next Monday, but not in regards to SuperNet. It's of a more personal nature. I'll be in meetings all day, and would prefer to meet in the late afternoon. Please let me know if you can fit me into your schedule. Be well, and know that I am thinking of you.

Ted

Victoria thought it was cute that he referred to her as V, the way she'd penned her previous email for privacy. But she wondered what he wanted to meet about? If not SuperNet, then what? *"A more personal nature?"* she repeated to herself, reading his email again. After a moment of contemplation she typed a reply. "This is going to be interesting," she mused, then headed to bed.

Ted checked his email one last time before turning in for the evening. He'd sent Victoria an email and was hoping that she'd stayed up long enough receive it and respond back before she went to bed. To his delight, he had incoming mail.

Date: Mon. October 11, 11:01 p.m.
To: ted1.runer@email.net
From: iamSMALL@mailnet.com

Subject: RE: Other Subjects

Ted,

Thought you'd appreciate not having our emails censored by the IT Department. I can always make room for you in my schedule. Monday afternoon sounds fine. I love a good mystery so I'm curious to know what you want to talk about??? But please know that whatever you need to discuss, I'm there for you with a listening ear and an open mind. See you next week.

V.

Wrong Address......

The next morning Victoria rose early, taking extra care to attend to her leg, which was continuing to heal nicely. After breakfast she sat at the desk in her home office, going through several files for upcoming events in the next two months.

So far, Divine Occasions had three parties lined up for the holidays. The first was for Sherry Smith, her realtor. The second was a dinner party for one of her Black Business Women's Coalition members, and the last event was the granddaddy of them all, Tyler's YFI Christmas fundraiser.

It would be YFI's first "elaborate" affair in the organization's eleven-year history. Victoria had been planning the event for the better part of a year, and it was shaping up to be a winner. Many of Tyler's fraternity brothers were buying tables and selling tickets. The Single's Ministry at Victoria's church had purchased a table, as had two members from her Black Business Women's Coalition group. Through her father's connections, John had arranged for his friend's nephew, Gary Hicks, the star point guard for the Atlanta Hawks, to serve as the keynote speaker for the event. Victoria knew that an NBA star's name on the ticket was sure to draw a crowd. She had already chosen everything from the decorations in the ballroom to a delectable menu of culinary perfection.

She was reviewing the list of donated items for the fundraiser's silent auction when the doorbell rang. She hobbled back downstairs and made it to the door. When she looked through the peephole and saw a delivery man holding a large basket, she thought he must have the wrong address. Slowly, she opened the door.

"Delivery for Victoria Small," the man said.

Victoria looked happy and puzzled at the same time. "This is for me?"

After the delivery man helped her bring the large basket inside, she examined its wine and Godiva Chocolate-filled contents. "My favorites!" she smiled. She opened the attached envelope and read the note inside...*Hope this makes you smile. Get well soon...Ted.*

"This man is too much," Victoria said out loud. She picked up the phone and dialed his cell.

It was late afternoon and Ted was wrapping up a meeting with the directors of the engineering and supply chain departments. It was the first opportunity he'd had all day to check his cell phone messages. He was delighted when he heard Victoria's voice ring loud and bright into his ear.

Thanks so much for the basket of goodies, you're so sweet. You really didn't have to do this. Um, anyway, thanks again and I hope your meetings go well. And oh yeah, I'm smiling.

After listening to her message, he found himself smiling too.

∽✺∼

Send Him Fast......

The sun was just going down when Victoria's next-door neighbor, Ms. Swanson, came by to check on her. Ms. Swanson was a silver haired, seventy year old widow who flitted around the neighborhood like the Energizer Bunny's twin. She had a wicked sense of humor and a heart big enough to fill the Grand Canyon. When Victoria first moved in a year ago, it was Ms. Swanson who had come over with a chicken casserole to welcome her to the neighborhood. She'd anointed herself Victoria's surrogate grandmother.

"Ms. Swanson, how are you? Victoria smiled…"and how are you, Caroline?" she asked flatly, greeting them at the door. She always felt uncomfortable when she addressed the old lady's dog. Not because Caroline was a five-pound Yorkie decked out in pink hair bows, pink nail polish, and a rhinestone studded collar, but because the canine was a dog with *attitude*, and a bad attitude at that.

"I wanted to come by and bring you these," Ms. Swanson said, handing Victoria a Ziploc bag. "Here honey, they're Macadamia Nut cookies."

"Thank you Ms. Swanson, would you like to come in? I can put on some tea."

Caroline shook her little head and yelped out a small bark. She was ready to go!

"No, I've got to walk Caroline. You know how she can be when she's ready for her walk," Ms. Swanson smiled. "I just wanted to drop these off and make sure you're doing all right since your accident." She started to turn around, but then stopped "Are you dating that handsome devil with the fancy car who brought you home last Saturday?"

This was the only thing about Ms. Swanson that grated on Victoria's nerves, she was nosy as hell! Ms. Swanson knew the low down on everyone on their street, and could write a tell-all book from the scuttle-butt she'd accumulated over the years. Victoria shook her head. "No, Ms. Swanson. He's a friend from work. Remember? I told you when you called to check on me that evening."

"Oh, that's right, you did say that. Well, it's time for you to start having gentleman callers again. It's been over a year since you broke up with that other fellow."

Caroline looked at Victoria, raised her cotton candy-colored paw, and yelped out another small bark. Victoria shot her a dirty look that quieted the pooch.

"I know you're going to tell me that it's none of my business, and that an old lady like me should stay out of yours, but you remind me of my granddaughter. She's a career woman too, and she's by herself just like you."

Ms. Swanson reached out and patted Victoria's hand. "Everyone needs a little companionship, honey."

"Thanks, Ms. Swanson. I'm working on that."

As Victoria watched the old lady and her dog stroll down the street, she thought about her mother's words—*someone to come home to at night, someone she could count on.*

That night as she lay alone in her bed, she said a prayer that was becoming a habit. "Lord, if it's not too much to ask again, can you please send me a good man…and send him fast?"

Go Your Own Way……

The next day Victoria called her father. Their relationship had been strained the first year after she'd left the bank, but slowly they'd been trying to patch things up. She'd finally come to her senses and decided that she would accept the money John had been offering her to cover start-up costs for Divine Occasions. But she still intended to finish her business plan because she liked having a roadmap to chart her course.

Just as with Steven, she'd been more angry with herself than she'd been with her father. She'd given in to his demands to please him, then blamed him for her inability to stand up for what she really wanted. With her new-found attitude, Victoria decided it was time to bury the hatchet and lay the childish grudge she'd been holding to rest. She held the phone tight as she dialed his number. John answered on the third ring.

"Hey, Daddy. Did I catch you at a bad time?"

"Hi, Queen," John said with surprise. "No, you're timing is perfect. I just finished up a meeting at the bank and now I'm headed out to lunch. Is everything okay?"

"Yeah. Um, Daddy, I'm calling to apologize for the way I've acted," Victoria began. "The things I've said to you and the way I've behaved over the years…you didn't deserve all that." There was a brief silence. She knew that she'd caught him off guard, and even though she couldn't see him, she knew her father was shaking his head, smiling on the other end.

"Queen, I can't fault you, after all, you inherited my stubborn streak," John chuckled. "I guess it's my turn to apologize. I was wrong to push you in the direction I wanted you to go, like my father did with me."

John let out a deep breath. "Growing up, my family had a lot more than most black folk during those times. We had money, land, and even investments. My father was a smart, industrious man, and one of only a handful in our town who had a college degree, black or white. But his education still couldn't get him the white collar job he wanted, so he put his schooling to use in a different way, buying land and growing a thriving tobacco business. Yes, he was successful, but he thought the tobacco fields and hard labor his money came from somehow tainted his wealth. Don't get me wrong, your grandfather was proud of what he'd accomplished. His success was unheard of for a black man in the segregated south, and believe me, he caught hell for it. But he wanted more for me, just as I wanted more for you. I didn't understand the importance of letting you go your own way. My father pushed me and I thought it was my duty to do the same for you," he told his daughter.

Until now, Victoria had never known what had driven that side of her father's incessant behavior. She'd just assumed that he didn't understand her, and didn't want to try. She was glad he'd finally opened up. After their conversation ended, she hung up the phone feeling grateful; grateful for her father's love, and grateful that she was growing.

Chapter Ten

He's A Smooth One......

Victoria's week had gone by fast, and tonight she was buried in work. Several business books were scattered across the table where she sat in the Emory University Library. She was in the stacks, and on Friday nights it was quiet there; like having the entire building to herself. When she started to yawn she knew that it was time to leave. She'd been there for almost three hours. She was closing her book when she felt someone standing over the table. She looked up and had to catch her breath. It was him!

She'd been thinking about him ever since their chance encounter at The Cheesecake Factory two weeks ago, and then seeing him while sitting at the stoplight last week. His smile had appeared to her in more dreams than she could remember, his lips had kissed her a thousand times, and his arms had held her through nights of peaceful slumber. Now, she had to blink hard to figure out if she had just fallen asleep and he'd slipped into her dream, or if she was awake and this was God's good grace in action. When he touched her shoulder she knew her prayers had been answered.

"Hi," he smiled.

Victoria was frozen, not saying a word but still gazing up at him.

"Are you okay?" he asked, his face showing concern.

"Oh, yes, I'm fine. I've just been reading for hours. It can bog down the brain," she finally managed to say.

"It's good to see you again," he smiled. The concern was gone and now all she could see was a set of perfect white teeth and glorious dimples.

"Thank you…it's good to see you too," Victoria smiled back.

He was holding a large book under his arm along with several issues of *National Geographic.* "Do you mind if I have a seat?"

Victoria cleared away her books to make room for him at the small table. Surprisingly, she didn't feel nervous at all. That night in the restaurant, she could barely look at him, and last week she couldn't move when he'd sped past her down the street. But now she was at ease, watching him carefully. She studied him as he slid into the chair in front of her. She thought his neatly creased khakis and black lambswool sweater made him look like a Banana Republic model.

Mr. Gorgeous spotted the pair of crutches leaning against the side of the table. "Are those yours?"

"Um, yes, I had an accident last weekend."

"Oh no, what happened?" He sat his books aside, not taking his eyes off her.

"I went jogging with a friend and had a bad fall. I was pretty banged up, but I've healed remarkably well."

"Sounds like you've had a tough time staying on your feet. As I recall, that's how we met," he winked. "But you're on crutches, it must've been some fall."

"Yeah. I had to go to the emergency room and get a few stitches, but I'm doing much better. I barely need the crutches anymore. I just have them for support more than anything." Even though there was nothing funny about what she'd said, they were both smiling.

"Which hospital?" he asked.

"Piedmont. The nurses in the ER were wonderful, and my doctor was great too."

"Oh, yeah, what was his name? I know a few folks over there in the ER."

"Dr. Obikwelu," Victoria answered.

"Obikwelu…Ah yes, Wole. I know him. He's a good man, a good doctor."

"It's a small world," Victoria said with curiosity. "How do you know people in the ER at Piedmont Hospital?"

"I'm a surgeon."

"At Piedmont?" She was impressed, but tried not to show it.

"No. I'm at Emory Crawford Long."

"What's your specialty?" she asked, trying to sound casual.

"I'm a cardio thoracic surgeon."

That explains the long slender fingers, she thought. The hands that she assumed belonged to an artist really belonged to a skilled surgeon. "You look too young to be a *cardiac thoracic surgeon,*" Victoria smiled, saying her words with emphasis. "But I bet you hear that from your patients all the time."

He nodded his head. "Yes, I hear that quite a bit. I'm sure you look too young for whatever it is that you do as well."

He's a smooth one, she smiled to herself. "I'm a senior director in HR at ViaTech."

"So, what's a beautiful woman like you doing in a library like this...on a Friday night?" Mr. Gorgeous asked.

If anyone else had delivered that tired line, Victoria would've rolled her eyes. But coming out of his mouth it sounded like a sonnet. She thought about telling him that she was on her way to meet friends for a late dinner so she wouldn't look like she had nothing else to do on a Friday night. She'd been alone on the Friday night they'd first met, and now here she was, alone again. But that was the reality of her life, so she spoke the truth. "I'm doing research for a project. When I come here I can get a lot done. How about you?"

"Research for a project? What a coincidence, so am I," he said, nodding toward his books. Mr. Gorgeous looked into Victoria's eyes. "I have to ask you a very important question...what's your name?"

She let out a small laugh, extending her hand. "I'm Victoria Small."

He took her hand in his. "It's a pleasure, Victoria. I'm Parker Brightwood, and now that we've been properly introduced, would you like to join me for a cup of coffee? Please say yes."

His eyes were so deep, she could see her reflection in them. Victoria remembered how he'd looked at her all night with those eyes. And then it came back to her. He had to steal glances because he'd been with another woman that night. Now, he was sitting across from her, eyeing her again, and asking her out for coffee. Even though she'd been fantasizing about him and wanting to see him, she didn't know if she could trust this man who'd visited her in her dreams. For all she knew, the same woman he'd been with when they first met could be waiting for him to come home at that very moment. Her attitude abruptly changed. "No thank you. That probably wouldn't be a good idea. It was nice meeting you Mr. Brightwood." And with that, she started gathering her books.

He was a little shaken, but remained cool. "Please, call me Parker. And why isn't it a good idea?"

"I don't think your girlfriend would approve. I know I certainly wouldn't."

"I don't have a girlfriend. What makes you think I do?"

"Oh, let's see…maybe it's the woman you were with at the restaurant the night we met." Victoria knew she was being sarcastic, but she couldn't help it.

Parker had almost forgotten about Sheila and their double date two weeks ago. All he'd thought about from that evening was his encounter with the beautiful woman who'd been holding his mind captive. He smiled.

"What're you smiling about? Did I say something amusing?" Victoria asked, clearly annoyed at this point.

"I'm smiling because I like your directness. And by the way, I don't have a girlfriend."

Victoria ignored him and was now gathering her books, preparing to leave.

"Victoria, please give me an opportunity to explain?" he asked.

He said her name with a familiarity that made her shudder. "Okay, you've got five minutes," she said, stopping to look down at her watch. "Go."

"You're a tough woman."

Victoria glanced down at her watch again, "Four minutes fifty-five seconds."

"You're really something," he smiled, with a brightness that could've put the sun to shame.

"Four minutes fifty seconds."

"Okay, I get the picture," he paused, "the woman I was with wasn't my girlfriend. We were on a blind date. I went out with her as a favor to the couple we were with that evening. They arranged the date, which by the way was a complete disaster. You were the highlight of my evening."

Now it made sense to her. She thought the two had made an odd couple, and she could certainly relate to being mismatched on a blind date! But she wasn't completely convinced, and he read it in her eyes.

"Listen, I'm going to lay my cards on the table. I've been thinking about you since we met. Wondering who you are, what you do, where you live, and when I'd see you again." He blushed, slightly embarrassed and startled by his honest admission. "Now that I've found you, I don't want to let you get away again. I don't have a girlfriend, fiancée, wife, or whatever else you're thinking."

Victoria's eyes still showed apprehension.

Parker leaned in closer across the table. She could feel his heat. "Victoria, I wouldn't be pleading my case to you if I wanted to play games. I'm far beyond that. If I wanted to be with that woman or any other woman of my choosing, I'd be doing just that, not sitting here in the library begging to share conversation and a cup of coffee with you. I'm a decent brother who wants to get to know you. That's the truth."

They both sat very still. The stacks were so quiet they could hear each other breathe. Victoria looked down at her books, then back up at him. "Are you buying?"

The Logistical Protocol......

Parker walked Victoria to her car. He was parked in a lot on the other side of campus, so he gave her directions and she headed to the Java Café, a coffee shop located in a trendy section of downtown. He watched her drive away, then headed in a fast sprint to his truck. He couldn't believe his luck. He smiled, thinking about how she'd gotten him to do something so uncharacteristic—begging.

The night they met, she'd shaken his normally cool exterior. He thought men who ogled women were weak and uncouth. Parker Brightwood was smooth, if nothing else. A man of his background, distinction, and good looks didn't have to hound women. Women hounded him. He came from a long line of self-assured men. His father was a retired judge, his grandfather, a retired surgeon, and his great-grandfather had been a family practitioner who'd run a successful medical practice out of his home. The Brightwoods were an established family among Washington, DC's black elite, and everyone who was anyone in the DC Metro area knew the family name.

That night at the restaurant when she'd taken a seat at the table across from where he'd been sitting, Parker felt something happen. It was instant. He knew he shouldn't stare, but he couldn't help himself. She'd drawn him in.

When his date came back to the table he'd almost forgotten he was there with someone. A week earlier, his best friend, Phil, had approached him with a proposition. Phil's girlfriend, Gayle, who was forever the matchmaker, wanted to introduce him to her cousin.

"Man, I'm not interested," Parker had said. "Right now the only thing I'm concentrating on is getting things in order for the Africa Project. This is a career opportunity of a lifetime, so I've got to stay focused."

"You've got the Africa Project in the bag so don't worry. Besides, you don't have to marry the woman. Just meet her and have a little fun," Phil urged.

During dinner Parker was frustrated. He didn't want to be rude or outright disrespectful to Sheila, but he couldn't take his eyes off the mysterious woman sitting across from him. He faded in and out of the group's conversation throughout dinner. At one point it became uncomfortably obvious that his interest lay at the other table.

Parker drove fifteen miles over the speed limit in his rush to reach the coffee shop. He pulled into the small parking lot adjacent to the building and scanned the cars. He didn't see Victoria's silver Audi. "*Damn!*" he said out loud. He rubbed his hand over his slick bald head, jumped out of his black BMW SUV, and looked around the parking lot one last time—still no silver car. He hoped that she hadn't ditched him.

The Java Café was a cozy, smartly decorated coffee shop with several small bistro tables, club chairs, and love seats sprinkled throughout the room. Neo Soul music floated over the soft buzz of patron chatter. Parker walked through the door and scanned the tables. Finally, he saw Victoria. She was sitting on a small loveseat in the far corner of the room. She waved to him and he felt relief give him a pat on the back.

"You made it," Parker said with a big smile as he sat down close beside her. "I was worried because I didn't see your car in the parking lot."

"When I got here all the spaces were taken, so I parked around the corner. It wasn't hard to find. And you were right, it's not far from the building where I work."

"This is one of the best coffee shops in the city. I come here almost every day because the owner's a good friend of mine, plus I only live a block away, so it's really convenient."

That explained why she'd seen him driving in the area on her way back to work. He lived nearby. Victoria almost laughed when she thought about the irony; she'd wondered over and over where he lived, and it turned out that he'd been close by all the time.

Parker ordered a regular coffee, Victoria ordered a cappuccino, and they decided to split a slice of chocolate cream pie. They sat facing each other; sitting so close they looked more like long-time lovers than two people just finding each other. Parker held the dessert between them as they each took small nibbles with their forks. It was a subtle, yet very romantic scene; they laughed and talked with natural ease. At times, Victoria touched Parker's arm for emphasis in her statements, purposely letting her hand linger a bit too long. He smiled each time she made the gesture.

As she observed him, it became clear that Parker knew he was incredibly handsome, and possessed a certain power over women. But he wasn't arrogant about it, he just knew he looked damn good and that was that! She wanted to know everything about him. "Can I ask you a question?" Victoria said, tilting her head with curiosity.

"Sure, ask me anything you like."

She was trying to think of a polite way to pose the question. "Do you shave your head by choice, or is it because, um…"

Parker finished her thought, "Because I have male pattern baldness?"

When he laughed, she knew he wasn't offended. Parker rubbed his hand over his glistening scalp. "I'm bald partly by choice, partly by vanity, but not because of necessity."

"Vanity?"

"Yes, I guess that's what I'd call it. Like all the men in my family, I have a full head of hair. But a couple of years ago I shaved it off, just to see how I would look, and I liked it. I got a lot of compliments so I've been shaving it ever since. Why do you ask? Do you prefer men with hair?"

"Oh, it's not that. I was just curious…I think *bald* looks very good on you," Victoria said, wanting to touch his soft-looking scalp.

"Thank you. And by the way, I think your hair compliments you perfectly."

"Thank you," she smiled. She was hoping he wouldn't make the *good hair* comment. To her comfort, he didn't.

They continued on in their conversation; asking questions, giving answers, and growing more and more in sync with each hour that passed.

"Sorry partner, but I gotta close up shop," the owner said as he approached their table. "It's one o'clock and we closed an hour ago."

Victoria and Parker looked around and realized they were the only two customers left in the coffee shop. "Sorry man," Parker said, standing to greet the owner. "Don, I'd like you to meet a very special lady. This is Victoria Small. Victoria this is Don Watkins, the owner of this fine establishment."

Don extended his hand. "I see why Parker doesn't want the evening to end. It's a pleasure," he bowed and smiled.

Don had a warm presence, and his angular face and long dreadlocks reminded Victoria of Bob Marley. "Thank you. You have a very nice place. The coffee and dessert were excellent," she complimented.

Don gave Victoria a humble nod. "I'm glad you enjoyed it. You'll have to come back."

"We will," Parker smiled.

Parker held Victoria's crutches under one arm while they walked slowly to where she was parked. They reached her car faster than either of them had wanted to. When they exchanged business cards, Victoria was pleased to see that Parker had written his full contact information on the back, including his home phone number and address. *Men don't usually give out this kind of information if there's someone else in the picture, too easy to get caught,* Victoria thought to herself. She shivered as the chilly night air made her teeth chatter. "This weather is really crazy, isn't it?"

"Yeah, I guess you need to get in from the cold." Parker took a step closer, and Victoria's heart started doing laps around her chest.

"Um, yeah. I guess so," she answered. They stood in the silence of the crisp air biting around their bodies. "Parker, I had a great time tonight. Thank you for inviting me for coffee."

He smiled and took another step closer until there were only a few inches separating them. "When can I see you again?" he asked.

"Call me. We'll work something out."

"Work something out? I like the sound of that."

Now came the awkward part of the evening. Victoria didn't know if she should hug him, kiss him, or shake his hand? She was deliberating the logistical protocol of first date goodbyes, when Parker brought her hand to his lips and kissed it ever so gently.

*D*on't Spare Any Details......

Victoria's phone rang at eight a.m. She turned over in bed and looked at the Caller ID. "Good morning, Parker. And by the way, I always check my caller ID before I pick up."

He laughed. "So do I."

"How're you this morning?" she asked, trying to tame the excitement she felt from hearing his voice.

"I'm fine. But I miss you."

Victoria sat straight up, gripping her comforter between her knuckles. "You miss me? You just saw me a few hours ago." She was smiling so hard her cheeks hurt.

"I know, and I can't wait to see you again."

She could hear Parker moving around, and she tried to picture him in his condo, wondering what his home was like. She imagined it to be just like him; sophisticated, well appointed, and seductively comfortable.

Victoria had gleaned from their conversation last night that Parker was a bit spoiled and used to getting his way. But he also possessed a very genuine nature she liked. There was no pretense about him. He didn't try to impress her or act cool and in control like some of the men she'd dated in the past. He was simply himself, full of natural born confidence and frank honesty. He wanted her to know that he really liked her, and he didn't care if it made him look vulnerable. That quality appealed to her.

"Do you have plans for later this evening?" he asked.

Victoria thought about the tentative dinner plans she'd made with Tyler and Juliet. "Kind of. An old friend of mine is in town and we'd planned on hanging out, but I'm not sure if we're still getting together. Um, why? Did you want to do something?"

"I was hoping to take you to dinner."

"Why don't I call you later and let you know."

"Sounds good," Parker said, trying not to sound disappointed. "I'll look forward to hearing from you."

After her morning wake-up call from Parker, Victoria got out of bed and started her day with a burst of energy. An hour later she was driving her car, bopping her head to the beat of her Jazzhole CD. She was headed to Tyler's house to have breakfast after Juliet called with the invitation. From the lilt in Juliet's squeaky, high-pitched voice, Victoria knew that Tyler had broken his "let's wait" rule.

Sitting around Tyler's kitchen table, the three laughed and reminisced about old times. Victoria was happy to see that Tyler's life was falling back into a happy rhythm now that he and Juliet were back together.

"Tyler's lawyer talked with Allison's attorney and she's not going to contest the divorce," Juliet said, hands tightly secured inside Tyler's. "So it looks like Mr. Jacobs here will be a free man in six months."

"What? I can't believe that Allison isn't going to make a stink. Are you sure she doesn't have something up her sleeve?" Victoria asked with raised brows. She knew that Allison was the type of woman who'd suck the life out of a vampire if given the opportunity.

"She knows it's over," Tyler said. "One of my frat brothers who knows her family told me that word on the street is that she's already seeing some dude. She's moving on and so am I," he smiled, planting a mouth watering kiss on Juliet's lips.

Victoria averted her eyes. "Before you two rip each other's clothes off like I'm not even here, I need to know if we're still on for dinner tonight?"

"I'm not sure, what's up?" Tyler asked.

"I might have a date," she said, casually sipping her coffee like it was no big deal.

"Excuse me? A date with who?" Tyler asked.

Victoria couldn't maintain her cool. A goofy grin swept across her face. "Remember the guy I met at The Cheesecake Factory two weeks ago? Well, I saw him at the library last night. I found out that the woman he was with that night wasn't his girlfriend, she was his blind date, and it didn't work out. Anyway, we went out for coffee and talked so long we shut the place down, literally," she smiled. "He wants to take me out to dinner tonight and I told him I'd let him know later today."

"Wow, sounds like you two really clicked," Juliet said.

"I can't explain it, but he feels so right. He's kind, considerate and he's honest about his feelings. That's a hard combination to find," Victoria said to Juliet, who nodded her head in agreement.

Tyler looked skeptical. "Victoria, do you believe this guy? I mean, how much do you really know about him? The brothah could be bullshittin' you. That could've really been his woman he was with that night."

"Tyler, don't be so pessimistic," Juliet said, clearing the table of their breakfast dishes.

"I believe him," Victoria countered. "We found out a lot about each other last night. Parker is different. That's his name, Parker Brightwood, and he's a surgeon," she smiled like a proud parent.

Juliet stopped in her tracks. "Parker Brightwood? Oh my goodness. Is he from DC?"

Victoria looked at Juliet with surprise. "How did you know that?"

"Yeah, how did you know that?" Tyler asked, just as surprised.

"If he's who I think he is, his brother is one of the senior partners at my firm. Did the Parker you're talking about go to Howard undergrad, and Harvard Med?"

"Yeah. What do you know about him, and girl, don't spare any details!" Victoria said, sitting on the edge of her chair, hoping that Juliet wouldn't tell her something she didn't want to hear.

"I don't know a lot. Only the basics; his profession, his age, family background, stuff like that. He used to date one of the associates at my firm, and his family is supposed to really be something. I've seen a picture of him in Mason's office, that's his brother. Girl, you've got a fine one," Juliet smiled approvingly.

"*Hey,*" Tyler kidded, pretending to be jealous.

"Did this woman ever tell you anything about him? And like I said, don't spare any details. It's me you're talking to," Victoria said anxiously.

"Okay, Victoria, I'll give you the scoop. But this is purely hearsay, and it's from *her* point of view."

Victoria held her breath, preparing herself.

"Her name was Pamela Presley. She and Parker dated for a little over two years. He broke it off with her right before he left New York and moved here. From what she told me about him, he's a good guy and a real gentleman. But she also said he was commitment phobic. She said he'd rather have a root canal than walk down the aisle. But to be perfectly fair, Pamela was high maintenance, a bit of a Primadonna, and a little on the needy side. As a matter of fact she left the firm last year to join some huge practice here in Atlanta. Everyone suspected it was so she could be near him.

"Hmmm, so she's local." Victoria said, digesting Juliet's information.

"Yeah, and from what I know, Parker has had a lot of women, but he's never made a real commitment to anyone," Juliet concluded as Tyler shook his head with disapproval.

"*Interesting*. I guess I'll just have to find out how he is for myself. I'm going to call him and accept his dinner invitation."

On The Physical Level......

Victoria looked at herself in her full-length mirror as she slipped on her beige-colored wrap dress. It was form-fitting, simple and sexy. She hated having to wear flats with such a fabulous outfit, but her bad ankle called for practicality over fashion. She wanted this evening to go well. All she could think about was Parker's endearing hand kiss from the night before. It was gentle and respectful, yet definitely sensual, and it made her wonder what this date would bring.

She was headed downstairs when the doorbell rang. "You're right on time," she greeted. She admired Parker's herringbone blazer, tan shirt, and black slacks. When he smiled, his dimples looked deeper than she remembered from the night before.

"You look amazing, Victoria."

"Thanks." Victoria could already feel her body throbbing, wanting to be touched, but she reminded herself that she was going to take it slow—if she could.

They went to the Cabin Room, a fine dining establishment known for its bold southern cuisine and exceptional service. Their table in the back was intimate; perfect for a romantic evening. Parker ordered filet mignon and Victoria had the grilled chicken. After their meal, they ordered coffee and dessert.

"This was another great choice, the food is delicious," Victoria said, biting into her key lime pie.

"I'm glad you're pleased. I still can't believe you love to cook. It's hard to find a woman who's interested in doing more than popping a frozen dinner in the microwave."

"Well, as you saw from my clean plate, I love to eat, so it's a good thing I know how to cook," she smiled, patting her flat stomach.

Parker's deep voice lowered to a sexy whisper. "I'd like to sample your...recipes sometime."

"That can be arranged."

They flirted shamelessly. Licking their forks seductively, throwing suggestive hints back and forth, letting their legs brush up against each other under the table. Victoria was loving it!

"I have to be honest," Parker said, "I'm shocked that you're not seeing anyone." He paused, giving Victoria a serious look. "You sure there's not some brother out there wondering where you are right now?"

Victoria gave him a nervous laugh. "No, Parker. There's no one. I was in a relationship that ended a little over a year ago. You're the first person I've been out with since then." Vincent didn't count!

Parker stopped eating his fruit tart in mid bite. "You can't be serious. May I ask why?"

"It's a long story. I'll have to tell you on our next date," she smiled, and he welcomed the suggestion.

They walked out of the restaurant and into the frosty night air. Parker drew Victoria in close, holding her hand in one of his, securing his other arm around her waist. He guided her toward a horse and carriage parked across the street. "I thought it would be nice to take a little ride," he winked, helping her up into the carriage. He sat down beside her, then covered them both with the thick blanket lying on the seat. She snuggled close to him, resting her head on his shoulder as they rode in contented silence.

They ended the evening back at her place, sharing a cup of hot chocolate to take the chill off from their romantic carriage ride. They talked again until the wee hours of the morning. Parker didn't want to leave and Victoria didn't want him to go, but it was past two a.m., and their eyelids were getting heavy. Finally, Victoria walked him to the door.

"Parker, thank you again for another wonderful evening." Victoria wished she could skip through the awkward good night dilemma. She'd told herself that she was going to take it slow, and even though she wanted to pull Parker down to her lips and explore the depths of his mouth, she didn't know if she could trust him, or herself, with such a deliberate move. As if reading her thoughts, Parker wrapped his arms around her waist, pulling her close to him.

"Victoria, I know we've only known each other for a very short time, but this feels so right," he whispered. "I'm feeling things I've never experienced before. We have a real connection, and I want to build a relationship with you." He paused for a moment. "I know I'm coming on a little strong, but I want to be straight up with you."

Victoria's breathing slowed. She clung to his words like oxygen as he continued.

"Like I said last night, I'm not interested in playing games. I'm telling you how I feel so there will be no confusion. Tell me if that's something you can handle?"

"I feel the same way, but..."

"But what?" he asked, pulling her in closer.

Victoria could feel his heart beating fast, pounding just like hers. Their bodies were pressed against each other. "Parker, I've been hurt in the past and it took a long time for me to heal. I want to take things slow...on the physical level. You need to know that before we go any further. When I told you that I haven't dated anyone in over a year, that means I haven't been intimate with anyone either. I don't want to rush into anything until I know that there's genuine trust and honesty in the relationship," Victoria said, searching his eyes.

"Then we'll take it nice and slow," he whispered, giving her a gentle forehead kiss. They stood in the doorway holding each other, ignoring the cold for what seemed like days before Parker finally headed home.

Chapter Eleven

He's Incredible......

Denise walked over to Victoria's desk carrying two cups of coffee. "Girlfriend, I'm glad you're back," she said, handing Victoria a mug.

"Thanks," Victoria beamed, taking a quick sip.

"So tell me, what's got you showing all your teeth this morning? If this is what being out for a week will do for you, I'm turning in my leave form today!"

Victoria gave Denise all the juicy details of her weekend with Parker.

"Wow, he's a catch. He's fine, romantic, and he's a surgeon on top of all that."

"I know, he's incredible, and I'm seeing him again tonight."

Victoria was impressed by Parker's gifted intellect. She learned that growing up he'd been quite the prodigy. He'd graduated from high school at sixteen, whizzed through undergrad at Howard in three years, then on to Med School at Harvard, completing his residency at Johns Hopkins. He'd been an over-achiever his entire life.

"You're seeing him tonight? *Hmmm,* sounds serious already," Denise said, throwing caution into her voice.

"I know what you're thinking..."

"How you figure that?"

"Because I know you. You're thinking; she hasn't had a date in a hundred years, and now she's head over heels for the first guy who comes her way."

"Okay, you're right this time," Denise laughed.

"Denise...I *really, really,* like him. And he's already told me that he's not interested in a one-night stand. This man wants a relationship."

"He said that?"

"Yeah, I mean, how many brothers are that forthcoming?"

"Well, I'm certainly looking forward to meeting Mr. Stud-muffin. And speaking of stud-muffins, I cleared your calendar so you'll have time to prepare for your *after-hours* meeting with Ted," Denise winked with a mischivious grin.

Every Last Detail......

When Ted returned from New York early yesterday morning, he'd instructed his driver to head straight from the airport to the office. It wasn't the way he'd originally planned to spend his first day back home, but he had to take measures to address the stagnant production issues of ViaTech's New York operations.

After plowing through a desk piled high with paperwork, he left the office to meet with his realtor and look at several properties in the area. He planned to be out of the house he shared with Trudy before she returned next week. The quicker he made plans to be free of her, the sooner he could be with Victoria. This was part of the groundwork for repairing his life. The first step was to get a divorce, the second was to move out, and the third and most ambitious step was to confess his feelings to Victoria.

Ted looked at his watch. It was five-thirty on Monday afternoon, and any minute now Victoria would be standing before him. He'd thought about asking her to meet him at a restaurant for dinner or some place away from the office. But this kind of pronouncement required a more private setting; one which he could control. He was uncharacteristically nervous. Not because he had doubts, but because this was the most sure thing he'd felt in his life, and the thought of Victoria not returning his feelings cut at him like a dull edged knife.

He planned to go slow. He wouldn't tell her how crazy he was about her right away; just that he was interested in pursuing a relationship that extended beyond the platonic confines of friendship. He would wait for her reaction and go from there. If she wasn't interested, he knew she would let him know. She was that kind of woman. So he prayed she'd give him the response he was hoping for.

"Ted?" Jen's voice caught him off guard. She was standing in the middle of his door. "I'm leaving now. I just called Victoria and she's on her way up," she smiled with knowing.

Ted looked up, giving her a nod. "Thanks, Jen. Have a good evening."

He watched his assistant as she walked away. He knew that she was on to him, but he wasn't worried. She was one of the few people he trusted, so her knowledge gave him comfort. Plus, she was good friends with Victoria's assistant, a connection he knew would serve him well in the future. A few minutes later, he heard a faint knock on the door.

"Hi," Victoria smiled, slowly walking toward him.

He took in her long, ivory-colored skirt and matching silk blouse, wanting badly to feel her body next to his. He came from behind his desk to meet her halfway.

"See how well I've recovered. No crutches."

"Yes, I see. And you look beautiful, as usual."

"Thank you."

Ted's desire was momentarily replaced by concern. "V, let's have a seat," he said, leading Victoria to the large leather couch on the other side of the room. He sat down close beside her. "I hope you don't mind me calling you that?" he asked tentatively. The way Victoria penned her email to him had become his private term of endearment for her. If she looked uncomfortable or objected, he knew it would be a sign for him to proceed with caution.

"I don't mind at all. I think it's sweet."

A green light—Proceed! "Are you feeling okay? How's your ankle and your leg?"

"They're healing well. All the swelling is gone."

"I'm glad to hear that you've been a good patient."

"Would you expect anything less?" Victoria teased. "I know I can be difficult and stubborn at times, but I eventually come around. It's a trait that I readily attribute to being my father's daughter," she laughed. It was a characteristic that until now, Victoria had not been willing to admit, but her stubbornness was matched only by John Small's. "And Ted, thanks again for the basket. Godiva Chocolates happen to be my favorites."

I was right! "Well, I'm glad you liked them." He took a deep breath, deciding to jump straight in. "V, I'm glad you agreed to meet with me."

"Sure," she nodded.

Ted felt his heart pound hard in his chest, like the drums he'd heard the tribal village men beat on the *Discovery Channel* special he'd seen the night before. He started to sweat. "V, can I get you something to drink?" he asked, standing to regain his composure.

"No thanks," she answered, noticing the shift in his demeanor.

Ted walked over to the mini bar on the other side of the room. *Dammit, what the hell is wrong with me? Okay, get a grip. Go over there, and get back on track,* he told himself. He took another deep breath to calm his nerves.

Victoria looked at her watch. She wanted to give Ted the opportunity to talk about whatever it was that he wanted to share because it was obviously something big, judging by his mood. But she was supposed to meet Parker for their date tonight and the clock was ticking.

Ted saw Victoria glance down at her watch. "Do you have to leave soon?" he asked, pouring himself a gin and tonic.

"Um, actually, I have a date tonight," she blurted out. "But I can be a little late. You still have something you wanted to talk about, right?"

Ted had to steady his hands to finish pouring his drink. *Did she just say she has a date?* He walked back over to the couch, reclaiming his seat beside her. "You have a date tonight?" he asked, trying to make his voice sound casual.

"Yes. But I already told him that I had a late afternoon meeting, so...."

"You've met someone?"

Victoria blushed. "Yeah, but we're not here to talk about me..."

"I'm curious. When did this happen?

Victoria told him about how she and Parker first met, then gave him a brief snapshot of the weekend they'd shared. Ted felt his heart sink. He didn't want to think about her with another man, but he knew it would kill him if he didn't ask questions. "Tell me about him?" he asked.

Victoria eyed him curiously. "Do you really want to hear all this?"

"Yes, V...every last detail," Ted forced himself to say. He took a long gulp of his drink and braced himself.

Oblivious to Ted's anguish, Victoria told him about each encounter she'd had with Parker from their first eventful meeting at The Cheesecake Factory, to their first coffee date, to their dinner and carriage ride, to their three-hour phone call last night. With each romantic detail she revealed, Ted's heart sunk deeper and deeper. He didn't know how much longer he could continue his charade of nodding politely and smiling appropriately, as if he were happy to hear about her new romance.

"So, that's my story," she concluded. "Now, let's change the subject to you. What is it that you wanted to talk about?"

"Sounds like you two are quite an item." Ted faked a smile, bringing the focus back to Victoria and her new man in question.

"Yes, there's something very special about him. But I'm exercising caution. My last relationship taught me a thing or two about rushing in."

"You're absolutely right," Ted encouraged. "That's a very wise approach to take."

She could see that he was stalling. "Ted, please tell me what you wanted to talk to me about? You said it was personal?"

"Yes…I've filed for divorce. My attorney drew up the papers while I was in New York last week. Trudy will be served when she returns to town. I'm looking at houses in the area, and in the meantime I'll be staying in a suite at the Ritz Carlton." Ted rattled off the life-changing events as if he'd just told her what he had for breakfast that morning.

Victoria was amazed by the casualness of his revelation. It was the same tone he'd used when he first told her about the details of his paper marriage. She could see that there was still something weighing heavy on his mind. "I know this must be difficult for you, but you're doing the right thing."

Ted drained his drink, desperately wanting another. "Yes, it was a decision that was long overdo, and I feel better now that I've made it." His mind vexed under the weight of Victoria's news. He wanted to prolong their time together, to keep her from her date.

"I'm glad you felt comfortable enough to share this with me," Victoria said in earnest, "and I'll be here for you whenever you want to share anything that's on your mind."

They talked for another hour about Victoria's ideas for SuperNet, Ted's week in New York, and their plans to go jogging again once her ankle was fully healed. Finally, she told him she had to leave.

He walked her to the parking garage, and on their way down she called Parker to let him know she would be there soon. Ted's ears burned as he listened to the sweetness in her voice, making polite apologies for running late. He resented and envied the man on the other end of the line.

Ted cursed himself after returning to his office. He was frustrated and angry, and he knew he had no one to blame but himself. "Why didn't I just tell her how I felt last week before I left for New York?" he said aloud, banging his fist on his desk. And in that moment, he knew what he had to do. He had to pursue her; quietly and patiently. He knew that her new relationship would fizzle, and when it did he'd be there to pick up the pieces.

He knew that because he knew Victoria was meant to be with him.

Professional Or Personal...

Victoria stood in the vestibule-like entrance of Parker's ultra-luxe building and rang the buzzer to his unit. "Is that you?" Parker's deep sexy voice floated out to her.

"Yeah, it's me."

"Thought you'd never get here. Come on up."

She heard a buzzing noise and a click of the double doors that gave her entry into the inner lobby. She stepped into the mahogany paneled elevator and rode up to the fifth floor.

"I'm glad you finally made it," Parker welcomed her at his door. His day had been long and hard, but now his mood was instantly brightened. He'd labored through three rough surgeries, each wrought with complications. After meeting with hospital executives about the upcoming Africa Project, he made his rounds, then finished the last of the paperwork on his desk. He was tired, but the sight of Victoria standing in his doorway was the perfect end to his day. Parker reached for her hand "Come in. Let me take your coat."

Victoria had imagined over and over in her mind what Parker's home was like, and as she looked around, it was pretty much what she'd expected. He had a generous size condo, especially for the city. The living room was furnished with a large entertainment center, outfitted with every kind of high-tech electronic gadgetry known to man. The brown leather sectional and mahogany armchair were perfectly centered, and situated in the middle was an iron and glass coffee table.

She walked across the pristine hardwood floor and ran her fingers over the hand-carved set of African drums that sat in the corner beside a large tropical plant. She examined the African prints and the collage of African masks hanging on the walls. It was *good* art too—originals. "Your place is really nice," she said.

"Thank you, coming from you that's a great compliment."

"Who decorated for you?"

"I did it myself."

"Really?"

"What....a brother can't have good taste?" Parker teased.

"I didn't mean that. It's just that most men don't get into decorating. They usually leave that kind of thing to their wife, girlfriend, or a designer."

Parker laughed. "I don't have a wife or a girlfriend...yet," he smiled, "and I'm much too practical to pay a designer to put together what I already know I like, so I did it myself."

Victoria looked at him and smiled. *Thank you God for answering my prayers!* She wanted to ask him if he was handy at fixing things around the house, but decided to table that question for later.

"Let me give you a tour," Parker motioned, leading Victoria through the front rooms and toward the long, wide hallway. Four beautifully framed Vanderzee prints hung on one side of the wall, while family portraits decorated the other. Victoria stopped to admire them.

"I like your Vanderzees. Very nice."

"Thanks, my oldest brother gave them to me as a housewarming gift."

Victoria turned to look at his family portraits. There must have been twenty pictures of various sizes covering the wall. As she examined each impeccably framed photo, she felt the air grow thin. From the two large portraits of who she assumed to be the family patriarch and matriarch at the top, to the many children, grandchildren, great grand-children, and other relatives scattered throughout, they all looked the same. They were all very light in complexion. Some even looked white. The older black and white portraits of Parker's ancestors depicted somber-looking men and women, devoid of any recognizable African features. They were dressed in what Victoria could see was the very finest in turn of the century attire. She imaged this was what a wall of pictures in the Sanders' home would have looked like. It brought back a painful past. One she'd only heard about...............

The week after Victoria had been born, her mother's family traveled to North Carolina to visit their new addition. But the first thing they all wanted to know was the infant's skin color. Everyone in Elizabeth's family was very fair in complexion, as were all the people who married into the clan. The Sanders' believed in the old fashioned practice of color-coding—making sure the pale hue in the family stayed that way. Elizabeth often recoiled at her family's ways. "Mother, how many times do I have to tell you, we don't use the term *colored* anymore. We're black," Elizabeth would say.

"We are colored, and mildly at best. We will never be *black*," her mother would throw back in a matter-o-fact tone.

John was the lone chocolate chip in the batch, and the only reason he was accepted into the Sanders family was because he and Elizabeth's brother, Maxx, were best friends, but more important, he came from a family with money and land. John never had a problem with the Sanders, but he knew how they were and he'd never liked it.

When the family came to visit, John tried to have patience with his in-laws because he wanted things to go smoothly, especially after all that he and Elizabeth had been through over the last couple of years; loosing their first baby, and nearly loosing Victoria as well. But when Elizabeth's mother made her now infamous comment, the shit hit the fan! Grace Sanders looked at her tiny one-week old granddaughter and started what was to escalate into a dramatic scene. "At least you can tell she's going to have good hair, she's actually a cute little baby to be so dark," she had the nerve to say.

John was fuming and Elizabeth was embarrassed by her mother's behavior. But Grace didn't stop there, "Don't get upset with me. I'm only thinking about her future. It's one thing to be a dark colored man, but who will want to marry a dark colored woman? Really, I'm just thinking about the poor little thing's future," she said.

Within five minutes, John had cleared his home of Elizabeth's entire family. Even though John was educated, successful, and came from a family with money, he was still dark. And down south in those days, having light skin was just like having money; it gave you a leg up. The fact that John was dark was a strike against him.

"You should be grateful that we even allowed you into our family," Grace spat out at John, then turned to follow her husband and other family members out the door.

John was normally a restrained man, but they'd pushed him over the edge. "You can all kiss my black ass!" he yelled, slamming the door on his mother-in-law's heels. After that, relations with Elizabeth's side of the family were non-existent. Her brother Maxx was the only relative who still remained close to them...............

"This is the Brightwood Clan," Parker announced with pride. "That's my grandparents at the top," he smiled, pointing to the two large portraits, "and the rest are their children and their children's children, along with others who've married into the family."

"You sound very proud of your family," Victoria said with an edge.

"I am. We're very close, and that's hard to find in many families today. We believe in tradition."

"Oh yeah, what kind of tradition?" *Keeping the darkies out?* Victoria thought. She could hear the sarcasm coloring her voice, and she was sure he'd heard it too.

"The tradition of family, hard work, and strong morals. Those kind of values." Parker paused. "Victoria, are you okay?"

"Uh, Yeah, I'm fine." Victoria tried not to judge, but she knew what that scene was all about. Looking at the pictures on Parker's wall took her back to that night when she was seven years old. The night she learned how to swallow hurt and rejection like bad medicine.

"Shall we continue?" he asked.

Victoria didn't want to ruin their evening because of a wall full of pictures. "Sure," she said.

"Now, on to the love den," Parker smiled, giving Victoria a wink. She looked at him suspiciously. "I'm only kidding," he laughed.

Parker's bedroom was a mixture of rugged masculinity and modern comfort, with deep colors and contrasting fabrics. His mahogany king-size sleigh bed was covered with a rich-looking paisley patterned comforter that made Victoria want to lay on top of it—with him. She walked over to inspect his large master bathroom and walk-in closet. She looked at Parker and wondered how many women had recently taken the Brightwood home tour, and if his bedroom was the main attraction.

She tried to put her negative thoughts out of her mind. "Since we're going to miss the movie do you want to go straight to dinner?" Victoria asked.

"To be honest, I really don't feel like being in a crowded restaurant tonight. I was thinking we could order something and stay in. Is that okay with you?"

"Sure."

After looking over several menus, they decided to order Thai. They sat next to each other at a safe distance on the couch, waiting for their food to arrive. Victoria could feel his heat and it made her want him. She had to find a distraction. Her eyes landed on a photo album sitting on the bottom base of the coffee table. "Do you mind if I look through your album?" she asked, hoping to uncover something that would contradict what she'd seen on his family wall of shame.

"Help yourself. But I must warn you, there are a few ex-girlfriends in there...all ancient history of course. Unlike women, men very rarely throw away anything." They shared an awkward laugh at his joke. Now Victoria was more curious than ever to see what she would find.

The first few pages were a repeat of the hallway, filled with noble looking, color-conscious Brightwoods of the past and present. Parker gave her a run down of who was who in each picture. They leafed through page after page of family gatherings, wedding photos, and pictures of Parker in various stages of development from Boy Scouts and Jack and Jill, to his college days at Howard. *He's a Kappa,* Victoria smiled to herself. He was a member of the same fraternity as Tyler. She hoped that being frat brothers would give the two men a good start, especially since Tyler was so skeptical about the men she dated.

They moved on to several pages of Parker posing with different women. Victoria remembered what Juliet had said about him having a lot of women, and even Parker had told her so himself. The women were all very attractive, well-bred looking BAPs, and they all looked like his relatives. Victoria didn't want to obsess over the color thing, but it struck her as too calculated to be coincidence. She wondered if Pamela, the one who had moved to Atlanta to be near him, was one of the women on the pages in front of her?

Parker could see Victoria's uneasiness. He put his hand over hers and reached to close the book. "Victoria, those pictures are old. I lost contact with most of those women years ago," he said in a serious voice, returning the book to the bottom of the table.

Victoria wasn't ready to discuss her suspicions of his possible color bias, or admit it to herself. *Why would I even be here if he felt that way? I need to just relax and enjoy the evening,* she told herself.

After their food arrived, Parker chose a smooth white wine from his collection to accompany their meal. He lit two candles, and they ate, serenaded by the soft, glowing light. Parker sat his chopsticks on the side of his plate, reached for Victoria's hand, and held it in his. "I'm glad we stayed in tonight."

"Me too," she smiled.

After they finished their meal, Victoria helped to put away the dishes before they returned to the couch. She felt amorous sitting so close to him. She'd been thinking about kissing him since she walked through the door. But she knew she had to be strong because Parker's seductive charm was like credit card debt...it could sneak up on you, and before you knew it you were about to go over your limit.

"How's your ankle feeling? You were walking so well when you came in, I almost forgot to ask."

"It's fine. As you can see, the swelling is completely gone, and so is most of the bruising on my thigh. But I still can't wear pants or pantyhose until it heals a little more."

"Oh, let me take a look."

Before Victoria could respond, Parker had lifted her long flowing skirt and was moving in for a closer examination. His quick action took her by surprise.

Parker saw the look on her face. "Don't worry," he said gently, patting her hand, "I'm a surgeon. I've seen it all." He glided his fingers over her leg and upper thigh. "Mild abrasions, several small lacerations, but not too bad.... probably negligible scarring...Obikwelu does clean suture rows," Parker said, almost to himself. He was talking in his professional doctor voice and it made Victoria laugh.

"What's so funny?" he asked, still examining her leg.

"It's interesting to see you totally disconnect like that. One minute you're Parker Brightwood, charming and sexy. And the next you're Dr. Brightwood, serious and methodical. It's an interesting dichotomy."

"There's a time and place for everything. As a medical professional it's critical that I separate my personal emotions from my professional responsibilities," he said, continuing to rub her thigh, but more slowly now.

"And what mode are you in now...professional or personal?" Victoria purred.

"I'll let you decide."

When his mouth met hers, Victoria thought she would melt. Parker kissed her gently, easing her body down into the sofa. His tongue searched for hers and found it. She ran her fingers across his scalp and he moaned, enjoying the feel of her delicate forefingers on his skin. She sucked his tongue into her mouth, then kissed him gently, slightly biting his lower lip before moving on to his neck. Parker tilted his pelvis and began to grind against her as they moved their bodies in synchronized motion. His hand searched beneath her skirt and cupped her firm, round behind. She gently sucked his tongue again, then tickled it with her own. Parker felt shock waves run through his body, and his erection rubbed hard against her leg.

Victoria could feel herself loosing control. "We need to stop," she panted, not wanting to *really* stop, but knowing she needed too.

Slowly, Parker withdrew from their embrace, lifting himself up while Victoria pulled her skirt down, hoping he hadn't seen the wet spot in the seat of her panties. He shifted in his place beside her on the sofa, trying to regain his composure. Victoria glanced down at the huge lump bulging at the seat of his wool trousers. *Damn!* she thought to herself.

"I'm sorry. I got carried away," Parker apologized.

"You weren't bumpin' and grindin' by yourself," she smiled, giving Parker a little relief. "I guess we need to slow things down."

"But why? Victoria, you feel the same thing I feel. I know you do. Why don't we just do what comes natural."

"For one thing, this is only our third date. It's too soon. Besides, sex has a way of clouding the issues."

"What issues?"

"My point exactly. Whatever issues we might have remain to be seen. We're still getting to know each other. When you introduce sex into the picture, it can cause you to overlook obvious flaws, and make excuses for certain behavior because the physical rewards are used as compensation."

Parker raised a brow. "Sounds like you're speaking from experience."

"I am."

He ran his hand across his slick scalp, then looked straight into Victoria's eyes as he spoke. "I'm already falling in love with you."

"What?..."

"I said I'm falling in love with you," he repeated.

There was silence

Victoria fidgeted. *What do I say? What do I do?* She felt a strong connection, but was it love...so soon?

"I don't expect a response...at least not tonight," Parker winked. "I know this seems sudden, and believe me, I'm surprised myself. But this is right, Victoria. I know it."

He cleared his throat and waited for a moment to pass. He hoped she would say something, anything. But she didn't. "Listen," he started again. "I don't want to scare you off, I'm just trying to be honest with you. I'll always be honest with you, Victoria."

She knew she had to say something. She couldn't let him confess his feelings and not respond. "Parker, everything is happening so fast. You're what I've been praying for, and that's why I want to take it slow... I don't want to mess things up. I want to enjoy discovering new things about you, and I want you to accept my quirky ways and crazy habits. I want to know that I can *really* trust you, and the only way I'll find out is with time."

"If taking it slow is what you want, then that's what we'll do." Parker lifted Victoria's hand to his mouth and kissed it gently, letting his tongue graze her skin. He felt her tremble and looked into her eyes. "You can't blame a brother for tryin'."

They shared a laugh before falling back into the sofa, cuddling in each other's arms.

Preferential Treatment......

Three weeks after Victoria's report had been submitted, the big SME meeting caused a raucous so explosive it could've been mistaken for a Fourth of July fireworks display. Midway through the meeting, Patricia spilled over with anger. She was upset because Bob Hoffman, the VP of HR, had used one of the failing evaluations as an example of how *not* to manage a team. No one except Victoria knew the identity of the person in question until Patricia went ballistic and removed all doubt that she was the culprit.

She jumped out of her seat and started yelling like a mad woman. She accused Victoria of setting her up. "You're jealous of me," Patricia scowled across the table in Victoria's direction. "I know what you're up to. You're trying to make me look bad. You're trying to get rid of me. I know you're the reason I wasn't nominated for EMP."

Bob tried to calm her down, but it was to no avail.

"I've watched you, cozying up to certain people so you'll get assigned to the best projects. I see right through your little act," Patricia raged, pounding her fists on the conference table. "You have everyone around here fooled, except me. You're a fake, and pretty soon people are going to find out all about you. I'll see to it!"

Bob quickly adjourned the meeting within a matter of minutes. After that, Patricia left for the day and her erratic behavior became the talk of the office. Bob let tempers calm before he called Victoria into his office a few hours later. He apologized for Patricia's outburst and made assurances that he'd talk to her.

But the real blow came when Victoria learned that Patricia would be joining her on an upcoming project in New York. And to her surprise and outrage, it was at Ted's request.

"Ted copied me on an email he sent to Patricia earlier this morning," Bob said. "He wants her to help the strategy team that you're working with to evaluate the New York office and the situation that's brewing up there."

Victoria was upset, but realized there was little she could do. An hour later, she and Denise went out for a late afternoon lunch. "I can't believe Patricia!" Victoria said with anger, crunching on her vegetable spring roll. "I don't know if I can work with her on the New York project."

"Well, you've gotta try."

"She said that I cozy up to certain people to get preferential treatment."

Denise rolled her eyes. "You know why she said that, don't you?"

"Yes. I know she was referring to Ted. And I'm not crazy, I know that people are talking."

"She's jealous, just like all the other heifers around there. They wish they were spending time with Ted and getting his attention instead of you."

"But all we do is work, work, work! SuperNet is a huge project, plus I've got my regular work to deal with," Victoria huffed. "And how I got dragged into the New York situation is still a damn mystery to me. If I'm receiving preferential treatment, why wasn't I able to get out of that assignment?"

Denise took a sip of her ginger tea. "Yeah, but you're missing the point. People are jealous because you're getting face time with the top dog."

Victoria shook her head. "If they want to trade places with me, they can have at it. Then maybe I'd be able to spend more time with Parker. He's always having to wait on me because I'm running late."

"Listen, Girlfriend. I hear you, but people are watching. Every time that you and Ted go out to lunch or have late afternoon meetings, people are keeping tabs on it. Jen told me so. And it doesn't matter what kind of projects you're working on."

"This is truly unbelievable! Patricia has fucked nearly the entire executive team, and people are questioning my ethics?" Victoria was so mad she had to sit back and take a deep breath. "Denise, what happened today really pissed me off. Patricia gets away with entirely too much shit, and the only reason they haven't fired her is because they're afraid of a lawsuit," Victoria huffed.

Denise raised her brow. "Why do you think Bob let's her do as she pleases?"

Victoria shook her head with disbelief. "Tell me you're joking."

"He's tappin' that. He's got to protect his interest."

"That's trifling," Victoria said with disgust. If it hadn't been for the fact that she was looking forward to SuperNet next summer, she would've handed in her resignation after the meeting. But she had to focus on the bigger picture. She'd made a commitment to herself, and she'd be damned if she was going to let Patricia fowl up her plans.

Lips Met Lips......

A week after the disastrous SME meeting, Victoria sat across from Ted at the conference table in his office. She was disappointed that he had yet to mention a word about the big blowout she'd had with Patricia, but more than that, she was ready to leave. It was Friday night and they were working late—again. She looked at her watch and saw that it was eight-thirty. She should have been at Parker's an hour ago because they had plans to attend Phil and Gayle's big Halloween costume party.

Even though work had been hectic over the last several weeks, Victoria's love life made everything seem like a breeze. She and Parker quickly fell into a routine like they'd been together for years. They saw each other at every opportunity their busy schedules would allow. They shared long romantic kisses, but were mindful not to let things go too far. She was amazed by Parker's self-control. Some nights she wanted him to rip off her clothes and ravage her body, but when he felt his urges grow too intense, he would withdraw and kiss her on the palm of her hand.

She was finishing her review of the updated schematics and booth design for the SuperNet show when she looked at her watch again. *After I finish this page I'm outta here*, she said to herself.

Tired from pouring over the tedious documents, Victoria stood to stretch. Ted studied her, and she caught him. They stared at each other for a few silent moments before he rose and walked over to where she stood. He reached for her, slowly pulling her into his arms. She embraced the sudden shock and thrill of what was happening.

Lips met lips. Hands met flesh. Her blouse came off, then his shirt. Within seconds they were both patially nude. With one sweep of his hand, Ted pushed the pile of documents and folders from the conference table to the floor, laying Victoria across the hard cherry wood surface. He rested his body on top of hers, kissing and licking until she moaned. He felt her wetness, smelled her hunger, and plunged into the comfort he'd been longing for. When he entered her, they both cried out a breathless, *"Yes."* She moved under his body as she moaned with delight.

"Ted, I'm finished here. You can review this to see if it meets your approval," Victoria said, handing Ted a folder. "Ted? Ted, can you hear me?" she asked.

Victoria's voice shocked him back to reality. Ted pulled off his reading glasses and rubbed his eyes. His fantasies were getting out of control. "I trust your opinion. Go for it."

"Are you okay?"

"Uh, yes. I'm fine."

"Okay, I'm outta here."

Ted didn't want her to leave. His attempts to keep Victoria busy with

SuperNet and the New York project weren't working. She was still finding time to see Parker.

But as Victoria's romance with Parker was growing, so was the intensity of her friendship with Ted. They worked long hours together, laughed at each other's jokes, and talked in more intimate detail about their personal lives. Victoria had even confided in him about the night her relationship with Steven had ended.

"You're leaving so soon?" Ted asked.

"Yes, I'm already late."

"For what?" he asked, putting down his pen. He knew that whatever her plans, they almost certainly involved Parker.

"Parker and I are going to a Halloween costume party tonight," Victoria smiled slyly. "I'm going as Catwoman."

Chapter Twelve

I Got It Off the Internet......

Parker buzzed Victoria into his building, then returned to the sofa. He'd left the door ajar so she could enter on her own. He was pissed! Her job was starting to wear thin on him, more specifically, her demanding CEO. Whenever they planned to meet, go somewhere, or do anything, it seemed that Ted Thornton always had a project that required Victoria's immediate attention. They'd begun to have small arguments about it. Parker hadn't met Ted, but already he didn't like the man.

"Victoria, he's the company's top executive, with a large staff at his disposal. Can't he find someone else to do some of the projects he's assigning to you?" Parker had asked.

"There are a lot of complicated situations the company is dealing with right now," she responded.

"You said that you're leaving next June to run your business full-time, just phase out the work to someone else. Or better yet, tell him no."

"That's not my style. I wouldn't do that, just like I wouldn't expect you to walk out on a patient who needed your help."

"That's different. You're talking about someone's life."

"I might not be saving lives, but my job is just as important to me as yours is to you. I never complain when your beeper goes off and you have to leave, or work late. I adjust my schedule around yours without complaint. Why can't you do the same for me?"

He knew that Victoria was right. "I'm sorry," he acquiesced, but still didn't like the imposition her work forced on their time together.

Victoria noticed that Parker's front door was open. She pushed through slowly and found him sitting on the sofa. He was dressed as a Greek Olympian in full regalia. His short, sexy toga made her want to devour him on sight. She walked over to him and dropped her duffel bag to the floor. "I love your costume," she smiled.

"You're late…again."

"Parker, I called and told you that I'd be late. I'm sorry, but I had some important documents to review before I leave for New York this Sunday."

"Victoria, why does this guy have you working on so many assignments?"

"I've explained this to you before. Most of the projects I'm working on are leading up to SuperNet, which is a great opportunity for me. Why can't you be supportive?" Victoria asked, looking dejected.

"I'm sorry, baby. I guess I just want you all to myself," Parker said, standing to his feet, pulling Victoria close to him. "I want to spend as much time with you as I can."

"We have plenty of time, there's no rush. I'm not going anywhere, are you?"

Parker quickly evaded her question. "You got your costume?"

"Yep, it's in my bag."

"Then let's hurry and get you changed."

They walked down the hallway and into Parker's bedroom. He stood in the doorway with his back turned as Victoria undressed. "I don't want you to think that I'm not being supportive," he said over his shoulder. "I'm glad that your new CEO is looking out for you. But I think that this Ted Thornton guy is being totally unreasonable, and he's taking advantage of your time."

"Asking me to work on SuperNet after turning down his EMP nomination was something he didn't have to do," Victoria countered.

"Well, all I know is that he's cutting into our time together. But listen, let's not argue about your job tonight. Let's just concentrate on having a good time."

"Fine with me." Victoria was glad to end the conversation. She finished putting on her costume. "So, tell me what you think?"

Parker turned around and smiled approvingly. Victoria's shiny, black bodysuit hugged every curve of her body, and her three-inch black patent leather Dolce & Gabanna knee-high boots gave the outfit sizzle. She adjusted the pointy cat ears perched atop her head and did a quick once-over in the mirror before they headed out the door.

When Victoria and Parker arrived, Gayle welcomed them with a big smile. "Hey, come on in. We were wondering if you two were going to make it." She was dressed as Alice in Wonderland, the café au lait version. She kissed Parker on the cheek. Victoria extended her hand, but Gayle drew her in for what felt to Victoria like a genuine hug. "I'm Gayle. It's nice to meet you, Victoria. I've heard so many wonderful things about you."

"Likewise, and it's nice to meet you too."

Phil came up from the back, giving Parker a customary brothahman dap. "You're late ass finally showed up," he yelled over the music. He was dressed as a Boy Scout, badges and all.

Parker introduced Victoria, and Phil gave her a light kiss on the cheek. "It's good to see you again, and formally meet you this time" he smiled, making everyone laugh.

"You have a lovely home," Victoria said, looking from Gayle to Phil. Parker had told her that the two had purchased their house six months ago, and planned to marry sometime next year.

"Thanks, why don't I give you a quick tour," Gayle offered.

As the two women headed off, Phil and Parker made a bee-line to the poker game underway in the den.

Gayle and Victoria walked around the first floor, going in and out of neatly decorated rooms packed with party-goers. They ended their tour with the master bedroom upstairs. "Victoria," Gayle started slowly. "I thought you should know…Sheila's here tonight."

"Oh, really? I didn't see her downstairs," Victoria said, feeling a little uneasy.

"She's down there somewhere. I'm just telling you because I don't want there to be any awkward surprises. I already told her that you and Parker would be here too."

"You say it like I should be concerned." Now Victoria was beginning wonder if Parker's relationship with this woman had been more involved than he'd led her to believe.

"No, there's no need to be concerned. Parker and Sheila only went out on that one date. I just know it was awkward that night at the restaurant because Parker was so obviously taken by you. Sheila's my cousin, but hey, I just wanted you to know."

Parker had said that Phil was crazy about Gayle, and now Victoria could see why. Gayle possessed a realness that made her trustworthy. "Thanks, and I appreciate you sharing that with me, but your cousin isn't going to do anything crazy is she?"

"Girl, please!" I just didn't want anyone to be caught off-guard. She knows I don't tolerate drama," Gayle said, hands on her hips.

Victoria was glad that Gayle had warned her, and wondered if Parker was aware that Sheila was on the scene.

Gayle smiled. "Victoria, I have to tell you, you're workin' the hell outta that cat suit."

"Thanks, girl. I got it off the Internet."

Back downstairs, Sade crooned out *Sweetest Taboo,* while the crowd of young, black professionals swayed to the beat, chit-chatting, mingling, and checking out the night's sampling of available potentials. The house was packed with people who'd arrived solo, but didn't plan on leaving that way.

Victoria didn't know if it was the two glasses of wine she'd drank, or the beat of the music surging through the room, but she was having a good time.

A few hours and another glass of wine later, she and Parker decided to head home. "I'll grab our coats from upstairs," she said. She moved slowly, trying not to let her wine buzz get the best of her. But on her way back downstairs, she stopped cold at the second landing when she saw something that gave her an instant chill. Parker was standing in the middle of the living room, talking to Sheila.

The vixen was stunningly dressed as Cleopatra. Parker's back was turned toward Victoria, while Sheila faced in her direction. Her hand was resting on Parker's elbow, and they were laughing as if they were the best of friends. Victoria quickly sobered up, eyeing them as she descended the staircase. Sheila spotted Victoria and decided to give her a little show. She leaned into Parker, put her hand on his chest, and whispered into his ear. He laughed at whatever she'd said and nodded his head, as if in agreement.

Victoria walked up to them. "Here's your coat." She tossed the suede jacket to Parker like a pitcher on the mound, steppping past them, barely slowing down or breaking her stride. "I'll be waiting at the door while you two catch up," she snapped.

Parker moved away from Sheila like she had leprosy and high tailed it in

Victoria's direction. He knew that she was upset. During the drive back home she only gave one-word answers to his questions, so he prepared himself for what would be their first big argument once they got back to his place.

*R*ight Here. Right Now. Today......

Parker threw his keys on the coffee table. "Okay, what's wrong?"

"You know what's wrong."

"Victoria, it was nothing. She just came over to say hello."

"Oh, really?" Since when does a casual hello involve touching and rubbing? I saw you two laughing like you were at a Chris Rock concert."

"You're overreacting."

"Parker, she was openly flirting with you, and you let her."

"No she wasn't."

"Yes, she was. She was touching you like you two were together."

Parker walked over to Victoria and led her to the couch. "She came up to me to say hello, but there was no flirting going on, just conversation. She put her hand on my chest when she told me a joke, and I laughed because what she said was funny. It was an innocent gesture. I even told her that you and I were there together."

Victoria looked at him closely, trying to determine if she should believe him. She wondered how Parker could exercise such strong self-control during their heavy petting sessions, yet couldn't manage to remove Sheila's hand from his chest tonight, or disengage her obvious flirtation. Victoria's head began to throb.

Over the last month she had come to realize that Parker was one of the most decent men she'd ever met, but she also knew that he was, or at least had been, a ladies man. In the back of her mind, she replayed the pictures of the women in his photo album. She wanted to trust him, but how could she believe a self-professed Casanova? And then there was Pamela, the one who had moved to Atlanta to be near him. Victoria had questioned Parker about her, but he'd insisted that his relationship with the woman was a thing of the past.

What Victoria didn't know was that Pamela was still very interested in him, and had only stopped calling two months ago after their last sexual rendezvous. Parker had realized that sleeping with her had been a big mistake, so he decided that it was time to cut all ties with her and put a permanent end to their on-again-off-again relationship.

Victoria couldn't shake the fact that a part of her felt insecure even knowing that Pamela lived somewhere near. All those thoughts, combined with the scene tonight were feeding into her insecurities. She didn't want things with Parker to end up as they had with Steven. No Repeats!

"How would you have felt if you walked up to me and I was canoodling with someone you'd seen me with in the past?"

Parker shook his head. "I wasn't *canoodling*...I don't even know what that means." He looked at Victoria and felt her distrust. "Baby, I have absolutely no interest in Sheila."

"You know my history, and you know what happened to me in my last relationship. I have to know that I can trust you in order for this to work. Letting Sheila fawn over you like that, touching you, letting her whisper in your ear...that doesn't instill trust."

As soon as Sheila approached Parker, he'd felt uneasy. He was on his way out to meet Victoria when she stopped him. His first reaction was to say hello and keep going, but she smiled and said it was good to see him again. She said she had no hard feelings about what happened on their blind date; she even wished him and Victoria the best. She rested her hand on his elbow to steady herself as she shifted her weight from one foot to the other, then touched his chest lightly, making a joke about how her high-heels were killing her feet. "Cleopatra never wore Prada," she laughed, and he followed.

"Victoria, I'm nothing like that asshole you dated before we met. I love you too much to ever hurt you like that. The only thing I'm guilty of is not thinking about how things may have looked to you, seeing me with Sheila."

"The next time, please think about how I feel."

"There won't be a next time. Baby, I don't want you to lose trust in me because of this. I want what we have to grow. You're like no other woman I've ever been with."

Over the past few weeks, Parker had repeated that phrase several times, and now those words were making Victoria's temples throb to the point of anger. "What kind of game are you playing?" she asked.

"What?

"Is this some kind of experiment?"

Parker looked confused. "I told you from the beginning, I'm not playing games. Just because this is happening so fast, it doesn't mean it's not genuine, or that you can't trust what I'm saying. I love you."

"Oh, so now that you've walked on the dark side you think you love me?" Victoria snapped, letting the alcohol give her boldness.

"What're you talking about?" Parker knew she'd had too much to drink at the party, so he tried to be patient.

"You're always saying that I'm so different from any of the women you've ever dated, that I'm like no other woman you've ever been with."

"It's true."

"Is it because I'm dark?"

Parker looked stunned. "Baby, why would you say something like that?"

"Because all the women in your photo album look the same, just like your family."

"I can't believe you're serious."

Victoria stared at him, waiting for his response. "Well?"

"Well, what? Baby, I told you those pictures are old. I've dated a lot of women over the years. But why are we even talking about this? Let's focus on our relationship, and this trust thing."

"You say that I can trust you?"

"Absolutely. I've been honest with you about everything that happened tonight."

"Okay, since you're being so honest, tell me, have you ever dated a dark skinned woman other than me?"

"Why?" Parker asked with growing irritation. "Where's this coming from? Just because you saw a few pictures in my photo album?"

"Have you?"

"Yes, I have. But what does that have to do with what happened tonight?"

"As dark as me?"

"Baby, come on. This is ridiculous."

"Parker, look at the evidence. The women you've dated, your family, and even your friends. They all look alike. And that makes me think that it's a conscious effort. This kind of stuff doesn't happen by accident."

Victoria was spent from the alcohol and the night's events. These were feelings and emotions she hadn't thought about in years. "Parker, I want to tell you about something that happened to me a long time ago," she said quietly. She began to tell him about her family history, and the painful truth she discovered one night when she was seven years old. The night she'd been carrying with her every day of her life...............

"Mommy, we always visit Daddy's family, and Aunt Phyllis and Uncle Billy come to see us and send me birthday gifts and Christmas presents. How come Granny Grace doesn't come to see me? Or Uncle Charles or Aunt Jean? Only Uncle Maxx comes. And why don't we go to see them Mommy?"

Victoria asked. She was an inquisitive child and she wanted to know.

Elizabeth looked at her daughter with loving eyes and told Victoria a half-truth. "Well, sweetheart, my family and our family see things different-ly. We think one way, and they think another."

"Mommy, I don't understand?" Victoria said. "Do they think wrong, or do we think wrong?"

Elizabeth looked at John with eyes that reflected a tortured heart.

"Listen, Queen," John's deep baritone eased into the air, "No ones right or wrong, we're just different. You don't understand now because you're much too young to know about these grown up things, but just remember that Mommy and Daddy love you very much, and so does all your other family, whether you see them or not."

Elizabeth took John's hand in hers and mouthed a silent, "I Love You."

Later that night when Victoria got up to use the bathroom, she heard her mother crying; her voice laced with tears. She grabbed her teddy bear and walked down the long hallway. She crept to the edge of their big spiral stair-case, her small feet curled under her as she knelt at the banister to see why her mother was so upset.

"It's going to be all right, Elizabeth," John tried to soothe his wife.

"But John, how do I tell my precious little girl that her own flesh and blood won't have anything to do with her because her skin's not light enough. That she's too dark for their taste." Elizabeth let out another sob. "Never mind that she's beautiful and smart, and happy and well behaved. That means nothing to them if her skin isn't light. It breaks my heart John, she's just a baby."

Victoria sat on the edge of the stairs, paralyzed with pain. She listened as her parents talked about the day the Sanders family came to visit the week after she'd been born. She heard the hurt in Elizabeth's voice that she still carried, and the anger John still held from that day. Small tears formed in the corners of Victoria's big brown eyes. She held her teddy bear tight, walked back to her room and crawled back into bed. She cried a stream of quiet tears until she fell asleep. The next morning she told her mother she didn't feel well enough to go to school. She never mentioned what she heard that night. The only person she'd ever shared that night with was Tyler. Now, she was telling Parker. She hadn't intended to, but she couldn't hold on to the hurt any longer.

They sat in silence after Victoria finished her story. "Tell me what you're thinking," she asked.

"I'm thinking, it's the twenty-first century, and we're still dealing with this skin color shit," he said with a heavy sigh. "I admit that back in the day some of my relatives were caught up in that messed up way of thinking. I'm a fourth generation Washingtonian from a prominent black family," Parker paused, shaking his head. "And my family…well…they are who they are, and I love them nonetheless. But that was then. Things are different now, and I definitely don't think that way. You know that, don't you?"

Victoria needed to hear him say those words. She believed him. Parker had been honest with her about his feelings since their first date, and his truthful admissions were beginning to slowly tear down the wall she'd been trying to hold up.

"Parker, I've been on the receiving end of other people's hang-ups about my skin. So you see, that's why I had to ask. When I saw your family pictures it brought back those painful memories. I thought I was over it, that I'd buried it long ago. But sometimes the hurt still manages to sneak up and bite."

Parker moved in close, wrapping Victoria in his arms. "I wish I could take back the pain you went through, but I can't. All I can do is tell you that I love you. Right here, right now, today. I love everything about you," he whispered in between soft kisses to her lips, "and I think your deep brown skin is absolutely beautiful."

Sleeping In The Same Bed……

"I better head back home," Victoria said, looking at the clock on Parker's wall. It was close to two in the morning and they were lying on his couch, feeling dreamy and relaxed from their make up kisses.

"It's so late, why don't you sleep here tonight?"

"No, I think I better go home."

"Baby, it's cold, it's late, you're tired, and quite frankly you've had too much to drink." Parker thought about how in spite of her best efforts, Victoria had stumbled when they came through the door after they got back to his place. "Just stay here tonight. You can go home in the morning," he said, rising from the couch.

Victoria thought about his proposition. "I *am* tired. And you're right, I shouldn't get behind the wheel. But I don't have anything to sleep in."

Parker smiled, pulling her to her feet. "I'll find something for you to wear." He took Victoria by the hand and led her to his bedroom.

"Where will I sleep?"

"Certainly not the couch. You can sleep in my bed," he offered.

Parker opened his drawer and pulled out one of his Howard University t-shirts. "Your nightgown, Madame," he smiled, handing it to her. "I'm going to get out of this toga," he said, heading to the bathroom to change.

Victoria undressed and placed her costume neatly in her duffel bag. She slipped the t-shirt over her head, grabbed her travel toothbrush from her bag and headed back to join Parker.

When she walked into the bathroom, he was standing at the sink—shirtless, save for a pair of blue and white striped boxers. His skin looked sunkissed golden, and his body, a work of art. Victoria tried not to stare too hard at his rock-solid abs and rippled muscles as he removed the last of the cleanser from his face. She knew that fine, well-groomed men like Parker always put time into their appearance. She remembered how Steven used to raid the Clinique counter for toiletries when they were dating. Parker's baby soft skin benefited not only from good genes, but from a healthy dose of meticulous pampering.

"Your negligee looks really nice," he teased, flashing Victoria his megawatt smile.

"Thank you. It's all the rage this season." She pointed to his toothpaste sitting on the counter. "May I?"

Parker picked up the tube and squeezed a perfectly straight line of Crest onto her purple Oral-B. After he left the room, she watched him from behind and prayed the night would go by quickly.

She finished brushing her teeth, then headed back out to the bedroom, but she stopped short when she saw a long, lumpy form under the comforter. "Parker, are you in bed?" It was an obvious question.

"Yeah, and it's warm under here. You better come in out of the cold," he said without an ounce of sleepiness in his voice.

"I thought you said I could sleep in your bed?"

"You can, and I am too. In case you didn't notice, this is a king-size bed. It's big enough for both of us." Parker propped himself up on his elbows. "What's wrong?"

"I didn't think we'd be sleeping in the same bed."

"Baby, you should know by now that I'm not going to take advantage of you." Even in the darkness she could see the intensity in his eyes. "Remember, we're taking things slow. Now come to bed," he said, gently coaxing her with his deep voice.

Victoria obliged and slipped into bed beside him, falling into a peaceful sleep.

The next morning she awoke to the feeling of Parker's long, hard body next to hers. The hair on his thighs tickled her smooth, bare legs. Not an inch separated his body from hers. She kissed him softly at first, not wanting to expose him to any unpleasant morning breath. But as their lips parted and their tongues embraced, Parker moaned, enjoying the warm saltiness of her mouth. After a few minutes they came up for air.

He looked at her, grazing her cheek with the back of his hand. "Victoria, what're we doing?"

"What do you mean?"

"Baby, last night was hard for me. When we're together, I try to act like holding you and touching you doesn't affect me, but it does. I want you so bad." Parker placed his hand under her t-shirt, tracing his fingers along the length of her back. "This is so damn hard for me."

"It's hard for me too," Victoria admitted.

He brought his mouth to hers and kissed her deeply, enjoying the way her growing wetness felt against his leg as she pressed herself close to him. He rubbed her breasts, gently at first, then with more force and deliberateness. She kissed his neck and flicked her tongue against his skin, arching her back to feel his impressive length against the wet cotton strip of her panties. *"Mmmm,"* she moaned.

"I can't take this any longer," he panted, grabbing her firm behind, massaging her cheeks in his hand. "Let me in, baby......"

Victoria thought, *what the hell!* "Do it. Make love to me."

Parker reached into his nightstand for a condom. "Let me put it on," Victoria purred, straddling his lap. He handed it to her. Just then his beeper went off and they both froze. They looked at the small device as if their stares would make it stop. But it kept making its repetitive sound. Parker reached over and grabbed it from the nightstand.

Victoria let out a frustrated sigh and rolled off him. She lay on her back, staring up at the ceiling, hoping the page didn't mean what she knew it did. Reluctantly, Parker reached for the phone and dialed the hospital. "This is Dr. Brightwood," he said in his professional doctor voice that always made Victoria smile. His sex appeal rose ten notches and all she could think about was how long it would take her to reach orgasm.

Parker had a disappointed look on his face when he ended the call. "Baby, I've gotta go in. This is shitty luck," he grumbled as he rose slowly.

Victoria wanted to scream, but she refrained. "I guess duty calls," was all she could say.

Chapter Thirteen

I Didn't Expect the Royal Treatment......

The next day Victoria sat in her seat, prepared for landing. The Sunday afternoon flight into LaGuardia was full, but thankfully the ride had been smooth. And that was good because she knew the week ahead would be bumpy, given that she had to work with Patricia.

She was headed toward baggage claim when she saw a chauffeur standing to the side. He was holding a white sign with her name written in big black letters.

"I'm Victoria Small," she said as she approached the man.

"Hello, Ms. Small," the stout Indian man greeted her. "I am here to take you to the hotel."

"ViaTech arranged for this?" she asked.

"Yes, Ma'am," the chauffeur said, taking Victoria's heavy attaché from her shoulder as they headed off to get her bags.

He led her to a black town car waiting at the curb. When he opened the door, she was surprised by who awaited her inside. "How was your flight?"

Ted asked.

"It was fine, but I didn't expect the royal treatment…a chauffeured ride? I was just going to cab it over. How did you know my…"

"Denise gave Jen your itinerary," he answered before she could finish. He'd actually instructed his assistant to get the information from Denise.

After arriving at the hotel, Victoria unpacked her week's supply of clothes and arranged her toiletries on the marble countertop in the bathroom. After a quick shower she changed into a pair of black palazzo pants and brown cashmere top, threw her heavy Alpaca wrap over her shoulders, and headed downstairs to meet Ted for dinner.

The grand lobby was flooded with people, so Victoria searched for Ted through the sea of activity. She spotted him sitting in an oversized high-back leather chair in the middle of the lobby. She stood for a moment to study him. He was dressed in all black; trousers, mock turtleneck and jacket. She thought he looked painfully handsome, and she could see women checking him out as they walked by. "Have you been waiting long?" she asked as she approached.

"Only a few minutes. You look lovely," he smiled.

Ted escorted her to the chauffeured car waiting outside. After they were on their way, he decided to address what he couldn't put off any longer. "V, I heard about what happened during the SME meeting."

Oh, so you finally want to discuss it? "Yes, it was quite a scene."

"You'll be working with Patricia on Wednesday, and as I'm sure you already know, it was my decision. We need her institutional knowledge of the old software protocols for our reports."

"That's fine. I'll work with her. But if she decides to give a repeat performance of what happened the other week, I won't be as diplomatic this time. I don't get paid to take abuse from anyone. I know that she's golden, and I know for what reasons. But I'm not trying to screw her, so I'm not putting up with her shit," Victoria warned.

To hear her speak this way, Ted knew that Victoria was angry. "V, I hate putting you in this situation. But the problems here in the New York office are urgent."

"I understand that business is business. But it pisses me off that she's able to get away with the things she does."

"She'll be dealt with, I promise you that. So, are you angry with me?"

"No. Not with you, just with the situation," she answered, looking into his penetrating eyes, trying to put a name on the strange feeling that was creeping up in the pit of her stomach.

Ted held Victoria's hand as he helped her from the car. He'd been looking forward to this all day. They'd had lunch together several times, but now he was finally able to share dinner with her. He hoped that spending an entire week together in New York would create an opening that would allow Victoria to see him as more than just a friend.

The maître d' seated them at a candlelit table in a cozy corner on the top floor of the restaurant. They made their menu selections and Ted ordered a vintage red wine to accompany their meal. Victoria loved a man who knew how to select a good bottle of wine. Parker had that talent as well. His taste, like Ted's, was impeccable. She found it strangely unsettling that they were alike in many ways.

As they laughed and talked throughout dinner, Victoria examined Ted more closely under the glow of the restaurant's soft lighting. She'd sat across the table from him on several occasions, sharing a meal, but had never paid attention to how smooth his skin was until tonight, or that he had a slight dimple in his right cheek that seemed to wave when he smiled really hard. *It's amazing how you see things differently when you're out of your everyday environment,* she thought.

Ted had been dying to find out what happened on her date with Parker. "So, tell me, did you have a good time at the costume party?" he asked casually, taking a sip of wine.

"Yes, it was lots of fun. But Parker and I had an argument. Our first *real* argument."

"What about? Ted's curiosity was piqued.

Even though they'd made up, the encounter between Parker and Sheila still bothered Victoria. She hadn't had a chance to talk to Tyler about it before she'd left town, and she wanted a male perspective on the situation. As she replayed the episode between Parker and Sheila in vivid detail, she could see that Ted was mulling it over in his mind. "Tell me what you think?" she asked.

Ted dabbed his mouth with his napkin while the server removed their plates from the table. He knew this was an opportunity to strike.

Ted had carried on affairs throughout the years, but had always been extremely careful, practicing the utmost discretion. No one could ever say they had seen him in any type of compromising situation with a woman. In his mind, Parker's public display confirmed that he was an asshole, and an idiot at best, to do such a thing when he had a woman like Victoria. "I think you were right to be upset," he finally answered. "Even if it was innocent, the appearance was questionable. He should've put a stop to it before it got to that point…her putting her hands on him. That only leads to trouble," he said, letting the suggestion linger.

"You're right. I told him the same thing, and he admitted that he'd made a mistake."

She's defending him, he thought. Ted knew he'd said too much, so he kept the rest of his negative opinions to himself. "So you made up?" he asked.

"Yes," Victoria smiled to his disappointment.

He didn't care to hear details about their make up so he quickly changed the subject. After their meal, they ordered coffee and dessert to accompany their intimate conversation. Victoria found that being with Ted was easy, and she realized that she was enjoying the evening a little more than she cared to admit.

After dinner they drove around the city, taking in the bright lights and moonlit sky. As they rode in silence, admiring Manhattan's sights and sounds, Victoria thought about what she was doing—riding around the city in a chauffeur-driven car, after having a fantastic meal at a five-star restaurant, with a handsome millionaire. This would have normally been her idea of a perfect date. But this was different, and she had to remind herself that she had a boyfriend, and that the man sitting next to her signed her paycheck.

She also thought it was supremely ironic that under any other circumstance her mother would have cheered things on, but not in this case. Initially, Elizabeth had been a big Ted Thornton fan. She'd delighted in the news when Victoria shared with her that Ted had asked her to spearhead the SuperNet show, even after she'd turned down his EMP nomination. And when Victoria told her about her jogging accident, and how Ted had stayed with her at the hospital and brought her breakfast the next morning, Elizabeth saw grandchildren on the horizon.

"Oh sweetheart, it sounds like you've found a nice new friend. How old is this Ted fellow?" Elizabeth had asked with excited curiosity.

"He's in his mid forties."

"You know your father is ten years older than I am," she hinted.

Victoria decided to ignore the comment because she knew what her mother was up to.

"It's so nice to see black men doing well in corporate America. It was so much harder when your father and I were coming along."

"Mom, Ted isn't black," Victoria said. It had just occurred to her that she'd never mentioned Ted's race to her mother. She just assumed that Elizabeth would know that most Fortune 500 telecom executives were white males. But then again, most of her parents' friends and associates who ran independent businesses and large companies were black. All her life, Victoria and her family had associated with highly educated, very successful African-Americans. So it was natural for Elizabeth to assume that the kind-hearted CEO was of the darker persuasion.

"Oh, he's not?" Elizabeth said with surprise.

"No. What made you think he was?"

"Well, from all the things you've shared with me about him, I just assumed he was black. Very rarely do white men in that kind of position take such an interest in the career or personal well being of a young black woman, unless..."

"Unless what?"

"Well, unless they're getting something out of it—you know what I mean?" From that moment forward, Elizabeth's attitude about Ted changed.

But riding around Manhattan with him, Victoria knew that Ted's heart and motivations were genuine. During dinner she'd asked him to volunteer with Tyler's organization, YFI, and he'd gladly agreed to it. "The teenage boys you'll be working with are minorities from underserved neighborhoods. It's not at all what you're used to," she'd warned.

"I guess it's time for me to learn something new," was his response. "Until meeting you, I didn't even think about these kinds of things. For so long my life's been about business, and more business. Now I'm beginning to see all that I've missed out on," Ted paused, lowering his voice to a soft whisper, "I'm glad you're a part of my life."

Victoria had felt moved. Moved in a way that excited her, even though she knew it wasn't the kind of emotion she should have been feeling. She thought about that feeling as she looked out the car window, avoiding Ted's intense stare and the woodsy smell of his cologne. She tried to ignore the tingling sensation in her stomach, and prayed the driver would get them back to the hotel soon so she could clear her mind.

I Haven't Told Her Yet......

"So, how're you holdin' up, man?" Phil asked Parker as they talked over coffee and danishes in the hospital cafeteria.

"Man, I'm beat. I had four surgeries on Saturday. I was here for sixteen hours yesterday, and now I'm sittin' here talking to you at five-thirty in the damn morning," Parker answered with weary eyes, although he loved every minute of his work.

"That's the kind of heroics that helped you get the green light for the Africa Project."

"How'd you know I got the green light? They just told me yesterday."

"Man, you know word travels around this place. Congratulations my brothah!" Phil raised his cup, giving Parker a congratulatory nod.

"Thanks, man. But I'm so tired, it hasn't really sunken in yet."

"When your ass is knee deep in insect repellent and mosquito nets, you'll have a better appreciation." They both laughed at Phil's silly joke.

The Africa Project was a medical relief mission developed by the U.S. government and a panel of prestigious doctors from Emory Crawford Long. Only the top doctors from around the country were selected to participate. The Africa Project would enhance Parker's career, giving him international exposure and humanitarian relief experience. It had been one of the reasons he'd decided to move to Atlanta two years ago. The hospital was a founding member of the world renowned project, and boasted a third of its participants. Parker knew that calculating this move would pay off, and it was no secret that he was one of the most ambitious and talented surgeons on staff. He had big plans for himself.

"By the way, how does Victoria feel about all this?" Phil asked.

Parker shrugged. "I haven't told her yet."

"You haven't told her…have you discussed it at all?"

Parker hesitated. "Um, not really."

"Man, you're leaving in two months, and you haven't even talked about it?"

"Look, I just got the official word yesterday."

"Yeah, but you were chosen for the project back in July. You've just been waiting for final approval of the paperwork. I can't believe you haven't told her that you're going to Africa for six months on this project. This isn't good."

"I didn't want to say anything until I was a hundred percent sure."

"Man you're fucked. You better tell her soon, like today. And I'm tellin' you, she's gonna be pissed that you didn't say something before now. Trust me."

Parker knew that Phil was right, and that he should have told Victoria before now. He'd almost told her that first night at the Java Café, because his gut told him that she'd be a part of his life. But instead, he decided against it. And then there were other times when they were alone, talking about life and sharing their dreams, that he'd wanted to tell her, but couldn't. He didn't want Victoria pulling back from him, and he knew that if she'd known of his upcoming departure, her emotional wall would have been harder to penetrate.

Parker had never loved a woman the way he loved Victoria. But he wasn't oblivious to her shortcomings, like the way she obsessed about putting everything in its proper place; picking up behind him if he sat his glass down in the wrong spot. And it drove him crazy the way she always questioned him on everything, determined to know the tiniest details of information because she couldn't just accept what he told her and let it go. He didn't know whether that behavior came from her trust issues, natural curiosity, or a need for control. But there were two things Parker knew for sure—despite Victoria's quirks, he loved her, and that the Africa Project was going to be a sticky issue.

We Have Plenty Of Time......

Victoria quickly wrapped herself in the soft, hotel bathrobe and scurried to answer the phone.

"Good morning beautiful," Parker's deep, sexy voice hummed on the other end.

"Parker!" Victoria screeched with delight.

"Did I wake you?"

"No. I've been up for a while. "I just got out of the shower when I heard the phone ring."

"Just got out of the shower, huh? What're you wearing?" he asked in a low, seductive tone. He was in his office, taking a final review of his patient's chart.

"You're so bad. I'm wearing a bathrobe."

"What's underneath?"

"Nothing, I'm bare to the bone."

"*Mmmmm.*"

"And I'm wet," Victoria purred, sitting on the edge of the bed.

Parker put down the chart. "If I was there, I'd take care of that."

"Oh yeah, and what would you do?"

"Lick you dry."

"Where?"

"Where you're the wettest."

"Licking me there could make me wetter...it could be quite a job to handle"

"Then you're in luck. That area happens to be one of my other specialties."

Victoria felt hot and flush. "Too bad we couldn't finish what we started the other morning."

"Don't remind me," Parker groaned.

"Well, maybe it was a sign that we should continue to take things slow. I have a feeling it'll be worth the wait," she said, "besides, we have plenty of time ahead of us."

Parker was disappointed. Being called away for emergency surgery hadn't been a sign, it was an *unexpected interruption*. He felt uneasy listening to Victoria talk about all the time they had, so he quickly changed the subject. "Sorry I didn't call you last night. Things got pretty busy here. We're short-staffed and I had a ton of things to do."

"You're at work now?"

"Yep."

"You're schedule has been grueling lately. Please don't overdo it, you need your rest."

Parker couldn't remember any other women he'd dated who had shown the kind of genuine care and concern for him that Victoria did. She'd even begun preparing him home cooked meals, a treat he looked forward to at the end of his busy days. "Yes Ma'am," he said, smiling into the phone. "By the way, are you still meeting Juliet for dinner tomorrow?" Parker remembered Juliet from his brother's firm. He liked her, but he wished she hadn't told Victoria about Pamela because he wanted sleeping dogs to lie.

"Yeah, I'm meeting her at her office after work," Victoria answered.

"Can you ask Mason to send me the tickets for the Knicks game?"

"Sure."

"Thanks, baby." He left his office and walked down the hall toward the scrub area. "I have to go. I just wanted to call and hear your voice."

"Oh, I have a quick question I forgot to ask you before I left."

"Sure, what's up?"

"My church is having our annual winter cruise in February. Can you go with me? I think Tyler and Juliet will want to go too, and I need to let the church secretary know my final headcount by mid-week." She smiled into the phone, thinking about the fun they were going to have.

Going on her church's cruise was something Victoria wouldn't have even considered a month ago. But now that Parker was in her life, she couldn't wait to sail the romantic seas.

Parker felt panic. It would be impossible for him to go on a cruise in February because of the Africa Project, but he wasn't prepared to give an explanation over the phone because he knew that Victoria would grill him like she was conducting a homicide investigation, firing one question after another. "Baby, I've got to scrub in for surgery. I'll get back to you later."

"Okay, love you."

"Love you too."

Victoria hung up the phone and reached for her bottle of orange juice. She was definitely in love. Sometimes she felt like her relationship with Parker was a dream. He was the man she'd prayed for. Her mother was beside herself with happiness when she'd called to tell her about their first date.

"Is he black?" had been Elizabeth's first question.

Victoria finished her juice and watched the local news. Crime, drugs, and corruption; a typical day in New York City, and it was only seven a.m.

A New Kind Of Asshole......

Victoria took a seat on the small leather sofa next to a leafy ficus tree. The office suite of Stern, Cohen, Donaldson, and Baer was opulent. Juliet came out smiling from ear to ear. "Hey, girl. How're you doing?" she greeted Victoria with a big hug.

"I'm great. How're you?"

"I'm fantastic," Juliet squeaked in her high-pitched voice.

"Is that big smile on your face because you're happy to see me, or do we have Mr. Jacobs to thank for that?"

"Both! But I can't even lie, Tyler has a lot to do with it," Juliet beamed, leading Victoria from the lobby and back through a set of glass double-doors. "I'll take you back to meet Mason now."

Mason's door was open, so Juliet gave it a light knock before entering. She reached for Victoria's hand and ushered her into the large corner office. "Mason, I have someone I'd like you to meet."

Victoria instantly saw the resemblance between Parker and his older brother. They both shared the same confidant, sexy air. Mason Brightwood was handsome. His full head of thick, curly black hair, square jaw, and inviting smile made him the kind of man who deserved a double take. He was impeccably dressed and smelled of European cologne. Victoria's curiosity about meeting him was fueled by the fact that while Parker was closer to Mason than to any of his three other brothers, they shared a serious sibling rivalry.

"Mason, it's so nice to meet you, I'm Victoria," she said, extending her hand.

Mason accepted her hand into both of his, giving her a warm welcome. "It's a pleasure to finally meet you, Victoria. I see why my brother can't stop talking about you. You're every bit as beautiful as Parker said you were."

"Thank you," Victoria smiled.

The three stood in the middle of Mason's office, chit-chatting. But Victoria soon became uncomfortable when she noticed that Mason was checking her out, roaming his eyes over her fitted black suit as if he were inspecting a choice cut of meat. Juliet noticed too.

"Parker tells me that you and your wife have two children, how old are they?" Victoria asked, smiling hard enough to choke. She knew that bringing up anything that escorted a married man's wife and children into a conversation would quickly shut things down. Juliet gave her a knowing glance of approval.

"Our son is four and our daughter will be two next month," Mason answered, motioning toward their pictures on the credenza across the room. "Please, have a closer look," he smiled, continuing to eyeball her.

He's a new kind of asshole, Victoria thought. "I can see from here that you have a lovely family." This time she spoke without a smile. "How long have you been married?"

"Ten happy years," Mason responded in a voice as smooth as silk.

"Isn't that special," Victoria said sarcastically. She couldn't believe that he was actually proclaiming marital bliss while looking at her ass! "We better go, we have dinner reservations," she nodded toward Juliet, ready to get out of Mason's sight.

She and Juliet said their goodbyes, then headed out the door. They were down the hall when Victoria remembered that she'd forgotten to ask Mason about Parker's tickets for the game. She headed back to Mason's office while Juliet went to gather her things.

"I hate to interrupt, but Parker wanted me to remind you about the tickets for the Knicks game," Victoria said, standing in his doorway.

Mason was happy to see her back in his office—unaccompanied. He rose from behind his desk and walked toward her, standing a little too close. Victoria didn't move away. She stood her ground and looked him in the eye. "My boyfriend just wanted me to deliver the message." *You pervert!* she wanted to scream.

Mason liked her boldness. "My little brother has done well for himself. I'm glad I didn't have to wait until the game to meet you."

Victoria gave him a puzzled look. "What do you mean?"

"Parker said you were coming with him, that's why he asked for two tickets. The firm gets court-side seats," Mason grinned. "You *are* coming, aren't you?"

Victoria thought that Parker was getting the tickets for himself and Phil. *Maybe he's trying to surprise me with a weekend in the city? But if it's supposed to be a surprise, why would he ask me to talk to Mason about the tickets?* Victoria tried to pretend she was excited. "I'll be there," she smiled.

"Parker's a lucky man."

"Yes he is," she said with an icy tone, this time not even trying to fake cordiality. She turned abruptly and headed back down the hall without saying goodbye. She knew that Mason was standing in his doorway, watching her as she walked away. She knew it because she could feel his eyes on her like the sun bearing down in the afternoon sky. When she reached the end of the hall, she turned and waved goodbye. He waved back.

Victoria and Juliet remained silent until they stepped into the elevator. Miracle of miracles, it was empty. "Can you believe that asshole? He was checking me out," Victoria fumed.

"Girl, that's just Mason. He has a weakness for women."

"Well, this woman is taken, and by his own brother no less. I can't believe his audacity!"

"Mason is used to getting what he wants, he's a player. And it's a shame because his wife is actually a nice woman. She was an attorney too, but after they had the first kid she quit her job to stay at home."

"This shit really bothers me. I think I'm going to tell Parker."

Juliet looked at Victoria like she was crazy. "Don't do it. It'll just cause trouble."

"But Mason was out of line. You saw him. He was so disrespectful."

"I'm not arguing that, but until he does something blatant, and I mean really concrete, you better keep a lid on it. Trust me. You should never try to make a case without indisputable evidence."

They stepped out of the building and into the crisp November air. Juliet walked hurriedly up to the curb and raised her arm to hail a cab.

"We're over here," Victoria motioned, walking toward the black Lincoln Town Car that was double-parked a few feet away. The chauffeur came around to open the door for them. "Ted, my colleague...he arranged for a car for the evening," Victoria said.

"Tyler was right," Juliet smiled, raising a brow.

Can I Give You a Ride?......

Victoria was glad it was Wednesday. She was halfway through the week, and to her relief, she hadn't had to work too closely with Patricia. Her day was breezing along, and by afternoon she planned to finish her employee interviews with the disgruntled New York staff, then complete her report when she returned to the office next week.

Over the last three days she had enjoyed working with Henry Cleveland, the New York office's newly hired VP of Operations. Henry had been the "go-to" operations man at Vanguard Systems, and Ted had recruited him shortly after he transitioned over to ViaTech last spring. She and Henry cliqued instantly. He was an engaging, confident brother, knowledgeable in his work. And he'd given her valuable information that would help with the reorganization plan they were developing.

The ten-member group assigned to the New York strategic team met in the boardroom at the end of the day. Ted conducted the meeting in his usual succinct manner. He thanked the New York staff, along with Victoria and Patricia for their hard work and efforts. Patricia sat next to him, smiling, and nodding her head approvingly at Ted's every word. He adjourned the meeting and reminded the group about their wrap up dinner later that evening. "I'll see you all at seven sharp," he said.

On their way out, Henry stopped Victoria before she left the boardroom. "Victoria, can I give you a ride over to the restaurant tonight? I can swing by your hotel and pick you up," he offered.

Victoria looked at Henry with slight hesitation, but his charming demeanor made her give in. "Thank you, Henry. That's very nice of you. I'll see you in a few."

Ted, Victoria, and Patricia rode back to the hotel together. Ted wished that Patricia hadn't invited herself along on the ride, but since they were all staying at the same hotel there was little room getting around it. He wanted to ask Victoria what her conversation with Henry had been about, but Patricia was sitting beside him, going on and on about the crime in New York. He knew that Henry was single and had a reputation for being quite the ladies man.

The three arrived at the hotel and strolled through the lobby toward the bank of elevators. "What time should I meet you in the lobby?" Patricia asked Ted, flashing her three-dollar smile, disregarding Victoria completely.

Ted turned to Victoria. "What time will you be ready?"

"You guys can go ahead without me. Henry's picking me up."

Ted bit his lower lip as they rode the elevator in silence, save for Patricia's blabbering about the rudeness of New Yorkers. She held the door open at her floor. "Ted, I'll meet you downstairs at six-thirty," she grinned before getting off and strutting down the hallway to her room.

"I'm so glad the meetings are over," Victoria said as the doors closed. "Things actually went better than I thought they would."

"Why is Henry picking you up?" Ted tried not to sound accusatory, but his question came out short and curt.

"Because he thought I might need a ride. It's just employee camaraderie."

"Yeah, I'll bet," Ted smirked with an attitude.

"What's that supposed to mean?"

"Forget it," he snapped.

"Fine!" Victoria snapped back. She stepped off the elevator at her floor without saying another word.

Two hours later, Ted sat in the restaurant, glancing at his watch. It was nearly eight o'clock and everyone was there except Victoria and Henry. The group had started with a round of drinks and appetizers. *Where could they be?* he wondered. Just then he saw the pair walking in the group's direction under the escort of a hostess. He watched them carefully, but Victoria refused to make eye contact.

She took a seat at the table, but she was in no mood for dinner. She was pissed, not only by Ted's earlier behavior, but because Henry had shown up late—in a taxi! His excuse was that he'd been having engine trouble for the past week, and had to drop his car off at the shop on his way over to the hotel. *If he knew that he was having car problems, why would he offer to pick me up?* Victoria had silently fumed on their cab ride over to the restaurant.

Dinner dragged on like a turtle chasing a snail. As the evening wound down, everyone headed out the door and said their goodbyes. Victoria declined Henry's offer to take her back to the hotel, and stopped short of giving him the hug he wanted, substituting it with a firm handshake. Knowing that she couldn't stay mad at him, she walked over to Ted and looked him firmly in the eye. "Do you mind if I ride back to the hotel with you guys?"

"I'd like that," he smiled.

"Victoria, do you have a minute?" Henry called out, standing under the restaurant's canopy, waiting for the valet to hail him a cab.

Victoria hoped he wasn't going to ask her if she wanted a ride back to the hotel again. She'd discovered that he possessed slickness, not charm, and she had no tolerance for his game. But she didn't want to ignore him, so she let out a deep breath and excused herself, heading in his direction.

Ted wanted to walk over with her to see what Henry was up to, but at the risk of ruining what he saw was a truce, he went to the car and waited.

"What are we waiting for?" Patricia asked, already sitting in the backseat. She was anxious to get back to the hotel for a chance to seduce Ted on her last night in town.

"Victoria had to speak with Henry about something, she'll be here in a minute," Ted answered without looking in her direction. His mind was busy thinking about how he would formally apologize to Victoria once they returned to the hotel.

"We should just leave her…she's holding us up. Besides, you know how black people are, always late and never on time for anything. Look how late the two of them showed up for dinner. Hmph, *those people*," Patricia shook her head.

Ted's body became still, but Patricia was too busy talking to notice.

"And I bet she's doing more than just talking to him. They're probably making plans to finish whatever made them late in the first place. Victoria doesn't fool me for one second. I know she's been trying to get on your good side, but Ted," she paused, placing her hand on his knee, "you really should be careful around her"

When Ted finally looked at Patricia, his stare was one that could've done less damage if he'd taken a knife and slid it across the delicate expanse of her porcelain hued throat. Patricia drew her hand back as if avoiding hot coals.

Just then, Victoria appeared. She was relieved that Henry's request had been legitimate. "Thanks for waiting. Henry wanted me to give you this," she said, handing Patricia a CD ROM. "It's the information for your report. He forgot to give it to you during dinner."

"Oh, thank you. I think everything went well today, Victoria, don't you?" Patricia said, exposing her genuinely fake smile.

On the ride back, Victoria could sense that something was very wrong. From the moment she'd stepped into the car, Ted's body language had been rigid and gruff; almost angry. And what made her antennae go up even more was that Patricia was being nice to her, actually engaging her in pleasant conversation!

Back at the hotel, Patricia stepped off the elevator at her floor. "Good night," she smiled nervously, "I hope the rest of your meetings go well. See you two back at the office next week," she waved before disappearing down the hall.

"Good night," Victoria said, but Ted remained silent. Before the doors closed, Victoria turned to face him. "What's going on? You didn't say a word the entire ride back."

Ted shook his head. "Nothing's wrong."

"You're not telling the truth. What happened in the car between you and Patricia?"

"V, it's nothing…really."

The door opened at Victoria's floor. "Good night, V. I'll meet you in the lobby tomorrow morning," he half-smiled, ushering Victoria out of the elevator.

Once he returned to his room, Ted undressed, throwing his clothes to the floor. Even after all the manipulative things Trudy had done to him over the years, he had never felt as mad or as angry as he did tonight. Patricia had crossed the line. The only reason he hadn't addressed her was because for the first time in his life he didn't trust himself to control what he might do.

He knew it was time to deal with Patricia once and for all. He logged on to his laptop and sent out several emails, then made a few phone calls, leaving voice messages for his intended recipients. Satisfied that he'd accomplished his mission, he took a hot shower to relieve his stress.

*S*he Would Keep A Lid On This Too……

After a long relaxing shower, Victoria sat on the sofa with the TV remote in hand. She couldn't sleep. She didn't know what had gone on between Ted and Patricia, but she saw the lie in Ted's eyes. She reached for the phone.

Ted picked up on the first ring. "Hello."

"Are you up?"

"Yes."

"Can I come up?" she asked.

"Um, sure."

Ted felt exhilarated at the thought of having Victoria in his room—with a bed only a few feet away. He rushed into the bathroom, quickly gargled with mouthwash, and brushed his hair. He inspected himself in the mirror.

He didn't know what he should wear. It was eleven-thirty at night, so he hoped his pajama bottoms and t-shirt were appropriate.

Victoria walked in wearing a baggy sweatshirt and gray leggings. Ted poured them both a glass of wine from the mini bar before joining her on the couch. Victoria leaned in close, looking into his eyes. "Please tell me what happened in the car before I got in," she asked, taking a small sip of wine.

Ted was disappointed that this was Victoria's reason for coming to his room. "I'd rather not discuss it."

"Did Patricia come on to you?"

"No."

"Then what happened?" Victoria probed. "We're supposed to be friends. We've shared some very personal things with each other, enough for you to know that you can trust me."

Ted put his glass down and let out a sigh. "Patricia made some comments that I didn't appreciate, and it irritated me."

"What did she say?"

"V, I don't want to talk about it."

"It must've been pretty bad," Victoria continued to probe.

"Can we change the subject?"

Victoria couldn't imagine what Patricia could've said or done that was so unspeakable, but it was apparent that Ted had no intention of discussing it. She decided not to push the issue any further, at least not tonight. "Okay, I'll let it go, for now," she acquiesced.

"Good. Um, listen, I want to apologize for my behavior this evening. I acted like a jerk."

"Actually, *asshole* is a more accurate description," Victoria said as they both laughed at her joke.

Ted hesitated for a moment. He'd promised himself he would play it cool, but her closeness, and his heightened feelings empowered him to take a chance. "How do you feel about me, V?" His eyes were fixed on her, waiting for her response.

Victoria didn't want to admit that she found herself attracted to him. After all, she had Parker in her life. But there was something about Ted that aroused her. She liked watching his eyes dance when he laughed, watching his upper lip disappear when he smiled, and the warm comfort she felt when she was with him. "Ted, what makes you ask me that?"

"I'm just curious. I want to know what you think of me, of our *friendship?*"

She wasn't about to tell him that although she had initially questioned his orientation, that she now found herself thinking about him in very familiar, even intimate ways. Just as she was going to keep quiet about Mason's flirtation, she would keep a lid on this too. "I guess I'd have to say it's interesting. I've never had a friend like you," Victoria answered honestly.

"What do you mean, *like me?*"

"Well, you're a man."

He nodded. "And so is your best friend, unless there's a secret that Tyler's hiding."

Victoria laughed, "Let me qualify that. You're a white man, and the first I've ever been close friends with."

There was a moment of complete silence.

"So, I take it you've never dated a white guy?" Ted asked with new awareness.

She shifted in her seat. "No, I haven't. Have you ever dated a black woman?"

"Yes, I have."

"Oh," was all Victoria could say. There was another moment of silence. "It's getting late. I...um...need to go," she stammered, clearing her throat as she stood to leave.

"V, don't leave. I didn't mean to make you feel uncomfortable..."

"I'm not uncomfortable," she lied, walking to the door as Ted followed her. "It's just that it's late, and we have a busy day tomorrow." She gave him a quick smile before retreating to her room, trying to hold back the strange feeling in her stomach that was getting harder to ignore.

Long after she'd left, Ted was still thinking about what Victoria had said—that she'd never dated a white man. He wondered if it was because the situation had never presented itself, or if it was by deliberate choice. Finally, he went to bed, but he stayed up all night.

Chapter Fourteen

What's Going On?......

Parker finished his visit with one of his patients in the open-heart intensive care unit, then headed to his office to review cardiac catheterization and fluoroscopy films in preparation for his eight o'clock surgery. His vibrating cell phone, which he'd meant to turn off five minutes ago, broke his concentration. He looked at the caller ID. It was Victoria—again. He'd managed to avoid her calls since Monday, but now it was Thursday, and he knew he couldn't keep putting her off. "Hey beautiful," he answered.

"Good morning, are you busy?"

"Yeah, I have to scrub for surgery in a few and I'm reviewing charts now."

"I just need a minute of your time. We've been playing phone tag all week."

"Well...I..."

"I miss you," Victoria cooed softly.

"I miss you too, baby. I'm sorry I haven't called, but it's been so busy around here." It was a statement that was partially true.

"Parker, about the cruise..."

"Hey, Mason told me that you guys met the other day," he interrupted, trying to change the subject. "You really made an impression on him."

I bet I did, Victoria wanted to say, but then a thought came to her. How had Parker found time to talk to Mason but not to her? "Speaking of Mason," she said, "Why didn't you tell me that the Knicks tickets were for us? I thought you were getting them for you and Phil."

"I thought we talked about going?"

"No, I'm pretty sure we didn't discuss tickets to the game."

"Oh, I thought we did. Sorry. Can you go?"

"Yes, but..."

"Good. Listen baby, I've gotta run."

"Wait!" Victoria said quickly before he could hang up. "Since I didn't hear from you about the cruise, I reserved our tickets before they sold out. Now we can have a little getaway like we've been talking about."

Parker was silent.

"Parker? Are you there?"

"Uh, yeah, I'm here."

Victoria heard the shift in his voice. "You can go, can't you?"

Damn! I can't lie to her, and I can't tell her now, not over the phone, Parker thought. "Let's talk about it when you get back home," he said in a rush.

"I thought that since it's several months away, you'd have plenty of time to clear your calendar."

"Baby, you know how busy I am."

"Do you have a medical conference or something?"

"Uh, no, not exactly," he hesitated. Again, he hated that she never let things go with just one question. Now he was beginning to sweat.

She heard another shift, a crack in the smooth veneer of his polished baritone. "Parker, what is it? What's wrong?"

"Victoria, I have to scrub in," he said forcefully. "We can talk about this at another time."

"Oh, no we can't. We're gonna talk about it right now. Something's wrong. I can hear it in your voice. Talk to me."

"Victoria, it's not a phone conversation. I think it's better if we discuss it in person."

Victoria sat on the edge of her bed, wrapped in her bathrobe. She brought her hand to her forehead, bracing herself for the bad news her stomach sensed was coming. "Dammit, Parker, you can't do this to me. You can't say some shit like that and expect me to walk around New York for the next two days wondering what kind of terrible news will be waiting for me when I get back." Victoria could feel herself about to lose it, but she was determined not to break over the unknown. "Parker, be a man. If you want to breakup with me, just tell me now and you won't have to worry about…"

"Baby, no," Parker's voice softened. "You know that I love you more than anything. I don't want to break up with you. Why would you even think that?"

"Because you've been avoiding my calls all week, and the things you're saying now…if that's not it, then what? What's so terrible that you can't tell me over the phone?"

"Baby, it's nothing terrible. It's just complicated."

"Parker, you're scaring me. Tell me what's going on right now," she demanded.

He spoke slowly. "I've been selected for a project at work…it's called the Africa Project. It's a government-sponsored program that selects only the top doctors in the country to participate. So, the timing will prevent me from going on the cruise with you."

Victoria stopped holding her breath, letting relief wash over her body. "Parker, that's great news! Sweetie, I'm so excited for you. Why was that so hard for you to tell me?" She didn't allow him to answer before she started firing away with questions. "So, when does the project start?"

"In January."

"You can still go on the cruise. Just bring your paperwork with you."

"Uh, the project isn't exactly in this area."

"You mean you have to go away?" Then it dawned on her. "Parker, is the Africa Project…in *Africa*?"

"Yes."

Her next question tumbled out slowly. "How long will you be gone?"

"Six months."

Victoria didn't know what to say. He'd be gone for six months, and his departure was only two months away. But it didn't make sense to her. She knew the type of long range planning that went into special projects and employee programs. That's what she did for a living. And she knew that coordinating a government-sponsored program took time. Applications had to be submitted, interviews conducted, decisions made, and visas arranged. *This has been in the works for months,* she thought.

"Parker, we've talked about everything under the sun. From me leaving ViaTech next June and running Divine Occasions full-time, to your family reunion next summer, and somehow you never mentioned going to *Africa for six months!*" Victoria's voice became loud and animated. "This isn't like, oops, I thought I told you about the Knicks tickets."

"Baby, I'm sorry. I didn't want to tell you until I found out for sure, and I just got the final approval a few days ago."

"But you must've known there was a possibility that you'd be going. This is obviously a very important project. I know how committed you are to your career, yet you never mentioned this to me?"

"There was never a good time to tell you."

"Never a good time? How can you even say that?"

Parker didn't want to deal with this right now, he had a surgery to perform which required his focus. Victoria's questions were irritating him, and his tone reflected it. "We can talk about this when you get back," he snapped. "I have to scrub for..."

Click...

"Hello?...Victoria?...Baby, hello?...Damn!"

Even though they hadn't been dating very long, Victoria thought that Parker was the one. He was everything she wanted in a man, and then some. But now she was beginning to doubt her judgment, thinking that she'd been wrong about him. *Why do I always make such bad decisions when it comes to men?* she lamented. But for now, she would put those thoughts out of her mind. She had less than fifteen minutes to get dressed and meet Ted downstairs for their meeting with a prospective client for SuperNet.

A Pleasant Surprise......

Ted grabbed his black leather portfolio and glanced at the Raymond Weil timepiece on his wrist. He was running late. He walked out of his room and headed for the elevator. His eyes were heavy; evidence of the two hours of restless sleep he'd managed to get around four a.m. He'd been unsettled since his ill-fated attempt last night to find out Victoria's true feelings for him.

But now, he knew he had to focus. He realized it had been a mistake to try to initiate a conversation around feelings of romance. It was a shock to him that Victoria had never been involved with a white man. But he wasn't deterred, he'd just have to remember to take things slow. And as he did whenever he made a mistake or faced a crisis, he collected himself and moved forward. "It's not about the mistake, it's about the recovery," he told himself as he walked toward the elevator.

Ted looked for Victoria in the crowded lobby. "Good morning. Sorry to keep you waiting," he apologized as he approached. Immediately, he sensed that something was wrong.

"No problem," she said in a low voice. "Let's get moving."

As the driver sped them through the maze of morning traffic, Victoria gave Ted the quick and dirty version of her conversation with Parker. "I was ready to trust him, to finally give in to him...physically. I was such a fool."

Ted hated the way he felt at this moment. He didn't want to see Victoria hurt in any way, and he'd do anything to make her happy. But he was elated that Parker had fucked up, just as he knew he would. First with Sheila, and now with this. "V, I'm sorry. It sounds like you two have a lot to discuss, but it's not a situation you can resolve while you're here in New York. Try to focus on what you can control and the day ahead."

"You're right, there's nothing I can do about things until I get back home."

"I'll strike a deal with you. If I show you a good time over the next two days, do you promise to cheer up and try not to think about the situation?"

She nodded her head. "I'll try."

After their morning meeting, Victoria and Ted lunched at Tavern on the Green. She enjoyed a salad of fresh shitake mushrooms and mixed field greens, while Ted polished off the last of his ginger salmon. They were about to order dessert when Victoria looked up and saw Mason Brightwood headed in her direction. Ted continued to talk, but instinctively followed Victoria's eyes, which were focused on the tall man approaching their table.

"My, isn't this a pleasant surprise," Mason said, full of smiles.

Victoria stood to greet him. Ted couldn't help but notice that when the man hugged her, he held her a little too close for comfort. He was about to stand and introduce himself to the stranger, but Victoria moved in front of him, gently placing her hand on his shoulder, motioning for him to stay in his seat and out of site. *What is she doing?* he wondered.

Both men tried to get a better look at each other, but Victoria stood in between them. Ted fought to maintain a calm outward appearance, but he wanted to know who this man was that Victoria obviously didn't want him to meet. Whatever his identity, Ted knew that he was someone she didn't like. Her body language told him that from her stiffly arched back to her tightly crossed arms.

"Are you enjoying your lunch?" Mason asked, focusing his attention away from Ted and back to Victoria.

"Yes...I am."

"You look very lovely today."

"Thank you." *You Bastard!*

An awkward silence passed between them before Mason spoke up. "I'm meeting a client here for lunch," he offered, explaining his presence and expecting Victoria to do the same.

Instead, Victoria grabbed his hand and shook it quickly. "I hope you and your client have a good lunch," she said. That was his cue to keep moving.

Mason gave her a sly grin. "I guess I'll see you at the game."

"I'm sure you will."

He walked away, but not before turning around to give her one final look.

"Who was that?" Ted asked, trying to sound casual, even though his curiosity was burning a hole in his head.

"That was Mason Brightwood......Parker's brother."

At that moment, Ted knew there would be trouble.

Spoon Feed Him......

It was late Saturday morning as Victoria left the airport and headed down Interstate 400. She'd enjoyed the last two days in the Big Apple, and Ted had done as he'd promised—shown her a good time. After their meetings they'd visited museums and shopped at some of Fifth Avenue's finest stores. But now that she was back home she knew she'd have to deal with Parker. They hadn't spoken since their argument. But she needed to talk to her touchstone first, to get advice, so she dialed Tyler on her cell. "What're you doing?" she asked.

"Chillin'. You back in town?"

"Yeah, I just passed Phipps Plaza, so I'm about five minutes away. Can I come over?"

"The door will be open."

Victoria sat on the soft upholstered sofa she'd helped Tyler pick out several years ago, and sipped hot cocoa. It was cold outside and the hot drink felt good going down. "Is this instant?" she asked.

"*Swiss Miss*, baby. And don't say a word. Not everybody can make shit from scratch."

"I wasn't going to say anything. Instant is fine," she lied.

"Juliet told me about Parker's brother."

Tyler barely liked Parker, and after hearing about Mason, he thought

Victoria should stay clear of the Brightwood boys altogether.

"Can you believe that bastard? He's my man's brother, and he was trying to make a move on me."

"You gonna tell Parker?"

"I don't know. Juliet said I shouldn't. What do you think?"

Tyler rubbed his chin, as if studying the situation. "Even though the shit was foul, I don't think you should say anything, at least not now. But don't act like you like that mothafucker either, and the minute he tries to make a serious move, bust his ass."

"I saw him again on Thursday, when Ted and I were having lunch. I know he wanted to know who Ted was, but I didn't introduce them, and I'll bet money that he called Parker as soon as he sat down at his table…only I'm sure he left out the part about pressing his dick up against me when he gave me a hug."

"You lyin?"

"I wish."

"That's truly fucked up."

"Tell me about it."

"So…he saw you havin' lunch with Prince Charming, huh?"

"Yeah."

"Juliet told me about the limo. He's smooth."

Victoria shook her head. "It was a town car, and it was no big deal."

"Oh, don't try to front. You know he wants you. And don't give me that bullshit about him bein' gay."

"I don't think he's gay…anymore," Victoria conceded.

Tyler peered at her with suspicion. "Did something happen between you two while you were in New York?"

"I just saw him in a different light, that's all."

"A different light? What happened?"

"Nothing…let's drop it, please."

Tyler shrugged his shoulders. He'd known his best friend long enough to know when to back off. "Okay, we'll come back to that subject later."

"Thank you," Victoria said with relief.

"So how're things with you and the dashing Doctor? I know somethin's up. Otherwise you would've high tailed it over to his place as soon as you hit town, instead of sittin' on my couch drinkin' instant cocoa that I know you don't like. So whassup?"

Victoria told him about Parker's deception with the Africa Project, although she neglected to tell him about the Sheila incident. She had to spoon feed him information a little at a time, especially since she had a strong feeling that he didn't like Parker. She remembered the way Tyler had acted when she invited him to join them for dinner one night. She wanted the two men in her life to meet, but she didn't want Parker to know that she was putting him through a litmus test, so she invited Debbie and Rob as cover.

She made a simple meal of chicken parmesan, spinach lasagna, and garlic bread, Tyler's favorites. But almost right away she noticed how his eyes darted over Parker with disapproval, how his lip curled slightly when Parker made jokes that she found hilarious, and how he'd asked Parker questions, then listened to his responses with a placid expression.

"I don't know what to do," Victoria said. "I love him, but I just don't know if I can trust him."

"Well, this is what you do know," Tyler began. "It's almost certain that he's known for some time that there was a very good possibility he'd be going to Africa for six months. He knew it the first day he met you. He knew it while you've been spending practically every day together. And he damn sure knew it when he sat his ass down at your dinner table and took second helpings of *my* spinach lasagna at your inspection dinner."

"Tyler, I need advice, not sarcasm."

"Just talk to the brothah. Put it on the line and tell him exactly how you feel." Tyler looked Victoria in the eyes and reached for her hand. "But whatever you do, don't avoid him, or not talk to him. Don't run away. Get things out in the open so you'll know what you're dealin' with."

Unilateral......

When Victoria turned into her driveway she saw Parker sitting in his SUV, parked in front of her house. She drove around to the car pad in the back, and when she got out Ms. Swanson appeared, walking up to the fence line. "Your gentleman friend has been parked out front for over an hour. Is everything all right?" her nosy neighbor asked.

"Thanks for letting me know, Ms. Swanson. Everything's fine." Victoria knew that the old lady had been watching the comings and goings of Parker's vehicle since they'd started dating.

Victoria walked into her house and headed straight to the front door. Her heart raced when she opened it and Parker was standing there—looking good. He was holding a box of Godiva Chocolates, knowing they were her favorites. "These are for you," he said, handing Victoria the gold foil box. As soon as she closed the door, Parker drew her into his arms and kissed her. She hated that she didn't have the will power to resist.

"Baby, I missed you," he said.

"I missed you too, but we really need to talk." She took the chocolates to the kitchen and ushered him back to the den, putting distance between them on the couch so she could think clearly.

"Baby, I'm sorry about this whole mix up."

Victoria looked at him squarely. "This isn't a mix up. This is a lack of communication and a total disregard for my feelings, our relationship, and the trust we were starting to build."

"Victoria, I love you and I would never do anything to intentionally jeopardize our relationship," he pleaded.

"Clearly that's not true. You knowingly kept something very important from me, and that jeopardizes everything."

Parker shook his head. "Listen, I'll be honest. The reason I didn't tell you about the Africa Project from the beginning was because you had this huge wall up when we first met. And even though you said you were ready for a relationship, you were very guarded. I knew that if I told you I was leaving so soon, you wouldn't have given me a chance," he confessed.

"So you thought about your own feelings, about how you wanted me, but not about how your deception would affect me."

"It wasn't deception," Parker defended.

"You're used to getting what you want, when you want it, but you can't manipulate others to your advantage."

"I wasn't trying to manipulate you…"

"What country are you going to anyway?" Victoria interrupted.

Parker let out a deep breath. "Kenya. We'll be set up in a nomadic village about four hours outside Nairobi. But Baby, I wasn't trying to manipulate you, honestly."

Victoria shook her head, trying to control her emotions that were vacillating from sadness, to anger, to forgiveness. "Well, what are we going to do…about us?"

"Continue to let our relationship grow," Parker said, reaching over to hold Victoria's hand. He held it tight, showing his sincerity.

"If you want me in your life, you have to include me in the decisions you make. A relationship between two people shouldn't be unilateral, it's no way to build trust or respect. I've been through that before and I won't put up with it again."

Parker kissed her to make her quiet. All he wanted to hear was that she wouldn't give up on their relationship.

He brought her luggage in while she freshened up and then went through a week's worth of mail. Before they knew it, the afternoon had slipped into evening. They ordered pizza and opened a bottle of wine for dinner.

"I tried to call you several times. Did you turn off your phone?" Parker asked, taking a bite of his veggie slice.

"You know I did. I was avoiding you like you avoided me."

"Fair enough," he said, clearing his throat. "Mason told me that he saw you at Tavern on the Green."

Victoria had been anticipating this line of questioning. "Yeah, I love that place. The view of the park is spectacular."

Parker knew what she was doing, so he let the pause linger until he couldn't take it any longer. Seeing that she wasn't going to cooperate he plunged ahead. "Mason said you were having lunch with some guy. Who was he?"

"Why, are you jealous?"

"Should I be?"

Victoria laughed, but Parker didn't. "Relax, it was just Ted."

"Ted who?"

"Ted Thornton, silly."

"But Mason said you were having lunch with some white guy?"

"Yeah, that was Ted."

"Ted's white?" Parker sat up straight, letting his pizza fall to his plate.

"Yes," Victoria said with surprise. And for the first time, she realized that just as in her conversations with her mother, she'd never mentioned Ted's race when she talked about him. She assumed that Parker would know that Ted was white for the same reasons she thought her mother would. But the truth was that Parker had very little interest in professions or business happenings outside of medicine—including her own budding business.

Parker was speechless. All this time he'd assumed that Ted was black. The fact that he was white suddenly changed his perception of the man and his assessment of Victoria's relationship with him. "I thought he was a brother."

"Well he's not," Victoria said in a *"let's drop it"* tone.

Parker didn't want to have another argument so he backed off.

They slept in Victoria's bed that night. Parker held her close, wanting to make love, but thankful for the chance to lie next to her, especially after narrowly escaping a break up. They'd gotten over a major hurdle tonight. He was confident that she loved him just as much as he loved her. But her relationship with Ted disturbed him. From the beginning, he had a bad feeling about Ted Thornton. And now, his spider senses tingled even more. Mason had told him that when he ran into Victoria, it definitely seemed that she and her lunch companion were more than just casual acquaintances. Now, Parker was very interested in meeting Ted. His opportunity would come next month at the ViaTech Christmas party; a party he planned on attending, come hell or high water.

Chapter Fifteen

That's Where You Come In......

It was Sunday afternoon, and Victoria was lounging around the house, glad to be home from her week in New York. She and Parker were back on track. They'd made up last night, and after a large breakfast she'd prepared this morning, he headed back home.

She decided to call Denise to catch up on the office happenings since she'd been gone, but she wasn't prepared for what she heard. Denise told a story that left Victoria's mouth hanging open. "Patricia was fired? I can't believe it!" Victoria said.

"Yes, Girlfriend. When the heifer came in on Friday morning, Bob Huffman told her to pack her shit and hit it!"

"I wonder what finally got her fired?"

"I don't know. It's all very hush hush."

"What do you mean, *hush hush?*"

"All they're saying is that her services were no longer needed."

"Jen is your girl. Did you ask her what happened?"

"Sure did, but for the first time since I've known her, she wouldn't give me the scoop. I asked her a few questions and you would've thought I was trying to investigate the Kennedy assassination. Her lips were tight."

"Interesting."

"Yeah, I thought so too. So I figured that whatever got Patricia fired must've happened while she was in New York, and that's where you come in. What happened up there?"

Victoria's head was spinning. "I knew something happened between the two of them. I knew it!"

"Details, details, please!"

Victoria told Denise about the car incident between Patricia and Ted.

"Damn, Ted fired Patricia over you," Denise said.

"What makes you say that?"

"What else could it be? The man told you that she said something that pissed him off, and you know it was probably something about you because she talks shit about you every chance she gets. That's what got her ass fired."

"I don't think Ted would fire her over something as trivial as bad mouthing me."

"Girlfriend, you're truly in denial. Stop making excuses, it's really not cute anymore."

"I resent that," Victoria quipped.

"Look, he's getting a divorce and you'll be leaving the company soon. There won't be any roadblocks, so just go ahead and admit that you two have a thing for each other. Is it because he's…"

"My boss," Victoria cut her off. "And besides, there's something very important you forgot about…my boyfriend."

Denise wanted to roll her eyes so badly her lashes hurt. She'd met Parker two weeks after he and Victoria had started dating. He'd come by the office one morning, surprising her with flowers. Denise thought he was one of the best looking men she'd seen other than on the pages of her *Ebony Man Calendar*. But when he requested coffee, it pissed her off. Not only didn't he wait to be asked if he wanted a cup, he *told* her to get him one. He'd treated her like domestic help, and his arrogance and superior air made her want to spit in the freshly brewed French Roast before handing it to him.

Even though he apologized, and only because Victoria had gone off on him the moment Denise left the room, the damage had already been done. He'd torn his drawers as far as Denise was concerned, and no forced apology could mend that hole.

"I know you have Mr. Wonderful, but let's pretend he doesn't exist. What then? What would be your excuse?" Denise probed.

"I'm in love with a good man who loves me back. Ted isn't in the running."

"Girlfriend, who you think you foolin'?"

Victoria paused for a moment. "Okay, so maybe there's a small attraction…but it's not going to lead anywhere."

"If that's the way you see it."

"That's the way it is."

Fork In The Road……

1701 Summerset Lane was rockin' the night that Victoria threw Debbie and Rob a spirited going away party. Victoria had decorated her downstairs with rubber palm trees she'd rented from a local party store, giving the house a Miami Beach feel. The living room, dining room, and den were aglow with candlelit hurricane lamps filled with sand and seashells. She'd hired a bartender for the evening who served delicious tropical drinks, and she prepared a variety of mouth-watering delights that had all the guests devouring the food as soon as it hit the buffet table. She secured two new clients by the end of the evening.

Debbie and Rob had a ball, Tyler managed to act civil toward Parker, and Denise and Vernon danced like they were on *Soul Train*. The only tense moment of the evening came when Parker followed Victoria into the kitchen when she went to refill a serving tray with more hors d'oeuvres.

"Why didn't you hire a wait staff to serve the food?" she asked. "You shouldn't be doing this kind of menial labor. You should've told me. I would've paid for it."

Victoria breathed hard with irritation. "This isn't *menial labor*, it's what I do. I told you, this is my passion. This is my business, Parker. It's who I am.

Parker's unsupportive attitude made her downright frustrated at times. But that comment aside, everyone had fun.

Debbie was happy and glowing; comfortably into the beginning of her first trimester of pregnancy. Victoria was going to miss her. She was closer to Debbie than most of her friends she'd grown up with, and they'd become like sisters over the years.

Although Rob was excited, Debbie still had reservations about the move. "Atlanta held your memories, but Miami holds your future. Good things are on the horizon for you, Rob, and my godchild," Victoria assured her friend.

Victoria was hoping that her future would hold good things too. Her life was taking twists and turns down an unexpected and unfamiliar path. She wasn't sure where it would lead, but she had a feeling that wherever it took her, Parker and Ted would be standing at the fork in the road.

Driving Him Crazy......

Parker steered the rental car onto Interstate 40 from the Raleigh/Durham International Airport. He and Victoria were spending Thanksgiving with the Smalls. After many discussions, they'd finally come to an agreement about how they would divide up the holidays. Since he was leaving for Kenya the first week of January, they wanted to spend as much time together as they could. That meant dividing the holidays between each others' family; Thanksgiving with hers and Christmas with his.

Although the Brightwoods weren't pleased that Parker wasn't coming home for Thanksgiving, as was tradition in their household, they would have been even more upset if he missed Christmas. The Brightwoods, as Victoria was coming to learn, were big on family traditions.

As they entered the up-scale community where Victoria had grown up, she looked out the window with anticipation, excited about seeing her parents. Grand houses, pristine lawns, neat sidewalks, and stately trees graced the streets. She practically bolted out of the car as Parker pulled into the driveway in front of the large Colonial on Savannah Circle Drive.

"John, they're here," Elizabeth yelled back to her husband as she opened the front door. She grabbed Victoria and hugged her tightly. "Sweetheart, I'm so glad you made it," she said, giving her daughter a kiss on the cheek before reaching for Parker. "And you must be Parker. It's so good to finally meet you." Elizabeth gave him a hug too.

Parker had seen dozens of pictures of Victoria's parents, and he always marveled at her strong resemblance to her mother. Seeing Elizabeth face to face, he smiled. She'd just given him a close-up glimpse of what Victoria would look like in the years to come.

"Where's my Queen?" John's voice came roaring from the back.

"Daddy!" Victoria yelled like an excited little girl. She embraced her father as they rocked back and forth in each other's arms.

Parker was glad to see Victoria and her father so happy together because family was very important to him. Victoria had told him about the differences that she and John had battled in the past, and that she was trying to rebuild their relationship. Parker encouraged her to work on regaining the closeness they once had, and on his advice, she'd begun calling her father regularly. They shared open and honest conversations that had been hard at first, but were healing in power. She even opened up to both her parents about the painful night that she'd discovered the truth about her mother's family. John knew that his daughter's new boyfriend had a lot to do with her change in attitude, and he liked Parker if for no other reason than that.

"You must be Parker," John said, extending a hand that looked the size of a baseball mitt.

"Nice to meet you, sir," Parker greeted him.

Victoria was surprised; Parker actually seemed nervous.

"Elizabeth and I are glad you could join our family for the holidays," John said.

"Thank you for having me, sir." Parker felt small in comparison to the older man's mass. John Small was in his late sixties, but was still fit thanks to good genes and regular exercise. He was an intimidating figure.

"Please call me John, and let me help you with the luggage," he offered, trying to put Parker at ease.

Victoria and her mother headed toward the kitchen while the men unloaded the car. "He's very handsome," Elizabeth winked.

Elizabeth had designated the spacious downstairs guest room with private bath for Parker. Victoria was relieved that he'd be sleeping down there and not in the guest room upstairs, right beside her old bedroom. The temptation of giving in to a sexual love fest with him was growing greater by the day. The holidays and change of environment, along with her growing desires, were a potent combination for testing her self-imposed abstinence.

Parker finished unpacking his clothes and pulled a box of Trojans from the bottom of his bag. He was looking forward to putting them to use over the next couple of days.

During their weekend trip to New York when he and Victoria went to see the Knicks play the Hawks, Parker had hoped he would finally be able to make love to Victoria. Mason had invited them to stay with him and his family in their Harlem Brownstown, but Parker declined. He told his brother that he and Victoria needed privacy, and made reservations for a romantic suite at a luxury hotel in midtown. That night after the game, they held each other under the feather down comforter and did the usual, kiss passionately, touch and caress to the point of erection and wetness, then fall asleep in each other's arms. Not having her was driving him crazy, but this weekend he planned to change that.

Happy Turkey Day......

Victoria and her mother had been in the kitchen from the minute she and Parker arrived. They worked together, peeling potatoes, dicing vegetables, snapping beans, marinating the turkey, and baking desserts. Although they both prepped the food, it was Victoria who did most of the actual cooking. Parker entered the kitchen a few times to observe Victoria in her element. Food preparation was a new thing for him; his mother had never cooked the family meals when he was growing up. They had a woman named Francis who'd been cooking and cleaning for them for as long as he could remember.

Thanksgiving Day in the Small household was full of laughter, old stories, and enough food to feed a small island of people. John's sister Phyllis, and her husband, along with their two grown children and grandchildren, were all gathered for celebration and thanks. Elizabeth's brother Maxx, who had never married but always seemed to have a new woman on his arm, was there with his most recent flavor of the month—twenty years his junior.

Victoria was delighted that Parker blended in like he was a member of the family. Even her cousin Jeremy, who was now next in line to take over at the bank after John retired, and who happened to be a major-league asshole, liked Parker too. It was a relief to Victoria that her family welcomed her new boyfriend, especially since none of her friends seemed to care very much for him.

Back in the family room, Victoria and her cousins were laughing about old times when her cell phone rang. She walked over to the end table where she'd left it earlier and answered uncharacteristically, without checking the caller ID. "Hello," she said in mid-sentence laughter.

"Hi V, it's Ted. Happy turkey day."

She felt a jolt of excitement at the sound of his voice. "Happy turkey day to you too." She quickly turned her back to the group to give herself a little privacy. The laughter and conversation continued in the background, but Parker was silent. He listened carefully because he noticed a change in the tone and inflection of Victoria's voice.

Who's she talking too? he wondered. He watched Victoria flip her hair behind her ear, and heard the smile in her voice. He knew this wasn't just an ordinary friend she was talking too. Parker's antennae was at full alert. *I bet it's that mothafucker Ted on the other end,* he said to himself.

Ted could hear the commotion in the background. "How're you enjoying the holidays with your family? Sounds like there's lots of activity around you."

"We're having a great time. My entire family is here. How's your family?" Victoria asked.

"Everyone's fine. My brother and his wife and kids came, so did my sister and her family. My mother's happy to have all of us here. It's been hard on her since my father died a couple of years ago."

Ted knew that his mother hadn't been herself since his father passed away, but when he told her that he was divorcing Trudy, it had put a smile on her face that he hadn't seen in a long time. He also told her about his feelings for Victoria, and that she had been instrumental in his decision to finally file for divorce.

"I can't wait to meet this special young woman," Carolyn Thornton said warmly. "So, tell me about her?"

Ted smiled. "She's amazing. She's intelligent, ambitious, kind hearted, and she's a southern girl like you," he teased. "I could go on and on. Victoria's wonderful."

"She sounds like a fine young woman."

"She is, and she's beautiful. Inside and out." Ted knew that his mother would appreciate Victoria's beauty because her own good looks had been legendary in her day and had won his father's heart.

Carolyn Thornton was a beautifully frail seventy-five year old grande dame. But in recent years, grief had taken its toll. Her five foot seven-inch frame now looked much smaller with each passing year, her complexion had darkened, and her wrinkles had deepened. But her spirit was still strong. Carolyn Thornton had endured tragic episodes in her life, many of which she would carry to her grave, she'd vowed. Her will and resilience were the weapons that had kept her going.

Ted continued to smile as he talked about Victoria. "She's tall, with incredibly thick, long black hair. She has intense brown eyes, and the most beautiful deep brown skin."

Carolyn blinked her eyes, "What do you mean deep brown?"

"You know…brown. Kind of like chocolate," he answered. He knew that his mother would have some sort of reaction after learning that Victoria was black, but he wasn't prepared for the response she gave.

"Theodore…is she a *colored* girl?"

The hairs stood up on the back of his neck. "Victoria is African-American. Does that make a difference?"

"Well, I…I'm just surprised."

"Why? You know that I've dated all types of women in the past."

"You were young back then. Even so, I didn't know you fancied colored girls."

Ted shook his head, letting his frustration spill out. "Mother, I told you, Victoria is African-American."

"In my day we called them colored," Carolyn corrected.

"Well, it's a different day."

"So it seems," she said through pursed lips.

Ted hadn't expected his mother's reaction to be so hostile. "I can't believe you have a problem with the fact that Victoria is black."

"Theodore, I just don't know what to say. What brought all this on?"

"I fell in love with her because of who she is, and how she makes me feel. I can't believe you're acting this way."

Although Ted had never known his mother to have a diverse social sect, neither had he known her to ever express any prejudice views. She'd always been a progressive thinker. But he had to remember that she'd been raised in Louisiana, and maybe some of the things she'd experienced as a young woman still clung with her today.

"You think I'm a racist?" Carolyn said defensively.

"I didn't say that."

"You certainly implied it."

Ted raised a brow. "You must have a guilty conscience."

Carolyn looked into her son's eyes. They were the same ocean blue as the man she'd married and loved for over fifty years. "Theodore, I know what it means to love someone the way you say you love this young woman. That's what your father and I had until the day he died, God rest his soul. But I also know how hard it is," she hesitated, "for *blacks* and whites when they decide to intermingle…to marry. I've seen things in my day. The road you'll travel won't be an easy one, not even in today's time," she warned her son.

Ted thought about his mother's warnings as he listened to the voice of the woman he loved. He wasn't naïve. He knew there would be bumps ahead, but he was ready for the challenge.

"Sounds like this visit is just what your mother needed. I'm glad things are going well," Victoria said. She wanted to tell him that she missed him, that it would've been nice to have him at the dinner table when her mother brought out her delicious sweet potato pie. But somehow it didn't seem an appropriate thing to say.

Just then, Parker came up behind her. "Ted, thanks for calling, but I've gotta go," she said in a rush. "Enjoy the rest of your holiday with your family." She pressed the end button on her phone and turned to face Parker. She could see that his mood had turned sour at the mention of Ted's name.

"Why is he calling you?"

"To wish us a happy Thanksgiving."

"No, he called to wish *you* a happy Thanksgiving, not us. Victoria, what's the real story with this guy?"

"What do you mean?" she asked, pulling Parker over into the living room when she noticed that her cousins had quieted their chatter to observe what they saw as the beginnings of a lover's quarrel.

"You're always working late at the office, conveniently with him. It's like he's trying to find ways to keep us apart. Now he's calling you during the holidays. What's up?"

"Working late is part of the job. You of all people should know that by the hours your job requires. And he called to say happy holidays, that's it."

"I think he's showing an unusual amount of interest in you."

Victoria stiffened her back. "What are you trying to say?"

"I think it's strange that a man who's running a company as large as ViaTech, somehow always finds time for his *favorite employee*." Parker's tone was accusatory. "Is there something I should know?"

Victoria became furious. "I would never do anything to jeopardize our relationship. I don't have anything to hide. I have no surprises that I'm going to shock you with at the last minute," she said with heated anger.

"Baby, I'm sorry. I didn't mean that."

"Too late," she said. Victoria pushed past him and walked back into the family room with her cousins.

A Man Will Say Anything......

It was ten o'clock when Victoria awoke from her nap. She was exhausted from the past two days of activities. Parker was still asleep in the guestroom downstairs. After their argument they both needed to cool off and rest. The house was empty now, and the stream of relatives and friends had gone home with full stomachs and happy memories. Victoria came downstairs and found her parents sitting at the kitchen table.

"You guys still up?" she asked.

"Yes," Elizabeth said with a tired smile. "Your father and I were just talking about what a good time we had today."

"Yeah, it was great seeing everyone again. It's been too long."

"You know, I think Parker's still asleep," Elizabeth hinted while John gave her a look that said, *honey, stay out of it.*

Victoria knew that her parents had heard about the argument she and Parker had earlier. After their heated exchange, they'd come back into the family room, but had barely spoke two words to each other. Everyone felt the tension. A few minutes later they each retreated to their rooms.

"Oh, really?" Victoria shrugged as if she could care less. "Aren't you two tired?"

"Pooped," John said. "And your mother and I have to get up bright and early for the community fair that the Bank is sponsoring with the Boys and Girls Club tomorrow."

"You guys need to go to bed and get some rest. I can handle kitchen clean up," Victoria told her parents. Just then she looked up and saw Parker coming into the kitchen. He was wearing a ratty old t-shirt and a pair of severely faded Levi's. She thought he looked scrumptious, and suddenly had the urge to lick the underside of his neck. But she remembered that she was still pissed with him, so she acted as if he wasn't even there.

"Yeah, we can take care of this," Parker joined in eagerly, walking over to the kitchen island where Victoria stood.

Victoria looked at him with disbelief. She knew that Parker hated housework of any kind, and had a cleaning service that kept his place immaculate. *I can't believe he's offering to clean my parent's kitchen!* She knew this was his way of trying to make up.

"You kids have a good night," John said, then he and Elizabeth headed upstairs.

They worked quickly, cleaning in silence. A half hour later, Victoria and Parker were finished, leaving the kitchen with a sparkling shine. She was standing at the edge of the counter when Parker walked up behind her and stood close, pressing his pelvis into her behind. He pulled her hair away from her shoulder and rested his head in the crook of her neck. His breath was warm and made her legs weak as he pressed his body closer into hers. "I'm glad we're finally alone," he whispered, kissing the side of her neck.

Victoria's anger melted away, oozing down her leg like a carton of ice cream left out on a counter.

He turned her around to face him, pressing his groin into hers as he eased one hand under her t-shirt. He lifted her bra and rubbed her breasts, taking turns to ply each nipple until they were hard and rigid. He cupped his other hand over the front of her leggings, massaging her through the protective layer of cotton and lycra, the only barrier separating him from what he wanted.

"Parker," Victoria said between heavy breaths, "We should stop."

"Baby, let me make love to you. I know you want me to."

"I do, but, my parents…"

He wrapped his tongue around hers and pulled her in for a kiss that was so long and deep, she felt she'd drown it in. "They're upstairs asleep. This is a huge house. They won't hear a thing. I'll be quiet…I promise," he said, leading her to the guest bedroom.

They undressed frantically, grabbing at each other's clothes and exchanging hungry kisses as if their lives depended upon one another. "Baby, I love you so much," Parker whispered as he laid her down across the smoothness of the bed. He explored her body with his tongue, kissing her ankles, and then her knees. He moved up her leg, journeyed to her thighs, and worked his way to her delicate middle, spreading her legs like eagle wings. She was dripping wet, so he licked, and sucked, and kissed every inch of her soft folds, enjoying her hypnotic taste and the sensual sound of her low moans. Victoria thought she would burst.

He slipped on a condom and parted her thighs further with his knee. He rubbed his fingers against her moistened lips, massaging them before opening her wide for his admission. She squirmed beneath him, begging him to enter her.

He arched his back and guided himself inside her. When he entered, her warmth welcomed him in like an old friend. He took his time, filling her inch by inch until she'd taken his entire length. He looked down on her with loving eyes, thrusting with slow and steady control. She moved in sync with his hips, grinding herself tightly around him. She rolled over and straddled his lap, sliding down on top of him, making him moan too. He held her by her hips as she rode him, and fought back the urge to make the primal sounds his body demanded from her sensual movements. When he couldn't take it any longer, he returned her to her back and buried himself deeper inside, relishing each stroke of his re-entry. He felt as if his body would explode, but he concentrated and held back, wanting to make sure he satisfied her first.

Victoria felt her body melt into his. His love and his passion rendered her helpless, like a child. She closed her eyes and allowed herself to receive the gift she'd held out for. He was going deeper and deeper, and she moaned, enjoying the pleasurable pain she felt below her waist. She opened her eyes and found him staring at her, a mixture of determination and devotion on his face. At that moment, her stomach fluttered, her thighs shook, and her internal warmth spasmed around him, holding him in tight for dear life. She trembled, and that was his signal to join her.

Afterwards, they lay together, hugging close, trying to catch their breaths. Parker kissed her softly. "Baby, I'm sorry about the things I said earlier, and about the situation with the Africa Project. I know you're still upset about it."

Victoria wriggled her body from under him and walked over to the bathroom. She came back out with a determined look on her face. She wasn't going to have this conversation with Parker in the nude. Tyler had once told her to never have a discussion with a man while she was naked. "A man will say anything when he's got ass in the palm of his hand," he'd said.

Victoria quickly dressed herself and grabbed Parker's boxers from the floor, tossing them onto the bed. "Get dressed, we need to talk."

They sat at the kitchen table drinking orange juice. Victoria's legs still trembled, but she needed to get things off her chest. "We've discussed the Africa Project so much that I'm sick of it. I really don't want to talk about it tonight," she said to Parker's relief. "But I do want to address your accusations about Ted. How could you think there's something going on between us? Don't you trust me?"

"I trust you. But I know how men are. Especially men like Ted."

"What do you mean, men like Ted? You've never even met him."

"I don't have to meet him to know his kind. Powerful, money hungry, arrogant white men who believe the world is theirs for the taking. He sees you and he wants you. And just like anything else he sets out to acquire, he's orchestrating a plan to get you. All the late nights at the office, the business trips, the special projects, the phone calls?"

"Parker..."

"Baby, he's trying to spend time with you so he can ease his way in."

"You have such double standards," Victoria countered. "I never question you when you're working late, or on the few occasions when I've come by the hospital to meet you, and seen those nurses openly flirting with you."

"That's different."

"How so?"

"I'm a man, I can rebuff that kind of behavior. It's different with women."

"Oh my God, you sound so chauvinistic. I didn't know I was dating a caveman!"

"Call me what you will, but I know how things work." Victoria opened her mouth to speak, but Parker continued. "Mason is a good judge of character, and he told me that Ted looked like a man who's after pussy, not friendship," he said with bluntness.

Victoria sucked in a deep breath of air to calm herself because she didn't want to yell and wake her parents. She couldn't believe that Mason had the nerve to talk about what anyone was after. "What Mason thinks is of no concern to me."

"Has Ted come on to you?"

"Absolutely not. Do you really think I would continue to work with him if he were making sexual advances toward me? I wouldn't tolerate something like that."

"I'm sorry, I trust you, baby. But like I said, I know how men are. Plus he's white."

"What does race have to do with anything?" Victoria said, surprising even herself with the comment.

Parker stared at her, "Maybe it doesn't matter when it comes to Ted. You didn't even tell me he was white. I had to find out from my brother."

"Ted's race doesn't matter in my friendship with him, just as Debbie and Rob's race doesn't matter. And besides, Ted is my boss, so there's a certain separation I have to keep. But Parker, he's no threat to our relationship." Victoria looked him dead in the eyes. "We've got to have trust in this relationship, otherwise we may as well end it now before you leave for Kenya."

Parker rose from his chair and pulled Victoria to her feet, wrapping his arms around her waist. "I trust you. I just don't trust him."

"Is trusting me enough?"

"It'll have to be…because I love you." He kissed her until he felt the familiar rise in the front of his pants. He led her back to the guestroom, and she willingly followed.

Bon Appétit……

Parker dropped Victoria off at her house when they returned to town. He wanted to spend the night, but they both had a busy Monday ahead. They were worn out from traveling, visiting, and making love. So despite Parker's yearning, he went home to his own bed.

Victoria needed to relax because she knew the next couple of weeks would be hectic. She had two parties for clients in the next few days alone. Then there was ViaTech's annual Christmas party at the end of the week, Tyler's YFI fundraiser the following Saturday, and her own holiday party the weekend after that. And last but not least, spending Christmas with the Brightwoods in Washington, DC. The last event registered a zero on Victoria's top ten list of things to do.

She unpacked her bags and drew herself a hot bubble bath. She sank down into the soothing water and replayed her stolen moments with Parker. That's what they were, stolen moments. Each time her parents left the house or went to bed, she and Parker would steal away to whatever room was convenient at the moment; the guest room, her old bedroom, the couch in the family room, up against the wall in the kitchen, and on top of the washing machine in the laundry room. She felt like a teenager, and it added to the excitement of their lovemaking.

After a long soak in the tub, Victoria slipped into her nightgown and crawled under her soft sheets. She sat up in bed and flipped through her *Bon Appétit* magazine. She was searching for a sparkling champagne recipe when she came across an advertisement that grabbed her attention. It was a wine ad, and in it a couple was toasting to the holidays. The man reminded her of Ted. She reached over to her nightstand, picked up the phone and dialed his cell.

"Hello," he answered.

"Hi Ted, it's me."

"V, I'm so glad you called. Are you back in town?"

"Yes, I got in this afternoon. How about you?" she asked.

"Yeah, I flew in early this morning. So, what're you doing?"

"Lying in bed, looking at you," she giggled. "Actually, I'm looking at a picture of a guy in one of my magazines who looks a lot like you."

"Really?"

"Yeah, tall, handsome, terrific smile, great teeth, nice body..." Victoria stopped herself, throwing her hand up to her mouth. She hadn't intended on going so far.

Ted smiled on the other end. She always told him what a sweet guy he was, what an intellectual mind he had, and what a supportive friend he'd become. But she'd never told him that he was handsome, or even good to look at. "You think I'm handsome?"

"Yes," Victoria said, slowly letting out a deep breath. "Ted, I feel awkward talking to you like this. You're my friend, but you're also my boss."

"V, I tell you that you're beautiful all the time, and honestly, I'm flattered by the compliment." Ted's heart was racing. He found himself pacing the floor of his suite. "But please do me a favor. Can you stop referring to me as your boss? It makes me cringe when I hear you say that."

"But Ted, essentially you are my boss. What else should I call you?"

"I'm your friend, call me that."

"This is very strange for me. Like I've said, I've never shared a friendship with someone like you, and I want to make sure I don't overstep any boundaries, as if it weren't already too late for that." They both laughed slow and easy at her statement. "I'm glad we've become so close, and our friendship means a lot to me, but sometimes even I don't quite understand it, so I know it's difficult for other people to. That's why it's hard for me not to think of us without certain boundaries in place."

"Other people like who? Ted asked.

"Parker."

"He doesn't understand it, or he doesn't like it?"

"Honestly, both. We really bonded over the holiday and he made some valid points. I'm in a relationship with him and even though you and I are just friends, he feels like you're the other man. Just think about it from his perspective."

"Does he feel the same way about your friendship with Tyler?"

Victoria didn't answer.

Her silence confirmed his thoughts. "So, you two bonded?" Ted's pacing stopped, but his heart raced faster.

"Yes…we did."

Ted knew what that meant, so he ventured to ask the question he already knew the answer to. "You slept with him?"

Her response was slow, mixed with a strange wave of guilt. "Yes."

Ted sat down on his bed. His head was swimming and his throat went dry.

"Ted, are you there?"

"I'm here," he managed to respond, holding back his despair. He made up an excuse about having to finish some last minute paperwork, then said a quick goodbye.

Victoria tried to shake the confusion in her mind. She put her magazine away, turned off the light, and forced herself to sleep.

Ted went to bed with what felt like a sledgehammer in his head and rocks in the pit of his stomach. The woman he loved was sleeping with another man. He knew it was inevitable, and in reality, he'd been bracing himself for this from the moment he found out that Victoria was seeing Parker.

Parker had beaten him to the draw, claiming Victoria first, while he sat back and pondered over what he should do. But once again, Ted reminded himself that it wasn't about the mistake he made, but how he recovered from it. Parker would be gone in another month and Ted planned to use that window of opportunity to grow closer to getting what he wanted.

Chapter Sixteen

Circling In On His Prey......

It was a bitterly cold Friday night for ViaTech's annual Christmas party. Ted was shaking hands and making polite small talk as he worked the room of employees. He surveyed the large, festively decorated ballroom and smiled. Victoria had done a grand job of organizing the company's holiday event. He looked for her, but he didn't see her anywhere. Finally, he spotted Denise across the room and headed in her direction.

Denise greeted him with a warm handshake, then introduced him to her husband, Vernon.

"Have you seen Victoria?" Ted asked. "I wanted to speak to her before I go onstage." He had been in and out of town on business all week, and each time he'd tried to meet with her she'd already left for the day. They hadn't seen each other since before Thanksgiving.

"She called a few minutes ago and said she was a few blocks away. She should be here any minute," Denise said, looking at her watch.

Just then Victoria strolled through the door wearing a sexy, red chemise that paid homage to her curves. Her sparkling rhinestone-studded earrings and large rhinestone bangle completed her outfit. "Sorry I'm late," she said, leaning in to hug Denise and Vernon.

Victoria looked at Ted, admiring his black, Italian cut suit and red bow tie, which she thought added just the right touch of holiday color. She wanted to embrace him, but instead she squeezed his forearm. "It's good to see you," she whispered, leaning toward his ear.

"You too. You look beautiful," he whispered back. He noticed that she was a bit distracted, drawing her eyes and attention toward the front entrance. "Are you looking for someone?" he asked.

"Yes…Parker. Since we were running late he dropped me off, then went to park."

Ted tried to put on a good face. "Great, I finally get to meet him."

"This should be interesting," Denise said under her breath.

Jen came over wearing a stylish winter white pantsuit, greeting everyone with hugs. "I hate to interrupt, but Ted, it's time for you to go onstage and make your speech."

Ted excused himself as he and Jen headed toward the podium across the room.

"Girlfriend, what took you so long? Denise asked once Ted and Jen were out of earshot.

Victoria didn't want to relive the drama a second time by telling Denise that she and Parker had gotten into another argument over the infamous Africa Project. Parker wanted her to come to Kenya in March to spend two weeks with him, but she told him no. March was quickly shaping up to be a busy month for her with work at ViaTech and several events she was coordinating for her business. Divine Occasions already had two parties lined up for that month, and she couldn't turn away clients while she was trying to grow the business. A two-week vacation was out of the question. But Parker insisted that visiting him in Kenya would be a more enriching experience than the American Business Women's Association Banquet and the retirement party for one of her father's colleagues, two events that Victoria was planning.

It was starting to bother her more and more that Parker didn't encourage her business aspirations. All week she'd been leaving work early every day, rushing around town to make sure things were set up for the two holiday parties she'd been planning for months. But Parker hadn't seemed to notice that she was practically worn down trying to run her business, make time for him, and still show up for work at ViaTech. He often commented that he didn't understand why anyone with an MBA from an Ivy League school, making a six-figure salary, would want to plan parties, cook food, and God forbid, sometimes have to serve it for a living. To Victoria, he sounded like her father of old.

"Parker and I had an argument. It's a long story," Victoria said to Denise.

"It usually is with him," she smirked.

When Parker entered the ballroom it was clear that he wasn't a happy camper, but he looked like a million bucks in his tailored black suit. His red and white snowman tie, compliments of Victoria's need for festive holiday attire, was the only thing about his appearance that looked cheery. Parker hated the tie! He shook Vernon's hand and gave Denise a quick hug. To Victoria's relief she'd gracefully accepted it.

"You still mad at me?" Parker whispered in Victoria's ear, slipping his arm around her waist.

"Let's discuss it later," she said with agitation.

Parker didn't flinch. Instead, he drew her in closer.

"Ladies and gentlemen, may I have your attention please." Ted's voice resonated over the sound system as silence fell across the room. Everyone turned in his direction.

"That's Ted," Victoria said, trying to sound nonchalant.

Ted gave a pep speech detailing the company's progress, quoting impressive statistics and figures. He received a large round of applause when he announced that Christmas bonuses would be handed out a week early this year.

Parker watched Ted as he spoke. *So this is the sonofabitch who's trying to take my woman?* He didn't like the man on sight.

After Ted ended his speech, he left the podium and headed back to where Victoria was standing. He spotted Parker beside her and approached like a hunter circling in on his prey.

"Parker, I'd like you to meet Ted Thornton. Ted, this is Parker Brightwood," Victoria smiled. She followed the introduction with a quick and silent prayer that both men would behave.

They shook hands like adversaries, each gripping the other's palm with a force that was much too hard to be considered a friendly greeting.

"So," Parker began, "I finally get to meet the man who's been keeping Victoria away from me with late night business meetings."

"Yes, some projects are complicated, and require time and patience to seal the deal," Ted smiled. "But in the end it's worth the long hours once you've accomplished your goal." His voice was so even you could balance a drink on his words.

Parker nodded his head. "I agree. Over the last couple of months I've been working on a very important project too," he smiled back, positioning himself even closer to Victoria, wrapping his arm more securely around her waist, "and very recently my hard work finally paid off, and I was rewarded for my efforts…quite handsomely."

Denise looked at the three of them. "Looks like everybody's workin' hard these days."

Victoria simply looked straight ahead, hoping things wouldn't escalate.

"Nice meeting you, now if you'll excuse us," Parker smirked, ushering Victoria to the dance floor, leaving Ted to stew in his juices. Parker held her close as they danced to *The Christmas Song*. "I don't like him," he said flatly.

"Why not? What did he do to you?"

"I didn't like his tone."

"You two barely even had a conversation. And by the way, what was that little exchange about?"

"I had to let him know that I know what he's up to. I'm not going to let anything come between us. Not him, not work, not distance, not anything."

What's The Occasion?……

Several hours later, Victoria and Parker left the ViaTech party and returned to his place. Parker was in his study, checking his email for Africa Project updates, and Victoria was in the bathroom, taking a relaxing and much needed hot shower. She hated that she and Parker had been arguing so much lately, but at the same time she knew that he was crazy about her. One side of his medicine cabinet was filled with her toiletries, two of his dresser drawers were filled with her clothes, and several of her business suits hung in his walk-in closet. Whenever his phone rang, she was free to answer it. Yes, she knew that Parker loved her, but every time she thought about the Africa Project, she felt second to that mission.

She was reaching for a towel when she heard the soft stream of music flood her ears. She walked into Parker's bedroom and to her surprise, it was aglow with candles; atop the dresser, windowsill and nightstands. Victoria stood in awe of the soft light radiating warmth throughout the room. The comforter was pulled back, revealing a new set of satin sheets. A bottle of Veuve Clicquot, two champagne glasses, and a box of Godiva Chocolates sat on the nightstand. And the best treat of all was Parker. He was standing in the middle of the room wearing nothing but desire and a smile.

Victoria dropped her towel where she stood and walked into his waiting arms. "Parker, I can't believe you did all this! What's the occasion?"

"Just that I love you. I know the last couple of days have been stressful with the parties you had earlier this week, then the ViaTech party tonight. You've been working really hard, so I wanted to do something special for you, to show you how much I appreciate you, baby. I was afraid that I'd ruined things earlier this evening...."

"Shh," Victoria whispered, bringing her finger to his lips.

Parker guided her to the bed. He poured the bubbly, then made a romantic toast. They sipped champagne while resting on the soft satin beneath their naked skin. "Turn over," he whispered.

Victoria obeyed and rolled onto her stomach, burrowing her face into the luxurious sheets. Parker massaged the back of her calves, the pressure points behind her knees, the length of her hamstrings, and the sensuous small of her back. She felt her stress float away like doves.

"Turn back over, baby," Parker whispered again. This time he had another kind of massage in mind. He cupped her breasts together, kissing her nipples softy, sucking them with attentive care. He worked his way down as she moaned under his touch. Her hands palmed the back of his head, holding him between her legs. His gentle licks sent her body arching further into his waiting mouth, giving her pleasure until she felt her body slipping away into a warm, familiar place.

Breathless, and ready to return the favor, Victoria eased Parker onto his back. She tried to swallow his entire length; a difficult task even for her advanced skills, so she took him into her mouth as far as she could, using her tongue and lips to bring him to within an inch of orgasm. She pulled back instinctively, not wanting him to explode until he was deep inside her. She reached for a condom from his nightstand and took pleasure in sliding it on him. He entered her like water breaking a damn, crashing in and out with slow, deliberate thrusts. He worked diligently, sweat pouring off his body, mixing with hers. She let out a low whimper when she felt him hit the glorious spot that always made her tremble with sweet relief. Her inner walls closed in around him as she came, and he continued to make love to her until she came again.

*A*ny Of Your Tricks Tonight......

From the selection of Petite Filet Mignon and Salmon Steak, to the elegant floral arrangements, to the sparkling holiday decorations and tasteful give-aways in neatly decorated goody bags, Victoria had left no detail to chance. She'd even gotten a popular, local jazz trio to play throughout dinner until the guest speaker took the stage.

The first annual YFI Christmas Fundraiser had turned into a notable affair, evidenced by the large crowd gathered at the Buckhead Westin. Many distinguished private sector and non-profit business leaders were milling around the silent auction tables, enjoying pre-dinner cocktails, networking in lively fanfare.

A few YFI volunteers didn't show up, so Victoria stepped in to pick up the slack. She greeted patrons, directed guests to the silent auction tables, and did anything else that needed attending to, all while overseeing the smooth operation of the evening.

She was pleased that so many people had turned out for the event, and she knew that Ted was partially to thank. Once he found out how important the fundraiser was to her, he spread the word in the business community. He'd also seen to it that ViaTech gave a very generous corporate donation to the organization. Between helping YFI and putting in a good word with the Stanley Group, a law firm in the city that had hired Juliet and relocated her back to Atlanta, Ted had won over Tyler as one of his biggest fans. And therein lay the only snag of the evening.

Victoria bit the inside of her jaw when she found out that Tyler had changed the seating arrangements to include Ted at the head table. She knew it would make for an awkward situation to have Ted and Parker break bread in such close proximity, but at this point there was nothing she could do, after all, this was Tyler's function—she was just the event planner.

Victoria made her way around the room, smiling and greeting well-dressed attendees. "Where's Juliet? I need a big favor," she asked, walking up to Tyler with an envelope in hand.

"She and Gigi were over at the bar with your parents a few minutes ago," Tyler said, looking dapper in his tuxedo. "I gotta give your father props for the Gary Hicks hook-up."

"Yeah, he came through on that one. But now I have to get Gary straight for his speech," Victoria said, in exasperation. "Do you know he showed up without a prepared speech, not even notes or anything...ball players! I had to write this for him," she huffed, holding up the envelope.

Just then, Juliet and her best friend Gigi appeared. Juliet's black, strapless gown flowed around her petite frame, transforming her cute, girlish looks into that of a sophisticated style maven.

"Victoria was just looking for you, babe. She needs a favor," Tyler said.

"Sure, what do you need, Victoria?"

Victoria's eyes darted toward Gigi, momentarily stunned, but not surprised by her outrageous appearance. She quickly refocused her attention back to Juliet, handing her the envelope. "I'm short staffed on volunteers, so I need some extra help. Can you deliver these notes to Gary Hicks in room 702, and see if he needs anything, and schmooze him a bit. You know how NBA stars like to be catered to."

Gigi perked up, snatching the envelope from Juliet's hand. "I can take care of that," she grinned.

Victoria took a deep breath. She was happy that she and Gigi had reconnected since Juliet had returned to town, but this was one task she didn't trust to her old college friend. Gigi was a man-eater, often devouring her victims in one fell swoop. Tonight, she was decked out in an outfit so tight it looked as if it had been spray painted on. Her candy-apple red colored dress was loud! And the split up the front was so high it nearly revealed her crotch. Victoria gasped at her plunging neckline that exposed her voluptuous 34DD's. All she needed was a pole and a good beat, and she could've performed onstage at Magic City.

"No offense Gigi, I love you to death, but I can't have any of your tricks tonight," Victoria said, taking back the envelope. "Gary Hicks is off limits. I don't want you jammin' up the keynote speaker before he even hits the stage."

"Victoria, how could you say such a thing?" Gigi smiled, pretending to be wounded by the accusation. "I'll be a good girl, scouts honor," she said, raising her right hand.

Against her better judgment, and because she didn't have time to argue, Victoria gave in. "Okay, but no funny business...Juliet, watch her."

And with that, Gigi and Juliet were off. Victoria and Tyler were going over last minute details of the evening's agenda when Denise walked up. "Aren't you looking sexy tonight," she smiled, admiring Victoria's dress. "Girlfriend, I'm scared of you."

Victoria was wearing a black, backless, floor-length gown. "Denise, you look fantastic yourself," she complimented, taking in Denise's simple yet elegant A-line number. "How's Vernon feeling?"

"Better, but he's still nursing that cold. He sends his love."

Victoria looked at her watch; it was ten minutes to show time. She instructed Denise and Tyler to head inside the large banquet room as she glided off into the crowd. She found Parker near the silent auction table. He was striking in his tuxedo. "Where did Phil and Gayle go?" she asked.

"Phil was called in to the hospital. They left a few minutes ago. They told me to tell you they're sorry they had to leave," Parker said, planting a soft kiss on Victoria's cheek.

"Are we going to your place tonight?"

"Well, since your parents will be at your house, and we're already downtown, we can be at my place in five minutes," he smiled, then whispered, "and I can have you out of that gown in less than thirty seconds."

"Sounds like a plan," Victoria winked. "Why don't you go in and take a seat at the head table. I'm going to make sure everyone gets ushered in."

Parker's sexy mood was suddenly broken. "Victoria, why're you running around like a gopher?" he scoffed. "I've been watching you since we got here; greeting people and showing them around. You're not the help you know, let them do that."

Victoria stared at him with penetrating silence. Parker regretted his words even before they settled into the air, like sandpaper meeting wood.

She was furious. "There's nothing wrong with helping people, being gracious, and more important, making sure that this evening goes smoothly because my best friend's reputation as well as that of my business are riding on it. This event was a huge contract for me, and I've worked my ass off to make sure it's a success," Victoria hissed through clenched teeth, trying to maintain her composure. "This may not mean anything to you, but it means the world to me. Now if you'll excuse me, I have to perform a few *menial* tasks before the ceremony starts."

"Baby, I just want the best for you."

"I already have the best. And in case you haven't been listening to me over the last couple of months, this is who I am."

"Let's not do this. I don't want to argue," Parker retreated.

"Then don't. Now please take your seat inside. And don't worry, I won't be serving the food...I'd hate to embarrass you."

A few minutes later Victoria stood out front, cooling off while she surveyed the empty lobby. Nearly everyone had taken their seats inside the ballroom when Ted showed up. "Sorry I'm late," he apologized.

"Look at you," she softened, admiring Ted in his custom-made tuxedo. He appraised her, roaming his eyes over her gown. "Thank you, and I must say, you look incredible."

"This old thing?" she blushed.

When Victoria and Ted approached the head table, all eyes were on them. They claimed the last two seats, sandwiching her between him and Parker. "Good evening everyone," Ted greeted. They all spoke except for Parker.

Ted glimpsed the pretty woman with the perfect melon-sized breasts seated beside him. He didn't want to stare too hard, so he looked beyond her and was nearly rendered speechless. Sitting next to the bombshell was the attractive older woman he'd seen in the photo at Victoria's house several months ago. She was fashionably radiant in her soft-pink sequined gown. When she laughed, she revealed an explosive smile just like her daughter's. Beside her was the man in the picture, and even sitting down he looked commanding. Ted leaned forward, "You must be Victoria's mother?"

"Yes, I am," Elizabeth smiled proudly at the stranger. It took a moment before she realized who she was speaking to.

"The resemblance is striking. Now I know where your daughter gets her exquisite beauty. It's a pleasure to meet you, I'm Ted Thornton. I work with Victoria," he said modestly, bowing his head in respect.

"It's nice to meet you, Ted. Let me introduce you to my husband." Elizabeth made the introductions as Ted and John nodded in each others' direction.

"Mr. Small, it's a pleasure to meet you. You're a very lucky man to have lived in the company of two such beautiful women," Ted said in a polite and respectful tone.

Victoria looked across the table at Tyler and Denise. They were enjoying this, she could tell.

"Yes, they are my Queens," John boasted.

"Ah, yes, like the name of your bank."

"I see my daughter has given you a bit of our family history."

"Yes, and actually I'd like to sit down and pick your brain about a few business strategies I've been tossing around."

John perked up. "That sounds very interesting. Let's see what we can arrange while I'm in town next week."

Look at him, Victoria thought. *He's working Daddy!* She knew that bonding through business talk was a surefire way to ingratiate ones self with her father.

After a few pleasantries, the evening spiraled downhill when Elizabeth innocently thanked Ted for taking care of Victoria after her jogging accident. "I don't know what Victoria would have done without your help. You were a life saver," Elizabeth said.

Victoria had never told Parker that Ted had been the friend she was jogging with that day. She could see the glint in Parker's eyes at hearing the news.

The next thunder cloud came when Tyler casually announced that Ted had been volunteering with YFI for the past month, serving as a mentor to Jermaine Johnson, an eleventh grader with promise. "I talked to Jermaine yesterday and he's excited about the new computer you got him last week. He just set-up his email account yesterday," Tyler said, waiting for Ted's reaction.

Ted had asked Tyler not to mention his volunteer activities to Victoria because he wanted to give it a few months to see if the whole mentoring thing worked out. Initially, his primary reason for volunteering was to score big points, knowing it would go a long way with Victoria. But after working with Jermaine his intentions changed, and he found himself benefiting just as much from the experience as his young mentee. So he continued to volunteer, and continued to keep it private, as he'd become accustomed to doing about many things in his life.

He smiled to himself, not surprised that Tyler had managed to let Victoria know his secret without actually telling her. "Uh, yes, he emailed me this morning," Ted nodded as he ladled the vinaigrette dressing over his salad.

Victoria rolled her eyes in Parker's direction. This was yet another bone of contention in their relationship. She'd asked him several times to volunteer with YFI, but he'd said that preparing for the Africa Project and spending time with her kept him far too busy.

"I think it's wonderful that you're helping young people," Gigi purred, inching closer to Ted at the edge of her seat. "It's such honorable work."

"Thank you," he nodded.

Gigi extended her petite, perfectly manicured hand, "I'm Georgina Howard, but my friends call me Gigi."

"Nice to meet you Gigi," Ted smiled.

Juliet and Victoria exchanged glances. They both knew that Gigi was on the hunt and had found her target. They watched as she subtly licked her bottom lip—a trademark move she'd perfected during their junior year.

Ted could see that the woman was experienced in the art of seducing men. Her large brown eyes were boring holes through him with a look that he recognized all too well. He studied her as she twisted her reddish-brown hair between her fingers, as if beckoning him to her. Her skin reminded him of a gleaming copper penny. She leaned forward, giving him a full view of her abundant cleavage as she scanned his left hand for traces of a ring—as if that meant anything.

"So, Ted," Gigi smiled, placing her hand on his forearm. "What does a handsome man like yourself like to do for *fun?*"

Elizabeth let out a small, lady-like "Umph", while Denise rolled her eyes in astonishment of Gigi's bold moves. Parker was glad that the scantily clad seductress had turned her attention to Ted. The two chatted in familiar tones as the servers brought out the entrées.

Victoria could feel herself sinking. She didn't like the way Gigi kept touching Ted's arm, or the way she laughed and leaned into him for a little "accidental" body contact. She fought back her agitation because she knew she had no right to those feelings. But halfway through dinner, Gigi's non-stop flirtation, combined with Gary Hicks' fumbling speech, and her frustration with Parker had all gnawed on her last nerves.

She tried to ignore it; tried to concentrate on her food, on the beauty of the elegantly decorated room, on the good time everyone was having, and on anything else she could think of that would take her mind off Ted. But she kept coming back to him. By the end of the evening she was drained. She blamed her mood on her hectic schedule, telling a disappointed Parker that she needed to rest in her own bed tonight.

Lying under her warm sheets, Victoria prayed that the confusing emotions she'd experienced during dinner was just stress and nerves, but deep down she knew they weren't. Not wanting to dig any deeper into her thoughts, she drifted off to sleep.

Chapter Seventeen

He Was Marking You......

The theme was *A Winter Wonderland Christmas*, and since a light snow had already blanketed the ground, it was the perfect scene for Victoria's holiday party. Her house was illuminated with dozens of white pillar and tea light candles. Intricately designed crystal snowflakes accented the fireplace mantel, while white wicker baskets filled with snow-dusted pinecones sat in the corners of each room. The large vase of white tulips on the buffet table gave way to the delicious holiday spread that Victoria had prepared. And the crowning touch was the nine-foot Frazier Fir she'd decorated with vintage ornaments, handed down to her by her mother.

The house was full of family, friends, and good food. Everyone was enjoying John Small's secret recipe eggnog, spiked so strong it could ignite if placed close enough to an open flame. Victoria was glad to have her parents in town for the holidays. They had been there since the YFI fundraiser last week, and had proven to be holistic medicine to their daughter's soul. Having them around was a source of comfort, especially since her frequent arguments with Parker were starting to depress her. Victoria knew it was a result of the pressure surrounding their upcoming six-month separation. They found themselves bickering about little things, from coordinating their work schedules to how long they would stay in DC when they went to visit his family in a few days. But their most heated exchanges centered around Ted Thornton.

After the YFI fundraiser, Ted had arranged to have lunch with Victoria's father while he was in town. The two dined at the Ritz Carlton, where Ted was living until he closed on his new house. They'd spent over two hours discussing everything from the ups and downs of running a company, to the handicap of their golf game. When Parker found out about their lunch he was furious.

"Why did that sonofabitch have lunch with your father?" he'd fumed.

"It was more of a business meeting. Ted told me that Daddy gave him some sound financial advice."

"With all the bankers in this city, why was it suddenly imperative that he meet with your father to discuss financial management?"

"You've known since Thanksgiving that my parents were going to be here for this entire week. But you never once asked Daddy to have lunch or dinner, so why are you upset that someone else did? Especially since it was just business!" Victoria shot back.

"Baby...don't you see what's happening? He can't wait until I leave so he can make a move. I see it in his eyes."

Initially, Victoria had reservations about even inviting Ted to her party; not knowing how Parker would react. But it was the holidays, he was her friend, and she wanted him there. She was sitting in the living room talking with her parents, Ted, and a few neighbors when Parker entered the room. "Who wants in on a friendly game of poker?" he asked, zeroing in on Ted.

Elizabeth looked at the two men, then at her daughter. She leaned over and whispered into Victoria's ear. "Sweetheart, I think you have your work cut out for you tonight."

Up until now the evening had gone smoothly. Victoria's only worry was the scene brewing in the den. Tyler, Phil, Ted and Parker were engaged in what had turned into a not-so-friendly game of Poker. Victoria and Denise eased into the room to watch. The testosterone in the air was so thick that Victoria could feel the hair growing on her chest just standing in their presence.

Tyler and Phil cashed out and the game had come down to Parker and Ted. At this point, several people had gathered around to observe the card duel. Parker reached his hand out for Victoria and she came to his side. "She's my good luck charm," he smiled, at Ted.

Ted didn't move a muscle. He wanted to come across the table and punch Parker in the nose, but instead, he sized up his hand. It killed him to see Victoria with this man, but for now, he knew all he could do was receive the blows as they came. They played their final hand. After all the cards were on the table, Parker was the victor. He stacked his cards neatly to the side. "I guess that old saying is true," he grinned.

"Oh…what's that?" Ted tried his best to appear unfazed. He hated loosing at anything.

"Bet on *black* and you'll win every time."

Ted had a retort for that comment, but he held it back.

Victoria had had enough. "It's time to bring out more hors d'oeuvres," she said, hurrying off to the kitchen. Denise and Tyler followed in tow.

Victoria took the extra pitcher of eggnog out of the refrigerator and poured herself a glass, gulping it down like spring water. Denise had to pull the glass away from her lips. "Whoa, Girlfriend, slow down. That stuff is potent!"

"Yeah, and I need it to get through this night. Parker's driving me crazy. Did you hear that smart-ass remark he made?"

"He should've just pissed around you," Tyler said.

"*What?*" Victoria glared, hands on her hips.

"He's right," Denise jumped in. "He was marking you like dogs mark their territory."

Victoria threw Tyler an annoyed look, "You talk a lot of shit, you know that?"

"Girlfriend, at least he's honest and he'll tell you the truth."

"I know. But it's just that these are the holidays, my favorite time of year. I shouldn't be stressed like this!"

"Speaking of stress, when do you leave for DC?" Denise asked.

"Four days and counting. I want to come back the day after Christmas, but Parker wants to stay longer."

"Let him," Tyler jumped in. "He can stay and you can come back early. Just change your ticket."

"But we want to spend as much time together as we can before he leaves," Victoria whined. Denise and Tyler looked at each other, rolling their eyes with a look that said, *Why?* "And don't say anything smart," Victoria continued, "I guess he's just upset about having to leave soon, and so am I. We're both on edge."

"Is everything okay in here?" Juliet chirped, entering the room.

"We're consoling our dear friend," Denise said with a heavy sigh.

Juliet crossed her arms and shook her head. "Parker and Ted troubles?"

"You got it," Tyler nodded

"Don't worry, Victoria," Juliet said, "your problems will soon be solved. I was walking by and I heard Parker on his cell phone talking to someone at the hospital, he's got to go in. And I think Ted has more than he can handle. Gigi was on him like stink on shit when I passed them in the den."

Denise wrinkled her nose. "I know you all are friends, but I wouldn't trust that one with the Pope, let alone my man."

Victoria walked up to her bedroom and found Parker getting his coat out of her closet. "You're leaving?" she asked.

"Yeah, I just got paged. I was headed back downstairs to tell you. I'm sorry baby, but duty calls."

Victoria was actually glad he was leaving. It was too much stress having him and Ted under the same roof. She walked him to his car out back and felt guilty about breathing a sigh of relief after he'd gone.

The snow had started falling in thick, heavy flakes, prompting the party goers to head home. Victoria walked her last guest out, then came back in and searched for Ted. He and Gigi were seated at the breakfast table in the back of the kitchen. *Why are they tucked away in here?* Victoria said to herself as she entered the room.

Gigi's chair was pulled close to Ted's. She was in rare form tonight and her tight, leather mini-dress had captured the attention of nearly every man at the party. She ran her fingers through her free-flowing hair, coming on to Ted with no shame. Victoria saw the determined flash in her friend's eyes which meant only one thing—she had no intention of letting her prey elude her grasp this time.

"There you two are. I thought you'd both left already," she lied, trying to smile as if their presence together didn't bother her.

Victoria forced herself to smile as she walked over to the sink and started loading the dishwasher.

Gigi tried to spark a flame, but Ted acted as though his pilot light had burned out. He hadn't responded to her overtures last week, and tonight he still seemed unaffected by her charms. Finally, Gigi decided to give up. "Ted, it was good seeing you again. Maybe I'll see you around sometime," she fawned, giving her seductive powers one last try. Ted stood and gave her a cordial goodbye hug, careful not to touch anything critical. With that move, he'd successfully extinguished the vixen's last bit of hope. Victoria was uneasy when she saw their embrace, but was glad that Gigi was on her way out.

Gigi walked up to Victoria and gave her a warm hug. "Girl, this was a great party, as usual. I'm so glad we're back in touch."

"Thanks, Gigi, me too." Victoria hugged her back, feeling silly for being jealous of her friend, again, knowing she had no right to those feelings.

Gigi whispered into Victoria's ear. "Juliet told me that you used to think Ted was gay. Well, I don't know about all that, but something's definitely wrong with him. I pulled out the big guns and he didn't budge. No man in his right mind refuses Gigi," she quipped.

After walking Gigi out, Ted was Victoria's lone remaining guest. They sat on her sofa, falling into relaxed conversation as they usually did. Victoria wanted him to stay but knew it was probably best that he leave because their stares were beginning to linger a little too long. Finally, she walked him to the door. She was startled when he reached for her, bringing her into his arms for an embrace. "Good night," he said, holding her in a lingering hug.

Victoria closed her eyes, enjoying the woodsy smell of his cologne and the feel of his arms around her back. She couldn't trust what might happen next, so she pulled away. Reluctantly, he let her go. "Drive safe," she said before closing the door.

That night Victoria tossed and turned in her bed. It was no use in denying it any longer. For months she'd dismissed her friends' assertions, and her own feelings. But after being in Ted's arms and feeling the rush it brought, she knew that all she could do was pray. "Be careful what you ask for, you just might get it," she said aloud. She thought about the talk she'd had with God several months ago. She'd asked him to send her a good man, and he'd sent her two. As she drifted off to sleep, she vowed to never ask for too much, ever again.

Just Say It......

Christmas at the Brightwood's was festive. Their large, stately home was decorated in full holiday grandeur from the bright, clear-colored lights framing their front door, to the beautifully decorated Blue Spruce in the living room. The Brightwoods lived in Northwest DCs, Gold Coast community, known for its beautiful homes and affluent residents. Victoria was glad to see how happy Parker was to be with his family. Their bond was close on both sides; she secretly envied him that.

When Fred and Dorothy Brightwood welcomed Victoria into their home, she could feel the inspecting eyes of Parker's father and the disapproving ones of his mother. Fred Brightwood was a tall, handsome gentleman with a head full of curly salt-n-pepper hair. He was proof of where the Brightwood men inherited their sex appeal and charm. Dorothy Brightwood was a large bodied woman who in Victoria's estimation, could stand to lose a good fifty pounds or more. But her sophisticated comportment and stylish flair was a cross between Lena Horne and Nancy Wilson, making her a striking woman just the same. Still, almost immediately, Victoria could sense that her man's mother didn't like her.

Dorothy was incredulous when she discovered that Victoria didn't belong to a sorority, but forgave her when she learned that Elizabeth was a fellow soror. She dug into Victoria's family background, and from the questions she posed, it was evident she'd done her homework. She was pleased that Victoria wasn't first generation educated or second generation wealthy. The only piece of the puzzle she hadn't been able to figure out was how John's father had come into his money. When Victoria told her that it was by way of tobacco farming, and in South Carolina no less, Dorothy looked as though someone had just urinated on her favorite Persian rug.

But his mother's attitude aside, Parker's brothers were polite and their wives and girlfriends were civil. And even though she was prepared for it, Victoria still found it amazing that they all looked like brothers and sisters. His cousin, Samantha, was the bright spot of the clan, because albeit a little on the wild side, she was genuine and warm. She'd also gone to Spelman, and she made Victoria feel relaxed with her hilariously gritty sense of humor.

All in all Victoria was handling the visit well, but she was patiently counting down the hours until the Christmas dinner would be over and she and Parker could return to their hotel room.

"Victoria, I need to talk to you for a minute," Parker said with a serious look. He led her away from the den of merry-making relatives and out toward the sunroom in the back.

"What is it?" she asked.

"I don't know how to tell you this except to just say it. My ex, Pamela...well, she's coming to dinner this evening."

"What?" Victoria asked with shock. She couldn't believe Parker had just told her that his ex-girlfriend, the one he'd almost proposed to, would be sitting at the dinner table with them.

Victoria had been curious about Pamela Presley ever since Juliet had told her about the woman several months ago. She was the only woman from Parker's past who had ever come close to getting him to the alter, and for Parker Brightwood that had been something! When Victoria had probed him about his ex, she learned that the two had grown up together, their mothers were best friends, and it had been a HUGE deal when he'd broken up with her. "Our mothers were devastated," he'd said, "not to mention Pamela. But I had to be honest with her and with myself. You know when it's right and when it's not. She was a decent woman, just not the woman for me."

Yes, Victoria had been curious about Pamela, but she had no desire to meet her today, and especially not on the woman's home turf. "Parker, why are you just now telling me that your ex is coming to dinner?" Victoria asked, feeling her temples begin to pulsate.

"I didn't know she was coming over. Mother just told me a few minutes ago."

"I guess keeping secrets and last minute surprises runs in the family," she said in a curt tone, looking at him with growing anxiety.

"Baby, that's not fair. My mother invites Pamela and her parents to our Christmas dinner every year. I kind of figured her parents might come but I didn't think she would, especially after knowing that I was bringing you home to meet my family."

"How do you know that she even knows I'm here?"

"Because I'm sure that mother told her when I let her know that you'd be spending Christmas with us."

"Are you sure your mother told her?" Victoria asked with raised brow.

"Of course I'm sure, why wouldn't she? Listen, baby, Pamela and I are ancient history. I'm with you, and I love you, okay?"

An hour later, Pamela and her parents arrived. Victoria wanted to gag with disgust at the way Dorothy gushed over Parker's ex, like she was visiting royalty. Victoria looked the woman up and down. Pamela was petite, and sported a short, stylish pixie cut. Her hazel eyes twinkled with delight as she looked in Parker's direction, aligning her profile so he could get a good look at her curvy figure, neatly tucked inside her cashmere sweater and wool skirt.

"Parker, dear, come and greet the Presleys," Dorothy said with a wide grin.

To Victoria's comfort, Parker took her hand in his and walked toward the group. Pamela's disposition changed with lightning speed when she saw Victoria by his side. He hugged Pamela's mother, shook her father's hand, then reached for Pamela's. When he did, she threw her arms open, pulling him in for a big hug. "Parker, it's *sooo* good to see you," she cooed.

"I want you all to meet my girlfriend," Parker smiled, withdrawing from Pamela's embrace. It was clear by the surprised look on everyone's face that Madame Brightwood had not disclosed the fact that her son was bringing his new woman to meet the folks.

I knew that bitch didn't tell her, Victoria quietly seethed.

The introduction was met with a chilly reception. But as Victoria quickly discovered, although Pamela was initially taken aback, the princess was quick on her feet. She adjusted her game, ignoring her competition, not even acknowledging Victoria's presence. "Shame on you, Parker," she teased, "we only live two blocks from each other, so why haven't I seen you since Labor Day?"

Victoria bit the inside of her cheek. This was late breaking news! Parker had never told her that Pamela lived in such close proximity, or that he'd seen her within the last few months. It sounded like they had a recent history, not an ancient one as he'd said.

"The hospital keeps me very busy, and when I'm not there I usually spend my free time with Victoria," he said firmly. They all stood in uncomfortable silence, save for the Christmas music playing in the background. Ready to end the awkward moment, Parker spoke up again. "We're glad you could make it this evening," he nodded to Pamela, then to her parents. And with that, he took Victoria's hand in his and walked away.

"I thought you said you two were ancient history," Victoria said through clinched teeth once they left the room.

"We are. Ancient history doesn't always mean time. In this case it means feelings," Parker sighed, running his hand over his scalp. He looked into Victoria's eyes, knowing he had to tell her the complete truth. "We hooked up a few months ago, before I met you. But I put an end to it…for good. That's the truth."

Victoria realized that Parker didn't have to divulge that information, but he told her anyway. He told her because he was trying to be honest. "Okay, so why didn't you tell me that she lived a few blocks from you?"

"For the same reason you never mentioned that Ted was white, or that he's the friend you were with when you had your accident," Parker responded. "Because it's no big deal. Isn't that what you told me?"

Victoria had to check herself. He'd just given her a taste of her own medicine. The only thing she could do was nod her head. "Yes, I guess you're right."

"Baby, you know I love you, and as you can see I have no interest in

Pamela. Now, let's get back to enjoying your favorite time of year." He kissed her on the lips, quieting her fears.

Thicker Than Water......

The Presley's left right before dinner, even though Dorothy had begged them to stay. "I've lost my appetite," was Pamela's short response.

Sitting at the large banquet table in the Brightwood's ultra formal dining room, with more than twenty of Parker's relatives, Victoria watched as Francis, the help, set the last of the holiday feast on the buffet table. Victoria balked at the fact that Parker's mother had actually made the poor woman wear a gray maid's uniform, and cringed even more when Parker said he didn't find anything wrong with it. "It's just formality," he'd said.

"Victoria, I have to say that I'm surprised my son brought you home to meet the family after dating for only three short months," Dorothy said with icy skepticism. Everyone around the table looked uncomfortable after her comment.

"Aunt, Dot, you can't put a time table on love when you find that special someone," cousin Samantha spoke up, giving Victoria a wink. She leaned over close and whispered in Victoria's ear, "By the way, she hates it when anyone calls her *Dot*. I do it just to fuck with her."

Victoria smiled at Samantha's little gab, then lifted her glass of Pinot Grigio to her lips in favor of giving Parker's mother a piece of her mind.

"Victoria, I think you're a lovely young woman," Fred Brightwood jumped in. "My blessings are with the two of you. Welcome to the family, dear," he said as if it were a foregone conclusion that Victoria would soon be hyphenating her last name to add Brightwood to her title.

"Let's not jump the gun," Dorothy scolded in a playful, yet serious tone. "You don't want to rush these two."

"Dad's right," Parker nodded, "when it's right you know it. And believe me, I know it this time."

"Yes, you're a lucky man to have such a beautiful woman," Mason added.

Parker looked squarely at his older brother, and Victoria sensed an unsettlinge edge in his body language that screamed something was wrong. "That's the third time today that you've mentioned my girlfriend's obvious beauty," Parker said in a threatening tone.

Now everyone at the huge table was aware that something wasn't right.

Mason's wife looked at her husband with growing irritation.

"I didn't know you were counting little brother," Mason replied with sarcasm.

Parker smirked, trying to control the anger that was rising in his voice. "I have to keep an eye on you big brother."

"What's gotten into you boys?" Dorothy snapped, looking at Parker. "Your brother's just trying to pay your dinner guest a compliment."

Victoria had to take another sip of wine. Dorothy had just referred to her as a *dinner guest*. She knew that Victoria was more than that, she was Parker's girlfriend. And from what Parker's father, and Parker himself had just said, she would soon be a member of the family. But Victoria knew the comment was Dorothy's way of letting her know where she stood in her book.

"Nothing's gotten into me, Mother. Why don't you ask Mason what's his problem?" Parker said in an accusatory tone.

"What are you trying to say, Parker?" Mason asked, shielding the suspicious eyes of his wife.

"You know exactly what I'm saying."

Mason cleared his throat. "I think you better calm down. Clearly you're letting the wrong head do your thinking," he volleyed smoothly as he buttered his freshly baked dinner roll. Victoria almost choked!

"I know you'd like to have what I have and that's your damn problem, Mason. Don't think I didn't see you looking at Victoria today. I saw you watching her when she was standing in front of the tree, helping the kids unwrap gifts."

"Parker!" his mother shouted. Fred simply looked on in astonishment.

But Parker continued. "And I saw you looking at her last night when we were doing the champagne toast. Let's not pretend. We all know how you are."

"You can say that again," cousin Samantha slid in, under her breath.

Parker stared directly at Mason's wife, who looked as if she could spit in her husband's face because she'd witnessed first-hand the truth of Parker's words. "I know what you're capable of, so I'm warning you, back the fuck off because in this case, blood isn't thicker than water my brother!"

"Now that's quite enough!" Fred finally stepped in.

Parker had just called his brother out in front of the entire family, and his wife, who'd already jumped down his throat about her suspicions. Mason was green with envy and mad as hell. He ignored his father's attempted intervention. "My, aren't we bold these days. You better tread lightly," he threatened.

"You're jealous," Parker snarled.

"And you're pussy whipped."

"See what happens when you bring just anyone to dinner," Dorothy said, shaking her head with anger.

"*Excuse me?*" Victoria shouted, giving Dorothy a look that could melt ice. "I'm not the one talking about pussy at the dinner table!" she corrected, letting her words fly out like darts in Dorothy's direction.

"*Damn,* this is gettin' good!" Samantha chuckled, watching the fiasco unfold.

Parker leaned forward in his seat. "Yeah, I'm probably whipped, and you wish you could be too. It kills you that you can't have her. I heard it in your voice when you called to rub it in my face after you saw Victoria that day at Tavern on the Green. Well, she's with me and we love each other. For once in your life can't you be happy for anyone other than yourself? Why do you always have to be the top dog? You have a wife who loves you and two beautiful kids sleeping upstairs who adore you. Why can't you be satisfied with your happiness?"

Mason threw his linen napkin on the table. "You don't know shit about my happiness," he yelled.

"See the trouble you've caused," Dorothy glared at Victoria.

"I've had it," Victoria huffed, "this unwanted dinner guest is gettin' the hell up outta here." She rose from the table with Parker following on her heels. They left the rest of the Brightwoods sitting at the well-appointed table in complete silence.

I'm Stating Facts…

Later that night in their hotel room, Parker and Victoria were lying in bed. "Baby I'm sorry about what happened. Mason's behavior was completely uncalled for. This competition thing between us goes way back, but I never knew it was this deep. He's obviously going through some things," Parker said.

"I had your brother's number the first time I met him. But I'm not half as upset with Mason as I am with your mother."

"My mother? Why are you upset with her?"

Victoria searched Parker's face. He was truly clueless. "Did you not here the insults she hurled at me from the minute I walked through the door? All the inappropriate questions, her *dinner guest* comment, the way she blubbered over Pamela, not to mention the fact that it was obvious she hadn't told anyone that I was coming home with you. She even blamed Mason's womanizing on me! Were you not a witness to all that?"

"I think you're overreacting. She's always treated the women we've brought home with a judging eye, but it's nothing personal. She's just protective of her boys. I've never known mother to be insulting, at least not the way you're suggesting."

"I'm not suggesting, I'm stating facts." Victoria paused. "She's probably never made off-handed remarks to any of the women you've dated because none of them have ever looked like me. They all look like Pamela and the rest of those bitches in your photo album."

"Here we go with that again."

"You think this is just something that's in my head. You think I'm *overreacting*?"

Parker nodded his head, irritation spreading across his face. "At times, yes."

"Didn't you hear the way your mother talked to me? Or were you too wrapped up in your pissing contest with your big brother to notice?"

Parker got up, his naked body bouncing off the light reflected from the window across the room.

"Where are you going?" Victoria demanded.

"To take a shower; I think one of us needs to cool off."

Victoria listened to the sound of running water that filled the room, and thought about her past that never quite seemed to go away. She felt seven years-old again, lying in bed, preparing to cry herself to sleep.

❦

Buried All The Love......

It was the day after New Years, and Hartsfield International Airport was buzzing with activity. Parker and Victoria stood at the private gate reserved for the Africa Project participants and their families, and waited for the boarding announcement. Their Christmas holidays had been rocky but the last few days had made up for it.

After their argument on Christmas evening, Parker felt terrible that Victoria had been brought to tears and he knew that he was partially responsible for her state. He apologized over and over. After they made up he went downstairs to the gift shop to get her Tylenol for the headache that he and his family had caused. When he returned to their room, he massaged her back and kneaded the tension from her shoulders. Then he laid her across the feather down bed, opened her wide, and buried all the love he had inside her.

They decided to leave the next morning, putting an abrupt end to their catastrophic visit. But before they headed to the airport, they made a quick stop by the Brightwood house. Victoria remained in the car while Parker went inside. He confronted his mother and made it clear that Victoria was going to be a permanent part of his life, then told her that she needed to change her attitude toward the woman he loved if she wanted to see her third born child during the holidays again. Reluctantly, Dorothy Brightwood acquiesced.

As for Mason, who'd already packed up his family and headed back home to New York, that was a more sensitive subject. After a long phone conversation with his brother, Parker confided to Victoria that Mason's home life had been unhappy for years, and that his marriage was speeding fast toward divorce. He and Parker made amends, but they both acknowledged their unresolved issues that still lingered, and made a pact with each other to work toward resolving them.

After they came back to Atlanta, they made the most of the short time they had left. Although Parker was pissed when Ted called Victoria on New Year's Day, he didn't say anything. The last thing he wanted to do was leave the country for six months after having an argument over Ted Thornton.

The flight attendant began boarding passengers.

"I'm gonna miss you so much, baby," Parker said as he held Victoria in his arms.

She sniffled, trying to hold back the tears that came anyway. "I'll miss you too."

Parker rocked her back and forth, savoring the memory of the love they'd made the night before, something he knew he was going to miss in the months to come. "I'll email and call when I can," he told her.

"Promise?"

He nodded and smiled. "I promise." He inhaled her sweet perfume, already missing her. "I know we've had our disagreements, but I love you, Victoria."

The flight attendant announced the final boarding call for all passengers as they shared one last kiss. Parker gently wiped the tears from Victoria's eyes, fought back the urge to openly shed his own, then walked onto the plane.

Chapter Eighteen

A Mixed Blessing......

Victoria was clad in her white bikini, stylish high-heel sandals, and *Jackie O style* sunglasses. She and Juliet were lounging on the cruise ships' upper deck, enjoying the protection that their wide umbrella provided from the hot Caribbean sun. She was working on her second strawberry daiquiri, compliments of the generous male admirers sending drinks her way.

"Girl, I wish this wasn't our last day of the cruise," Juliet said, sipping her melon margarita.

"I know, but I'm glad your job let you have time off so soon."

"Before I started, I told them that I already had this cruise planned. And besides, I needed the break. Between renting out my apartment in New York, moving in with Tyler last month, and starting the new job, it was time for a break."

They both looked up as Tyler approached. "You ladies have been out here for hours. You ready to head back in?" he asked Juliet.

She smiled, giving him a peck on the cheek. "We'll see you later, Victoria," and with that they were off.

As Victoria watched the two lovers stroll back to their cabin room, she thought about Parker and how he should've been there with her, enjoying the cruise. He'd only been gone for a little more than two months, but it seemed like an eternity. The first few weeks, even with the village's limited communications equipment, they'd emailed and talked on the phone at least twice a week. But once the pace of the clinic started to pick up, their emails and phone calls slowed.

Life without Parker was lonely at times, so Victoria was grateful she had the SuperNet project and her growing business to fill her time. Her schedule had become so busy, it forced her to finally open up to Ted about her plans to leave ViaTech and run Divine Occasions full-time. It had been a big weight off her shoulders, and she was glad she didn't have to continue keeping something so important from him any longer. And although he was completely supportive of her plans, offering to help her in any way he could, Victoria had come to view her relationship with Ted as a mixed blessing.

He was thoughtful, a good listener, and he made her laugh until her sides hurt. But day by day he was forcing her to reevaluate beliefs she'd held all her life, deep rooted beliefs about the foundation of relationships between men and women, based on race.

But the thing that bothered Victoria the most, the thing she couldn't get out of her mind as she lay under the warm Caribbean sun, with her many admirers looking on, and a handsome and successful boyfriend who loved her, was that all she could think about was Ted.

Later that evening, Victoria walked out onto the balcony of her cabin. She breathed in the salty ocean air for clarity, but her thoughts still felt crowded and confused. She picked up her cell phone and called her mother, pouring her heart out about her dilemma. This was the conversation that Elizabeth had known was coming for some time.

"What do you think about your daughter falling in love with a white man?" Victoria asked. She shocked herself, realizing this was the first time she'd admitted that she loved Ted.

"What matters is what you think," Elizabeth answered.

"Mom, come on."

"Sweetheart, I can't tell you who to love."

Victoria's voice was quiet and unsure. "How can I choose?"

"Listen to your heart. Choose the man who makes your heart sing. The man who makes it ache when you're not with him, and feel full when you are, the man who knows your flaws and still loves you anyway, and above all, the man who will be your friend and cherish and protect that relationship."

"But I feel that way about both of them."

Elizabeth was silent for a moment. She knew she had to measure her next words carefully. "I've had to fight the same demons you've fought. Some used to say you were too dark...well, some used to say I was too light. Growing up I caught hell. I was called everything from half-breed to white girl. I was too white to be black, and too black to be white, for some folks' taste. That's a terrible in between."

"It wasn't until I fell in love with your father, that I felt for the first time in my life that I was totally and completely accepted for just being me. There was no dark or light, no good or bad, just love. And Sweetheart, in the end, nothing else matters but the love."

"What are you saying, Mom?"

"I'm saying that whoever you choose, make that decision based on who *you* want. Don't look for permission or approval from anyone. You've always known what was best for you, even when your father and I couldn't see it, and you know what's best for you now. Just trust yourself."

"Mom, you say that I know what's best for me, but this is one time I don't."

"You know more than you think. Just pray and the answers will come.'

Get A Substitute......

The Monday after Victoria returned from the cruise, her body was in shock from experiencing the warmth of the Caribbean sun one day, and Atlanta's unusually cold February freeze the next. She got through the long work week, glad that it was Friday night. She made a quick dinner, then checked her email and answering machine. She didn't have any messages from Parker, so she sent him a quick email. Not quite ready to turn in so early, she grabbed a handful of chocolates and settled onto the couch before dialing Debbie's number.

"Hey, Debbie. It's me," Victoria said, munching on a roasted almond truffle.

"Stop eating in my ear," Debbie teased. "How was the cruise?"

"It was great. I really needed the getaway. How're you feeling?"

"I'm good, but hungry as hell! I've never eaten so much in my entire life. I'm bigger now than I was in the pictures I emailed you a couple of weeks ago. You should see me!" Debbie said with a joy that Victoria had never heard in her friend's voice.

"I can't wait for my godchild to arrive. I'm so excited."

"You and me both. Hey, have you heard from Parker?"

"Not since before I left for the cruise," Victoria said, trying to stay happy, but not feeling it.

"You miss him bad, don't you? I can hear it in your voice?"

"Yeah, I do. Even though we had our disagreements, especially right before he left, we had so much fun together. Parker is the most gentle, romantic man I've ever known, and some nights I get so lonely without him," Victoria paused, "once you've gone without sex for a long time and then you start again, it's hard as hell to go cold turkey, especially when it's good. And let me tell you, Parker is good!

"How good?"

"I'll put it like this…I think he got his degree in How to Eat Pussy, not Cardiology," Victoria said, making Debbie burst into laughter.

"Damn, that's a tough act to follow. The only thing I can tell you to do is get a substitute."

"Are you crazy? Let me remind you that the consumption of alcohol is ill-advised during pregnancy."

"What I mean is that you need to hook yourself up. Make a trip to that sex shop I used to go to downtown."

"I hate going into those places."

"Well, my dear, you've got three choices. You can either stock your shelves with some battery operated goodies, find a live and willing participant, or block it out of your mind."

"Great," Victoria said, depressed with the prospects.

"There's one other option."

"What's that?"

"Call Ted. I'm sure he'll be glad to come over and knock the edge off."

"Please…"

"You know I'm right. Why can't you just admit that he's crazy about you and that you like him too? I hear the way you sound when you talk about him."

"Debbie, it's complicated."

"Why? Because he's white?"

"Yes, partially. But also because I have a boyfriend. I love Parker and I couldn't cheat on him. I know what that's like and I'd never put him through that."

As only a true friend could, Debbie spoke frankly; from her heart. "I understand what you're saying, Victoria, really I do. But I think that Ted's race is the bigger issue for you, not your love for Parker. At some point you just have to say fuck it! You have to look beyond the man's skin and look at how you feel about him."

Victoria sighed. "Listen, it's late so I'll let you go."

"You're not letting me go, you're brushing me off, but that's all right. I still love you anyway."

"I love you too…and thanks," Victoria said before they ended their call.

She Called Out……

Two weeks later Victoria found herself standing in the large upper-floor gallery of the ViaTech building. Last March Ted had arrived at the company, and now, a year later, he was the official Chief Executive Officer and fifty percent owner of ViaTech, Inc. Tonight's affair not only marked that occasion, it also celebrated the fact that while other telecom companies were beginning to take a hit, Ted had managed to realign ViaTech's business model, putting them securely on top of their competitors. Senior managers and directors from the company's remote locations across the east coast were all in town for the event.

After a few hours of mixing and mingling, Victoria was ready to leave. "Denise, I'm going to call it a night. I have an early morning meeting with a prospective client," she said.

"Are you going to say goodbye to Ted," Denise asked, giving her a devilish grin.

Victoria had been trying to keep her distance from Ted all evening. This was a big event with lots of prying eyes, so she wanted to be careful about their contact. "No, I'm just going to slip out. If you see him, tell him I said good night."

Later that evening, Victoria ran herself a hot bath and tried to relax. She was lonely, and her body ached for attention. She toweled off and walked over to her nightstand. She opened the drawer and pulled out the vibrator she'd brought last week when she went "girl shopping" with Juliet and Gigi.

"You need to find one that's true to his size and form," Gigi had suggested from her vast experience in such matters.

Victoria's eyes scanned the selections until she came across what appeared to be a close match to Parker. She pulled it from the shelf and examined it through the clear plastic packaging.

"That's true to Parker's size?" Juliet asked.

Victoria held it out as they all studied the sex toy. "Yeah, pretty much" she finally concluded.

"My, aren't you a lucky one," Gigi smiled devilishly.

It still doesn't beat the real thing, but beggars can't be choosers, Victoria reasoned as she lay back on her fluffy comforter, parted her legs, and put the toy to work. She squirmed with pleasure as she fulfilled her needs, gently fondling herself in places she'd been deprived. Her body grew warm and full under her own touch as she moaned, enjoying the feel of her soft wetness. Her inner muscles tightened as the intense feeling of orgasmic euphoria filled her body. She moaned loudly, gave in to it and allowed the rush to come. *"Ooohhh Teeeddd,"* she called out.

Her eyes sprang open. The moaning—halted. The sensations—stopped. The euphoria—gone. Victoria sat up fast, letting the vibrator fall to the floor with a hard thud. She moved to the edge of the bed, naked and stunned, yet fully aware of what had just happened. A few minutes went by before she slipped on her nightgown and climbed back into bed.

When the phone rang, she didn't have to look at the caller ID to know who it was. "Hello," she answered.

"I was calling to see if you're all right," Ted's voice eased into her ear. "You left before I got a chance to see you tonight."

"Um, yeah. I have an early morning meeting with a client…"

"V, are you okay? You don't sound well."

His concern was choking her. "I'm fine, just tired," she said, pretending to yawn into the phone.

Reluctantly, Ted let her go. But now she was wide awake, as if the sun had just come up. She thought about her situation and all she could do was pray that the answers would come.

Let's Make A Deal……

The next morning, Victoria put her night behind her and concentrated on her nine a.m. meeting with Eva Masters. As she pulled into the driveway of the impressive brick home, she took in its intricate landscaping and detailed craftsmanship, hoping its occupant would be as inviting. Eva served on several boards and was one of the city's most notable socialites. She'd heard about Divine Occasions when she attended the YFI fundraiser with a friend whose husband was a major donor of the organization.

Victoria had received a frantic call from Eva three days ago. Initially, Eva's daughter had been adamant about not having a sweet sixteen birthday party, but after months of pleading, the disgruntled teenager finally gave in. "We've wasted valuable time and my little angle's birthday is only a week away," Eva had told her.

Victoria didn't know if she could work this miracle, but with the type of money that Eva Masters was willing to spend, and the exposure and contacts this event would bring for Divine Occasions, she was going to do her best to pull it off. She stood in front of the mahogany double doors and rang the bell.

"Good morning," the housekeeper greeted her. "Mrs. Masters is expecting you, please come with me."

Victoria followed the woman into the light-filled living room where the lady of the house was waiting. Eva Masters was fiftyish, but it was apparent that she was fighting like hell not to look it. She was tall and ultra-thin, the latter being a coveted asset in her social circle. Victoria thought she looked like the society types she'd seen at the spa who spent thousands of dollars on seaweed wraps and other sorts of age-defying remedies, only to come out looking like middle-aged women who were barely holding on.

"Ms. Small, it's nice to meet you, I'm Eva Masters," the socialite stood and greeted, extending her frail hand.

"Please, call me Victoria."

"Then I insist you call me Eva."

They sat across from each other in identical French Provincial high-back chairs. "Victoria, I'm so glad you agreed to see me on such short notice. Celeste's birthday is only a week away and as you can imagine, I'm at my wits end. I hope you can help us."

Victoria nodded her head, whipping out her notes from their phone conversation. "I'll certainly do my best."

"Celeste is going to be a debutante, and I think this party will be the perfect precursor to her formal debut; a lovely sweet sixteen party," Eva mused. "Ah, here's my angle now."

When Victoria looked up she nearly fell out of her chair. Celeste was decked out in a long-sleeve black t-shirt that boasted a peace sign emblem, tattered low-rise jeans that were falling off her hip, and a pair of run-over shoes that looked two sizes too big; not at all the polo shirt and plaid skirt Victoria had expected.

"Dear, this is Ms. Small, the event planner I told you about," Eva said with a nervous smile.

"Hey," the teen said, plopping down onto the sofa. She smacked hard on her gum, blew a big bubble, then sucked it back into her mouth. "I'm Celeste." Her long chemically darkened tresses peeked through the sides of her black sculley. Victoria didn't want to stare, but she couldn't help it.

"Hi, Celeste. It's nice to meet you," Victoria nodded with smile.

Celeste looked at Victoria and leaned forward. "I don't know what my mother told you, but if I *have* to have this dumb party, I want something that's gonna rock, not some lame sugar and spice crap. That's totally WACK!"

Eva smiled uncomfortably, shifting in her seat while Victoria regained her sense of focus. "Okay, let's start by establishing a theme. What do you like to do for fun, Celeste?"

"I like clubbing and chillin' with my friends," she grinned, playing with the string hanging from her black wristband. Eva shifted in her seat again.

Clubbing! She probably has a stash of phony IDs and a bag of weed under her bed. Victoria thought.

"You like the beach too, don't you dear," Eva encouraged, looking for a more suitable answer to give.

Celeste rolled her eyes. "That's the only reason I'm agreeing to this party in the first place. I do the party and make you happy, and you give me a week in South Beach."

Eva shifted in her seat again, growing more uncomfortable by the minute.

Victoria shot Eva a look. She was appalled that the woman was playing *Let's Make a Deal* with her own child.

"And I like to paint," Celeste continued. "I'm really good with gouache, and I kick ass at video games too," she smiled, blowing another bubble. At that moment, the housekeeper entered with a tray of tea and cookies, just in time to save Eva from fidgeting a hole through her chair.

As Victoria studied the rebellious teen, she realized that Celeste reminded her a lot of herself at that age; creative and bold, marching to the beat of the drum playing inside her head. But as she drank her tea and listened to the rebel without a cause, she became aware of a big difference between this girl and her younger self—Celeste Masters had already learned the art of negotiating to get what she wanted.

"Well, that gives me something to work with," Victoria said, turning to Eva. "Since you'd like to host the party here, I'll need to have a look around your property."

"Certainly, this way," Eva motioned as they stood, glad for the reprieve from her daughter's rantings.

A half-hour later after touring the massive grounds out back and more conversation with the debutante in waiting, Victoria had come up with a theme that made both mother and daughter happy. Celeste was going to have a sweet sixteen beach party centered around the mosaic tile pool out back. They'd have to rent a tent and portable heaters to off-set the forty degree temperature outside, but that was okay because Eva said she would spare no expense to ensure the party's success.

When Celeste suggested having male servers wear Speedos and serve Jell-O shots to her guests at poolside, Victoria's eyes widened, and Eva got so upset she started hiccupping. "This party is gonna be killer!" Celeste smiled, smacking her gum.

"Celeste!" her mother finally hissed. "If you don't stop this nonsense your father and I will take away your weekend dress privileges. No more Woodstock clothes! Is that understood young lady?"

Another bargaining tool, Victoria thought. Seeing that Eva couldn't handle her daughter, Victoria knew she had to take control. "I'm not tryin' to go to jail over indecent exposure and under-age drinking. This is how the party's gonna roll," she told Celeste, "we'll hire co-ed servers, dress them in cargo shorts and t-shirts, and they'll serve non-alcoholic tropical drinks on surf board shaped trays," she concluded with authority.

Celeste thought about the proposition for a moment. "Okay, I can live with that."

You better, Victoria thought to herself.

Eva wrote Victoria a check and thanked her a hundred times before saying goodbye.

❧

H is Full Admission......

When Victoria returned home that afternoon, she saw the package on the door step when she turned into her driveway. She drove around back, parked her car, and rushed through the house to the front door. It was a package from Parker. She was so excited! She went to the kitchen, grabbed a pair of scissors and ripped into the box like a kid on Christmas morning. Inside, she found an Africa Project t-shirt, a letter, and a photo.

The sight of him took her breath away. Parker was standing in front of the clinic, wearing a pair of shorts and the ratty, Howard University t-shirt that she thought made him look so adorable. The top of his head was covered with black curls. Victoria turned the picture over and read the back.

Haven't had time to keep up my grooming regime, hence, the hair. Miss you, Need you, Love you......Parker.

His letter and his picture made her feel warm inside. When she thought about what she'd uttered the night before, she felt like an adulterer.

The next morning she decided to call Parker. Luckily, and to her delight, she was able to reach him. "I got the box yesterday. The letter was so sweet, and the picture...Parker, I love your hair."

"You do?" he smiled into the phone.

"Yes, I do. Just when I didn't think you could look any more handsome you proved me wrong."

"Baby, I miss you," Parker said, "life just isn't the same without you."

"I miss you too. But hey, we're half way through this. In three months you'll be back home, and I'll be in your arms."

"Ooohhh, baby, I can't wait," he breathed into the phone.

"Dr. Brightwood, the bags have been loaded onto the van and everyone is waiting. We need to leave now if we're to make it to the city by the scheduled time," a man with a thick accent called out in the background.

"Where're you going?" Victoria asked.

Parker hesitated "Um, Nairobi."

She heard the break in his voice. "Why're you going to Nairobi?"

He hesitated again, forcing himself to answer her question. "We've been given a two week break and I'm going on Safari in Nairobi."

There was silence on the line. *A two week break?* Then it dawned on her. "Parker, is this the reason why you wanted me to visit you for two weeks this month? I just thought you wanted to see me. I had no idea you were actually going to have a two- week break...and to go on a safari trip! Why didn't you tell me?

"Well, I..."

"I'll tell you why," Victoria said, cutting him off, "it's because you knew if I found out you had a two-week vacation, I'd want you to come home to be with me. But you kept it from me because you wanted to go on that damn Safari trip so you could go looking for masks and artwork for your collection," she fumed.

"Baby, I'm sorry. Yes, I wanted to use the break to go on the safari, but I also wanted you here with me too." Parker paused, knowing he had to push on with the selfish truth. "I didn't tell you because after we got into that terrible argument right before your office Christmas party, and then at my folks', I didn't want you being more angry with me because I knew you wouldn't understand why I'd choose to stay in Kenya, rather than come back home."

His full admission calmed her. Victoria appreciated that Parker never tried to bullshit his way out of situations the way Steven used to. He was completely forthcoming about any wrongs he may have committed. It was one of the things she'd grown to love about him. But what disturbed her was that his honesty was always marred with deception.

"I know it doesn't excuse the situation. I'm just telling you how I felt. I love you, Victoria."

"If you love me, why didn't you change your plans and come home to be with me?"

"I couldn't. I tried right after I got here. But this government program is so fucking bureaucratic. The paperwork was too much."

"Parker, this is crazy. Why do you keep things from me that affect our relationship? You always try to control things."

"Dr. Brightwood, we have to leave now," the man in the background called out again.

"I'll be right there," Parker said.

"Just go," she told him. "Enjoy your safari."

"Wait, baby, don't hang up angry. I'm sorry."

Victoria let out a loud sigh. She could hear the regret in Parker's voice. She was mad, but she didn't want to waste precious talk-time arguing.

"Forgive me?" he asked. "Baby, I do love you, and I'm sorry."

"I love you too."

As she lay in bed that night, Victoria felt like a hypocrite. She'd blasted Parker for keeping secrets that might hurt their relationship, knowing all the while that it was she who was keeping the biggest secret of all.

If I Wanted Jokes......

Victoria only had two days before Celeste Masters' sweet sixteen party, and she couldn't wait for it to be over. The stress of dealing with what seemed like a hundred calls a day from a nervous Eva Masters, her day-to-day workload at ViaTech, and battling her mixed emotions about Parker and Ted were all taking their toll. She was glad that she and Tyler were having dinner tonight because once again, she needed to consult with her touchstone. Juliet was working late, so she'd have Tyler all to herself.

"So, whatcha know good?" Tyler asked as the server sat his lime margarita and Victoria's Pellegrino on the table.

"I'm stressed like hell."

"I can see why. You're dating the ebony surgeon of the year, but you're falling in love with the white shadow," he laughed.

"It's not funny. If I wanted jokes I would've stayed home and watched the damn *Comedy Channel*."

Tyler held up his hands. "Calm down, I was just tryin' to make you laugh, to lighten the mood," he apologized. "Okay, no more jokes. I'm here to listen."

"I just don't know what to do. Parker's everything I've dreamed of in a man. But then there's Ted. And he's so sweet and caring, but he's…"

"White," Tyler finished her thoughts.

"Yeah," Victoria said slowly.

"You want me to shoot it to you straight?"

"No, I want you to blow sunshine up my ass! Of course I want you to give it to me straight," Victoria snapped in frustration. She took a deep breath to even out her tone. "Tyler, I'm sorry. I'm just at the end of my rope. I'm exhausted and confused. I miss Parker and I want to be true to him, but my feelings for Ted are growing so strong."

Tyler could see the struggle on Victoria's face. "First, I'll set the record straight by saying that although I have issues with him, I don't doubt that Parker loves you. He's smart, and professionally speaking, his shit's on point. The brothah's tight, I'll give him that. But I don't think he's right for you."

"Why not?"

"'Cause it's all about him. He's the kind of man who needs a woman who'll be submissive, which by the way, you ain't," Tyler said in between bites of his steak fajita. "In return, he'll provide stability and a good life because he's a responsible brothah."

"Then there's Prince Charming. He's a good guy and has serious bank. He's the type who's used to being in control and runnin' things, but there's a side of him that's willing to compromise. I see that in the work he's doing with Jermaine at YFI."

Victoria stopped eating. "I've got to make a decision. A part of me wants to be with Ted, but at the same time I can't cheat on Parker, I love him."

Tyler shook his head. "Let's be honest, the main reason you're not with Ted right now isn't as much about your love for Parker, as it is about the fact that Ted is white, and you know it. You even put it out there that the man was gay instead of admitting that he was feelin' you." Tyler leaned in close, giving Victoria a stern look. "You were straight up wrong for that. Don't you know you can ruin a man's reputation by sayin' some shit like that?

You're my girl, but that was fucked up."

"Tyler, you're supposed to be helping," Victoria said, embarrassed by the truth. "But you know how difficult it is for interracial couples."

"I'm not sayin' it's cut-n-dry."

"You're wrong about one thing. I do love Parker."

"You love that you and Parker make the perfect buppie couple, you love that he loves you, and you love that the brothah's sexin' you the way you like it."

Victoria raised her brows.

"Juliet told me about your shopping trip to get a lil' sumthin' sumthin' to hold you over till ole' boy gets back," Tyler teased, making them both laugh.

Victoria stabbed her fork at her partially eaten pollo asada. "When I see a brother with a white woman, the first thing I think is that he's a sell out, or that he suffers from low self-esteem. I know that's not always the case, but that's how I feel. Then I think, damn, what about preserving the black family…you know?"

"Why are you worried about what people will think?"

"You like Ted don't you?" she asked, avoiding his question. "I take it your vote is for him?"

"I didn't say that. I'm not voting for either one of them. I'm in your corner."

"After all that, that's the best you can come up with?" You're almost as bad as my mother."

"Then I'm in good company," Tyler smiled. "But on the real, even though I'm not convinced that Parker is right for you, I'm not sure that Ted is either. I'm just sayin' you have to do what makes you feel good, and don't worry about what other people might say. Roll the dice and see how they land."

Full Disclosure……

Ted was frustrated because Trudy was putting up a small fight to keep the house. Even though she didn't get half of what she'd wanted in the divorce settlement, she'd gotten more than he thought she was entitled to. She was determined to "stick it" to him one last time, going back and forth over who would retain ownership of their house in LA. Finally, Ted decided to let her have it because it was a small price to pay for his freedom.

Today was his forty-sixth birthday, his divorce had become final three days ago, and as he turned down the street headed to Victoria's house, he couldn't wait to celebrate both occasions with her by his side. He was excited because he knew the fact that she'd invited him to her home for the evening had to mean something.

Victoria busied herself with last minute details; lighting the candles she'd sprinkled around the room, cueing up the CDs in the stereo, and putting the champagne on ice. She hoped Ted would like what she'd planned for his birthday. During one of their dinner conversations, she'd learned that he had never been on a picnic. She couldn't believe he'd never experienced the joy of eating out of a wicker basket while sitting under the open sky, surrounded by nature. "That isn't natural. How did you get through childhood without picnics?" she'd asked.

It was too cold to have a picnic under the stars, so she decided to bring the outdoor experience inside. She'd pulled off a successful beach party last weekend in forty-degree weather, so she knew she could manage a picnic in the comfort of forced heat.

This is as close to natural vegetation as he's gonna get, Victoria thought to herself as she sat the vase of fresh cut flowers on the blanket she'd laid on the floor. With the exception of his jogs in the park, Ted wasn't an *outdoorsy* kind of guy. She smoothed out the ripples in the blanket and tossed down two large pillows for seating. She sat a picnic basket in the middle, next to the bottle of wine and small tray of fresh fruit and imported cheeses. She rearranged the two Villory & Boch place settings, Waterford crystal wine glasses, and antique silver flatware, giving an elegant touch to the picnic scene she'd created. After she finished, she set the small, neatly decorated cake she'd baked on the coffee table.

Victoria looked around the dimly-lit room and smiled. The three ficus trees she'd moved into the room lent an outdoor feel, and the star-shaped floor lights she'd placed in each corner cast the spectacular illusion of a star-filled night sky on the ceiling above.

The doorbell rang and her heart jumped. *Okay, just roll the dice and see where they land,* she reminded herself. "Happy Birthday," she greeted Ted at the door. He was wearing his signature dark denims, and even though the temperature was in the low-forties, he wore no coat, only a wool sweater.

She led him back to the den and down to the picnic blanket on the floor. He took off his shoes and counted his blessings, finding a comfortable position as they both settled against the pillows, enjoying the soft jazz serenading them in the background.

Ted held up his glass and made a toast. "V, you've made this the best birthday I've ever had. To a wonderful evening ahead."

They sipped wine and ate fruit and cheese from the same plate, giving each other subtle but lingering stares. Victoria moved the tray to the side and opened the picnic basket. "What do we have here?" Ted asked. "Smells delicious."

"Good old fashioned southern fried chicken, baked beans, and potato salad. Picnic staples on fine china," Victoria winked.

"Sounds good, and I'm starving."

She prepared Ted's plate and then her own. He lowered his head while she said grace, a habit he'd come to enjoy. After they finished their meal, Victoria lit a small candle she'd place in the middle of his birthday cake.

"Boy, you know you're old when there's not enough room on the cake for the number of candles that mark your age," Ted joked.

"It's a small cake. Besides, forty-six isn't old."

"No, but it's not thirty-three."

"It doesn't have to be."

"I'm glad you said that," he smiled.

Ted made a wish, which he now felt had a strong possibility of coming true, then blew out the candles. They ate birthday cake and toasted with champagne. He smiled when he heard the twinkling of ivory keys being romanced by the rhythm of a seductive saxophone. *In a Sentimental Mood* was his favorite song, and her's too. "They're playing our song," he said, holding out his hand.

He led as they danced. Gently, he drew Victoria into his arms, letting his hand rest on the small of her back. She wrapped her arms around his neck and nestled her head on his chest as he pulled her in even closer. His pelvis rubbed lightly against hers as he closed his eyes, nudging his growing erection into her. Not only did she not stop him, she enjoyed it, pressing her body further into his. His hands slid down to the roundness of her behind and rested there. He lowered his head, bringing his mouth toward hers.

In a flash, Victoria's mind turned to Parker. She tried to push him out, but she couldn't. Slowly, she pulled away.

"V, what's wrong?"

She withdrew from his embrace, realizing this had been a bad idea. "I think you better go," she said in a weak voice, trying not to look at him.

"Why?"

"Because this isn't right," she answered more firmly this time. "I'll walk you out." She turned and started to walk away, but Ted reached for her hand and held on.

"V, don't do this. Please don't do this."

Victoria couldn't look at him. She couldn't look into his eyes for fear that hers would betray the hard stance she'd just taken.

"Don't pretend as if nothing just happened, or that nothing's been happening between us since the first day we met," Ted urged, finally coming forth with the truth.

"I'm in a relationship, you know that. I can't do this."

Fuck Parker, Ted wanted to shout. But instead, he continued to hold on to her hand. "Why? Because he's the safe bet and I'm not?"

Victoria finally raised her eyes to meet his. She knew she had to hold his stare. It was hard, but she did it. He searched her eyes, but she gave him nothing. This was it. The moment for full disclosure had come. Ted's heart was beating fast. "I love you," he said.

His words rang so loudly in Victoria's ears, she could no longer hear the music playing in the background. Ted put his hand around her waist and drew her back into his arms. "I love everything about you. I've been waiting, just wanting to be with you. V, I need you in my life."

Ted's voice was intense and low, and his breath smelled of butter cream frosting and champagne—a tantalizing effect on Victoria's senses. Her eyes focused on the ruddy pinkness of his lips and she wondered if they felt as soft as they looked. This time she had to look away. "Parker and I are in love, and you and I...we can only be friends. That's the way it has to be."

"No it doesn't."

"Ted, please just accept it."

"You can't even look at me," he said, searching her face. "V, look me in the eye and tell me that you don't feel something for me?" Then he spoke slowly, letting the full impact of his words settle over both of them. "Tell me you don't love me," he demanded.

Victoria couldn't continue to deny the truth. She loved the man standing before her. He'd seeped his way into her heart like a slow and steady pinhole leak. But something held her back.

"Answer me, V," Ted demanded.

"But, Parker and I..."

"Dammit, V," he hissed in frustration. "Let's just be honest here. Do you have a problem with the color of my skin?

Victoria pulled away from him and this time he let her hand go. "You don't have a clue," she glared at him. "No, I don't have a problem with your color. After all the shit I've been through with skin color, that's the least of my worries. I have a problem with your race. There's a difference!"

Ted shook his head in disbelief. "We're the same race, the human race!" he yelled.

Victoria let out a cenacle laugh. "What a trip."

"You think it's funny?" he asked, starting to grow angry.

"No, I don't think it's funny. It's just idealistic and almost ridiculous. Is that some bullshit you heard on TV, or read in a magazine, because it's not reality and you know it. The reality is this…you're a white man, I'm a black woman, and in our society the two still don't mix."

"I can't believe you would let race be an issue between us."

"Race matters. Isn't that why you had Patricia fired?"

Ted looked away.

Victoria put her hands on her hips. "What? You didn't think I would find out? ViaTech is a rumor haven and eventually all things come out in the wash. She called me a nigger and you fired her for it."

Ted shook his head, trying to explain, but Victoria cut him off.

"Well, I've got news for you. Being black is a twenty-four-seven, three hundred sixty-five days a year gig, with no time off. When I'm discriminated against or mistreated because of how I look, I can't just make someone go away and pretend that it solves the problem. I have to deal with it."

Ted sucked in his breath, then exhaled deeply. "Patricia didn't call you," he hesitated, "the *N* word, that's just a nasty rumor. But yes, she did make a racially insensitive remark that angered me."

Victoria rolled her eyes, but Ted continued.

"And to answer your question, no, I didn't fire her because of her comment. I fired her because she was a terrible employee. She served her purpose in New York and once her work was complete, the company no longer had use for her services," he said, mouthing almost the same official sounding response Denise had been given when she inquired about the situation months ago.

"I believe you would've eventually had Patricia fired, but the bottom line is that race made you mad enough to do it much sooner. Race dominates everything. People think *race* before they think color, gender, or anything else."

"Since when do you give a damn about what anyone thinks?" Ted asked, incredulous. "You're one of the most independent, strong-willed people I know. Why are you letting this stand in the way of us being together?"

Victoria stepped back even further away from him. "You really don't know me do you? I'll give it to Patricia. She was right. I'm a fake. I pretend that I don't care, but I do," she paused, "I didn't make the rules. Besides, I have a man who loves me. A *black* man who loves me!"

Ted walked up to her and stood within an inch of her face. "This is bull-shit and you know it! Tell me you don't love me. Look me in the eye and say it," he demanded.

Victoria could feel the heat bouncing off his body. She began to trem-ble with anticipation and fear. The cheerful birthday surprise she'd planned had turned into a tidal wave of an evening. She felt all the energy drain from her body.

When Ted looked into her eyes, he saw her turmoil but he pushed on because it was now or never. "Say it, dammit!" he demanded, "tell me you don't love me and I'll walk away. I'll leave you alone and never bother you again."

"I...I need time," was all Victoria could manage to squeak out. She was trembling from head to toe.

Ted pulled her into his arms and held her against his chest. "Shh," he whispered, stroking her hair. "I'm sorry, V. I'm not going anywhere. I won't pressure you. I'll give you time."

Chapter Nineteen

H ow Clever......

The last three months of Victoria's life had passed by quickly. March had sped into June without much fanfare, but she knew the next two weeks would bring significant changes. Parker was coming home in two days, she'd be at the SuperNet convention the following week, and finally, her resignation from ViaTech would be official.

Although Victoria had mixed emotions about the future of their relationship, she was looking forward to Parker's return. It had been six months since she'd seen him, and she missed him. His emails had crept in like time standing still, and when he did have time to pen a letter, it took weeks for it to reach her. But he tried to call once a week, even if they only talked for a few minutes.

On this side of the world, Ted had been true to his word. He hadn't pressured her since the night of his birthday. They still saw each other whenever they could, went for long jogs in the park, and shared frequent lunches and dinners. All the while he was respectful; careful to uphold their unspoken rule of not hugging for too long, sitting too close, or initiating anything that might resemble romantic intimacy. Victoria was both grateful and disappointed by his actions.

It was a hot and muggy Saturday evening in south Florida, and Victoria was standing in front of the mirror in her hotel room, getting dressed for dinner. She was at the end of her visit with Debbie and Rob. She'd flown down earlier that week, just in time for the arrival of her friend's first born. Debbie gave birth to a fat, red-cheeked little boy. The pregnancy had been a breeze, but the twenty-seven hour labor had been hell. Finally, cesarean section brought little Brandon Robert Long into the world. Victoria found it hard to tear herself away from her godson and made Debbie promise to send pictures every month.

As she slipped into her linen sheath dress and spritzed a small puff of Cartier behind each ear, Victoria thought about the night ahead. Ted was conveniently in Miami for a meeting at their ViaTech office and had asked her if she would have dinner with him. Even though she found the last minute meeting highly suspicious, she'd said yes. *How clever,* she thought. She had to admit that Parker had been right. Ted had been trying to get close to her all along. He knew what he wanted, and like anything else he desired to have, he waited until the time was right and went after it.

Later that evening, Victoria and Ted enjoyed a delicious meal together at an outdoor café. It was almost midnight before he escorted her back to her room at the Mandarin Oriental Hotel. He didn't have far to go because amazingly, he'd managed to get a room there too—on the same floor. "It's ironic that we're both in Miami at the same time, staying at the same hotel, on the same floor," Victoria said, giving Ted a knowing look as they walked through the hotel lobby.

"Yes, isn't that something," he smiled. "How about joining me for a nightcap?"

Minutes later, Victoria found herself in his suite, sitting on the sofa by the balcony. She tried to relax, giving him a nervous smile as he sat down beside her—no drinks in hand. "I thought you invited me over for a nightcap," she said, even though she knew that wasn't the real reason he'd asked her to come to his room.

"V, this is silly. We've been tip-toeing around our feelings for months. You know that I love you, and I know you love me too. You haven't said it yet, but I know you do. And it doesn't matter about race, or color, or anything else. When it comes down to it, it's just you and me that matters."

"You think it's that simple?"

"No, but if you're going through it with the right person it's a hell of a lot easier."

Victoria touched her palm to his face. She could feel the fine hairs along his jaw line, which meant he'd need to shave in the morning. "What am I going to do with you?"

"I can think of a few things," he winked.

"Parker's coming home on Monday."

Ted moved back, letting her hand fall from his face. "I know. What are you going to do?" he asked, looking down at the six inches of space that separated them.

"Have a long talk with him. I'm going to tell him about what's been happening between us. Beyond that, I honestly don't know."

They sat in silence. Victoria looked at the clock. It was late, and she was growing tired. "I'm flying out in the morning, so I should get going."

"Don't go. Stay with me tonight."

Victoria looked away. "Ted, you know I can't do that."

"I promise nothing will happen. I just want to sleep next to you and wake up with you in the morning, that's all."

Victoria knew this might be her last opportunity to be this close with Ted. Between Parker's return in a few days and her resignation in a few weeks, their future contact was uncertain. She knew she shouldn't do it, but her feelings for him made her say yes. She decided that if she could sleep in the same bed with Parker and abstain, she'd certainly be safe with Ted.

Laying in the darkness, he held her close, breathing in the sweet scent of her perfumed skin. Her body was warm and soft next to his. He tried with all his might, but he couldn't stop the erection growing in the crotch of his pants. He was sure she felt it because she was lying spooned next to him. But she didn't move. She just lay there—perfectly still, as though she were a statue. "I love you, V," he whispered into her ear.

Victoria pretended she was asleep. But she heard him, and it made her heart beat a mile a minute.

I Wish I Had......

It was seven o'clock on Monday morning, and Victoria was waiting nervously at the baggage claim area. She'd taken the day off so she could be with Parker on his first day back home. She watched as passengers began to trickle in.

Yesterday she'd returned from her Miami trip, and today she was more confused than ever. She'd slept in the same bed with Ted, and although nothing sexual had happened during the course of the night, she knew that they'd entered into a new level of intimacy that rivaled anything she could have experienced with him physically. It wasn't her body that he had penetrated, it was her heart. She loved Parker, but she loved Ted too, and she wished like hell she wasn't stuck in the middle.

Her knees grew weak as Parker walked toward her with outstretched arms. He looked even more handsome than she remembered. His dimples were perfect, his smile was bright, and his sexy aura suffocated the air around her. He was wearing the khaki pants and polo shirt she'd sent him two months ago for his thirty-eighth birthday. He looked like he'd lost a few pounds, but his muscles still reflected those of a man in great physical shape. And his hair! His hair was a mop of heavy black curls.

He embraced her, lifting her off her feet and spinning her around, legs flying in the air. His mouth couldn't stop kissing her lips as she ran her fingers through the soft pile of silky cotton atop his head.

"Baby, I missed you so much," Parker smiled, taking in Victoria's dark Capri pants and yellow halter top. He wanted to devour her on the spot. He knew he'd made the right decision by purchasing the two-carat diamond engagement ring before he left six months ago. And tonight, no matter how jet lagged he felt, he planned to make passionate love to Victoria, get down on one knee to propose, and wake up the next morning beside his new fiancé.

On the ride home they went by the bank, dropped off ten rolls of film at the photo shop, then made a quick stop by the hospital to let them know that he'd arrived back in town. Parker picked up several folders of paperwork to take home. Even though they'd given him a two-week hiatus upon his return, he wanted to get a jump on the work ahead.

After they arrived at his place, Parker and Victoria finished unloading his luggage and settled into his condo. "Do you want anything?" she asked, walking over to the refrigerator.

"What do I have?" Parker grinned, following her into the kitchen. He'd left it empty before his departure six months ago.

When Victoria opened the refrigerator he saw that it was fully stocked. She'd gone shopping for him last night. "I'm so lucky. You think of everything." Parker wrapped his arms around Victoria's waist and pulled her into him. He planted small, sweet kisses on her lips as he pressed her up against the counter near the sink. "*Mmmmm*, let's make love right here," he whispered, his familiar breath cascading over her mouth. "Let me show you how much I missed you," he panted, gently sucking her earlobe.

He reached behind her neck, untied her halter, and began giving her breasts the same attention he'd given her lobe. His tongue assailed their targets, sending darts of pleasure through her body. Victoria felt the throbbing between her legs as she reacquainted herself with Parker's heat, giving in to how much she'd missed his touch. He pulled off his shirt in one quick motion, rubbing his hardness against her leg. She threw her head back and closed her eyes, trying to put Ted out of her mind. She'd awoken next to him yesterday morning, and now she was dry humping her boyfriend on the edge of the kitchen counter.

"Parker, I can't," Victoria said slowly, trying to release herself from his embrace.

Parker leaned forward and pulled her back into him, "Okay, we can go to the bedroom," he breathed heavily, already unzipping his khakis, ready for action.

She gently pushed him away and pulled the front of her top up to cover herself. "I'm on my period."

After she stocked Parker's refrigerator last night, Victoria had driven home with rumblings in her stomach and mixed emotions in her heart. She could still feel Ted's breath on her neck and the weighted guilt that clung with it. She knew that after being away for six months, regardless of how tired Parker would be, he would want to make love. When she returned home her stomach was queasy just thinking about her predicament. *Parker's my boyfriend. I shouldn't feel guilty about making love to him,* she'd told herself.

But when she took off her clothes to soak in the bubble bath she'd drawn, she discovered that it wasn't just her nerves that had her stomach twisted in knots, she'd just started her period. She wasn't due for another couple of days, but her stress level apparently dictated changes. She was thankful that Mother Nature had stepped up and intervened. This, at the very least, would buy her more time.

Victoria tried to avoid Parker's eyes. "My stomach is cramping. I started my period last night."

"Oh, I thought you weren't due for a few more days," he said, like he'd been keeping track of her cycle in his PDA!

Victoria paused with surprise. She knew that being a physician, Parker was well aware of how to chart her twenty-eight day menstrual cycle, but that he'd actually been doing it was a shock to her. She was going to question him about his mastery of her reproductive system's schedule, but he looked disappointed so she let it go. He wanted her badly, she could tell because he cupped his hand firmly at the crotch of her pants, continuing to gently massage her between her legs. A crippling mixture of guilt and lust settled around her.

"Do you want some Motrin?" Parker asked in his professional doctor voice."

"Yeah, thanks."

After Victoria took the medicine, she and Parker laid across his bed and cuddled. She ran her fingers through his hair, enjoying the warmth of his body next to hers. "I love your hair."

"You do?"

"Yes, it gives you a whole new look."

"I thought you liked me bald," Parker said, kissing her on the neck.

"I do. But I like it this way too. Keep it like this for a while. It's sexy," Victoria smiled.

He stroked her hair, pulling her down on top of him. "I know I've made some really selfish mistakes. But I've had time to think about a lot of things over the last six months, and you know what I discovered?"

"What?"

"That without a doubt, you're the best thing that's ever happened to me, and being apart for the last six months made me realize that even more. Baby, I want us to take the next step," he said, looking deep into Victoria's eyes.

She looked back at him. "What do you mean?"

"We love each other. I don't want anyone else, and hopefully you don't either," he paused, "I think we should take our relationship to the next level."

Victoria spoke slowly. "What exactly are you saying, Parker?"

"I want to marry you."

He waited. There was silence. She didn't say a word, she just stared into his eyes as if she wanted to tell him something, but couldn't.

Parker searched her face and saw something that he couldn't place. "Baby, I know there are a lot of things going through your mind right now, and I know you're still a little pissed at me, but we love each other and we're good together. You don't have to give me an answer right now. We'll work things out," he said.

Parker was exhausted from his travels and the disappointment of knowing that Victoria had doubts. Victoria was exhausted from her travels and the task of avoiding sex with the two men she loved. Their combined pressure was enough that they soon found themselves drifting off to sleep.

Several hours later, Victoria awoke to the sound of running water. Parker was in the shower. At the foot of the bed was a vibrant, red-colored traditional wrapper skirt, and beside it was a small gold box. She opened it to find a beautiful beaded necklace inside, with a note that read, *With All My Love, Parker.*

The water stopped running and Victoria sat up on the bed, holding the necklace in her hand. "Parker, this is beautiful," she yelled toward the bathroom.

"You like them?" he yelled back.

Victoria was smiling from ear to ear as Parker walked into the bedroom, still damp in his nakedness. He was a sight to behold. *Damn, he looks good!* she thought. She blocked out the slight cramping in her stomach and began calculating what would be the better move; taking him back into the bathroom and making love to him in the shower so it wouldn't be so messy, or dropping to her knees and taking him deep into her mouth? She was weighing her options until he got closer. Suddenly her smile went flat.

"I have another surprise for you, and I hope you'll accept it as enthusiastically," Parker said, thinking about the big, sparkling ring in the little blue box tucked away in his closet. He sat down next to Victoria on the bed. "And in three to four days, if memory serves me correctly," he smiled, reaching down and rubbing Victoria between her legs, "I'll give you a really big gift that I'm sure you'll like." He kissed her on her lips. When she didn't kiss him back, he studied her face and saw her frown. "Baby, what's wrong?"

"You shaved off all your hair."

Parker ran his hand over his freshly shaven scalp. "Yeah," he grinned. "Why?"

"I don't know. I just like it better this way," he shrugged playfully, grabbing Victoria around the waist and pulling her close to him.

"But I told you I liked your hair the way it was. I thought it made you look adorable."

"You also said that my bald head was sexy, remember?" He tried to nuzzle her neck, but she moved away.

"I asked you not to cut it, but you didn't even listen to me." Her voice was getting louder.

"It'll grow back in a couple of weeks. It's no big deal."

"It's a big deal to me. You made another decision without even talking to me."

"It's *my* hair!" Parker shot back, staring at Victoria. He got up, opened his dresser drawer, slipped on a pair of boxers, and braced himself for the argument that was sure to come. He returned to the bed and sat down next to her.

Victoria stood up. "You're right. It is your hair. But this really isn't about hair. Sometimes you have to think of others before you do things. But it seems that you only care about yourself."

"Baby, calm down. You're just emotional because you're on your period."

Victoria drew in a deep breath and narrowed her eyes. "Don't patronize me. I know exactly what I'm saying and it has nothing to do with my period. This is about your need to control and inability to compromise," she said, raising her voice.

"Okay, you want to talk about compromise, let's talk about it. Let's talk about someone asking *you* to do something and *you* disregarding it completely."

"What're you talking about?"

"Ted. That's what I'm talking about. You've been spending time with him, even though I asked you not too," Parker said, raising his voice to match hers. He was standing now too.

"You never asked me not to spend time with him."

"But you know I don't like him. He's been tryin' to get in your pants from day one. I told you that. But did you keep him at a distance? No! You've been having late night dinners with him."

"How do you know what I've done with him?" Victoria asked with boldness, feeling the pit of her stomach twist with discomfort.

"Phil and Gayle saw you two at Pano's and Paul's one night. He told me when he emailed me last month."

"If he saw us, why didn't he come over and say hello? We were just having dinner," she said calmly, as though it were nothing.

"Are you fucking him?"

"What!"

"Don't play dumb with me." Parker let his words trickle out with growing anger. "Are you *fucking* him! Is that why you won't make love to me? Are you really on your period? Or is that just an excuse because you've been with him?"

Victoria couldn't believe that Parker was speaking to her this way. Then it suddenly became clear why he kept rubbing the seat of her pants. Now her full anger came boiling to the surface. "You have so little faith in me that you think I would cheat on you?"

"Just answer the question."

Victoria stood with her hands on her hips, her chest heaving up and down. "I haven't *fucked* anyone except you in almost two years. So to answer your question…NO! But now I wish I had."

Parker took a deep breath, shaking his head. "Victoria, you just got back in town yesterday from your trip to Miami. I just got back this morning after a hell of a long flight. We're both tired and we're both angry. This isn't the time to have this conversation because we're saying things that I know we'll regret later. We need to talk about this after we both calm down"

"You're right. I'll give you some alone time," she hissed, storming out of the room.

Parker followed behind her. "Baby, don't go. I'm sorry for what I said. Stay here tonight so we can talk."

Victoria ignored his plea, grabbed her handbag and slammed the door behind her.

That night she thought long and hard about her relationship with Parker. He'd made another decision to do something without talking to her. *Is that what married life with him will be like?* she asked herself.

She thought about what he'd done. He knew she didn't want him to cut his hair, so he'd waited until she was asleep to do it. The thought of him waiting until she drifted off, getting up, plugging in his clippers and shaving off the soft curls she'd briefly enjoyed running her fingers through, made her livid. But worse than that was the nagging question that rolled around in her head; she didn't know if Parker had intentionally waited until she was asleep to do it, or if he'd just taken it upon himself to cut his hair simply because he wanted to. Either way, she knew his decision had been made with no regard for her wishes.

Live As A Hypocrite......

The next morning Victoria called Denise. "I'm not coming in today," she said, fatigue clouding her voice.

"Girlfriend, what's wrong? Did you get a little too much of a good thing last night?" Denise giggled. "Oh, excuse me, I mean a lot of a *big* thing."

"No, just the opposite," Victoria sighed, explaining yesterday's events to her friend. "That wasn't exactly a good homecoming, was it?" she finally said.

Denise shook her head. "No," she responded, but didn't make further comment, although the words on the tip of he tongue were, *I told you he was selfish.* Instead, she focused on the business of the day. "So you're not coming in, huh?"

"No. I need a mental health day."

"Girlfriend, are you sure you're okay? I can come over after work?"

"No, I'll be fine. I just need to clear my head."

"All right, I'll reschedule your afternoon appointments."

"Thanks," Victoria said, breathing a sigh of relief before hanging up the phone.

Next on her docket was a call to Ted. He'd left for Chicago this morning and wouldn't be back in town until the end of the week. She'd told him that she would let him know how her discussion with Parker had gone. She picked up the phone and began to dial, but then put it back down. She didn't know what she was going to tell him because things were still up in the air. But even though she couldn't bring herself to talk to Ted, she knew she needed to face Parker. She had to tell him that her feelings for Ted ran far beyond friendship. If he chose to end their relationship, which she knew was understandable, then she would deal with the consequences, but he needed to know the truth.

The Java Café was packed with people. Victoria stopped in to pick up Parker's favorite blueberry muffins, and two cups of coffee. "Hey Don," she waved to the proprietor as he walked back toward the employee-only entrance.

"Oh, hi Victoria. You're looking lovely as usual," Don smiled.

"Thank you. Parker's back. I picked him up from the airport yesterday. He's at home resting so I thought I'd get us a late morning snack."

"Uh...well...um...that's good," Don said as he busied himself by opening the door for the girl coming out on the other side. "It's busy in here today. Gotta run," he said as he waved goodbye, then disappeared through the door.

Victoria paid for the food and headed out the door toward Parker's building. After his long flight and their heated argument, she knew he was probably exhausted. If he was still in bed, she would set their breakfast on the table and wait. If he was up, she would try to be calm in their conversation. But more than anything, she would tell him the truth because she was determined not to live as a hypocrite for another day.

Chapter Twenty

I Can Explain......

From the moment Victoria opened the door with her spare key, she knew that something was wrong. Slowly, she walked into Parker's condo and surveyed the living room. Her heart sank. Sitting on the coffee table were two wine glasses; one empty, the other half-full and stained with lipstick around the rim. She walked over to the side of the couch and looked down at the cute pair of strappy Manolo's tossed about, as if their owner had hurriedly kicked them off. Her ears strained, listening to the soft, seductive lyrics of Will Downing's voice trickling over Parker's stereo system.

Victoria gripped the bag of pastries and cardboard coffee tray holder as she started her descent toward inevitable destruction. She knew what awaited her once she reached the end of the hallway and made a right toward Parker's bedroom. She could turn around and walk away, or she could confront what was sure to be an ugly scene. Her legs pushed her forward.

She found him sitting on the edge of the bed in his boxers, leaned forward, elbows on his knees, head resting in the palm of his hands. The bed was in total disarray. The sheets hung off the sides and the comforter was jumbled; the aftermath of a wild tryst. Victoria stared in disbelief at the skirt and pink blouse lying on the floor. A tattered condom wrapper lay at the foot of the bed. She stood in the middle of the door unnoticed, taking in the details of the room, playing out in her mind what had happened prior to her arrival. It wasn't until the petite woman dressed in a lacy bra and panty came out from the bathroom and let out a small, startled scream, that Parker realized Victoria was there. He jumped to his feet.

His voice was filled with panic. "Oh shit! Baby, I can explain."

Emotion overcame Victoria, causing her legs to give way under her. She fell to the floor like dead weight as Parker rushed over to her. The hot coffee spilled on her leg, but she didn't cry out. She endured the pain to her leg, which was overshadowed by the pain that was hammering her heart. She felt dizzy. So dizzy she became nauseous. "I'm gonna be sick," she said, bending her head forward.

Parker reached for the bag on the floor beside her and brought it to her mouth. Before she could heave again, he quickly scooped her up in his arms as if she were a small child, and carried her to the bathroom down the hall. Victoria sat crouched on her knees, head over the toilet, arms hugging the edge of the bowl, heaving awful tasting bile from the pit of her stomach. Parker knelt over her, rubbing her shoulder, whispering apologetic words she couldn't hear.

When she finished, he handed her a cold cloth. It took Victoria a few minutes to recover, and when she did she looked at him with disgust. "Get away from me," she hissed in a low and angry voice as she pushed past him and out into the hall. She looked straight ahead and saw the woman again. She was fully dressed now, standing in the entrance of Parker's bedroom door with a smile on her face.

"You!" Victoria yelled as she stared into the face of the woman Parker had been with the night they first met.

Parker rushed into the hall to find Sheila standing there with a grin on her face. He looked at Victoria, "Baby, I'm so sorry. I can explain. This didn't mean anything. *A-N-Y-T-H-I-N-G*," he pleaded.

Sheila craned her neck so hard it nearly popped. "Oh, so this was just a mercy fuck? You didn't act that way when you were on top of me."

Victoria steadied herself against the wall, looking from Parker to Sheila. It seemed like a dream but she knew it was real, the pounding in her head told her so.

"What's it gonna be Parker. Her or me?" Sheila asked, tossing her hair back as she threw Victoria a nasty look.

Parker glared in her direction. "Don't try to make this seem like something it's not. This was a one time thing and you know it. It was a mistake. Now get out of my house!"

"After what I just laid on you, I know you're not tryin' to put me out?" Sheila hissed.

"I told you, get out of my house!" he growled.

Sheila rolled her eyes. "Fine!" she shouted. She walked out to the living room, gathered her things, then slammed the door so hard it rattled the hinges.

It Just Kind Of Happened...

Several minutes later, which seemed like hours, Victoria sat on Parker's sofa taking small sips of water. She barely remembered washing her face again and walking out to the living room. Parker had quickly thrown on a pair of jeans and a t-shirt. He sat on the opposite end of the sectional sofa, holding his head low. Little by little Victoria started to regain her senses. She had flashbacks of Steven, and that terrible night that seemed to be replaying itself in the present, but this time things were different. This was a different man. She was a different woman. And sitting there on Parker's Italian leather sectional, she decided to handle this situation differently. Running from the truth, from hurtful situations, and from facing her own shortcomings had been her trademark and her downfall. This time she wouldn't run. She was going to deal with this head on. "You dirty sonofabitch," she said with venom.

"Baby, I can explain..."

"You accused me of screwing around, but then I walk in here to find that you've been fucking someone...Sheila of all people? How long has this been going on, Parker? Huh? Were you fucking her when she rubbed all over you at the Halloween party last year?"

"No," he said in a pitiful voice. "This was the first time, I swear. It just kind of happened."

"Bullshit. Things like this don't *just kind of happen*. A woman ends up in your bed, fucking you on your sheets? Please, that doesn't *just kind of happen*." Victoria was furious. "How dare you question my virtue. Your ass hasn't been in town for more than twenty-four hours and you're already searching for new pussy!"

"Baby, it's not like that. I wasn't searching for anything. I was mad at you and I…"

"So you fucked Sheila because you were mad at me? If I fucked some-one every time I was mad at you my legs would stay open. You're gonna have to do better than that."

"It was a *terrible* mistake. I'm so sorry. I was mad because I wanted you, I needed you, but you left. You weren't here."

"So you fucked Sheila in my absence?"

Parker shook his head. "Please stop saying that."

"Don't you dare tell me what not to say!" Victoria finally screamed.

"I'm sorry. But I just want to explain. Please let me explain."

Victoria crossed her arms and stared at him in controlled silence. Parker's smooth veneer had chipped away like a cheap paint job as his words tumbled out. "I was hungry, so I went to the Java Café to get some coffee and muffins. Sheila was there and…"

"You have a refrigerator full of food. I saw to that. Why didn't you take your ass into your kitchen to get something to eat? I'll tell you why, because you were too busy on the prowl."

"No, you're wrong. That's not how it happened. I felt bad because of our fight yesterday. And when I told you that I wanted to marry you, you didn't say anything. Then I didn't hear from you last night, and I was lone-ly without you. Anyway, I felt really miserable, so I went down to the coffee shop and Sheila was there."

Victoria twisted her face when she heard Parker say the woman's name, but he continued. "We started talking and I told her about my work in Kenya. She was really interested, and she was being so nice to me. And well, we ended up back here, and it just kind of happened."

"So you fucked her because she was nice to you and she listened to your safari stories?"

"No. Well, yes…I mean…I was weak," Parker stammered. "I needed someone to talk to, to be with. And we'd had that fight, and you just walked away from me, and…"

"So it's my fault? Because I wasn't nice to you?" Victoria glared at him. "Who the hell do you think listened to you go on and on about the Africa Project through phone calls and emails for the last six months? Who do you think baked your favorite brownies and shipped them to you every month? And who picked up your ungrateful ass from the airport yesterday and lis-tened to you talk about yourself for two consecutive hours?"

"Baby, I didn't mean it like that. I was talking about how I felt after you left. I know you're good to me. You're the best thing in my life."

"*I am?*"

"Victoria…baby, you know I love you."

Victoria threw her arms in the air. "Oh, I'm sorry. I didn't know that when your man goes out and fucks another woman that it's a sign of his undying love. That slipped right by me. I'm so silly!"

"Baby, I do love you. What happened with Sheila is totally separate from us. It was a terrible mistake at a weak moment. It didn't mean anything."

"What kind of person can go around fucking women with reckless abandon, and it not mean anything?"

"It only happened this once."

"So, did you fuck your female colleagues on the Africa Project? Or did you prefer those beautiful Kenyan women? I'm sure they were more than willing to give it up to the handsome American doctor with the big dick."

"No, it's not like that. I only love you, and I only want you. I was hurt and the thought of you being with another man pissed me off."

"*What?*"

"The thought of you sleeping with Ted…I just couldn't take it."

"I told you, I haven't slept with anyone except you. I can't believe you're even bringing Ted into this discussion. What you did has nothing to do with him."

"But you said you wished you'd slept with him, and I couldn't bear the thought of it."

Victoria looked at Parker dead on. "I'll be honest with you. I've developed deep feelings for Ted that go far beyond platonic friendship. And I've had plenty of opportunities to cross the line with him. But I didn't because I wanted to be faithful to you. I loved you and I thought you loved me too."

The room fell silent.

"Do you love him?" Parker asked, holding his breath.

Victoria nodded. "Yes…I do."

Parker let out a heavy sigh. "I knew this shit would happen. I knew that the minute I left, that that mothafucker would try to ease his way in. That sneaky sonofabitch!"

"He's not the issue we're dealing with. I'm not even thinking about Ted right now. I'm thinking about what just happened here," Victoria fumed.

"But Baby, don't you see? That's why I felt so bad. Because I knew I was losing you. Otherwise you would've never left me like you did yesterday, and then you didn't even call me last night or pick up the phone when I called you. I knew something was wrong. That's why I felt so low today, and all of this happened."

"Let me get this straight. You can't bear the thought of me with another man, so you go out and fuck another woman? That's your strategy?"

"No!" Parker yelled.

"Don't you dare raise your voice at me!" Victoria yelled back.

"Baby, I keep telling you, it wasn't like that. I didn't plan this. I was at a weak point and it just kind of…"

"*Happened!*" Victoria finished his sentence. "Yeah, you told me that already. You must think I'm stupid," she huffed.

"Listen, I know it's hard to understand because it's hard for me to explain, but baby, it was a mistake and I wish I could take it all back," Parker pleaded as he stood to his feet and came toward her.

Victoria rose from her seat, extending her arm out in front of her. "I've never been in a fight in my entire life. But so help me, if you come one step closer, I'll kick your ass right here in this living room," she threatened.

Parker knew she meant every word coming from her lips so he backed off.

Victoria sank back down into the sofa, trying to gather herself. They sat on opposite ends staring at each other. "I've got to get out of here," she finally said, then stood to leave.

Parker pleaded with her again. "Please don't go. Please…"

"It's over, Parker."

"Baby, I know things look bad right now, but we can work through this. I'll do anything you want. I'll fix this, but please don't leave."

Victoria looked into Parker's eyes. "You know what I went through with Steven. You know what he did to me, how he hurt me. How could you do this, Parker? It was so hard for me to learn to trust again. And now you treat me like this? You make me sick," she said, spitting out her words.

Parker's face grew desperate. He wanted to reach for her but he knew it wouldn't be a good idea considering the threat she'd already made. "Baby, do you still love me?"

Victoria stopped just short of the door and turned around to face him. They stood across from each other, both looking like they'd just survived a train wreck. "Yes Parker, I love you. But I at this moment, I can't stand you."

*A*re You Threatening Me?……

Ted made it to the end of the week by sheer will. It was late Friday afternoon and he'd just left the airport, headed over to see Victoria. She'd called him the day of her traumatic break-up with Parker. When he learned of the betrayal, he was furious. He didn't want to see Victoria hurt in any way, and especially not at the hands of Parker Brightwood. "I can cancel my last two meetings and come back a day early. You shouldn't be alone," Ted had told her.

"Please don't do that," Victoria croaked, still hoarse from tears. "I'd feel even worse than I already do if my drama interfered with your priorities."

"But you are my priority."

She tried to bring a smile to her voice. "That's sweet, but I'll be okay, really. You need to take care of the problems in the Chicago office. Promise me you'll do that?" she asked. Finally, he agreed.

Ted stopped by La Madeleine, one of Victoria's favorite restaurants, then headed to her house. He rang the doorbell and waited a few minutes before she answered. She was dressed in a pair of shorts and a cut-off t-shirt. She raked her fingers through her hair, which looked as though it hadn't been combed. Looking at her sleep-deprived eyes, Ted knew she was in bad shape. He took the bags back to the kitchen, then returned to the den and sat beside her on the sofa.

Victoria was appreciative that Ted hadn't commented on her appearance. She knew she looked rough, and that was putting it mildly. She'd hoped to have herself together by now; certainly before he came over. But her mood had been gloomy all week. "I just don't feel like doing anything," she'd told Tyler when he'd come by earlier that day.

She looked at Ted. "I know I look awful. I've been lying around the house trying to get my head together. I guess I'm not there yet," she said.

"You always look beautiful to me." He stood and reached for Victoria's hand, bringing her to her feet. "Why don't you go upstairs and relax with a nice hot bath while I take care of dinner."

Victoria soaked in a soothing bath of lavender and jasmine sea salts, washed her hair in herbal shampoo, and slipped into a delicate cotton sundress. She returned downstairs feeling more refreshed than she had in days. "What're you cooking in my kitchen?" she teased playfully. "Something smells *delish*."

"What am I heating up in your microwave is more the question." Ted had removed his coat and tie. His crisp white shirt was unbuttoned at the neck and his sleeves were rolled up to his forearms. "You look lovely," he smiled as she entered the room.

Victoria looked down at her blue cotton sundress and bare feet. "I clean up okay," she winked.

Just then the phone rang. She looked at the caller ID, studying it before answering. She'd been screening Parker's calls all week. "What's up?" she said to the person on the other end. "Yes, I'm much better. Um…Ted's here."

At the mention of his name, Ted listened carefully.

"Uh-huh…*Noooooooo*," Victoria giggled, then lowered her voice. "We're getting ready to eat dinner now, just drop by later."

When she hung up the phone, Ted was looking at her with questioning eyes. "That was Tyler, she said. "He came by earlier to go over the hotel contract for this year's YFI Christmas fundraiser, which I can't believe is coming up in six months. Anyway, he left it over here so I told him he could stop by and pick it up later tonight."

They sat down to a dinner of Victoria's favorite selections. After their meal they made their way back to the couch in the den. She put on Wynton Marsalis' *Blue Note* CD, then settled into Ted's arms. "The meal was fantastic. Thanks for this evening. It's nice to know you care," she said.

"V, I don't just care about you, I love you."

Victoria looked at the handsome man who had come into her life and made her love him despite her misgivings and hang-ups. She thought back on all the times he'd given her small signals about his true feelings and how she'd intentionally ignored them because she didn't want to entertain the thought of a white man loving her, or beyond that, her loving a white man. The complications were too great.

She thought about her college days when she and her girlfriends stood firm against dating white men, saying they had small penises and didn't know how to please a woman in bed. Even though none of them had any first-hand experience to either prove or disprove the myth, they talked about the subject with great authority. Now, she was lying on her couch in the arms of a white man. A white man she loved. And as she snuggled next to him, feeling his erection poking into her side, she couldn't believe how amazingly normal it felt to be in this situation, in this moment, with this man.

This was the third time Victoria had felt Ted's erection, and just as before, she couldn't quite determine his size. Parker was "blessed" in that regard, and had given her pleasure that was close to paradise. She wondered about Ted. *But they say that size doesn't matter, it's what you do with it,* Victoria reminded herself. Then she remembered what Gigi had said about the size theory. "It's complete bullshit, and can't possibly be true," she'd scoffed. "If a woman says that size doesn't matter it's because she's got a man with a little dick, and you better believe she's got somethin' on the side to pick up the slack."

As she snuggled even deeper into Ted's arms, Victoria wondered how he was in bed. How did he kiss? How did he move his pelvis in the throes of passion? Could he work it? And then she thought about her own sexual prowess. She prided herself on being a good lover. She knew how to please a man; how to make him moan until she had him calling out her name. But she wondered how Ted would receive her. *Will he expect me to be an exotic fuck? To perform like a member of Cirque du Soliel?*

"V," Ted whispered, "what's wrong? You have a strange look on your face."

"I'm fine. Just thinking," she smiled.

He pulled her onto his chest and brought her face closer to his. She could feel his mouth inching closer toward her own. She prepared herself for his kiss...their first, but the sound of the doorbell drew her away. Ted wanted to ignore it, but Victoria was already on her feet. She grabbed the hotel contract from the coffee table. "That's Tyler, I'll be right back. And hold that pose," she winked.

Out of habit, Victoria looked through the peephole, and what she saw almost made her heart stop. Parker was standing on the other side of the door. *Shit! What's he doing here?*

He'd been calling her several times a day leaving messages, pleading for her to pick up the phone and talk to him. He'd sent her ten dozen roses two days ago, which she promptly donated to a local nursing home. And just yesterday he'd managed to get Gayle to call, to help persuade Victoria to talk to him. She agreed to speak to him, but once they were on the phone she told him not to call her or come near her ever again.

Victoria could see that he was about to ring the bell again, so she sat Tyler's documents on the console and quickly opened the door.

"What the hell is that mothafucker doing here?" were the first words out of Parker's mouth as he looked back over his shoulder at Ted's car.

Victoria spoke low, through clenched teeth. "No, the question is what the hell are *you* doing here? I told you to stay away from me."

"How're we supposed to work things out if we don't communicate? We need to talk."

"You should've thought about that before you started spreading your dick around."

"Baby, we can work this out. I made a stupid mistake, but you can't deny that we love each other. We have since the first night we met."

Victoria nodded her head. "It's interesting you bring that up. I've been thinking about that night, and you know what? I realized that you were an inconsiderate asshole, even back then. You had one woman on your arm while you openly gawked at another. How I ever found that charming or even remotely flattering makes me sick to my stomach. Why don't you go back to Sheila, or better yet, go to the city pound where they keep the rest of your kind."

"You can hurl all the insults you want. I deserve it. But I don't want Sheila or anyone else."

Victoria gave him a cynical smirk.

"Victoria, I'm not giving up on us." Parker paused, looking at her with frightening sincerity. "Do you really think I'm going to just walk away from what we have? You know me better than that."

"You walked away from what we had when you cheated on me. Just leave."

"I'm not leaving, especially not as long as that mothafucker's in your house. Where is he?"

Just then Victoria looked past Parker and saw Ms. Swanson and Caroline walking by. They were finishing up their regular evening stroll. *"Leave"* Victoria repeated, trying to keep her voice low because she knew her nosy neighbor was watching. At the same time she saw Parker's eyes narrow in concentration on something over her left shoulder. She didn't have to turn around to know that Ted was coming up behind her. She backed a few steps away from the door, trying to slow his approach.

"She doesn't want to see you or talk to you. I suggest you leave now," Ted belted out.

"Fuck you and your suggestions!" Parker barked back. "If it wasn't for you, we wouldn't be going through this shit!"

Ms. Swanson heard the yelling and came to an abrupt stop on the side-walk in front of Victoria's house.

Ted moved away from Victoria, planting himself closer to where Parker stood. "Don't blame me because you couldn't keep your dick in your pants!" he glared.

"Mothafucker, do you know who you're talkin' to? I'll kick your ass."

"Let's go!" Ted growled, making a quick movement toward the door.

Parker came forward at the same time, but Victoria reacted quicker than both men by jumping in between them. "Stop it!" she yelled. She glanced over and saw Ms. Swanson frantically reaching into her fanny pack.

"Can't you both see that you're hurting me?" she pleaded from one man's eyes to the other. Both Parker and Ted relaxed their stance and backed away from Victoria's outstretched arms. She looked up again and saw Ms.

Swanson rushing up through the yard. She hurried in between the two parked vehicles and up toward the portico, carrying Caroline under one arm and a small canister of pepper spray in her free hand. Parker turned around quickly to face the woman coming up behind him.

"It's okay Ms. Swanson," Victoria called out, stopping the old woman before she began to spray. "Everything's fine…really. They were just about to leave," she scrambled nervously, trying to convince her neighbor.

Ms. Swanson looked at the three of them. "Are you sure? I can call 911?" she said, still waving her pepper spray in the air.

"That won't be necessary. We had a little disagreement, but everything's fine now. You can put the pepper spray away," Victoria coaxed.

Reluctantly, the old woman put the spray back into her fanny pack as she tried to calm Caroline. The pooch's pink hair bows were standing on edge. "I'll call you later to make sure everything is okay," Ms. Swanson offered.

"Thank you," Victoria sighed as she watched her neighbor walk away. The old lady glanced back, shaking her head, mumbling something every few feet until she was out of site.

The muggy Atlanta heat loomed like Victoria's anger. She could feel the sweat beading up between her breasts, trickling down to her stomach, which felt like it was in knots. "I can't believe you two," she raged through clenched teeth. "Look at you; an internationally respected surgeon and the CEO of a fortune five hundred company, standing in my front door acting like schoolyard bullies. You should both be ashamed of yourselves."

"He needs to stay the fuck away from you," Parker said. "He shouldn't be here in the first place." He stared with anger in Ted's direction. "You couldn't wait could you? You wanted her all along. I saw through your bullshit from the start."

Ted clenched his fists at his side. "You better leave now, while you still can."

"Are you threatening me?" Parker's tone turned eerily calm, sending panic through Victoria's body. "I'm not one of those punks at ViaTech that you can order around. You don't know who the fuck you're dealin' with."

Ted glared back at him. "You sonofabitch, I know exactly who you are. Now get the fuck outta here or there's gonna be trouble. I'm not asking you again," he threatened.

Victoria stomped her foot. "Damnit. Shut the hell up! Both of you!" she nearly screamed, pushing Parker further out the door. "You've got to go. I told you not to come here."

Parker was incredulous. "You're putting me out? And letting him stay?"

"You're lucky you weren't doused with pepper spray, or worse, Ms.

Swanson could've called the police, and you could've been arrested. Parker, you know better than this."

"Baby…please…"

"Leave now, or I'll call the police myself." She pushed him back one step further, then slammed the door in his face. She rested her head against the door, trying to recalibrate.

Ted came up from behind and rubbed her shoulders. "It's over now," he said softly.

Victoria spun around to face him. "And you! What the hell were you thinking, challenging Parker to a fight? Are you crazy? Why didn't you just stay in the den? I could've handled him by myself. You made matters worse."

Ted was stunned. "V," I was trying to protect you. Parker was angry."

"Yeah, but he would never physically hurt me. He was in more danger of me than I was of him."

"I'm sorry. I was only trying to help. But he asked for it, and I'd do it again if I thought you were in any danger, physical or otherwise."

Victoria raised her hands to her throbbing head. "I know you meant well, but after what just happened I need to be alone, please understand." She took him by the hand and led him to the den. They gathered his things, then walked back to the front door. When she opened it, she jumped when she saw Parker still sitting in his truck, parked in her driveway.

"I can't believe that sonofabitch," Ted spat out, ready to go to blows.

"Don't make another scene. Just get in your car and drive away…*please.*"

When Victoria saw the last pair of tail lights drive off in the distance, she resumed her breathing, inhaling the thick, sticky air engulfing her lungs. Just then, Tyler's Jeep pulled up.

"Was that Parker and Ted I just passed?" Tyler asked.

"Yep."

"What was Parker doing here?…Oh no…don't tell me…I know some shit just went down."

"Come on in, you're not gonna believe this."

The Real Question……

It was the last day of the SuperNet convention, and from the minute Victoria stepped off the plane almost a week ago, she'd been working hard, trying to put her recent drama out of her mind. Thankfully, the convention had been the welcome reprieve she needed. She and Ted had arrived in Washington, D.C., on separate flights, but once she checked into the Mayflower Hotel, she discovered that they had adjoining rooms. "Is this why Jen offered to make my reservations," she'd asked Ted. His answer had been a simple smile.

As Victoria looked around the large meeting room on the second floor of the DC Convention Center, she breathed a sigh of relief that she hadn't run into Steven the entire week. He lived and worked here, and she'd heard through colleagues that he was there. But he'd used good judgment and stayed as far away as possible. Things had turned out better than she'd expected. ViaTech had been the talk of the show. People raved about the sleek booth design, golf outings, capitol tours, private dinners at the city's hottest restaurants, and other activities she'd planned for perspective clients. Victoria had made sure that everyone was catered to.

Even though the week had been a good distraction and a huge success, and Victoria was sure to get many new corporate clients from the event, she was ready to go home. She was tired from all the work and the stressful scene last week between Parker and Ted. The day after, Denise had come by to offer her a shoulder to lean on.

"*Umph, umph, umph, Girlfriend!* That's just ridiculous. I can't believe they were acting like common street thugs, right in your front door!" Denise had said.

Victoria rubbed her throbbing temples. "You should've seen them, it was awful. And when poor Ms. Swanson tried to pepper spray Parker, I almost fainted."

"That's the stuff reality shows are made of."

"Tell me about it. Intelligent, civilized people don't behave this way. I can't believe this is my life."

"Well, what I can't believe is that Ted was over here acting like a hoodlum. And Parker…the great almighty surgeon himself, was carrying on the way he did. I'm sorry, but that was some straight up trailer park drama if I've ever heard some."

"I know," Victoria flinched. "How do I get myself into these kind of situations? I wanted to crawl into a hole and hide."

"I can't say that I blame you," Denise agreed.

"And I'll never hear the end of it from Tyler."

As it was, Parker was already on Tyler's shit list, and once Victoria cried on his shoulder after telling him how she'd walked in on him and Sheila, Tyler was through. When he came over to her house to pick up the YFI contract he'd left and she told him about the scene that Parker had caused right before he drove up, Tyler hit the roof. "He's lost his damn mind, showin' up like that! I should drive down to that fancy condo of his and beat the shit outta him," Tyler yelled.

But Victoria pleaded with him, finally making the case that physical violence wasn't the answer. She made him promise that he wouldn't go near her ex-boyfriend.

Tyler didn't confront Parker physically, but he came close. That night, he called Parker and threatened him. "Stay your punk ass away from Victoria, 'cause if you ever attempt some weak bullshit like you pulled tonight, you'll end up in the fuckin' emergency room where you work," Tyler said, then slammed down the phone.

Denise looked at her friend and shook her head. "I can't believe Parker had the nerve to come over here after what he did to you. Who does he think he is?"

"He's used to getting what he wants, but this is where it ends," Victoria vowed, then paused. "But the real question now is what am I going to do about Ted?" She was looking to her friend for answers.

Denise raised her brow. "You've got to be kidding me. Girlfriend, you better take care of that serious drought you've got goin' on in your pants 'cause I know you're about tired of your little toys by now."

"I tell too much of my business," Victoria said, joining Denise in a much needed laugh. "But seriously, like I told Debbie, it's complicated."

"Show me a relationship that isn't."

"And he's white."

"*Really?*" Denise feigned shock. "And?…"

Victoria let out a deep breath. "I've never been with a white man, never even considered it until now. What if Ted's just infatuated and wants to fulfill some kind of taboo fantasy? You know, jungle fever, wild sex with a black woman. That would just devastate me," Victoria groaned, falling back into the couch.

"Girlfriend, you've got to stop being so damn dramatic," Denise scolded, rolling her eyes. "If the man wanted to fulfill a fantasy he could do that at anytime, with anyone he wants to. But he wants you."

"You have all the answers don't you?"

"Most of them," Denise winked. "Now go ahead and get you some vanilla lovin'," she laughed.

"So you're encouraging me to be a ho', and just give my stuff away?"

"Absolutely, and I want all the juicy details when you get back," Denise said, making them break into laughter again. Then she became serious. "If you love him, open up your heart to him and forget about all this black and white shit. You've loved black, now you have to learn to love without restrictions."

As Victoria prepared to wrap things up at the convention center and head back to the hotel, she thought about Denise's advice and what the evening ahead might bring. After the team dinner, she and Ted had plans to spend some "alone time" together. Her mind told her to take it slow, after all, she'd just broken up with her boyfriend. But her heart and her body were telling her something entirely different.

Chapter Twenty-One

Hallelujah......

The team dinner at The Palm restaurant was going well. The food was great and the company was lively. Everyone was high on the success of ViaTech's showing at SuperNet. As the wine and conversation flowed, Ted sat next to Victoria barely able to contain his longing to be alone with her. Finally, after an hour into their meal, Victoria leaned over and whispered into his ear. "Are you ready to leave?" They said goodnight to everyone, then left the restaurant with his hand on the small of her back, a smile on both their faces, and gossip on the lips of their colleagues.

Back at the hotel, they rode the elevator in silence and anticipation. But the higher they ascended, the more nervous Victoria became. When the doors opened, her throat was dry with second thoughts. They reached their adjoining rooms and stood in front of Ted's door. She knew that once she walked into his room, things would change. She knew she'd do things tonight that both excited and frightened her.

Ted sensed her trepidation and reached for her hand. "V, there's no pressure to do anything you don't want to do."

They walked in hand-in-hand. She made herself comfortable on the edge of the bed, not the sofa where she would have normally sat. She saw Ted's surprise at her deliberate action. He walked over and stood in front of her, his face bearing a serious stare. "V, the last couple of weeks have been hard for you. I know you need time, and I'll give you that."

"I'm scared," she whispered.

"I know."

Victoria looked into his eyes again. "I love you, Ted. I'm scared out of my mind. But I know that I love you."

She stood and went into his arms. He pulled her in close as she closed her eyes and readied herself for his kiss. She felt his cool lips on her warm ones. They were soft and moist, just as she'd imagined.

He kissed her gently, searching her mouth with his tongue, allowing the bright sensation to flood his body. His hand eased its way down to her behind as he rubbed his pelvis against hers. They started removing each other's clothes. She kissed his shoulder, his bare chest, and the adams apple of his neck. He unbuttoned her blouse, letting it fall to the floor, then slid her skirt down her legs, tossing it to the side.

They finished undressing one another, standing bare and exposed for mutual inspection. Ted took a step back to admire her, taking in the full scope of Victoria's naked beauty. His eyes washed over her body, ready to explore its elegant terrain.

Victoria scanned his body and braced herself for the view she'd been curious about for months. As her eyes journeyed over his midsection, and then down to his groin, her smile widened. She wasn't sure what she'd expected, but all she could think was *hallelujah!*

He took her breast into his mouth, gently kissing one while massaging the other. His tongue flicked her nipples until they were as hard and erect as he was. He glided his finger between her legs and felt her wetness, sending shivers through both their bodies. "*Ooohhh, V,*" he moaned. She secured her hand around him, massaging his hardness with the same gentle strokes she would use if touching her own flesh.

"Make love to me," she commanded.

Ted wanted nothing more than to grant her that wish, but after waiting for so long, he didn't want to rush in. He wanted to take his time and pleasure her in ways that until now, he'd only dreamed about. Gently, he guided her to the bed.

He buried his head between her thighs, lifting her legs over his shoulders. His tongue was gentle and skilled, and his kisses were sensual and intoxicating to her heated flesh. He took his time—sucking, nibbling, and licking with care. He parted her delicate folds with his fingers, exposing her bare middle, devouring her in small, savory bites as she moaned with pleasure. The softness of his lips and the precision of his tongue made her thighs tighten and her body tremble.

Ted knew she was ready for him. Slowly, he worked his way back up to her waiting lips. She kissed him hard, tasting herself on his tongue. His erection was centered at her point of entry as he pressed his lower body against hers, hungry for what was next to come. He parted her thighs, ready to enter her. He reached over to the nightstand, opened the drawer, and removed a handful of condoms. They looked at each other and smiled. He read her mind and answered her thoughts, "I'm an optimist," he whispered.

When he entered her, he moved slowly, plunging inch by inch until he filled her. And just as they did whenever they jogged together, after a few quick paces, their bodies fell into step.

"Mmmmmmm," Victoria moaned, lightly biting Ted's shoulder, clinging to him. They moved up and down, left and right, in and out, and side to side—reaching, searching, and stroking each other. Their bodies were slick with perspiration and excitement.

Finally, Victoria gave in to the ecstasy overtaking her body. Ted arched his back, thrusting harder, as she was begging him to do. *"Ooohhh Teeeedddd,"* she moaned, releasing the orgasm she'd been waiting for. Hearing her call his name, in that way, was music to his ears.

They Climbed Mountains......

He lay spooned to her in the morning dawn. His limbs were tired, fatigued from pleasure. After all the months of waiting, Ted had finally experienced his heart's desire. Looking at Victoria sleeping soundly next to him, he thought about last night.

After their second round, they were both exhausted. His only goal had been to please her and his only desire was to love her. He knew he'd accomplished both. He loved hearing her moan, and feeling her body quiver under him. He loved the way her legs felt against his skin, wrapped around his body as she clung to him. She exposed the whole of herself, bold and uninhibited.

Ted knew more than ever how much he loved Victoria. She was complicated, yet apparent. Serious, yet silly. Confident, yet vulnerable. Easy, yet edgy. But he wasn't blind to her faults. He knew that she could be obsessive and stubborn, with a tendency to nag until she got what she wanted. She was a bit spoiled, and could shut you out just as quickly as she could reel you in. And she was dramatic at times, almost to the point of annoyance. But these were the things that made her who she was, and he loved her for it. He lifted the sheet, admiring her form. Before they made love, she'd reached over to turn off the light beside the bed, but he stopped her. "I want to see you," he'd said.

He scanned her dark body next to his pale one. It reminded him of the picture of her parents that sat prominently on her living room table. He thought about how their children would look, whether they'd be a mixture of them both, or if they'd inherit her strikingly dominant features. He smiled at the thought of having a little girl who looked exactly like Victoria, just as she looked like her mother. The vision made him smile as she stirred, turning over to face him.

"Good morning," she whispered.

Ted kissed her forehead, her nose, and then her lips, relishing in the brackish taste of her morning breath. "Good morning," he smiled.

Victoria trembled when she thought about last night. She could feel his unselfish love in every movement he made. Somehow, he knew the deepest corners of her essence and the geographic route to her internal pleasure. He knew when to bite and when to nibble, when to lick and when to suck, when to thrust hard and when to ease out. At one point, he pinned her wrists above her head, nibbled her earlobe and whispered in erotic detail how he was going to pleasure her. All the things he'd said he would do were things she'd hoped for.

As Victoria lay in Ted's arms, she let out a small sigh. "I wish we didn't have to go back today. Before last night I couldn't wait to get back home, but now, I could stay here in bed with you a few more days," she smiled.

"Consider it done." Ted picked up the phone, called Jen, and had her change their flight arrangements. Next, he dialed the front desk and extended their stay through the weekend.

"I love you, I love you, I love you" Victoria squealed, showering him with small kisses.

"V, I've waited so long to hear you say those words."

A knock at the door interrupted them. "Does housekeeping come this early?" Victoria asked, looking at the digital alarm clock on the nightstand. "It's not even seven o'clock."

Ted rose from bed and walked over to where he'd dropped his trousers the night before. Victoria watched him; his narrow hips jotting out as he bent over to pull the tailored pants up the length of his legs. He opened the door and exchanged a few cordial words with a voice ladled in a Spanish accent. "I can take it from here," Ted told the man. He walked back toward the bed pushing a small cart of food. "I ordered last night right after you fell asleep. I figured we'd need it this morning," he winked.

They sat in bed feeding each other, enjoying the food and the thought of the next two days together. Ted studied Victoria closely as she dug into her syrup drenched waffle. "When did you know you loved me?" he asked.

Victoria wiped her mouth and placed her plate on the cart. "I was in denial for a long time, but after the Christmas party at my house, I finally admitted it to myself. And it's funny; all my friends saw it from the beginning."

Ted brought Victoria's hand to his mouth and kissed it softly. "Love is difficult to hide." He lowered her back onto the bed, covering her body with his. His breath whistled a sultry lullaby in her ear as his heat blanketed her. He slipped on a condom and guided himself inside her. Slowly, they climbed mountains. Her low whimper told him that she was at her breaking point—and he was there to meet her.

The next day they finally ventured out of the hotel. They strolled through the trendy Dupont Circle neighborhood in Northwest, the upscale shops in Georgetown, and then on to the luxury of Mezza Gallery on Wisconsin Avenue. Victoria was prepared for the disapproving eyes of the brothers in Chocolate City, but to her surprise, no one gave them angry stares.

She thought about how difficult it was for black women to find a good man because the statistics were stacked against them. She knew she was blessed that she'd found one...a very good one. She'd fallen in love with a man who happened to be older, and who happened to be white. She remembered the contented look on Ted's face as he held her while they lay in bed earlier that morning, and she made up her mind at that moment that she wasn't going to apologize for loving him.

Interrupting My Shopping......

Victoria shopped at Neiman Marcus while Ted stood outside the store, engrossed in his cell phone and blackberry, taking care of business for the upcoming week. She was about to make her purchase; four Jo Malone candles, when she saw Mason Brightwood appear.

It was reminiscent of New York, only this time she wasn't completely caught off guard. She'd been prepared for something like this. DC was Parker's city, and she'd imagined scenarios of being out and running into any number of people like his parents, one of his siblings, cousins, or family friends. And she knew that Mason conducted business between New York and D.C., and was frequently in town—his mistress lived on Capitol Hill.

"Victoria, funny how we keep running into each other," Mason smiled.

"Hello, Mason," she managed with distant cordiality. "If you'll excuse me, we're on our way to dinner," she said, looking outside the store in Ted's direction. She was glad that he was still on his phone, immersed in ViaTech business.

Mason looked in Ted's direction. "Can I have a few minutes of your time?"

"I'm really in a hurry…"

"Just a few minutes…please?"

Against her better judgment, Victoria followed Mason over to the far corner of the store. But she wasn't in the mood for his nonsense and immediately became agitated and regretful the moment he opened his mouth.

"You look stunning as usual," he complimented, appraising Victoria in her strapless sundress and strappy summer sandals.

"What do you want, Mason?"

"I'd like to apologize for my rudeness during your Christmas visit. Some of my comments were uncalled for. You just happened to get caught in the middle of a little sibling rivalry. It had nothing to do with you, personally."

"That's what you wanted to talk to me about?" Victoria snapped, starting to walk away.

"And…I have a message for you from Parker."

She stopped.

"He knows you're here on business. He told me if I happened to run into you, to tell you that he wants to talk to you. He said he's been trying to contact you, but you won't return his calls."

Victoria shook her head. "Well, I have a message for your brother too. Tell him that we have nothing to talk about."

"You can tell him yourself. He's over at the house."

Victoria froze. "He's here in D.C.?"

"Yes. He's been here all week."

With all that had transpired, she'd forgotten that Parker had planned to spend time with his family after coming back from Kenya. Before he'd left for the Africa Project they had agreed that the week of SuperNet would be perfect timing for a family visit, that way they'd both be in town together. Just knowing that Parker was less than ten minutes away from where she stood made Victoria's stomach feel weak.

"Victoria, the only reason he's not here with me now is because he's sitting at home, sulking and thinking about you. He's miserable without you. I've never seen him like this."

Victoria rolled her eyes. "Honestly, that's none of my concern."

"Listen, I know whatever I say probably won't hold weight with you, especially after some of my actions. But I've seen a change in Parker since you two started dating, a change for the better. He loves you."

"If he loved me, why did he cheat on me?"

Mason sighed. "He made a stupid mistake, but he never meant to hurt you. He still loves you and he's sick over this. Do you know he actually cried last night!" Mason's voice was incredulous, mimicking the old sarcasm that was his customary tone. But then he stepped back into the kinder, gentler Mason. "We all make mistakes, and yes, his was a big one. But I'm telling you, that white guy out there isn't for you."

Victoria was about to blow her fuse. "How the hell do you know who's right for me!"

"I know that anyone other than Parker is wrong for you, and you know it too."

"I thought that Parker was the one. But it's over. He disregarded my feelings and violated my trust. Tell your brother to move on, and to leave me the hell alone. And if he even thinks about coming by my house again, I'll have him arrested."

Mason shook his head. "Yeah, he told me about that. It was an irrational thing he did…coming by like that," he shrugged, "but you're making him act crazy. He's lost his cool."

Victoria narrowed her eyes in amazement. "Don't turn this around to be my fault," she hissed, trying to keep her voice low. "This is unbelievable. Parker's in this situation because he couldn't control his wondering dick."

Mason raised a brow at Victoria's choice of words, but continued to press on. "He loves you Victoria. Give him another chance."

"I should slap you for interrupting my shopping with this bullshit."

Mason was shocked, but wanted to smile at the same time. He loved a woman with bite. "Victoria, I know it's not much coming from me…in your eyes. But my brother loves you. Black love is powerful, remember that."

✑

That's What She Used To Say...

Parker and Mason sat across from each other at a small table in the Mocha Hut, a popular coffee shop in the trendy, 13th and U Street corridor. Mason was glad that his brother was finally up and out because he hadn't left their parent's house since arriving in town last week. It seemed all Parker wanted to do was lay around and sulk, which was uncharacteristic of the man Mason knew; the man who had always been his best-loved brother. He'd been trying to make amends with Parker since last December, and now they were finally on a good footing again.

To his reluctance, and at Parker's insistence, Mason told his brother about his run in with Victoria. "She damn near cursed me out right there in Neiman's," he said. "She even threatened to slap me!"

Parker smiled, remembering how feisty Victoria could be. "You got off easy, she threatened to kick my ass in my own living room." The two men shared a laugh, each for different reasons.

"So, little brother, what're you going to do?"

"Man, I don't know. She won't return my phone calls or emails. I'm at a loss."

"Parker, you can't continue to let yourself go down like this. I don't care how good the pussy is."

Parker shook his head. "You might not understand this, but that's not all there is to Victoria, or our relationship. I love her. I feel lost without her."

Mason smirked, taking a small sip of his freshly brewed coffee before he spoke again. "You need to get a hold of yourself. You look like shit, you haven't shaved in days, and you're letting your hair grow back again. Hell, this is the first time you've left the house since you got here."

"I'm goin' through some serious shit right now so excuse me if I don't get decked out and hit the town."

"Well, you better do something if you intend to get your woman back. Like it or not, you've got competition little brother."

Parker huffed. "I can't believe she's leaving me for that mothafucker. She doesn't even approve of interracial dating. At least that's what she used to say."

"I know what you mean. You hate to see your woman with a white boy. But Parker, she didn't leave you. You fucked it up. Getting caught like that?"

Parker looked away. "I know," he said quietly, shaking his head.

"It was so *messy*. What possessed you to fuck another woman the day after you got back? You were on the other side of the world for six months, free to get all the pussy you wanted. But *noooo*, you waited until you came back home, under your woman's nose, to get caught?" Mason said, truly puzzled.

"I didn't mess around while I was in Kenya, I was faithful to Victoria. I never even thought about another woman while I was over there."

Mason narrowed his eyes on his brother. "So why did you do it?"

Parker raised his hands to his head in frustration. It was a question he'd asked himself a thousand times since that morning. All he thought about the night of his return was his love for Victoria and his disappointment over her not wanting to accept his marriage proposal, and added to that, her revelation that she wished she'd slept with Ted. When he saw Sheila in the coffee shop, he knew she was trouble. Just as his instincts had told him to avoid her at Phil and Gayle's Halloween party when she'd approached him, he knew he should've grabbed his coffee and muffins, and walked away. But he was lonely, and before he knew it he was making the biggest mistake of his life.

"Stop, Mason. I feel bad enough," Parker said, his head held low. "The look on Victoria's face when she walked in...it tears me up every time I think about it."

"This shit is ridiculous. Stop acting like a damn punk. You're a Brightwood man for God's sake. Pull yourself together!" Mason scoffed, having no sympathy.

Parker looked at his brother with tired eyes, unaffected by his outburst. "Mason, I don't know what to do."

"Thanks to the Africa Project, you have international recognition. You're young, good-looking, single, no kids...please. You've got it made. Actually, Victoria did you a favor. She gave you a get out of jail free card."

"But I only want her."

"Then stop sitting around here crying and moping. Clean your ass up and go after her." Mason paused, then calmed himself for the sake of the broken man in front of him. "Listen, little brother, if you love her, step up and get her back. But you better act fast before it's too late."

A Solitary Word......

Victoria smiled when she turned onto Summerset Lane. Even though she didn't want the last couple of days to end, and waking up with Ted was something she was now looking forward to, she was glad to be home. After seeing Mason, and knowing that Parker was there, it made her more than ready to leave D.C. She planned to unpack, go through her weeks worth of mail, and then relax until Ted came over later that evening.

As Victoria turned into her driveway, she agreed with Dorothy, "There's no place like home," she said aloud. She steered around back to her car pad and nearly lost control of her vehicle. There, parked in the extra space, was a shiny black BMW truck. She managed to regain control of her car and parked without hitting him. She was furious and anxious at the same time.

She sat in her car with the engine running for twenty minutes before she opened her door. When she did, Parker stepped out and walked up to her. She walked around to the trunk, he got out her luggage, and they went into the house—all without speaking a solitary word to each other. Ten minutes later they were sitting in the den on opposite ends of her couch, still not saying anything.

"I want us to be together. Whatever you want me to do, I'll do it. Just don't leave me, Victoria," Parker finally said.

"It's too late."

"It's never too late. Not when two people love each other. I love you, and whether you want to admit it or not, you still love me too."

"Yes, Parker, a part of me still loves you. I won't deny that, but love's not enough. The only thing I ever asked you for was honesty and respect, but you couldn't give me that. There's nothing left for us to talk about."

"Baby, I can't tell you how many times I've thought about what a completely selfish and incredibly stupid thing I did. I'm so sorry."

Victoria put her head in her hands. "I loved you," she whispered.

Parker moved over and held her in his arms. He put his hands on her shoulders, turning her around to face him. "I'm not giving up on us."

Victoria pulled away. "You need to leave."

She watched as Parker put his truck in reverse and backed out. She thought she'd cried all the tears she was going to shed over this man, but standing at her backdoor, watching him drive away, the tears rolled, and rolled, and rolled.

Chapter Twenty-Two

I Can't Want It By Myself......

It was now September, and three months had passed since Victoria had resigned from ViaTech. She was running her business full-time, and even with all the headaches of growing a start-up company, she was happy. She was pursuing her dream, her friends were doing well, and she was in love with a wonderful man who loved her back. Her only problem was the nagging fear invading her thoughts; the fear that things were too good to be true. She was waiting for something bad to happen, for the other shoe to drop.

One morning she awoke from a restless sleep, her mind battling with the troubled thoughts that seemed to cling to her lately.

Ted felt the tension in her body. "V, what's wrong," he asked, his voice still heavy with sleep. They were lying in their usual position—him spooning her from behind. He turned her around to face him.

"I feel like things are too good to be true," she said, looking him in the eye. "When you're this happy, things don't last."

Ted stroked her hair, "Honey, don't think like that. You deserve happiness. And sure, every day won't be sunshine and roses, but when things get rough I'll be here for you."

Ted kissed her chin, then found his favorite spot on her neck before moving on to her breasts. Tenderly, his tongue circled her nipples, sucking until her fears were replaced with moans. He rubbed his growing erection against her thigh. Victoria closed her eyes, tilted her head back into the pillow and enjoyed his loving tongue. Their bodies began to move together in anticipation of early morning love making.

She ran her fingers through his hair, delighting in his hardness as she pressed her body against his. She opened her legs and moved against him in a slow rotating grind. He slipped off his pajama bottoms and removed her teddy, kissing her slowly as he reached into his nightstand for a condom. He slipped it on. "Are you ready for me?" he asked, knowing that she was, feeling her wetness smeared against his leg.

"Yes."

"Are you sure?" he teased, wanting to hear her say it again.

"Yes, yes!" Victoria panted. She reached for him, guiding him to the meeting between her thighs.

Their erotic sounds filled the room as he penetrated her, gliding in and out with controlled ease. She wrapped her legs around him, bringing her lips up to his for a passionate kiss. He knew she was almost there. A few more strokes and he would again bring her to orgasm. He could feel his own climax about to unleash, but he wanted to wait until he felt her thighs tense and her nails dig into his back. He wanted to hear her call his name in *that way*. Her hips moved with his, receiving his powerful love blows, as she sank into the feeling. "Yes," she cried out, *"Ooohhh, Teeeddd."*

That was his favorite sound.

Afterwards, they lay cleaved to each other, their bodies tingling with slippery perspiration. Ted stroked her shoulder and kissed her forehead. "You mean to world to me."

She searched his face and saw that his eyes carried a different intensity than she'd ever seen before.

"Do you know what that means?" he asked.

She hesitated. "I think so."

"V, we need to talk about our future." His tone was deep and serious.

Now she became serious too. "What do you want from me?"

"I want to marry you, spend the rest of my life with you, and have children with you. I want us to build a life together."

This was the thing that scared Victoria most about her relationship with

Ted—what their future was going to be? Their present was fine, wonderful in fact. But it was what lay ahead that gave her pause.

She'd always wanted to get married and have a family someday. She'd imagined how her life would be; a handsome and loving husband, well behaved, neatly groomed children, a beautiful home, a happy life. A life much like the one she'd had growing up.

Victoria released herself from his arms. "Have you considered what that would mean?"

"Yes, and I'm ready for that commitment."

"What about children?"

"I'd like to have at least two, maybe three. Wouldn't you?"

Victoria shook her head slowly. "That's not what I mean," she paused, "our children would be bi-racial."

There it was. The elephant in the room they'd danced around for months. Not since his birthday had they talked about race in their relationship. Ted hadn't told her that he'd had a similar conversation with her father two months ago when her parents had come to town for a visit. Neither had he mentioned the conversation he'd had with his mother during his Thanksgiving visit last year. But the longer they ignored it, the larger the elephant grew, until it was unavoidable.

"Do you know what kind of obstacles and prejudice our children would face? They'd be too white to be black, and too black to be white," Victoria said, repeating her mother's words.

"But they'd also have the best of us. We'd just need to teach them how to be good people and surround them with love."

"That sounds so simple and easy. But the reality is that more than likely our children will look black, and they'll be treated like they're black."

"Okay?" Ted responded, shrugging his shoulders. He didn't want to have this conversation so early in the morning, and particularly not after an orgasm.

Victoria sat up in bed, pulling the sheet up to her chest. "What if we had a son? How would you raise a little black boy to be a man in this society? The rules for black men are very different," she said. "You don't know what it's like. You're the boy next door. How could you raise him to be a strong, confident black man, secure in his identity? You wouldn't have a clue."

Ted sat up beside her. "I would teach him how to be a good person, period. Love and guidance are what kids need, in any circumstance. I've learned that from spending time with Jermaine. I'm good with him. You've seen how well we get along."

"That's different. Jermaine is practically an adult. I'm talking about raising a little black child and dealing with all that comes along with it day in and day out."

Ted hated to admit it, but he knew that Victoria was partly right, and it scared him. He feared that there were things he might not be able to teach his black son.

Victoria continued. "Have you ever been followed through a store or pulled over by the cops for no apparent reason, or lost out on a job opportunity simply because of how you look?" she hammered away. "Well, plenty of black folk have. I have. That's the reality of what possibly awaits a child of ours. I can deal with it because I've had to all my life. But could you? Could you deal with those realities?"

They stared at each other. "Are you prepared for that? Are you?" she pressed.

Ted put his hand on hers. "I don't have all the answers, and sometimes the thought of it scars the shit out of me. But I'm prepared to deal with whatever comes our way," he paused, "but I can't want it by myself."

He had posed the question without having to ask it. Was it what *she* wanted? Was she up for the task? Would she be the hold up—not him?

Victoria searched Ted's eyes. She believed he would be a great father and a loving husband. She could be herself with him—goofy, silly, argumentative, quirky, vulnerable, and girlish. He knew how to please her, attending to her wants and needs. And although he wasn't handy at all around the house, which was a small disappointment, he more than made up for it with his sincerity and gentleness.

When she'd told her parents that she and Ted were "a couple", Elizabeth had shown quiet approval. But John, on the other hand, had been more vocal, spelling out his concern—something he'd never done before. He liked Ted, but all his life he'd fought men who looked like his daughter's boyfriend, so it was hard for him to separate his past experience from Victoria's present situation. He'd always wanted the best for her, and not allowing her to follow her dream, as his father had allowed him to do, still ate away at him. But as much as he wanted to support her now, he had serious reservations about her new relationship.

John and Elizabeth had come to town two months ago to celebrate Victoria's thirty-fourth birthday, and the grand opening of Divine Occasions' new office. They had a lovely time during dinner, but when they came back to Victoria's house for coffee and dessert, the serious show down began. John and Ted sat side by side and talked privately on the patio deck in Victoria's backyard. Both men were honest and to the point.

"What are your intentions with my daughter?" John asked. His voice was direct.

"I love Victoria," Ted answered, but not as forcefully as he'd liked. John made him nervous. He knew it was always a battle of wills and nerve when two powerful men engaged. He tried to be as commanding as John, but he felt himself slipping. "I'm very serious about our relationship and our future together."

"So you want to marry, Victoria?"

"Yes, I do. I see that you're not comfortable with that. Is it because you don't think I'll be a good husband to your daughter, or is it because I'm white?"

John chuckled. He heard the break in Ted's voice but admired his determination. "Ted, you're a good man. But as to what kind of husband you'll be, I can't speak to that. Marriage changes a man. Not every good man makes a good husband. But yes, I have concerns about my daughter marrying outside the race. Interracial relationships can be difficult and you'll need more than just love to make it work," John said.

Ted's response was swift. He uncrossed his legs and leaned forward in his Adirondack chair, positioning himself closer to John. "I can't promise that I'll always be a good husband, but I can promise that I'll always try. And I can't promise that we won't have problems, but I can promise that I'll work hard as hell to deal with them and take care of her. I love her as a man. Not a white man, or a wealthy man…just as a man."

John and Ted sat in silence, each thinking about what the other had said. Finally, John spoke his honest conclusion, "I'm going to hold you to that."

Back in the present moment as they lay in bed with Ted's statement hanging in the air, he held his breath, waiting for it to be answered. Victoria stared at him long and hard. He was asking her if she wanted him. Asking her if she wanted happiness, and children, and love. Asking her if she wanted a lifetime with him?

"I want it too," she said, snuggling close. "I guess we'll just have to ride this train as far as it'll take us."

*C*oloreds......

John and Elizabeth had warmed to the idea that Victoria and Ted were in a serious relationship. It had been a relief for Ted, and seeing that he was becoming closer to her family, Victoria finally told him about the maternal side of her genealogical tree.

Ted knew it was important that each of their families accepted the other. He wanted Victoria to know that she had nothing to fear, so he took her to Boston to meet the Thorntons. The visit had gone well, and he was especially pleased since he hadn't been one-hundred percent sure how his mother would receive Victoria after she'd expressed her concerns about their relationship.

Ted's brother and sister were gracious, glad that their brother had finally found happiness. The fact that Victoria was black hadn't seemed to be a big deal to them, and she was a natural with his nieces and nephews. And while Carolyn Thornton didn't seem to share the same enthusiasm as the rest of the family, she was, at the least, cordial.

Victoria sensed his mother's reservation, and nearly choked on her bread during dinner when Carolyn had actually referred to black people as *Coloreds*. She could see the embarrassment on Ted's face. But she kept her cool, responding to his mother in a tone a teacher might use when instructing a class of first-graders. "My people haven't been *colored* since desegregation." It was a tense moment, but they got through it.

After Carolyn's quick, but brief apology, the rest of the evening had rolled along. Ted assured Victoria that his mother had meant no harm, and was just old fashioned and slow to come around. "Remember, all that matters is you and me," he told her.

After they returned home, Victoria thought about what her life with Ted would be like; would they grow tired of each other, would they be able to stand the prejudice that would surely come their way? As she sat behind her desk in her chic new office, going over the final details of Tyler and Juliet's upcoming wedding, she prayed again that the answers would come.

*H*is Best Person......

"Okay Victoria," the wedding directress called out. "It's time."

Victoria walked up to the doors of the sanctuary as the wedding directress instructed. She couldn't believe that nearly a year ago, Tyler had been chained to unhappiness. Now, he was about to step into a bright new day with the woman he loved. And what made Victoria's heart swell even more was that she had a direct hand in the occasion. She had coordinated the entire event from the order of the ceremony, to the flavor of icing on the wedding cake. She would've directed it too if she hadn't been a member of the wedding party.

Victoria smiled with joy as she walked down the aisle in her ice-blue, Waters and Waters gown. She walked up to the front of the church, stepped into the space between one of the groomsmen, and took her place beside Tyler. Several people in the audience let out small gasps, looking down at their programs. Tyler and Victoria grinned at each other. She was his friend, his ace, his hangin' partner, and as the program listed, his "Best Person."

Gigi, Juliet's two sisters, and her cousin all made lovely bridesmaids, while Tyler's cousin and three of his fraternity brothers escorted them down the aisle. Juliet looked beautiful in her dazzling off-the-shoulder Nicole Miller gown, as she walked toward the alter. It was a simple and emotionally touching ceremony. After they were officially pronounced husband and wife, they strutted back up the aisle like peacocks with the wedding party bringing up the rear.

This Is Insane......

Thanks to a host of new clients, Victoria's schedule was full on most weekends. She'd coordinated Tyler and Juliet's wedding two weeks ago, and a luncheon for a children's charity last week. Now, it was Saturday night and she was beat. She'd just finished another big affair at the Masters' residence, coordinating an elegantly lavish meet and greet reception. The event served to usher in the Debutante season for Atlanta's young society ladies-in-waiting.

When the cotillion chair had told Eva Masters they were looking for a venue to host the meet and greet, the socialite eagerly volunteered her home for the affair. After the fabulous job Victoria had done with Celeste's last-minute sweet sixteen birthday party, Eva naturally called on Divine Occasions to plan her daughter's debut into social entertaining.

Glad that the event was over, Victoria breathed a sigh of relief that her long day had come to an end. She walked upstairs, peeled out of her clothes and ran a hot bath. She slid down into the bubbles and thanked God for the person who'd invented the Jacuzzi tub. Her arms and legs softened as the powerful jets massaged her tired muscles.

After toweling off, she slipped into her silk nightgown and crawled under her crisp sateen sheets. A minute after her head hit the pillow, the doorbell rang. "Who could that be this time of night?" Victoria said aloud, looking at the clock on the side of her bed. It was eleven o'clock. She tied her robe tightly around her waist and headed downstairs.

When she looked through the peephole she had to blink twice. She stood back, closed her eyes tight, then peered through the peephole again. But the image didn't change, so she took a deep breath and opened the door. "What are you doing here?"

"Victoria, it's been almost four months. I want...I need to talk to you. Can I please come in?" Parker asked.

"No, I can't believe you just decided to pop up on my doorstep like this."

"Please, if you let me in I'll explain."

Victoria shivered from the cool air outside and the feeling that came over her when she realized what she was about to do—let him in.

They stood in the middle of her living room. The air between them was heated. "Why are you here after I told you that I didn't want to ever see you again?"

"Baby..."

"Don't call me that! You lost the right."

Parker took a step forward. "Victoria, I still love you and I'm sick without you. There will never be enough apologies for what I did. I was so blind, I know that now."

They looked at each other for what seemed like an eternity. Victoria's mind flashed with memories of their good times, their laughter, their arguments, their make-ups, and their love. She looked closely at his lips, his eyes, and his hair. His beautiful curly black hair was as she had remembered it the day he'd arrived back in the states from Kenya. But that was before he had betrayed her. "Save it," she said, waving him away.

"Please, let me finish." Parker took a deep breath. "I take full responsibility for our break-up. That's why it's my responsibility to get us back together."

"You just don't get it do you? It's not gonna happen. In case you didn't know, I'm with someone else now."

"Baby, you're just with him on the rebound."

"I said don't call me that," Victoria glared "You know what, you're really starting to piss me off."

"It's not too late for us, we can make it work," Parker said, ignoring her comment, still pleading his case.

Victoria looked at him in amazement. "You need help, and I suggest you visit someone in the psyche ward at the hospital as soon as you can."

Parker shook his head. "You still love me. I know it."

"This is insane," Victoria said, throwing up her hands.

"Baby, don't deny it. You still love me."

"You've got to go," Victoria said in exasperation. Just as she turned to walk toward the door to show him out, Parker reached for her and pulled her into him. Her body trembled from his touch. "Parker, let go of me," she said, but made no attempt to pull away.

"I know you still love me." He brought his mouth to hers and kissed her more gently and with more love than she had ever remembered him doing. And slowly, she kissed him back, enjoying the familiar taste of his tongue and his body pressed against hers. They held each other tight as he whispered over and over how much he missed her. She'd missed him too, and her body was letting her know. She couldn't fight it any longer.

Before Victoria knew it, they were upstairs in her bed, removing each other's clothes. Parker hooked a finger on the side of her thong, sliding it down her legs. His fingers gently danced between her thighs, making her wet, preparing her for what he knew she liked.

She began to moan when she felt his rock hard erection gently rubbing against her swollen clit. "Baby, I love you," Parker told her, looking deep into her eyes. Slowly, he eased deep inside her as she arched into his thrust. She wrapped her legs around his back and moved to his pounding rhythm.

"I'm never letting you go," he told her in between deep kisses.

She held on to him, grinding her pelvis into his, letting him fill her with his heat. He took his time, reacquainting himself with the bend of her back and the curve of her hips. They moved slow and easy, their bodies slick and electrified. Finally, they both came.

Victoria gasped, trying hard to catch her breath as she quickly sat up in bed. Sweat poured off her body like she'd just run through a rain storm. She looked around the empty room, at the vacant space beside her, and at the damp and slightly tussled sheet wrapped tightly around her knuckles. She realized that none of it had been real. She'd made love to Parker, but only in her dreams. She was terrified and confused about what it meant.

With baby steps, she got up, went to the bathroom and ran a cold cloth across her face. She returned to the troubling comfort of her bed, trying to convince herself that crazy dreams were normal, that people had nightmares from time to time. But she knew this wasn't a nightmare, it was a fantasy. As she lay there, still and bewildered, she searched her heart and wondered if this was the other shoe that had finally dropped.

❦

Mr. and Mrs......

The wedding directress gave Victoria the cue. "All right *Miss* soon-to-be *Mrs.*, its showtime," she called out, getting everyone into place. The wedding directress had done such a marvelous job three months ago with Tyler and Juliet's wedding that Victoria decided to hire the woman for her own nuptials. Even though she only had a short time to plan, everything had come together nicely.

As the doors to the sanctuary opened, the sight made Victoria's heart jump. Assembled in the large church were 400 of her and her groom's closest family and friends. The candles in each window provided a light air to the cold December afternoon. Everyone oohed and awed as John escorted Victoria down the isle to Pachobell's Canon in D. She was radiant in her satin, Vera Wang gown. She wore her hair in a soft upsweep, and accentuated her bridal ensemble with a simple pearl earring and necklace set.

Victoria looked out over the audience on her side of the church and saw familiar faces she'd grown up with and many she'd developed friendships with in recent years. She looked to her groom's side and saw a few familiar, but mostly new faces that she was sure she would get to know in the years to come. Her heart swelled as they approached the altar. Denise, Debbie, Juliet, Gigi and her cousin Patsy, were beautifully dressed in their chic, lavender gowns.

John gave Victoria's hand to her groom, kissed her cheek, then took his seat next to a smiling and teary-eyed Elizabeth.

Tyler and Victoria had argued. "Why can't you be my Man of Honor? I was your Best Person," she'd told him.

"That kinda thing puts a brothah's manhood on the line," he'd told her. So they agreed upon a more suitable role for the man who would always be her "main man." Tyler read a beautiful poem, then took his seat in the reserved pew behind John and Elizabeth.

Victoria and her groom faced each other to say their vows and exchange rings. Looking into his eyes, she saw and felt all the love, all the happiness, and all the joy a woman could ever hope for in a man. She'd prayed for answers and without trying to work it out herself, she sat still and the answers came. No matter how much she fought the feelings of doubt, fear, and uncertainty about their future, she knew that she loved him. She'd loved him from the very beginning. Even through her most recent confusion and misgivings, she loved him, and she had no doubt that he loved her too. He slipped the shiny platinum band on her finger to accompany the flawless diamond engagement ring he'd given her.

"I do," she said.

"I do," he said.

The minister pronounced them husband and wife. He drew Victoria into his embrace, and they kissed as if for the first time. They turned to the congregation of cheering family and friends and beamed their love out to them. Victoria took her bouquet from Debbie as she and her new husband prepared themselves to walk back up the aisle, hand in hand as the minister announced, "It is my honor to present to you, Mr. and Mrs. Theodore Alexander Thornton."

The End

Reading Group Discussion Guide

1. Which character in Unexpected Interruptions, did you most like, and why? Which character did you least like, and why?

2. If you could sit down and chat with one character in the book, who would it be, and what unanswered questions would you ask them?

3. Tyler and Victoria were best friends from the start. Do you think it's possible for a man and woman to be "best friends" without the relationship becoming romantic?

4. As Victoria's relationship grew with Parker and Ted, she found herself falling for them both. Do you think it's possible to truly be in love with two people at the same time?

5. Parker and Ted were both successful men. What were some of their more favorable and less favorable qualities? Which one of the two did you think was ultimately the more controlling?

6. Family dynamics played a large role in the lives of the three main characters, Victoria, Parker, and Ted. In what ways, if any, do you think their family backgrounds impacted the decisions they each made in their romantic relationships?

7. Did you know who Victoria would choose in the end? At what point in the story did you know? Do you think she made the right choice?

8. In our society, it's not unusual to see black men with white women, but now we are beginning to see more of the reverse—black women with white men. What impact do you think this is having on the black community?

9. The issue of skin color has long been a prickly subject in the black community, as well as in other communities of color. Do you think the diversity of our multi-cultural society is changing that view, or do you think it is still a problem?

10. Has this book changed your views on interracial dating? If so, in what way? If not, why?

If you would like the author to make an appearance at your next book club meeting in person or by phone, please send an email to publicity@tricehickman.com.